SWEET SEDUCTION

Brie stared at Dominic, her heart pounding in her throat. The flickering firelight accented the hard masculinity of his carved features.

His thumb swirled lazily against her palm. "You know I want you," he murmured, his voice low and caressing.

The husky tone sent shivers up Brie's spine. She wanted to look away, to break the spell he was weaving around her, but her eyes seemed to be locked with his. Mesmerized, she nodded wordlessly.

Dominic reached up to stroke her cheek. His touch left her breathless, and when his gaze settled on her lips, Brie found herself unable to move.

Taking his time, Dominic ran his fingers through the burnished flame of her hair. Then, cradling the back of her head, he drew her closer. His lips touched hers softly at first, in a tantalizing butterfly kiss, and her token resistance soon faded beneath his gentle persuasion.

She felt herself losing all sense of reality, yet all her senses seemed infinitely sharper. She pressed closer against his hard, lean body, wanting something more from him but unable to name what it was . . .

VELVET EMBRACE

NICOLE JORDAN

ZEBRA BOOKS
KENSINGTON PUBLISHING CORP.

ZEBRA BOOKS

are published by

Kensington Publishing Corp.
475 Park Avenue South
New York, NY 10016

First printing: June 1987

Printed in the United States of America

To Candy and Vickie for the stars;
To Loretta for the rarest of wines;
To Paula and Marcy for the music;
And most of all,
To Jay for the romance.

Prologue

France, 1792

Although the fire in the grate burned steadily, its flickering light presented only a feeble challenge to the deepening shadows of the bedchamber. No candles had been lit to ward off the approaching dusk, nor had the velvet hangings of the windows been drawn against the night air.

Suzanne Durham failed to notice the increasing gloom, however, as she knelt before the hearth. Such things hardly mattered when her safe, serene world had shattered like fragile crystal in the space of a few days. Dead! Her mother was dead. And now it seemed her father's desire for revenge would result in another life lost. At the very least there would be bloodshed if a duel took place in the morning. Yet there must be a way to prevent it from happening!

Suzanne bent her dark head and clasped her hands, but she found herself unable to pray. Apprehension overshadowed even her grief as she remembered her father's rage that afternoon. Shivering as if the warmth of the fire were insufficient, she drew her shawl more closely about her slender shoulders. When a log became dislodged and crashed in the grate, she started violently and stared at the exploding shower of sparks. Then rising, she began to pace the floor, her black silk skirts rustling with each agitated step.

She paused from time to time, tilting her head to one side to listen intently. Where in God's name was Katherine? Would she never come? Together they might think of a way to avert the impending duel and thus prevent another tragic death.

At last Suzanne heard the anticipated footsteps. When the chamber door opened, she gave a sob. "Katherine!" she cried, flinging herself into the arms of the middle-aged woman who entered. "Where have you been? I have been worried to distraction, not knowing where you or Papa had gone."

Katherine pulled back, frowning. "Suzanne, please. This behavior is unbecoming." Her efficient gaze swept quickly around the room. "Why, whatever are you doing alone in the dark? Come, my dear, sit down."

Not waiting for a reply, she led Suzanne to a chair, then busied herself lighting the candles and removing her cloak. When she finally turned to the young woman, though, Katherine paused. Seeing Suzanne's pinched, white face, she felt compassion wring her heart. The girl was so young, so innocent. Certainly she didn't deserve to suffer such anguish.

Coming to stand before her, Katherine took Suzanne's chilled hands in her own. "My dear, we must talk. I fear what I have to say will come as a shock to you so soon after losing your mother. However . . ." She hesitated, gazing at the beautiful young face. "However, I must return to England. All the arrangements have been made. The coach leaves in a few hours. I should reach Calais by—."

"You cannot mean it," Suzanne protested, her dark eyes widening in fear. "You mustn't leave me, Katherine. I need you."

Katherine attempted to smile. "I know, my dear. But there is no possibility of my staying. Sir Charles—"

"What has Papa done? Don't tell me he has dismissed you. He cannot. I won't allow it."

Gripping the girl's hands, Katherine gave them a little shake. "Suzanne, you are behaving hysterically. Now listen to me, I beg you. Permit me to speak without interruption. This is difficult enough, so please do not make it any harder for me."

When Suzanne bowed her head submissively, Katherine continued with her usual briskness, although her tone held deep regret. "Yes, I have been given my notice. But Sir Charles was correct in his actions. You will return to school shortly and will have no need of me. The fact remains, however, that I am not fit to chaperon you. I was negligent in my duty to your mother, I will be the first to admit. As Lisette's companion, I was the one closest to her. Had I . . . had I been more on my guard, she would still be alive today."

Suzanne looked up in bewilderment. "How can you say that? You could no more have stopped Mamma than you could have commanded a butterfly to be still. I loved her, Katherine, but I wasn't blind to her failings. She was beautiful, but so very temperamental. If you must find fault, then blame my father. He was the one forever dashing about the continent, leaving poor Mamma alone. Why, he barely arrived in time for her funeral yesterday! Don't look so shocked. I am no longer a child. I can see things clearly. And now," Suzanne added bitterly, "now Papa has dismissed you, all because of Mamma's stupid letter. Heaven only knows what he intends for the comte!"

At the mention of the letter, Katherine's face drained of all color, her aging skin appearing harsh against the starkness of her black gown. "Dear God," she breathed. "How do you know about the letter?"

Freeing her hands, Suzanne rose and resumed her pacing. "I was outside the study this afternoon when you and Papa were arguing. After you left, Papa discovered me behind the stairs where I had hidden. He started shouting at me, brandishing the letter in my face, demanding to know if you had shown it to me. That was nonsense, of course—you never even mentioned it. Papa was hardly coherent, but I gathered somehow he thought Monsieur Philippe responsible for Mamma's death. Oh, Katie, it was horrible! Papa kept saying over and over again that the

9

Comte de Valdois was a murderer who had defiled the Durham honor. And then . . . then I said things I should not have said. I told Papa he was mad, that the comte would never have hurt Mamma. Papa was furious when I defended Philippe. I couldn't stop him from storming out of the house."

Suzanne whirled to face the older woman, tears glittering in her eyes. "Katherine, I am so afraid! I know Papa means to challenge the comte, and I've been trying and trying to think of a way to prevent them from dueling, but I don't know how. I will never, never forgive Papa if he hurts Philippe!"

Appalled, Katherine sank into the chair Suzanne had vacated, closing her eyes. The girl could not possibly mean to take the comte's side. Or could she? Suzanne Durham was the product of a self-centered English father and a beautiful, aristocratic French mother. By nature, she was generous and loving, but she could also be stubborn and passionate. And she was no longer a mere child, Katherine reflected. At seventeen, Suzanne was both old enough and naive enough to fall prey to the handsome Comte de Valdois. She had always had something of an infatuation for their titled neighbor, in fact, but since she had frequently been away at school, her attraction had never developed into anything serious enough for concern. Until now. Now Suzanne was defending that terrible man.

Yet how could she have known what the comte was like? It had only been a short time ago that Katherine herself had considered the French nobleman no less than the gallant gentleman he appeared. Katherine had even felt sorry for him when his English wife had deserted him earlier in the year. Indeed, Philippe Serrault, the Comte of Valdois, had fooled them all with his elegant manners and devasting charm. Especially Suzanne's mother, Lisette. How foolish Lisette had been! Katherine's stomach churned as she recalled what had happened. Thank God Suzanne had been well chaperoned during her infrequent visits home.

"Suzanne, you must have nothing more to do with the

comte," Katherine said abruptly.

Her voice, so unaccustomedly sharp, made Suzanne stare. "Why? What has he done?" Katherine's reply was a shudder.

Dismayed to see her pallor, Suzanne knelt before the older woman and began to rub her worn hands to return the circulation. "What did the letter say?"

Katherine shook her head. "I cannot tell you." Placing a hand protectively on the girl's dark hair, she held Suzanne's gaze. "I wish you to trust me, dear. It is better that you do not know. I can only say that your father has been deeply hurt. I cannot blame him for the anger he feels."

Suzanne's brows drew together in puzzlement. "You would condone the comte's murder? Papa will kill him if he can."

"Your father's honor is at stake," Katherine replied, looking away.

Suzanne pulled back and leapt to her feet. "What is honor, compared to a life? They will duel and Philippe will be killed! And . . . and what of his son? What will become of Dominic if his father dies? Can a seven-year-old understand the meaning of honor? Poor child! His mother an English witch who abandons him, and now this. No, Katherine. There has been one death too many. We must find a way to prevent the duel."

Katherine shook her head. From what she had heard in the village only a short while ago, there would be no duel. "Suzanne, your father has not challenged the comte. He has . . . submitted evidence to the authorities. The comte will be arrested."

Suzanne stared at Katherine in horror. "Arrested? But they will take him to Paris. He will be condemned to die without even a trial. No, I must warn him!" Not even waiting for a reply, she ran to the door and threw it open.

"Suzanne!" Katherine cried, coming to her feet. "Suzanne, I beg you, come back!" Her anguished words only echoed eerily as a rush of cold air invaded the chamber and made her shudder. "Dear God," she whispered. Then realizing she couldn't allow the girl to go rushing off like that, at night and alone, Katherine picked up her skirts and hurried out of the room.

Suzanne had already left the house and was racing across the rear lawn. She avoided the stables, heading for the woods that separated the Durham and Valdois lands. A narrow footpath led through the forest there, and she intended to save precious minutes by taking the path, rather than having a horse saddled.

When she reached the woods, Suzanne plunged recklessly into the dense vegetation and was immediately forced to slow her pace. Although it was autumn, the trees had not yet shed their leaves, and the light from the thin sliver of moon barely penetrated to the forest floor. Silver-black shadows danced all around her, making it impossible to see the brambles and low-hanging branches that choked the path.

The heavy growth impeded her progress as she tried to run. Gnarled roots and sharp rocks caused her to stumble; tough bark and prickly vines tore at her clothes and hair; branches lashed the tender skin of her face and hands. But she was oblivious to the pain. Her only thought was to go to the comte and warn him.

She was terrified to think what would happen if she were too late. Her sheltered life had not pretended her from learning what was happening elsewhere in France. The country was being swept up in the violent destruction of a long-abided social order. Chateaus were being burned to the ground by oppressed peasants, while noble families were driven from their homes and herded like animals into carts bound for Paris prisons. And in the capitol, hundreds of leagues away, the hideous instrument of the New Republic, La Guillotine, performed its grisly duty day after day without discrimination for the innocence or guilt of its victims.

For months Suzanne had listened to the horrible tales that filtered into the select boarding school she attended—tales of riots and massacres, of seething mobs demanding the country's noblest heads. But until now such incidents had touched her well-ordered life as only an extremely unpleasant dream might, and she had innocently clung to the belief that the horrors would soon end.

She had been shocked to be summoned from school in order to attend her own mother's funeral. Lisette Durham's death had not been remotely connected with the revolution, but it had brutally awakened Suzanne to what was happening around her. The revolution was spreading. Like a voracious predator, it was creeping across France, engulfing the country and its people. And now her father had harnessed the beast for his own purposes! She had been right to fear the hatred and rage she had seen burning in Sir Charles' eyes, even if she had mistakenly assumed he would abide by the strict codes that governed affairs of honor.

Suzanne's breath caught on a sob as she considered what would happen if she failed to reach Valdois in time. She had heard few people ever escaped with their lives once they had been imprisoned. Some simply rotted in the filthy cells where they had been incarcerated, while most felt the deathly caress of the knife. No matter what the comte had done, he didn't deserve such a fate.

Blindly, she raced on through the forest, while throbbing shafts of pain pierced her sides and her breath came in ragged shudders. Stumbling once again, she lost her balance and fell to the forest floor with an impact that left her stunned. She lay there a moment, her face pressed into the dirt. But her determination, born of fear, gave her the strength to clutch at a tree limb and drag herself from the ground.

For what seemed like an eternity, Suzanne compelled her legs to move. At last, though, she reached the end of the path that gave way to the side lawns. Beyond were the elegant, formal gardens and the magnificent Valdois chateau.

Suzanne drew up, gasping for breath, unable to go farther for a moment. When she recovered, she began to run again toward the great house. She could see a strange, flickering light coming from the front lawns, and it drew her like a strong magnet.

Threading her way past beautifully clipped hedges, she rounded the corner of the house, then stopped abruptly. Staring at the flaming scene in horror, she fought the scream that tore at her throat. She was too late! The drive was crowded with horses and soldiers, some of the men carrying pitchforks or other crude weapons but most brandishing firearms. Philippe Serrault, the Comte de Valdois, stood at the foot of the stone steps, his arms pinned roughly behind him by two of the soldiers.

Suzanne had a clear view of Philippe's proud profile, for his face was illuminated by torchlight. He held his dark head high, almost arrogantly, as he demanded to know the charges brought against him.

The captain of the troops swaggered up to the comte and spat on the ground at his feet. "Citizen, you no longer have the right to demand anything. Sacre! You aristos think you own the world. Much good the world will do you when you no longer have your head." Laughing at his own jest, he spat again. "But I will tell you," he added with obvious relish. "You are charged with acts of treason against the New Republic of France."

The comte raised a contemptuous eyebrow. "You know as well as I that I have committed no crimes against your precious Republic."

The grin of malicious enjoyment spread across the captain's face as he fingered the hilt of his sword. "But there is more, Citizen. You are also accused of the murder of Madame Lisette Durham."

Unable to move, Suzanne watched in frozen silence. She expected the comte to refute the accusation, but, oddly, he didn't appear to be surprised by the charge of murder. He only stared coldly at the captain. Just as Suzanne was about to take a step closer, however, the comte spoke again, asking who had accused him. Suzanne clearly heard the captain's reply.

"Why none other than the late woman's daughter," the man taunted. "Mademoiselle Suzanne has denounced you as a murderer and a traitor."

It was a moment before Suzanne understood the implication of what he had said. Then she gasped, realizing what her father had done. Sir Charles had used her name because she had tried to defend the comte!

"No," she cried, "it isn't true!" Outraged, she sprang forward, pushing her way through the crowd and startling the soldiers with her sudden appearance. The sneering grin on the captain's face vanished as she thrust herself in front of him. "You cannot arrest Monsieur le Comte," she insisted. "He has done nothing."

The captain glared at her as if he would have liked to make her disappear. "You should not have come, mademoiselle. We already have your signature on the arrest warrant."

"But it is a forgery! I signed no warrant—"

The captain cut her off, not giving her a chance to explain the part her father had played. "It is obvious that you are disturbed, mademoiselle. When you come to your senses, I am sure you will remember making the charges. Corporal, escort this man to his horse."

"No!" she said desperately. "I won't let you take him!" She threw herself at the captain, clinging to his arms while his soldiers looked on in astonishment.

The captain fell back several steps, swearing. When at last he gathered his scattered wits, he seized Suzanne by the arms and flung her to the ground.

She lay there a moment, sobbing, then raised a tear-streaked face to the comte. "I had nothing to do with it," she whispered hoarsely. "Please, you must believe me."

Philippe Serrault only stared down at her, his dark eyes void of expression. "It is of little consequence now, mademoiselle," he said tonelessly. Then his gaze swung to the captain. "Shall we go, monsieur?"

Suzanne wanted to beg, to plead, but she realized her entreaties would be useless. She watched helplessly as the comte was escorted to a waiting horse.

He went without protest. When he was mounted, however, a child's anguished cry made the comte glance over his shoulder. At the top of the steps, a very young boy was struggling wildly in the arms of a servant.

"Dominic," the comte murmured, giving a last, lingering look at his son. But he spared not a glance for the young woman who lay huddled and grieving on the ground as he was borne away by the soldiers.

Chapter One

England, 1818

Brie Carringdon clenched her teeth as she struggled with the stopper to the medicine bottle. When it wouldn't budge, she pushed a russet curl back from her forehead in exasperation. How, when she was capable of running the finest training stable in the country, had she managed to get herself in such a situation? It was nearly midnight, she was stranded three miles from home at a gentleman's hunting box, a snowstorm was raging outside, and the two elderly patients she had volunteered to care for were being more provoking than even invalids had a right to be.

Brie tackled the bottle again, trying to see the humor in her situation. She most definitely did not belong in a sickroom. She had neither the necessary patience nor the skill. But she would not be defeated by a medicine bottle!

Wrapping a fold of her brown kerseymere gown around the stopper for leverage, Brie tugged and twisted and at last succeeded. When the bottle was open, she wrinkled her nose at the unpleasant fumes. The medicine could have been poison for all she knew, but it had been prescribed by the doctor with orders to be administered regularly.

Carefully, Brie measured out a spoonful of the foul-smelling

17

potion, then sat beside the plump, gray-haired woman on the bed. "Please, Mattie," she urged, managing somehow to keep frustration out of her tone. "You must swallow a little of this."

Mattie Dawson coughed fitfully as she huddled beneath a mound of blankets. "My chest hurts," she complained in a rasping voice.

"I know, my dear, but this medicine is supposed to make you better."

"'Twill kill her, like as not," Mattie's husband muttered as he watched. Brie had arranged a cot for Homer beside the bed so that Mattie could rest more comfortably. He was lying on the cot with the covers pulled up to his chin, grumbling as he had been all evening. "Blamed doctors don't know anything. All charlatans, every last one of 'em."

Brie's blue-green eyes narrowed as she glanced down at Homer. He was the very opposite of his wife—tall, gaunt, and as cantankerous as a rusty hinge. He had always treated Brie with far more familiarity than was proper for a servant toward the daughter of a baronet, but since he had known her for the entire twenty-three years of her life, she was inclined to make allowances, especially now when he was suffering from such a severe head cold.

He looked a little absurd at the moment, Brie thought, with his grizzled hair sticking out from beneath his nightcap and his nose red and swollen. Realizing how miserable he must feel, though, she felt a twinge of sympathy. She herself was rarely ill. And in spite of her current annoyance, Brie was extremely fond of both Homer and Mattie. The couple had been in her parents' service, then hers, for more than twenty years before becoming caretakers at the Lodge. Brie had in fact been the one to recommend them for the prestigious position, and even though they no longer worked at Greenwood, she still felt responsible for their welfare. They were getting on in years and were more frail than either of them would admit.

Wishing she could do more to ease their misery, Brie sighed. Why had she ever agreed to stay with the Dawsons when she

18

knew so little about nursing? Her forte was training thoroughbreds for the hunting field, not soothing fretful patients. If Mattie and Homer had been suffering from colic, she would have known precisely what to do.

The irascible Homer seemed to think she didn't belong there either. "You needn't have come, Miss Brie," he said, sniffling.

"And who would have seen that you stayed in bed?" she asked, biting back a sharper retort as she held the spoon to Mattie's lips. "You wouldn't even have let the doctor in the house, had I not been here. At least Patrick had the sense to realize that and to come to get me."

Homer buried his red nose in a handkerchief and snorted. "Young scamp! Ought to take a rod to him to teach him proper respect for his elders."

Brie didn't reply since she knew his threat was empty. Patrick was the oldest and dearest of Homer's four grandsons, even though he was in disgrace at the moment. Patrick had been worried enough about Mattie's cough to defy his grandfather's express orders and summon the doctor, but afterward he had gone to Greenwood, hoping to gain Brie's support.

She had come at once, intending only to exert her authority. But Mattie's condition had turned out to be far more serious than even Patrick had suspected. When the doctor had ordered both elder Dawsons to bed, Brie had volunteered to look after them. It would have been wiser to send for Katherine, she knew, since her companion was far more qualified to preside over a sickroom. But Katherine's rheumatism had been bothering her again, and Brie hesitated to make her drive the three miles between Greenwood and the Lodge in such bitterly cold weather.

The situation had only become worse, though, for the snow that had been falling all afternoon had threatened to become a real blizzard. Since the small Lodge staff were all local people, Brie had allowed them to go home to their families. That had left seventeen-year-old Patrick and his three younger brothers in charge of the stables, and no one but Brie in charge of the house. Thinking of her abilities in the area of household management, Brie smiled ruefully. But at least the *horses* wouldn't suffer any discomfort because of the snow.

Trying to ignore Homer's grumbling, Brie made another attempt at getting Mattie to swallow the obnoxious liquid. When she succeeded, Mattie grimaced and sank weakly back against the pillows. "Pay Homer no mind, Miss Brie," she whispered hoarsely. "You're a blessed saint, just like your mother was."

Uncomfortable with such undeserved praise, Brie concentrated on pouring out more of the medicine. Being compared to her mother only made her feel guilty for the uncharitable feelings she had been harboring. Lady Suzanne had been known throughout the district for her selfless devotion to the poor and ailing. Had she still been alive, Brie knew, Lady Suzanne would have been doing exactly what Brie was doing now—only she would have done it with far better grace.

"I'll agree that Mama was sainted," Brie replied, "but I fear I'm not like her at all. Come now, Mattie, one more spoonful. You don't want your cold to develop into pneumonia."

Homer grunted. "'Twon't come to that. She just has a little somethin' in the lungs."

Nearing the end of her patience, Brie gave him a quelling glance. "It isn't a 'little something'. I may not know much about illness, but even I can tell Mattie's congestion is serious. And your condition is not much better."

Homer shrank back, but it was Brie's look, not her sharp tone, that made him regard her so warily. Her eyes, a smokey shade of blue-green, had a way of darkening and flashing when she was angry, as they were doing now. That peculiarity had been an advantage to her in the past. She wasn't particularly tall, nor was her slim figure very intimidating, but she had been in command of an army of grooms and ostlers since she was nineteen and had needed to use every means at her disposal in

20

order to run the vast estate she had inherited from her father.

When Brie got her patient to swallow again, she gave Mattie a sip of water, then turned her attention to Homer. Bending down, she held out the bottle and spoon to him. "I promised to see that you took your medicine, but I don't think you need me to administer it." Homer's scowl deepened, but Brie was determined to have her way. "Come now, Homer," she said warningly. "You don't want me to resort to Katherine's method. I've seen her with sick children. She holds their noses until they open their mouths and swallow."

Her threat managed to do the trick. Homer obeyed without further argument, only muttering a little about the bitter taste of the medicine. Relieved, Brie stoppered the bottle and set it on the bedside table as she rose. After checking the hot brick at Mattie's feet, she rearranged the pillows and tucked the covers around her patient. Mattie appeared to be asleep, Brie noted thankfully. She turned the lamp down, leaving the bed-chamber in a dim glow.

When she had made one last trip to the hearth to lay another log on the fire, she knew there was little more she could do. She picked up her candle and turned to Homer. "Good night," Brie whispered. "Patrick means to check on you in a few hours, but please call me if you need anything, or if Mattie gets worse."

"Very well, Miss Brie," Homer answered stiffly, still not admitting that his judgment had been in error. He let Brie walk all the way to the door before he called after her. "Patrick had best be looking after you, Miss Brie. I'll have his hide, else."

Brie smiled, realizing that despite his gruffness, Homer cared about her. "Patrick has been taking excellent care of me," she replied. "He's already kindled a fire in one of the guestrooms and brought up some water."

"'Tisn't right that you should be all alone in the house."

"It is only for one night. Julian should be here tomorrow—or the next day, if the snow delays him. With the number of servants he'll be bringing, there will be no need for me to stay. I couldn't remain here anyway with a bachelor in residence. Not

21

without giving rise to gossip, which Greenwood doesn't need."

Homer's bristled brows drew together in a frown. "Lord Denville won't be pleased to find me and Mattie abed."

Brie suspected that worry had been the root cause of his crankiness. "Heavens, Homer! Julian isn't a monster. He knows how hard you and Mattie have worked for him, and he certainly won't begrudge you a few days rest when you are both ill. If it will ease your mind, though, I'll tell him about the struggle I had to get you to stay in bed. Now don't worry and go to sleep. There's nothing for you to do at the moment."

Brie quietly let herself out of the room and shut the door. As she made her way down the service stairs, an icy draft nearly blew out her candle, reminding her of the storm raging outside. She shivered, cupping her hand around the wavering flame to shield it. The small county of Rutland rarely saw such severe weather, for it was located near the center of England, in the heart of the hunting country. But this snowstorm seemed particularly fierce. Hearing the sound of the wind swirling around the house, Brie was glad she wasn't out in the storm, even if it meant having to spend the night virtually alone in the big house.

It was only when she had reached the next landing that she realized she had no nightgown to sleep in. Not wanting to disturb Mattie again merely to borrow one, Brie detoured through Julian's room, looking for something to wear. She found one of his dressing gowns, as well as some tooth powder and a hairbrush, but his slippers were so large that she didn't bother to take them. Gathering up the other articles, she made her way back down the icy corridor to the bedroom she had appropriated for the night.

The room was only one of several guestchambers on the second floor, for although the Lodge was a hunting box, it wasn't small by any means. The house had fifteen rooms besides the servants' quarters and large kitchen, plus a number of outbuildings that included an excellent stable. There was also a dormitory in back that housed the male staff and the servants of visiting guests.

The Lodge was frequently occupied. Although most sporting gentlemen used their hunting boxes for only a few weeks a year, Julian Blake, Lord Denville, generally spent most of the hunting season at his, plus several months during the summer. Family concerns had kept him in London since the start of the new year, but he was expected any day now. Brie was looking forward to his return—in spite of the fact that he would also be bringing her cousin Caroline to visit her.

The room Brie had chosen served both as bedchamber and sitting room. A large canopied bed stood at one end, and at the other, flanking the fireplace, was a Sheraton chaise longue and a pair of overstuffed armchairs. The walls were paneled in walnut and lined with hunting trophies—antlers, stuffed heads, and the like—while a luxurious bear rug sprawled in front of the hearth. It was quite a comfortable chamber, Brie thought, or at least it would have been, if not for the cold. Despite the fire Patrick had lit, the room was still chilly.

Brie built the fire into a crackling blaze, then stood before the hearth to change, nearly laughing when she had donned Julian's blue brocade dressing gown. Far too large, the robe hung on her slender frame and reached several inches past her bare feet. But at least it was fairly warm. Tying the sash around her waist, she made quick use of the soap and water on the washstand to wash her face. As she pulled the pins from her auburn hair and began to brush it, she cast a deliberative glance at the bed. It was almost midnight, but she wasn't particularly sleepy and she dreaded the shock of climbing between stiff, cold sheets. When she spotted a leather-bound book lying on the bureau, she decided to read in front of the fire for a while. She had little time for such luxuries at Greenwood, for she was generally far too busy.

The book was a gothic novel, Brie realized upon seeing the title, and she wondered how it had come to be at the Lodge. She knew for a fact that Julian never read such stuff. One of his ladybirds had probably left it at the Lodge by mistake, she mused. Not that she would ever dream of pointing that out to Julian. She could just imagine what his reaction would be. He would color up to the roots of his blond hair and read her a blistering scold about how ladies weren't supposed to know about such things. Then they would argue as they always did, for Brie never let anyone scold her except Katherine or her head trainer at Greenwood. Not even Julian, who was her dearest friend and might have been her husband had she said "yes" only once to his numerous proposals of marriage. Her refusals had disappointed him, she knew. But even if Julian hadn't been more like a brother to her than a prospective husband, her one disastrous experience with love had taught her that she never wanted to marry. She never intended to give her heart to any man again.

Julian hadn't had any trouble finding someone to console him, though. Handsome, titled gentlemen usually didn't, particularly if they were rich enough to buy companionship—which Julian was. As Viscount Denville, he was wealthy in his own right, besides being heir to an earldom. He occasionally invited females to the Lodge, Brie knew. Even though Julian tried to be discreet about his ladyloves, not much happened in their small district that she didn't eventually find out about. After all, she was the largest landowner in that part of the country, as well as the possessor of one of the finest training stables in all of England.

Retrieving a blanket from the bed, Brie lit the lamp beside the chaise longue, then made herself a snug nest and settled down to read. The gothic turned out to be a blood-curdling account of a haunted castle, but she found it surprisingly absorbing. She had no idea that she had read for nearly an hour until she looked up from her book to find that the fire had dwindled to a dull glow.

When she shivered, though, it was due as much to the frightening tale she was reading as to the cold. Brie glanced nervously around the large room, finding it easy to imagine things lurking in shadows. Except for the crackling fire, the room seemed oddly quiet, for the wind had died down and was no longer howling eerily through the trees as it had been for hours. The dull thumping she had heard a few moments ago also had stopped. Probably a loose shutter or a limb striking the side of the house, she reflected. She would have Patrick see to it in the morning.

Throwing off the blanket, she went to the hearth and tossed another log on the fire, then scurried back to the chaise longue and buried herself under the blanket. Tucking her bare feet beneath her, she returned to the hair-raising story.

It was only a short while before she caught herself shivering again. Feeling ridiculous for scaring herself, she closed the book with a snap. She had to go to bed before she started imagining herself in a haunted dungeon with groaning ghosts and ghouls!

She blew out the reading lamp—a mistake, she realized at once. The dancing firelight sent shadows skittering across the room, making the stuffed heads on the walls come alive. Brie watched them warily, feeling a shuddery tremor race up her spine.

She was still trying to summon the courage to brave the shadows and the icy bedsheets when, without any warning, the door to her bedroom burst open. It slammed back on its hinges with a ferocious crack, nearly startling Brie out of her wits. She gave a cry that was half shriek, half choked gasp as she leapt to her feet and whirled to face the menace, her blanket and book tumbling forgotten to the floor.

She stood there quaking, her heart pounding violently in her throat. A man, a stranger, filled the doorway, looking as darkly ominous as the devil himself. He had obviously been out in the snowstorm, for the curly brim of his beaver hat was ringed with white, while the capes of his greatcoat glistened with frozen crystals. His eyes were what captured her attention, though. Narrowed beneath slashing black brows, they glittered like shards of ice, unnerving Brie with their piercing intensity. Yet even as she stared, his gaze changed subtly, becoming coolly speculative.

His eyes swept over her slowly, taking in every detail of her disheveled appearance. "So this is what Julian finds so appealing about the place," he said in a biting drawl.

His voice was pleasantly masculine, even if it did hold more than a hint of mockery. And it was a human voice. Which meant it was no specter who had invaded her bedchamber. Brie's knees went weak with relief. She groped for the little table beside the chaise longue, leaning against it for support as she let out her breath in a rush. "God's teeth, but you frightened me!" she accused, glaring at him. Her heart was still beating furiously, and she put a hand to her throat, drawing in deep gulps of air as she tried to calm her racing pulse.

The stranger made no reply, but stepped forward into the light, giving Brie the opportunity to see his features more clearly. Dark, sardonic, masculine, was her initial impression. Terribly masculine. He was a striking man. Too dark to be handsome in the classical sense, but certainly arresting. She could tell now that his eyes were gray, a chilly, penetrating gray. They were surveying her quite intently. In fact, he was subjecting her to a thorough—and thoroughly insulting—inspection.

Feeling color steal into her cheeks, Brie stiffened. She knew she must present a sight, with her feet bare and her unbound auburn hair flowing loosely down her back. She felt completely vulnerable, dressed in nothing but Julian's robe—and that was being stripped away by the stranger's insolent gaze. Brie's chin came up as she gave him a reproving frown.

Her quelling look didn't faze him. His blatant perusal continued to glide along her slender body, making every inch of her skin feel as if it were burning. A tremor ran up her spine when the stranger's gaze lingered on the swell of her heaving breasts, and Brie flushed with embarrassment. Snatching up the blanket, she wrapped it around her shoulders. "Don't you believe in knocking?" she asked irritably, still feeling foolish for reacting the way she had. He had startled her badly, but

26

there had been no reason to *shriek*, for heaven's sake! And she had sworn, too. Definitely not the behavior of a well-bred lady.

The stranger slowly raised his gaze to her face. His gray eyes studied her a moment longer, then his mouth twisted sardonically. "I did knock," he observed in a dry tone, "but no one responded. I had to pry open a window in the kitchen."

"You *broke* into the house?"

"It wouldn't have been necessary, had someone answered the door. Why the devil didn't you?"

He sounded impatient, as if he were in an extremely ill humor. Brie was unused to strangers taking that particular tone with her, however, and she didn't care for it at all. "Obviously I didn't hear," she retorted. "Not that I would have allowed you to come in. I don't know who you are."

"I'm Stanton," he replied curtly, as if that explained anything. He strode into the room, peeling off his gloves as he went. Brie took a nervous step backward, but the stranger didn't seem to notice. He tossed the leather gloves on the table, along with his hat, and went to stand before the hearth. Blowing on his chilled fingers, he held them out to the fire.

Brie eyed him with amazement. He had burst into her bedroom, and now, without permission, was making himself at home. "Stanton, who?" she asked perversely.

He flashed her a sharp glance. "I beg your pardon," he said, his voice again holding that faint hint of mockery. "Allow me to introduce myself properly. I am Dominic Serrault, Lord Stanton. Sixth Earl of Stanton, to be precise."

Brie gave a start. She had heard of Lord Stanton before. In fact she had heard some very unsavory rumors in London connected with him. Something about a duel and a man being killed. Brie had no idea how much of it was truth, but she could easily believe the man standing before her was someone to be wary of. He looked dangerous with his heavy, slashing black brows and waving ebony hair. His cheeks were faintly flushed with cold, but beneath the color, his skin was darkly bronzed. The faint shadow of a rising beard made him appear even darker. He probably had a temper as black as his looks, Brie concluded. She began to feel intensely uneasy, being here alone with him.

He had caught the flicker of recognition in her eyes, though. Watching the changing expressions on her lovely face, he wondered at its cause. But perhaps Julian had mentioned his name, Dominic mused. Pointedly, he raised an eyebrow. "And you are . . . ?" he prompted.

"Brie—" she started to reply, then thought better of it and clamped her lips together. It would be foolish to give him her name to bandy about in the London clubs. He had only to mention that he had found her here alone and she would have a scandal on her hands in an instant. It wasn't merely her own reputation Brie was concerned about, but that of her training stables. It had taken her years to earn the trust of her clients, for so many of them considered it beneath their dignity to work with a woman. She couldn't jeopardize all she had strived for. And she would have to be careful not to mention the name of her home. If Lord Stanton knew anything at all about horses, he would have heard of Greenwood. She would have to get rid of him at once, before he had a chance to ask any embarrassing questions.

He was waiting for her response. "Brie?" he repeated quizzically. "Just . . . Brie?" When she nodded, he regarded her silently for another moment. Then, almost indifferently, he turned back to the fire.

His presumptuousness astonished Brie, yet she couldn't help studying him as he stood warming his hands. He was tall and broad-shouldered, although she suspected his heavy greatcoat added breadth to his frame. His aristocratic features were unmistakably stamped with cynicism, but they were finely carved. He had a high forehead and a narrow, straight nose with slightly flaring nostrils. His chiseled lips were wide but a little on the thin side, and his firm chin had a slight cleft in the center. In profile, his high cheekbones were quite pronounced. He was quite attractive, Brie decided, if one liked dark, sardonic-looking men.

"Where is everyone, anyway?" he asked, interrupting her thoughts. "The lad in the stables told me the caretakers live here."

Brie hesitated. She preferred not to admit the only other people in the house were old and ill. "Mattie and Homer are . . . occupied at the moment, but perhaps I can help you."

Dominic's gaze swung back to Brie, and his eyes narrowed as he again caught himself staring at the vivid picture she made. The dancing firelight turned her silken hair to shimmering flame, while the sapphire brocade of the robe she wore brought out the blue in her eyes. Seeing that the blanket had slipped off her shoulders, giving him a tantalizing view of creamy skin, Dominic felt a tightening in his loins. He wondered who she could be. Such delicate beauty didn't belong to a serving maid, nor did her educated speech.

"You can't possibly be a servant," he said flatly.

Brie's long lashes came down, veiling her thoughts. "I am a friend of Julian's," was all she dared reply.

"A *close* friend?"

"You might say that."

Her answer was unsatisfactory, but Dominic didn't press the issue. He would eventually find out what he wanted to know—specifically, what her relationship was to Denville. The obvious conclusion was that she was Julian's mistress. Dominic was conscious of a distinct twinge of envy. "Is there no one else about?" he said, forcing his thoughts back to the problem at hand.

"The rest of the servants have left for the day," Brie answered with reluctance. "I gave them permission to go home when the storm grew worse."

One of his black brows lifted appreciably. "*You* gave them permission?"

She flushed at his tone. "Julian left me in charge," she prevaricated.

"And he neglected to tell you I was expected."

29

Realizing that Lord Stanton must have been invited to the Lodge, Brie stared at him in dismay. "Surely you don't mean to stay *here?*"

The corner of Dominic's mouth quirked. "I sure as hell am not going back out in the storm. Even if I were willing, my grays have had enough punishment for one evening. Besides, my coachman wouldn't stand for it. Jacques can be the very devil when he is denied his comforts."

Brie bit her lip, wondering what she should do. Stanton didn't look quite so . . . dangerous when he wasn't frowning. His harsh features softened a little, while his gray eyes appeared less chilling. And the snow on his greatcoat was melting, sending little curls of steam wisping about his dark head, somehow making him appear younger, even a little vulnerable. Brie felt oddly drawn to him. A damp lock of ebony hair had fallen forward onto his brow, and absurdly she wanted to smooth it back into place.

Realizing what she was thinking, Brie mentally shook herself. "There is a comfortable inn in the village," she suggested hopefully.

When an amused smile spread slowly across his lips, showing white, even teeth, Brie felt her breath catch. His smile was that of a fallen angel, devastatingly sweet with just a hint of devilry. It affected her all the way to her toes, creating a fluttery sensation in the pit of her stomach that was completely foreign to her. Staring at him, Brie hardly registered his next words, let alone the tolerant, condescending tone he adopted.

"My dear . . . Brie, if that is what you wish to be called, I intend to stay right where I am. My arrival is a few days early, but Denville did ask me here, I assure you. I wasn't proposing to stay here in your bedroom, if that is what concerns you. Although I wouldn't turn down an invitation . . ." Dominic's voice trailed off suggestively, but when Brie merely continued to gape at him, he sighed in resignation. "Just direct me to a room and I will manage for myself."

Making an attempt to regain her equilibrium, Brie swallowed

hard. "At th-the end of the hall," she stammered. "The one on the right. There should be kindling in the box," she added as an afterthought, "but if you want water to wash with, I'm afraid you will have to get it from the kitchen."

He shrugged his broad shoulders. "I've survived worse conditions. Although Jacques is probably receiving better treatment in the stables. At least he was offered a hot cider to take away the chill."

Hearing the pointed inflection in his voice, Brie glanced suspiciously at Lord Stanton. His expression was enigmatic, but there was a glimmer in his gray eyes that made her wonder if she were being teased. She felt vaguely ashamed, though, that he should have to remind her of her duties as hostess. Certainly no guest at Greenwood was ever treated in such a shabby manner. "I could make you something warm to drink," she offered belatedly.

His mocking glance slid down her body to encompass her bare feet. "You aren't exactly dressed to go traipsing about the house. Just tell me where Julian keeps his brandy and I'll be grateful."

"In . . . in the library, the cabinet next to the desk."

"I can find it," Dominic said, flashing her another melting smile. When Brie shivered in response, he lifted a dark brow and gave her a look of reproach. "You should be in bed," he remarked provokingly. "You must be chilled." Before she could even think of a reply, he had picked up his hat and gloves and walked from the room, shutting the door noiselessly behind him.

Brie let out her breath in a rush as she sat down heavily on the chaise longue. Whatever was she to do? For that matter, what *could* she do? She could order him to leave the house, but she very much doubted he would go. Perhaps Patrick and his brothers could throw him out? Brie shook her head. Lord Stanton was obviously not a man to cross, and he was probably accustomed to violence. He might actually harm the Dawson boys if it came to a confrontation. Besides, he was Julian's invited guest. She had no right to turn him away.

Brie sighed as she realized she had no choice, at least for tonight. She would have to let him stay at the Lodge. But it was rapidly becoming obvious she would have to leave. Very well, she would go home first thing in the morning. She didn't want to leave Mattie and Homer to fend for themselves when they were sick, but Patrick was capable of taking care of his grandparents for a few days. She would see to it that the doctor came daily to check on the Dawsons, though. And perhaps Lord Stanton would grow bored without any of his friends to keep him company. Perhaps he would even return to London, or wherever he had come from.

Indeed, she hoped so. She had little regard for London lords, for the ones she knew rarely took their responsibilities seriously, caring only for drinking and gaming and wenching. It was doubtful that Lord Stanton was any more admirable, Brie thought, recalling the way he had looked at her. With his title and striking good looks, he had at least two of the prerequisites for a first-class rakehell. He probably moved in circles where debauchery was a way of life.

Brie frowned, remembering her strange reaction to him. Yet she didn't trust his melting smile, no matter how attractive it was. Six years before, when she was seventeen, she had fallen in love with a man whose engaging smile had hidden his true designs. She had even agreed to elope with him, since her father had not approved of the match. Only by sheer chance had she discovered her suitor's intent before it was too late. It had been humiliating to learn he wanted her only for her fortune—and frightening. He had physically attacked her, attempting to force her submission. She would never forget that horrible night. Since then she had been extremely wary of men and their motives, if not actually afraid of them. Physical contact with a man still sometimes disturbed her.

But Stanton seemed to be a gentleman. Except for those first few moments, he had been polite enough. Nor had he given her any reason to fear him. Still, she was nervous about sleeping in

32

the same house with him. Not that she could sleep now. She had never been more wide awake in her life.

Determinedly, Brie lit the reading lamp and bent to pick up her novel. She had to have something to keep her thoughts occupied. Otherwise, she would spend the entire night wondering where Stanton was and what he was doing.

When a short while later a brief knock sounded on her door, Brie regarded the portal uncertainly. It had to be Stanton, but he would never believe she was asleep. "Yes?" she called out hesitantly. Somehow she wasn't surprised when he opened the door and strolled into the room, carrying a glass of brandy and a half-full decanter.

He had a hard, graceful body, Brie could see now that he no longer wore his greatcoat. His shoulders were broad and well-developed, while his waist and hips were rather slim. He was dressed expensively. An elegant coat of dark green superfine molded snugly to his lithe frame, while buff leather breeches hugged his long legs like a second skin, accentuating his muscular thighs before disappearing into knee-high top boots. He had loosened his neckcloth a little, Brie noticed, and the snowy linen looked startlingly white against his dark complexion.

He deposited the decanter on the table beside her. "Your room is warmer," he said offhandedly. "I trust you don't mind if I stay here until mine loses the chill."

Brie rather suspected it wouldn't matter if she did mind, but she wasn't even given an opportunity to reply. She watched incredulously as Stanton claimed the armchair near the hearth. He settled himself comfortably, stretching one long leg out before him as he brought his glass to his lips.

Brie's eyes narrowed as he sat there leisurely sipping his brandy. The audacity of the man was beginning to wear on her nerves. "Why don't you make yourself at home, my lord?" she asked with a hint of sarcasm. "Are you sure there isn't anything else you require?"

Meeting her flashing gaze, Dominic raised an eyebrow. "As a

33

matter of fact, I could use some help removing my boots. Would you like to volunteer?"

Brie's glance automatically moved down his buckskin-covered legs to his boots. The supple black leather was still wet and mud spattered. "No," Brie answered firmly. "Most *definitely* I would not."

He chuckled, and Brie was amazed at how his gray eyes softened with laughter. His features, too, lost that hard, cynical expression when he relaxed. "What kind of name is Brie?" he asked, surprising her. "I don't believe I have heard it before."

The question caught her unprepared. "I don't care for my real name, Gabrielle," she explained. "Brie is a shortened version."

Dominic nodded thoughtfully. "Somehow it fits."

It did fit, he thought, regarding her over the rim of his glass. There was a natural freshness about her that spoke of spring breezes. Yet her coloring belonged to fall—rich, warm, vibrant. Her hair was long and thick, with a few tousled curls framing her face, and the russet shade contrasted enchantingly with her apricot complexion. He was reminded of the red maples he had seen in America during an Indian summer. . . . Where the hell had Denville found her?

"I find it odd that Julian never mentioned you before," Dominic said casually. "Where is Julian, by the way? I expected him to be here."

"He is still in London, I imagine." That was all the information Brie intended to divulge. There was no reason to tell the arrogant Lord Stanton just why Julian was still in the city. It was none of his business, after all.

"Perhaps he decided to wait out the storm," Dominic commented, taking another sip of brandy.

Brie met his gaze deliberately. "That is indeed possible. Some people are sensible enough not to travel in a blizzard."

Dominic's eyes glimmered with something other than amusement. "You have a very sharp tongue, cherie. I wonder

34

that Denville tolerates it."

Brie flushed and lowered her gaze. She frequently spoke her mind too freely, but she had no call to be rude. Yet, Lord Stanton's remark had been just as cutting. It was clear that he thought she was here at Julian's invitation—and she could hardly set him straight without revealing who she really was. It was irritating, though, having to bite her tongue when she would have liked to tell Stanton to go to the devil. Lord, but this situation was becoming more complicated by the minute.

Dominic's reflections were running along different lines. He had a much more pleasurable occupation in mind than exchanging sharp words with Brie. She looked utterly enticing, he thought, sitting there curled on the chaise longue. That absurdly large dressing gown had fallen open at the neck, revealing a smooth, creamy throat and hinting at womanly curves. How very much he wanted to explore the hidden delights of her slender body. His gaze went to the bearskin rug before the hearth. He could easily imagine her lying there naked, her glorious hair spread beneath them like a carpet of liquid fire. And he would have her there soon, Dominic promised himself. Unless Julian had a prior claim. . . .

"Actually, I pressed on for a reason," Dominic remarked. "I thought Denville's hunting lodge, however remote, would provide superior entertainment than a wayside inn if I should happen to be stranded by the snow. I admit I expected to find better accommodations, or at least a few servants about the place. But I could forgive Julian if I thought he truly was thinking of my comfort. Did he arrange for you to be here for a purpose, by any chance?"

Brie didn't answer. She couldn't seem to think straight when Stanton was looking at her with those penetrating gray eyes of his. His assessing gaze was doing strange things to her pulse again, while his voice was sending shivers up her spine. In an unconsciously defensive gesture, Brie pulled the edges of her robe together. When Dominic rose from his chair with a lazy grace, she tensed, watching him warily.

He trapped her gaze as he slowly walked toward her. When he stood before her, Brie stared up at him, hypnotized. She was keenly aware of his proximity, of what his nearness was doing to her, yet it wasn't the raw hunger she could feel in him that shocked her. It was the primitive, entirely feminine response of her own body. A tingling, treacherous heat was snaking along her skin and gathering in places that, until now, she had hardly known existed.

He was regarding her intently, his gray eyes holding a strange glow as one of his dark brows rose slightly in question. He reached down to touch her cheek, then languidly trailed an index finger down her throat.

Brie jumped as if she had been scalded, suddenly realizing what his quizzical look meant. He was asking permission to seduce her! Obviously he considered her merely an object of pleasure, a diversion for his boredom.

His boldness infuriated her as much as the traitorous sensations he was arousing in her. Drawing back abruptly, she glared up at him. "I am *not* part of the accommodations, my lord!" she ground out through her teeth.

He stared down at her for such a long moment that Brie's heart began to thud. Not daring to move, she held her breath, waiting. Just as she began to worry if she would have to defend herself from a physical assault, Dominic stepped back, his mouth curving in a sardonic smile. "Pity," he remarked. "By the looks of it we'll be here together for some time."

Casually, he turned and picked up the decanter, then crossed to the door. He opened it before glancing back over his shoulder at her. "You really should lock this, cherie," he said, his voice once more holding a note of mockery. "You never know who might intrude." He left then, closing the door before Brie could manage to find her tongue.

She stared after him speechlessly, wanting to throw something. Why Stanton affected her so strongly, though, she couldn't imagine. There had been no reason to feel such fury at his suggestion. She had had propositions before, both honorable and not so honorable, and normally she was amused, sometimes even flattered. So why had she felt that intense anger toward Stanton? He had only acted as most red-blooded men would in such circumstances. He was the kind of man who used women only for pleasure.

Of course she didn't want to be used in such a manner. But why had she been unable to crush that odd tremor of excitement that had originated in the pit of her stomach? She had felt her body responding to him, to the blatant desire in his eyes, and for an instant, she had been conscious of an odd yearning deep inside her. She had wanted him to take her in his arms . . . and yet she had also been aware of a niggling sense of panic. She had been afraid of what would befall her if he did. Quite afraid.

Suddenly coming to her senses, Brie got up and locked the door, then let out her breath as she leaned back against the panel. It was becoming obvious that strange things happened to her equilibrium when that arrogant, cynical man was near her. She didn't know if she could handle any more such confrontations with him. One thing was certain, though. She wouldn't get much sleep tonight. Most certainly she wouldn't.

Chapter Two

Brie woke at dawn the next morning, feeling listless and bleary eyed. She stumbled out of bed and shivered as her bare feet hit the icy floor. The room was freezing. Her breath turned to little clouds of steam in the frigid air, while the goose bumps on her arms resembled small mountains. In the water pitcher there was even a layer of ice that had to be chipped away before she could wash.

Hurriedly, she poured water into the basin and splashed her face. Gritting her teeth against the shock, she decided that she actually envied the Dawson boys. They wouldn't have to wash with ice water, for the male servants' dormitory had an enormous stove that kept the place cozy and warm.

She made use of the few toilet articles she had, then ran a brush through her tangled russet curls. When she had tied the heavy mass back with a ribbon, she donned the same plain dress she had worn the day before. The empire-waisted gown was one of her oldest and wasn't at all stylish, but it was made of serviceable brown kerseymere and kept her warm. And the gown did mold nicely to her slender figure and complement the apricot color of her complexion, Brie thought, surveying her appearance in the cheval glass.

After pulling on her stockings and worn leather half-boots, she went to the window and drew back the curtains. Unable to see anything for the frost, she rubbed a circle on the pane, then stared out with dismay at the wintry landscape. The entire world was blanketed in a thick layer of white. It was no longer snowing, but the sky looked bleak and she could see great mounds of snow piled haphazardly against the house. Directly below the window, resembling moldy lumps of flour, were some odd clumps that she knew were rhododendron bushes. The line of oaks in the distance looked like a troop of decrepit old men with long gray beards, while the drive to the Lodge was unrecognizable.

Brie groaned as she viewed the frozen scene. The roads would be impassable and none of the staff would report to work. It also meant that the plans she had made the previous day would have to be altered drastically. She would have to find Patrick at once and decide what to do—but first she had to check on his grandparents.

Brie made her way upstairs, expecting Mattie and Homer's room to be as cold as hers had been. She was quite surprised, therefore, to find a fire burning cheerily in the grate. Mattie was still asleep but Homer was awake, buried beneath the blankets of the truckle bed. It seemed Mattie hadn't passed an easy night.

"She had a hard time of it, Miss Brie," Homer said in response to Brie's questions. "Been wheezin' something fierce. I be right worried about her. The medicine don't seem to be helpin'."

Although Brie was no expert, she could tell Mattie was getting worse. Her worn cheeks were flushed with fever, while her breathing was shallow and labored. Brie pressed her lips together, angry that Homer hadn't called her. But she realized it wouldn't do any good to scold him now. "I'll get some water to sponge her forehead," she said, disapproval creeping in her tone.

Homer sniffed and held his handkerchief up to his red nose. "I don't know, Miss Brie. We've already done t'once. His lordship said t'would be better for Mattie to sleep now."

"His lordship?" For the first time Brie noticed the basin and cloth beside the bed, and they puzzled her. She hadn't forgotten the man who had burst into her bedchamber the previous night, uninvited; she had even dreamed about Stanton. But she found it hard to believe that he would put himself out for an old, sick woman he had never seen before. "Do you mean Lord Stanton?" Brie asked. "He was *here?*"

Homer's answer was interrupted by a fit of coughing, but he managed to nod, which caused Brie's blue-green eyes to widen in amazement.

"And did he stoke the fire?" she asked skeptically.

"No, t'was Sheldon."

Brie was incredulous. To say that Sheldon Dawson was lazy would be like calling last night's blizzard a sprinkling of snowflakes. He never did any real work unless he was absolutely forced to. Even Patrick, who had the patience of an ox, had been known to give his brother a cuff on the chin when he grew tired of shouldering Sheldon's load. Surely Homer was mistaken. "Well, perhaps I could bring you some breakfast," she offered.

Homer shook his head. "Lord Stanton promised to see to it," he said, blowing loudly into his handkerchief.

Brie was conscious of a surge of resentment. Homer made the man sound like an angel of mercy. "Isn't there anything I can do for you?"

"Don't think so, Miss Brie. Thank ye, though."

Trying to hide her pique, she cast a glance at the sleeping Mattie. "Very well, then. Try to get some rest, Homer. I'll be up to check again in a little while—subject to his lordship's approval, of course."

The house was deserted, Brie discovered after a search of the ground floor rooms. A good fire was going on the kitchen hearth, though, indicating that someone had been busy, and a large caldron of water was slowly heating over the coals. The oven, too, was already warm.

Since Patrick was nowhere in sight, Brie went to fetch her

41

cloak from the hall closet, determined to brave the cold i
order to find him. She was tying the strings of her cloak whe
she heard a door slam. Glancing down the hall, she saw Stanto
beside the door. He had obviously just entered the house fo
the collar of his greatcoat was turned up and he was stampin
snow from his boots. She noticed at once that the growth on hi
chin was more pronounced than the previous evening, a sig
that he hadn't found time to shave yet this morning. There wa
also a grim expression on his handsome face that wasn't at a
pleasant. In fact, he appeared to be in a foul humor.

Brie decided she would be wise to avoid him if she could
"Good morning," she murmured, trying to slip past his ta
form. She didn't get far; Dominic's hand shot out to catch he
by the arm. Brie looked up at him, startled.

His gray eyes held hers for a moment before his gaze swep
down her body, taking note of her cloak. "Where do you thin
you are going?"

Brie stiffened at his curt tone. "The stables, if you mus
know."

"I don't advise it. The snow is too deep."

Brie stared pointedly down at the gloved hand holding he
arm. "Thank you for your concern, but I believe I ca
manage."

He didn't release her arm, nor did he beg her pardon for hi
boldness. If anything, his tone became more abrupt. "I expec
you to wait until someone shovels a path."

Brie felt a spark of anger ignite in her breast. Stanton wa
speaking to her as if he were disciplining a disobedient puppy
"I should like to see Patrick," she told him through tight lips

"Perhaps, but I doubt he wants to see you just now. He'
feeling quite a lot of pain."

Brie gasped, her eyes flying to Stanton's. "Why? What hav
you done to him?"

Dominic's mouth curled at the corner. "I served him to
pack of wolves this morning for breakfast, didn't I tell you? I'n
surprised you didn't hear the howling."

42

His dulcet tones dripped sarcasm, making Brie wince, but her concern was for Patrick, not herself. "Is Patrick truly hurt?" she asked, her eyes anxiously searching Dominic's face.

Giving a sigh, he released her arm. "The boy slipped on some ice and split his knee open. Jacques is sewing the wound now. I came back to the house to get some laudanum. Do you know where any can be found?"

For a moment Brie could only stare at him in dismay. "Mattie should have some," she responded finally. "She keeps a medicine chest in the upstairs pantry."

She turned and reached for the door handle, but Dominic gripped her arm again. "Just a moment. Perhaps you didn't understand me, but you aren't going outside."

"I *beg* your pardon," Brie said icily. "Release me at once, if you please."

"I don't please. I told you to remain here and I mean to be obeyed. I've had about all I can stand of this slipshod household so early in the morning. First my right leader turns up lame because that half-wit in the stables leaves a pitchfork in his stall, and now Patrick—"

He never completed his sentence. Brie jerked her arm away and gave Dominic a look of such fury that he momentarily forgot his own anger.

Brie did have some rationale for losing her temper. She was worried about Mattie and the news of Patrick's injury had greatly alarmed her. Besides that, she had had very little sleep the night before, all because of Lord Stanton. His presence in the house made her own situation untenable. She couldn't stay, yet she couldn't leave now that Patrick was hurt. She also resented Stanton's arrogant assumption of authority. The way he stood there, issuing orders and demanding to be obeyed, galled her. But to cap his sins, he had spoken derisively about a boy who was unable to defend himself. At eleven, Seth Dawson was the youngest of Homer's grandsons, but he had the mental capacity of only a five-year-old. He had a sweet nature, though,

43

and Brie had always been protective of him. She flew to his defense like a mother tigress.

"Seth is *not* a half-wit!" she spat furiously. "He can't help it if he's slow. He was born like that. Oh, how I detest it when people look down their noses at those who are less fortunate. Well, let me tell you, *your lordship*, Seth is as worthy in God's eyes as any of you well-born, titled, fashionable fribbles from London. And furthermore—" Brie's hands went to her hips as she drew herself up to her full, unpretentious height— "Furthermore, I don't need you to tell me what I can and can't do. If I want to go outside, if I want to dance *stark naked* in the snow, you have no right to order me otherwise. I intend to see Patrick and you had better not try to stop me. In fact," Brie added, her eyes flashing fire, "why don't you just take yourself back to the city? We don't want you here!"

Brie was too angry to notice the grim set of Dominic's jaw, but when she saw how his eyes had narrowed, she took an involuntary step backwards. The glittering chill in the gray depths frightened her. So did the silent pause which followed.

"Are you quite finished?" Dominic said finally, piercing her with his icy gaze.

The quiet menace in his tone was enough to make her shiver. "Yes," she replied, her own voice suddenly hoarse.

"Good. Now it's my turn. Sit down." Dominic took her arm in a firm grip and steered her toward the chair at the foot of the stairs. When Brie made a move as if to break away, Dominic put a forceful hand on her shoulder. "I said, *sit*."

Stealing a worried glance at him, Brie decided to obey. Those penetrating gray eyes were as cold as a winter's day and twice as savage.

When Dominic spoke, his tone was harsh and clipped. "In the first place, I wasn't speaking of Seth. As you said, the lad can't help being what he is. I was referring to the older boy, Sheldon. He was inexcusably careless. Since you're in charge of the place, you might like to know that I threatened to thrash him if he ever comes near one of my horses again. In the

44

meantime, I've put him to work chopping firewood. That should keep him occupied until I can attend to him."

"Oh," Brie said lamely, staring up at Dominic and realizing that she had misunderstood. Sheldon was the last person she would want around her own horses. And she could hardly fault Lord Stanton for being angry if one of his team had been injured. She felt like a royal fool now for shouting.

Dominic wasn't finished with her yet, however. "Second," he continued caustically, "you aren't dressed to go outside. You would never make it all the way to the stables in those skirts. The snow is four feet deep in places. We had to string a rope from the house to the barns merely to get some leverage against the drifts. Besides that, you'll get wet. With the Dawsons upstairs in bed and Patrick injured, we don't need another invalid."

"I don't get sick," Brie protested, although not very strongly.

"I'm not willing to take the chance," he said crushingly. "And last, you aren't needed at the moment." Brie's chin came up at that, and Dominic viewed her with mocking eyes. He had wondered how long that show of meekness would last. "Do you sicken at the sight of blood?" he asked abruptly.

"What?"

"Can you sew up a wound? Are you any good at nursing? Could you be of any real help to Patrick at the moment? His knee isn't a pretty sight. He's trying to be brave, but his injury is painful. I doubt that having a woman view his tears is the kind of comfort he wants."

Flushing, Brie lowered her gaze. She suddenly felt ashamed that she had been more concerned about her own pride than Patrick's condition. "Yes, you're right," she said humbly.

Dominic's harsh features softened a little. "Jacques is more than capable of handling the situation. He may not have studied medicine, but there is no one better at tending wounds. Patrick will be all right."

When Brie made no reply, Dominic put a finger under her

chin and tilted her face up. His eyes moved over her speculatively, lingering on her mouth. He was conscious of a fierce desire to taste her lips, to see if they were as sweet and luscious as they appeared. But this wasn't the time or the place.

"You and I have a number of things to discuss," he said instead, "but that can come later. At the moment I think it best that I get that laudanum for Patrick."

Brie nodded, unable to tear her gaze away from his. Her heart was beating too rapidly again, and there were hot little flashes running up her spine. She was conscious of an odd sense of disappointment when Stanton released her.

He had turned to mount the stairs by the time Brie came to her senses. "Lord Stanton," she called after him. He paused, one booted foot on the stair as he glanced down at her. As his gray eyes locked with hers, Brie felt a strange current pass through her body. It left her a little breathless.

"I . . . I beg your pardon for shouting at you," she managed to say.

A smile's shadow touched the corner of his mouth. "I must admit, no one has ever called me a 'fashionable fribble' before now, at least not to my face."

"I'm sorry."

"Very well, apology accepted."

"Is there anything I can do?"

One of his black brows rose. "Can you cook?"

"Not much, I'm afraid."

"You might see what food you can find in the pantry, then. We're cut off from the village and likely to remain that way for several days. Do what you can to start breakfast. It would be best for the Dawsons to have something bland like gruel, but the rest of us will need something more substantial. I'll be back shortly to help."

Brie nodded and rose. "There is one more thing," Dominic added, surprising her. When she looked up at him expectantly, she could see the mocking glint in his eyes. "If you do decide to dance naked in the snow," he drawled outrageously, "let me

46

now. I expect I would enjoy watching."

Brie opened her mouth to retort, but then thought better of and pressed her lips together. She had already made a fool of erself once this morning by losing her temper. She wouldn't o so again, no matter how deliberately provoking Stanton as. Instead, she squared her shoulders and turned to put her loak away in the closet. Fortunately for her new resolve, she idn't see the amused smile that was playing on Dominic's lips.

Brie went directly to the kitchen, determined to forget her npleasant confrontation with Stanton and regain her omposure. By the time she had finished checking what food he Lodge had on hand, however, she was feeling frustrated. ike the sickroom, the kitchen was not one of her areas of xpertise. She had been trained from an early age to manage a arge estate, but her training hadn't actually included learning ow to cook. She had merely needed to set standards for her ervants and see they were upheld. Now she fervently wished he had paid more attention when her mother had instructed er about household matters. Well, Brie thought with a defiant lance around the kitchen, she would just have to make the est of the situation.

At least the larder was well stocked. Her search through the toreroom revealed a large haunch of beef, several smoked ams, a side of bacon, and a variety of winter vegetables. There vere also a few loaves of bread, as well as some different heeses.

They could always have toasted bread and cheese, Brie lecided. And there was plenty of cider and ale. Tea and coffee, oo, if she could determine how much of each to use. But the nvalids needed a special diet. How did one make gruel, nyway?

Brie pushed a curl from her forehead and took a deep breath. This was no time to despair. At least she could find some ooking pots and set some plates out on the kitchen table. Besides, Stanton had said he would help, hadn't he?

Realizing she would be glad when he returned, Brie had to

47

smile. She never would have guessed that she'd be grateful for his presence at the Lodge. But he had been helpful, even if his manner had been rather high handed. And she supposed she had to make allowances for his arrogance. Earls were a different breed of men, after all.

Brie was still in a charitable frame of mind when Dominic entered the kitchen a few moments later. She looked up from her task of folding napkins at the table and gave him a friendly smile. For a moment she even thought he might return her simple greeting, for he had halted in the doorway and was staring at her intently.

But then his brows drew together in a frown. "Something is burning," he said abruptly, his searching glance moving quickly around the kitchen.

"The skillet!" Brie gasped, realizing she had set the pan on the hot stove. It was smoking now, darkening the air with greasy black fumes. Brie leapt to her feet and before Dominic could stop her, reached frantically for the skillet. She dropped it even more quickly, giving a cry of pain as the hot iron burned her fingers.

Dominic reacted by grabbing Brie by the arm and dragging her across the kitchen. In an instant, he had shoved her out the back door and down the steps, then tumbled her to the ground and thrust her throbbing hand into a snowbank.

Brie was too stunned to speak for a moment. Then realizing that she was sprawling in the snow, freezing, while Stanton forcibly held her there after he had practically threatened her life if she disobeyed him, she began to laugh.

Dominic liked the sound of her laughter. It was low and melodious and completely feminine. He grinned back at her. "You know, I was the one who told you not to go outside. But this will stop any blisters from forming."

"I didn't know the skillet would be hot," she said ruefully.

"You weren't jesting. You really don't know how to cook."

She nodded sadly. "I suppose I'm hopeless."

Dominic cocked his head, studying her. "I wouldn't say

that, precisely. I expect your talents just lie elsewhere." He didn't voice his actual thoughts—that warming a man's bed was probably what she was best suited for. Instead, he lifted her hand, turning it palm up to inspect the burn. The injury didn't seem too serious, just a couple of red marks on her fingers. "Does it pain you?" he asked softly.

Hearing the suddenly husky note in his voice, Brie looked down in confusion. Her hand wasn't hurting anymore, unless one counted the throbbing sensation where Stanton's warm fingers touched her skin. "No," she replied a little breathlessly.

"You'll live, then." He smiled, letting his thumb absently caress her palm. "And fortunately, I know a little something about cooking. Do you think you could chop some vegetables for a soup without cutting yourself?"

Looking up, Brie found herself staring blankly at Dominic. She had been admiring his long, graceful fingers and wondering how they had gotten so tanned, but his melting smile had scattered her thoughts, making her forget entirely what they had been discussing. "What did you say?" she asked.

Dominic regarded her with amusement. "Vegetables, cherie. For a soup. The broth will be good for our invalids."

Flushing at his knowing look, Brie pulled her hand away. "Yes, of course," she said hastily, feeling foolish for letting him affect her so. Struggling to her feet, she dusted the snow from her damp skirts and made her way carefully up the slippery steps to the house.

Dominic followed more slowly, letting his gaze linger on her trim hips. He hadn't had any trouble recognizing the look she had given him. That befuddled expression Brie had worn for a moment was no stranger to him, for he had often seen it on the faces of women he exerted himself enough to charm. Brie was most definitely susceptible to seduction, he decided, if not actually willing. And that meant it was only a matter of time before he had her in his bed.

49

Which was fortunate, Dominic thought with a grin. Otherwise being cooped up with her was likely to drive him to drink. He felt an ache in his groin every time he looked at her. Of course, he would have to make certain that she didn't belong to Julian. Honorably, he couldn't infringe on his friend's territory. But barring that, it should only be a few days.

It was a measure of Brie's innocence that she didn't guess what was being planned for her. She was aware that Dominic fascinated her, though. His nearness affected her strangely as she washed and peeled and chopped vegetables. Far too often she caught herself stealing a glance at him as he prepared breakfast.

He seemed almost a different man now from the one who had frightened her that morning with his cold anger, for there was a hint of gentleness beneath the cynicism that hadn't been present before. He was wearing the same dark green coat he had worn the previous night, although he no longer had on a neckcloth. His white cambric shirt was open at the neck, revealing a strong, brown throat. That, and the fact that his black hair was a little tousled, lent him an informality that was rather appealing, Brie thought. Even the stubble on his jaw didn't detract from his rakish good looks. A fallen angel, indeed. That suggestion of lost sweetness made a woman ache to take him in her arms and hold him. Not that she would ever do such a thing. But he fascinated her, all the same.

Brie found herself trying to guess his age. Something over thirty, she decided, wondering how had he spent those years. His deft movements suggested that at least he knew what he was doing with a skillet—and soon the appetizing aroma of bacon frying confirmed it.

The delicious smells made Brie realize how hungry she was, but she was content to wait. The kitchen radiated an intimate atmosphere that was cozy, warm, and welcoming. Brie smiled to herself, realizing she was actually enjoying working silently beside Stanton. How could anyone *enjoy* cutting up carrots?

Their intimacy was soon interrupted. First Ezra Dawson, the second youngest Dawson grandson, delivered a basket of eggs from the hen house. Then a moment later, the kitchen door swung open to admit a short, dark, heavy-set man.

He entered quietly without knocking, and his sudden appearance startled Brie, making her jump. His reaction to her was even stronger. When he saw her, he stopped dead in his tracks and stared at her as if confronting a ghost.

Brie stared back—although she hardly noted his black eyes or his olive complexion or the fact that he was dressed in rough, workman's clothes. Her gaze was fixed on the body of the young deer he had slung over his shoulders. Seeing that it was little more than a fawn, Brie was dismayed. With the heavy snow the animal must have come close to the house in search of food, and then this brute had killed it.

The man recollected himself first. Tearing his gaze from Brie, he nodded to Dominic who was watching them both curiously. Then he carried the deer to the corner behind the door and let the stiff carcass tumble to the floor. "Now we will have roast venison," he said, straightening.

His accent was heavy, French by the sound of it, but Brie wasn't concerned with his manner of speech. His callousness had made her furious. She was half inclined to bring charges against him for poaching on Julian's land. "How could you?" she demanded of the brawny Frenchman. "That helpless animal was unable to defend itself."

Bewildered, he looked to his employer. Dominic's expression remained bland, but there was an unmistakable glimmer of amusement in his eyes. "Jacques, this is Brie," he remarked in a dry tone.

Jacques eyed Brie warily. She was holding a paring knife in her hand, and at the moment, looked angry enough to use it. When she hesitated, he touched his cap respectfully to her.

Dominic found himself struggling to repress a smile as he watched the two of them square off like fighting gamecocks. Brie was beautiful when she flew into a passion; her eyes

51

turned a smoky, smoldering green, while her cheeks flushed with vibrant color. But Jacques' expression was comical. The man looked shocked to find himself facing such a lovely spitfire. Dominic could sympathize, for he knew what it felt like to be on the receiving end of the beauty's vixenish temper. Fortunately, Brie hadn't had a knife when she had raged at him earlier that morning. He had the uncomfortable feeling that he might be missing some vital parts now if she had.

Deciding that he had better rescue his coachman, Dominic inclined his head toward the door. "You'll find the Dawsons on the third floor," he told Jacques. "First room on the right."

The Frenchman looked relieved. He edged his way past Brie carefully, never taking his eyes off her until he reached the door to the hall. Then he slipped through quickly, leaving Dominic to face her alone. Dominic raised one eyebrow and waited expectantly for the explosion.

It didn't come. Brie was fuming, to be sure; she thought it incredulous that Stanton had dismissed his servant before she had a chance to speak to him about killing game on Julian's property. But she had also learned it was wiser not to challenge Dominic directly. She gave him one long, fulminating glare, then angrily turned her back to him and stabbed a potato.

There was a pregnant silence—a silence Brie found herself wishing would end. She could feel Dominic's intent gaze between her shoulder blades. She was about to take him to task for staring when he finally spoke. "The doe froze to death, Brie," he said gently.

"What?" she muttered irritably, not interested in anything he had to say.

"Jacques didn't kill the doe. She died last night from exposure after getting a leg caught in a crevice. That was how Patrick hurt himself—trying to carry the carcass across a patch of ice. I decided afterward to make use of the meat rather than leave it for the scavengers."

Brie felt a rush of mortification start at her ears and slowly burn a path downward to her toes. How could she have acted so

52

idiotically? She had jumped to an erroneous conclusion again, had made a spectacle of herself in front of Stanton for the second time that morning. Remembering her outburst, she was almost afraid to look at him. There would be a mocking gleam in his eyes, she was sure. He probably thought her a dim-witted rustic—certainly she had behaved like one.

She was not a coward, though. She turned to face Dominic, squaring her shoulders as if she were bracing herself to accept a particularly obnoxious dose of medicine. "I am sorry, my lord," she said stiffly. "I mistook the situation. Of course I will apologize to your servant at once."

Her expression was such an odd mixture of humility and belligerence that Dominic felt a curious tug at his heart. For once the mocking edge was missing from his voice when he spoke. "I doubt that Jacques requires an apology," he replied, "but it might be wise to let him know you didn't mean to carve out his liver. He's somewhat sensitive about such things."

"Yes . . . well . . . ," Brie stammered. The look Dominic was giving her made her knees feel weak. Flustered, she glanced over at the deer. "I felt sorry for it."

Dominic's lips twisted in a wry grin. "Somehow I got that impression. If I ever find any animals or little children in need of defense, I will have complete confidence in recommending you as their champion."

For a moment, Brie wondered if he was mocking her again, but she could detect only a strange tenderness in his tone. And since her heart had suddenly started doing odd little flip-flops in her chest, she was glad to turn her attention back to the carrots.

The rest of the morning passed in a blur. Dominic took charge of the household with the ease of a field commander, giving orders and organizing everyone, including Brie, into a surprisingly efficient staff. His own servants—a groom and two footmen who were part of his entourage—were assigned to the stables and general kitchen duty, while the younger Dawsons were left with their regular chores. Brie made no protest at any of Dominic's commands, even though she was a bit annoyed by his assumption of authority, for she could see he was more capable than she in dealing with such an emergency.

She was kept busy the entire time. When she finished the vegetables, she carried a breakfast tray upstairs to the Dawsons and discovered that her help was needed after all. She found Homer and Jacques involved in a heated discussion, arguing over how best to care for Mattie. The burly coachman was waving his hands in the air and swearing in volatile French, while Homer was brandishing a candlestick and stubbornly declaring that no God-forsaken Frog was going to touch his wife, sick or not. Jacques, it seemed, had recommended a mustard plaster for Mattie's chest but hadn't quite managed to convince Homer that his intentions were purely professional. When Brie solved the problem by offering her help, Jacques gave her a look that clearly said she might be more intelligent than he had first assumed.

Brie stayed with Mattie most of the morning, but she did find an opportunity to visit Patrick and allay her fears about his injury. She had no time to dwell on her own situation, though, or worry that she was risking her reputation by remaining in the same house with a man like Stanton. But she was no longer concerned that he would ruin her good name merely in order to have a topic of discussion at his club. He was not the frivolous dandy she had called him earlier, nor was he the sort of man to go bragging to his friends about his conquests. All the same, she didn't mean to volunteer any information about her identity. It really was none of his concern, after all.

Her first reminder of the real danger Dominic represented came that afternoon. Brie had gone in search of him because Homer wanted to speak to him about the Frenchman. When she couldn't find Stanton anywhere else in the house, Brie made her way up to his bedroom and knocked tentatively on the door. She was bidden entrance at once, but the sight that greeted her when she stepped into the room brought her up short. He was shaving.

Dominic stood before a mirror, razor in hand, a towel draped around his neck. His white linen shirt was casually opened to the waist, while a lather of soap covered his chin and one cheek.

Brie stared at him in fascination. She had never seen a man shave before, not even her father, and she found herself wondering if it hurt to scrape a sharp blade across his face, then wondering if the dark, curling hair on his bronzed chest felt as soft and springy as it looked.

When she simply stood there, silently gaping at him, Dominic raised an eyebrow. "Do come in. And shut the door, unless you mean for me to catch my death from the cold air you're letting in."

Realizing where her thoughts had been leading, Brie flushed and did as she was told. She was violating propriety with a vengeance by being in a man's bedroom with the door closed, but it really was freezing in the hall. She was shivering already—although she suspected her ailment had more to do with the way his gray eyes were roaming over her than with the temperature of the house. "Homer would like you to come and check on Mattie," Brie said a trifle breathlessly. "She seems to be getting better, but he wants your opinion."

Turning back to the washstand, Dominic casually resumed his shaving. "You would do better to call Jacques. He is the expert, not I."

"I know, but Homer has more faith in your judgment. Your coachman is French, you see."

Dominic eyed Brie in the mirror. "What does that have to say to anything?"

"Homer doesn't care for Frenchmen. He actively dislikes them."

That seemed to amuse Dominic, for his mouth twisted in a grin. "I doubt that I would be much of an improvement then since I'm half French myself."

His admission surprised Brie. Most people of French heritage were far shorter than he. Her own mother, for one, had stood just over five feet tall. Stanton had to be at least six feet. But then he might have gotten his height from the English side of his family.

"Homer really doesn't mean anything by it," Brie said, feeling a need to defend the old man. "It's just that he lost several members of his family in the war. His only son died fighting the French in Spain and two of his grandsons were killed at Waterloo."

"Ah, that explains it, then," Dominic said cryptically. When Brie gave him a puzzled glance, he returned her gaze in the mirror. "That explains why Jacques has had so much trouble getting information about you. All of the Dawsons have been as closemouthed as Napoleon's secret police. Even Patrick, whom I would have expected to be grateful to Jacques for sewing up his leg."

"Why should your coachman want to know about me?" Brie asked warily.

Dominic ran a thumb over his chin, testing for smoothness. "Probably because I asked him to see what he could find out. I don't care much for mysteries. And you, cherie, are a very big mystery."

Brie was growing extremely uncomfortable with the conversation. She took a nervous step backwards. "I'll tell Homer you were too busy to see him," she suggested, groping for the door handle at her back.

"Just a moment, Brie."

She stiffened at his command, but halted obediently, waiting. She remembered quite well what had happened that morning when she had tried to leave without his permission.

He watched her reflection as he scraped the last of the lather from his face. "Jacques is an expert at ferreting out information," he remarked in a cool voice, "but all he could learn was that your surname is Carringdon, that everyone calls

56

you 'Miss Brie', and that you live in a big house not far from here."

Brie's eyes widened. She hadn't expected to keep her identity a secret from Stanton forever, but she was amazed at how quickly he had found her out, especially since the Dawsons had tried to protect her with their silence. His presumptuousness piqued her, though. The nerve of the man, sending his coachman to interrogate the servants about her! "People here don't care for strangers asking questions," she said, bridling. "Especially *foreign* strangers."

Dominic ignored her gibe. "I once knew a Sir William Carringdon. Are you by any chance related?"

"Very distantly." That wasn't quite a lie, Brie thought defiantly. Her father had been buried in the village churchyard for the past four years now, and if her reply stretched the truth, it was only because she resented Stanton's probing.

He seemed willing to drop the point, however. Wiping his face with the towel, Dominic turned to face her. His gaze swept down her slender body, studying her measuringly, lingering on the soft swell of her breasts. "Julian has a good eye," he said, using a different tack, "but I thought his taste generally ran to more voluptuous females."

"I am not Julian's mistress!" Brie snapped, before realizing she would have been better off not admitting it. Being one of Julian's light-skirts would have at least offered her some measure of protection from Stanton's advances. Now it looked as if she would have to find some other way of putting him off. He was walking toward her, his gray eyes holding a glint that clearly warned her to flee. She couldn't move, though. Her limbs refused to obey.

Dominic halted before her, gazing down at her face. "Then perhaps you are open to suggestion," he murmured speculatively.

Brie stared up at him, unable to speak. His nearness was doing strange things to her pulse again. Not only could she feel the warmth of his body, but the scent of his shaving soap was

filling her senses, making her giddy. Her gaze fastened on h
mouth as he slowly, slowly bent his head.

His kiss was not what Brie had imagined it would be like. Sh
had expected his lips to be hard and demanding, like the ma
Instead, they were cool and firm and incredibly gentle. She fe
his tongue trace her lips slowly, as if he were memorizing th
taste of her. Then unhurriedly, he delved into her mouth.

If he had tried to force her, Brie would have bolted. But hi
kiss was curious and exploring. Brie was conscious of a singl
overwhelming sensation—she was melting. Her limbs wer
turning to warm, liquid heat. She parted her lips for hi
helplessly, opening to him as his tongue probed her mouth, n
even realizing when her hands crept up to his shoulders.

It was a long moment before Dominic drew away, his eye
dark and unreadable as they skimmed her face. Brie gazed bac
at him, mesmerized. And then his mouth came down on her
again.

His lips were no longer cool this time. They were hot an
fierce and passionate. And when his arms came around he
possessively, pulling her full against his hard length, she wa
robbed of breath. For a moment Brie even responded to hin
pressing against him, clinging. But then the sharp wave o
desire racing through her body alarmed her with its intensity
Moreover, a sudden memory of the physical violence she ha
once suffered at a man's hands made her panic.

Tearing her mouth away, she pushed frantically agains
Dominic's muscular chest. "No, please!" she cried, trying t
get away and finding it impossible; the door was at her back
leaving nowhere to run.

Dominic was surprised by her sudden reversal. When he fel
her struggling, though, he loosened his hold and tilted his hea
back to study her. "What is it, cherie?" he murmure
soothingly, stroking her cheek.

Hearing the gentleness in his voice, the panic that ha
gripped her subsided and Brie came to her senses. "I . . .
can't," she said, biting her lip.

She felt his warm breath caress her temple before his lips followed, tenderly brushing the sensitive spot. "Why can't you?" he asked in a voice thick with passion. "Are you married? Can I expect to find myself challenged by a jealous husband?"

Brie closed her eyes, feeling her heart pound. "No, but I . . . I am . . ."

His eyebrow lifted inquiringly. "Under some gentleman's protection?"

"Yes!" Brie latched onto that excuse with fervent haste.

"Then you can leave him."

"No! I mean, I don't want to leave him. I am happy with my current situation. He is kind to me, and . . . and I've been with him a long time, you see, and I don't want to—" Brie was aware that she was babbling, but she couldn't help herself. When Dominic pressed a finger to her lips to silence her, she was grateful.

He smiled at her then, the kind of smile that could lure a woman's soul from her body. "I can be quite generous," he said softly, persuasively. Brie swallowed hard. Her eyes were wide and shadowed when she finally shook her head.

Dominic deliberated a moment before releasing her. Then he stepped back. "Very well," he said lightly, his voice at odds with what he was feeling. "Tell Homer I will be up in a moment."

Brie felt relief flood through her. She fled, before he could change his mind.

Dominic stared thoughtfully at the closed portal. She was indeed a mystery—one he hadn't yet figured out. She was as skittish as a virgin, yet from the way she had responded to him, he would swear she was no stranger to a man's touch. But that flicker in her eyes had been fear. She was afraid of him for some reason. Perhaps he had been too harsh with her earlier. Or perhaps she was afraid of what her current protector would do to her if she were to accept the advances of another man. If she even had a protector. Brie's stammered excuses had given him reason to doubt that she was telling him the complet truth about that.

But why then had she not accepted his offer? He dismisse the possibility that she was merely being loyal to whomeve had her in keeping. Women were never loyal where money wa concerned. So who was she? She wasn't trained to be a servan although he had already seen she didn't mind hard worl Jacques had liked her, which was surprising, considering th way she had ripped up at him at first. Normally Jacques didn' care for women, unless they were in his bed. In fact, th coachman was even more cynical about women than Domini himself. Brie was lovely enough to attract a rich protector, s why was she dressed so poorly? She looked to be in her earl twenties, meaning she was old enough to have had half a doze protectors. . . .

Why that thought disturbed him, Dominic wasn't sure. Bu no matter, he reflected. He would just have to go slowly. Bri Carringdon couldn't be so far different from other women tha she would continue to refuse the generous terms he woul offer her. Nor so different that she could withstand a full-sca assault of her defenses.

Brie tried to avoid Dominic after that, but she found impossible. In the first place, he wasn't the kind of man on could ignore. In the second, they were forced by necessity t spend several hours a day together.

Little of it was leisure time. Had they been guests at houseparty, they would have occupied themselves with card chess, or billiards, or perhaps read poetry aloud, or entertaine anyone who would listen to their musical talents. But ther were no such activities. The only time Brie had a moment t rest was in the evening, after Mattie and Homer had gone t sleep.

Even then, she couldn't really relax. For when she retired t her room at the end of the day, Stanton followed her, just as t were the most natural thing in the world for him to drink his after-dinner brandy in a lady's bedroom. But then it probably *was* natural for him, Brie decided. More than likely he had spent a great deal of time in ladies' bedrooms. And she could hardly object to his presence without sounding oddly prudish. She couldn't be comfortable around him, though.

For one thing, he wouldn't give up his interest in her availability. Brie found her fabrication about having a protector becoming more and more complicated. During their first idle evening together when Dominic had probed her for information, she had felt a need to substantiate her story and had ended up describing an elderly gentleman who was very much like her head trainer, John Simms. John would have been horrified to learn he had been cast in such a role, but she had to tell Stanton something. As it was, Dominic looked at her with a mocking gleam in his eye and remarked that the man sounded old enough to be her father. The implication was, of course, that she would be better off with someone younger, more able to fill her nights with passion.

She did learn a bit more about him during those evening conversations, however, even though he was almost as reticent about his past as she was about her own. He had inherited his title from his maternal grandfather, she discovered, for his father had been French, his mother English. Her question about his parents obviously touched a sensitive nerve, though. Stanton's face darkened when he told her his father had been killed during the Revolution, and his lip curled in a sneer when he said his mother had remarried and was living in Hampshire.

Discomfited by the sudden charge of tension in the air, Brie had thought it best to change the subject. But Dominic's response, when she admitted that she was part French herself, disturbed her even more. His eyes swept leisurely down her body, and he asked, "Which part?" in a half-mocking, half-teasing tone of voice that made her well aware he was still interested in having her become his mistress.

He much preferred brandy over port, Brie discovered when

he related a humorous tale about some smugglers of hi
acquaintance. She also learned that he had been involved i
the war for several years, although in what capacity, she coul
only guess. She thought he might have been some kind o
diplomat, since he mentioned the Foreign Office once, and als
that he had met Julian in Vienna at the Congress.

That was really the extent of her discoveries about Domini
Serrault, Lord Stanton. Everything else was merely observa
tion.

He had two very distinct kinds of smiles, she quickl
realized. One was mocking and cynical, the other so sweetl
devastating that it made her heart melt. In addition to his har
mouth, his mobile black brows were mainly responsible fo
giving his expression a sardonic cast. The left one had a habit o
lifting nearly an inch higher than the right.

As for his character, he was arrogant and insufferable muc
of the time, but he could be delightfully, devilishly charmin
when he wanted to be. Occasionally he even showed traces o
real warmth. Sarcasm had absolutely no effect on him
probably because he was such an expert at it himself. H
tended to mock everything, unless he was genuinely amuse
and his assumption of masculine superiority often angere
Brie. His sheer male virility, on the other hand, made he
nervous.

In fact, being confined in the same house with him wa
beginning to wear on her nerves. He did no more than touc
her cheek as he left her each night, but that alone was enoug
to set her quivering. An urgent, inner voice warned her tha
she was starting to feel a permanent attraction for him. Yet sh
didn't see how she could change her situation until the sno
melted. The regular household servants would return then
and she could go home to Greenwood and never see him agai

Her situation did change, however, the fourth night of thei
enforced intimacy. Brie had already gone to bed, but she wasn'
asleep. She was too busy pounding her pillow and trying t
forget her annoyance with Stanton. She had waited two hour

or him to join her, but when he hadn't come, she had finally repared for bed.

It was nearly midnight when she heard Dominic rap softly n her door. Defiantly Brie turned away and pulled the covers p to her chin, determined to let him think her asleep. He ould try the handle, but he would find it locked.

It was with a sense of amazement, therefore, that she heard he bolt being drawn back. Feeling a chill breeze touch the back f her neck, Brie gave a gasp and sat up. Her eyes widened in stonishment when she saw Dominic standing in the doorway. e looked like a pirate, with his loose-sleeved shirt and skin-ght breeches. A *dangerous* pirate. His black hair and bronzed kin seemed even darker against the startling white of his shirt.

He shut the door behind him, giving her a casual grin. "I uppose I should have warned you. I'm an expert with locks."

When Brie remained speechless, Dominic found his own aze sliding over her appreciatively. Her russet curls spilled ver her shoulders in wanton disarray, while the firelight leant delicate golden hue to her skin. She was naked beneath the lue robe, he guessed, for he could just see the tops of milky hite breasts where her dressing gown gaped open. Looking at er, Dominic was conscious of some unmistakably erotic tirrings in his body. He wondered if Brie knew how very close he was to being ravished. He had bided his time, waiting atiently for her to lose her qualms about him, but he didn't ntend to wait much longer. Aware that he needed something o distract his thoughts, Dominic turned his attention to the randy decanter he had left on the table the previous evening.

Brie found her tongue while he was pouring himself a drink. 'Do you always barge into ladies' bedrooms uninvited?" she lemanded.

"Rarely," he replied, unruffled by her angry tone. "I enerally have an invitation. You, cherie, are the exception."

"Get out! Get out of my room before I—" She broke off as Dominic slanted a mocking glance at her. His look clearly told er she had no choice in the matter. She was powerless, and any threats she might make would be empty.

He surprised her completely by apologizing. "Forgive me for being late. Jacques had a matter that required my attention."

Brie frowned. "You might have sent me word."

"I know. I'm sorry."

He sounded genuinely sincere, Brie decided, but her anger was only slightly mollified. She didn't like being in such a helpless position. But she certainly couldn't remain in bed while he was in her room. Catching up one of the blankets to throw about her shoulders, Brie climbed out of bed, shivering as her feet touched the icy floor.

Dominic noticed her reaction to the cold, but he refrained from comment as she marched over to the chaise longue. He doubted that she would appreciate his offer to warm her just now. At the moment her cheeks were flushed with temper and her eyes were flashing green sparks. He greatly admired her eyes, Dominic reflected as he settled himself in the armchair across from her. They were large and darkly fringed, and they tended to change hues like an ocean. He found himself wondering what color they would be when they were glazed with passion.

That thought was uppermost in Dominic's mind as he set about soothing Brie's ruffled feathers. He put himself out to be charming, drawing on skills that had worked with reticent females in the past.

His strategy was successful. At the end of an hour spent discussing neutral subjects, Brie had totally forgotten her anger and was even enjoying their conversation. Curled up on the chaise longue with her feet tucked beneath her, she listened with unfeigned interest to Dominic's tale of how Elgin had brought his famous Greek antiquities to England.

And since she was unaware of Dominic's specific plans for her seduction, Brie wasn't particularly concerned when he rose to throw another log on the fire. Even when he settled himself on the bear rug at her feet, she didn't immediately recognize the danger. Dominic's movements were casual and

64

unhurried. He leaned back, bracing his weight on one hand, resting an arm on his upraised knee. When he stopped talking, the silence was comfortable and natural.

It was only when Dominic looked up at her, fixing her with those penetrating gray eyes of his, that Brie felt her heart skip a beat. He was so close that she could actually feel the heat that radiated from his body. She was suddenly afraid of their intimacy, of his nearness.

Thinking only of escape, Brie uncurled herself and swung her legs to the floor. But Dominic was faster. He caught her hand in his, preventing her from rising.

Brie stared at him, her heart pounding in her throat. The flickering firelight painted his carved features an orange bronze, accenting their hard masculinity. He was watching her with a heavy-lidded expression that she had no trouble defining.

His thumb swirled lazily against her palm, making his intent crystal clear. "You know I want you," Dominic murmured, his voice low and caressing.

The husky tone sent shivers up Brie's spine. She wanted to look away, to break the spell he was weaving around her, but her eyes seemed to be locked with his. Mesmerized, she nodded wordlessly.

Dominic was satisfied with her answer. He tugged gently on her hand, drawing Brie to her knees beside him. Then, slowly, he reached up to stroke her cheek.

His fingers were warm and reassuring, but his touch left her breathless, as if she had been running too quickly. When Dominic's gaze settled on her lips, Brie felt her heart start to hammer against her ribcage. She held her breath, unable to move.

Taking his time, Dominic ran his fingers through the burnished flame of her hair. Then cradling the back of her head, he drew her mouth closer. His lips touched hers softly at first, in a tantalizing butterfly kiss. Brie's palms instinctively came up to press against Dominic's chest, but his lips

65

continued to move softly over hers, and her token resistanc faded beneath the gentle persuasion of his mouth.

She felt herself losing all sense of reality as she knelt ther before him, yet all her senses seemed infinitely sharper. Sh was conscious of the steely strength of Dominic's muscle beneath her hands and the crisp linen of his shirt against he palms. She tasted the warm brandy on his breath as she opene to his probing tongue, then felt the ruffled thickness of his hai with her fingertips as her arms crept up to encircle his neck She was aware, too, when Dominic's hands began sensuousl kneading her shoulders. She shivered as a tremulous wave o longing flowed through her.

Brie wasn't prepared for his next move, though. His han slipped between the parted fabric of her robe before she eve realized what he planned. She was stunned to feel his warm seeking fingers on her naked breast. She stiffened automatic ally. Pulling away, she stared at Dominic with wide, frightene eyes.

Dominic was puzzled by her fear. He had felt her body's firs response to his caresses and was convinced that she wante him almost as much as he wanted her. "Are you afraid?" h asked softly, forcing himself to be patient.

Brie found it hard to answer. When he looked at her lik that, with eyes that were soft and glowing with desire, she fe like warm clay. But she was afraid. "Yes" she said, her voice n more than a breathless whisper.

He touched her cheek. "Don't be," he murmured tenderly "I only want to give you pleasure." Firmly then, he wrapped ar arm around her waist and pulled her against him. For moment she tried to twist from his grasp. But then Dominic' mouth covered hers once more, and once again she became los in the sensations he aroused.

Dominic felt Brie's melting response, but her previous reticence had challenged his masculinity. He wanted more now than to have her limp and pliant in his arms. He wanted to see her lips parted in ecstasy, to have her warm body straining

66

eagerly against him. He kissed Brie urgently, making her feel a fiery warmth that had nothing to do with the crackling fire in the hearth.

Brie was trembling by the time his lips slid hotly across her cheek to her ear. She made no protest when Dominic's fingers found her breast again and began gently stroking. Her hands only tightened convulsively on his muscled shoulders. He trailed a path of teasing kisses down her throat and lower, letting his mouth nuzzle gently at one soft breast. Brie gasped as she felt the hot flick of his tongue against her nipple, but her head fell back in an unconscious gesture of surrender. His touch burned her, yet she could no more have stopped him than she could have commanded her heart to cease beating.

Dominic could sense her defenses weakening. He lay back slowly, pulling Brie's unresisting body with him until she was draped across his chest. Her breasts pressed against him, making him throb, and he began to kiss her hungrily—long drugging kisses that left her weak and dazed. His tongue plundered her mouth, stealing away her breath, her will.

She was powerless against his half-tender, half-savage assault. The feel of his hard body beneath her sent ripples of excitement racing through her, while the hands caressing her back aroused emotions she never experienced before. She was too dazed even to notice when Dominic gently rolled her over on her back.

Supporting his weight on one elbow, he lifted his head to gaze down on her flushed face. He ached to possess her, but he forcibly curbed his impatience. Slowly, so as not to alarm her, Dominic eased Brie's robe open, baring her fully to his gaze. His breath caught at the sight.

She had the body of a wood nymph. Her shoulders were smooth and gently sloping, her breasts high and pointed with just a hint of tantalizing fullness. Her hips were slim, her legs long and slender. The curls at the junction of her thighs were dark, but they had the same reddish hue as her glorious hair. In all his experience, Dominic thought he had never seen such an exquisite body. He wanted to run his hands over every inch of her silken skin, to feel those taut, provocative breasts burning against his chest once more. He bent his head again, letting his mouth close over hers in a hard, possessive kiss.

Even with her senses drugged, Brie could feel the passion he held in check. She pressed closer against his hard body, wanting something more from him but unable to name what it was.

As she arched against him, Dominic gave a groan of satisfaction. Intending to arouse her even further, he swept his hand downward possessively, claiming her breasts as his personal property. His long fingers stroked and caressed the soft peaks, lingering over each quivering nipple until it throbbed at his touch. When he heard the soft whimper coming from Brie's throat, Dominic cupped her breasts in his hands and lowered his head. Drawing first one swollen tip into his mouth, then the other, he teased and sucked until Brie was moaning with pleasure.

Yet she wasn't aware of making a sound. A flood of heat and desire was sweeping through her, like nothing she had ever known before. When his lips began a sweet exploration of the rest of her body, time ceased to exist. There was only Dominic's hot, hard mouth working its magic, his warm sensuous fingers stroking her skin.

Quivering beneath his roving kisses, she was only vaguely aware when his hand roamed downward to caress her flat stomach and slender hips, then gently press her knees apart. But shortly, his mouth moved lower, to the cluster of curls between her thighs. When his tongue claimed her there, the resulting jolt awakened Brie from the spell he had cast over her and she stiffened in shock.

Dominic paid no attention to her sudden rigidity at first. Most women had never been pleasured that way, he knew, and it was natural for Brie to be surprised. When she began to pull frantically at his hair, though, Dominic realized that he had moved too quickly. For a moment he tried to soothe her by gentling his kisses. Since that had no effect, he reached up to pull her clutching hands from his hair.

Brie panicked when she felt him grasp her wrists. "No!" she whimpered, flailing at his shoulders with her fists. "Please, no!" When Dominic released her, she scrambled to her feet and fled across the room, sobbing.

Dominic watched her for a long moment, his eyes narrowed. Brie was shuddering and clutching her robe defensively about her as she tried to catch her breath. Someone had frightened her, he decided. And quite badly, from the looks of it. Unaccountably, the thought filled Dominic with anger, making him conscious of an oddly chivalrous urge to protect her.

For a moment he debated trying to comfort her, but then he decided against it. He was throbbing with desire, and in his present state he was more likely to attack her than soothe her fears. Besides, he would have other opportunities to overcome her reluctance while they were still snowbound.

Dominic gave a sigh as he thought of the cold bed that awaited him, but he rose to his feet. When he saw Brie cringe, he hesitated. "I mean you no harm, cherie," he said softly. "But to ease your mind, I will promise not to enter your room again without an invitation. You have my word on it."

Oddly enough, Brie believed him. She nodded mutely, unable to speak for the knot of apprehension in her throat. She heard Dominic's footsteps as he crossed to the door.

And then she was left alone with her fears.

Chapter Three

Brie stood at her own breakfast room window, staring disconsolately at the bright winter landscape. She had returned home the previous day—although *escaped* was probably a more accurate word. She had been unable to face Stanton after that late-night encounter with him in her room. As soon as dawn had broken, she had taken a horse from the Lodge stables and ridden home to Greenwood. But at least she hadn't had to feel guilty about abandoning her responsibilities. Mattie's condition had improved greatly and Homer had recovered sufficiently enough to care for her.

The weather had improved as well. Snow still covered the ground, but much of it had melted under yesterday's sun and this morning's cloudless sky promised another mild day. The view from the window was lovely, although Brie wasn't in the mood to appreciate it. The landscape, normally a sweeping vista of green hills and meadows, was a blanket of white dotted with coverts and patterned with hedges and stone walls.

There really was no reason for her to feel so depressed, Brie reflected as she stared at the scenic tableau. Indeed, she had very good reason to be cheerful. A letter from the Duke of Mobley had been waiting for her when she returned home. His grace had at last agreed to send a prize four-year-old and a promising yearling to Greenwood in the spring. His capitulation signified the achievement of one of Brie's greatest ambitions. With her loyal staff and a great deal of hard work, she had been able to maintain the excellent reputation of the training stables started by her father, but the patronage of the duke would seal the future of Greenwood.

She should have been delighted. Instead, she was a jumble of conflicting emotions.

Her eyes clouded as she thought of her last encounter with Stanton. True, she had escaped his attentions without coming to any real harm. But she had nearly allowed him to seduce her. If she hadn't panicked, she would have lost her virtue to exactly the kind of man she had done her best to avoid in recent years.

Hot shame flooded through her as she remembered the feel of Stanton's lips on her breasts. What in heaven's name had come over her? How could she have allowed him to kiss her like that, to run his hands so intimately over her body? She should have known better.

That scene before the fireplace had been familiar. On the first night of her long ago elopement, she had almost given herself to her fiancé in front of a hearth. She had pulled back at the last moment, wanting to wait until the marriage vows had been exchanged, but then her betrothed had savagely attacked her, saying that he didn't intend to risk waiting any longer to secure her inheritance. He had nearly raped her before she had managed to hit him over the head with a fire iron and render him unconscious. Fortunately for Brie, her family had been able to hush up the scandal.

But this time she had no excuse for her behavior. Stanton was obviously a master at seduction, but she never should have fallen for his practiced charm. How easily he had stirred her desire! Brie groaned, recalling just how wantonly she had responded to him.

Knowing she had to find something else to occupy her thoughts, she seated herself at the breakfast table. There was no one to serve her, for she preferred breakfasting in solitude thout an army of servants hovering over her shoulder. Yet it as evident that her household staff had been hard at work. A sket of warm flaky rolls, crocks of butter and jam, and a pot steaming hot coffee had been left on the table. There was so a good fire burning in the grate, and next to her plate, eatly arranged, was a stack of papers, a small notebook, and a n and standish.

Sipping her coffee, Brie held up a report from her head ainer, John Sims, and tried to read. She found herself totally able to concentrate. After several minutes of struggling, she thered all the papers in her hand and with an uncustomary srespect for her work, tossed the whole lot the length of the ble. "Devil take it!" she muttered in frustration.

"Gabrielle!"

Brie looked up in surprise to see Katherine standing in the orway. As usual, the elderly woman was severely dressed in a wn of drab gray merino, while her iron-gray hair was covered ith a white cap. Her carriage was lacking its usual stiff egance, however, for she was leaning heavily on a wooden ne. It was obviously a morning for disrupted routines, Brie flected wryly; Katherine rarely rose before nine, for the pain her joints was generally too severe.

Katherine composed her lips in a tight line as she eyed the sordered papers on the table. "It is highly improper for a lady swear," she admonished. "Particularly at this hour of the orning."

Wisely Brie avoided a direct reply. She poured another cup coffee as Katherine made her way slowly to the table with e aid of her cane.

At one time Katherine Hewitt had been her governess, but r the past several years she had been acting as Brie's mpanion. There was genuine affection on both sides, but eir relationship could more accurately be described as fond lerance. Having little in common but a mutual need of each ther, they had depended on one another since the death of rie's parents, for Katherine had no home of her own and

73

needed the income the position earned, while Brie's sing
state demanded the presence of an older lady to lend
respectability.

Brie was in no mood to listen to a lecture on propriety t
morning, though. "Couldn't you sleep?" she asked wh
Katherine was seated. "I thought your new medicine was mo
effective in relieving the pain."

Katherine grimaced as she tasted the strong coffee.
couldn't bring myself to suffer the usual dose last night. I a
paying for it now, though. I feel as if I slept on a bed of nai
The fault of the cold weather, I expect. But that wasn't wh
woke me. I had the strangest dream, not a bit of which I cou
remember. It left me with the oddest feeling that somethi
unpleasant was about to happen."

"Well, it is," Brie said matter-of-factly. "My cousin
coming."

Katherine slowly nodded. "It concerns me that Caroline a
Lord Denville have not yet arrived."

"I doubt if anything more terrible than the storm h
occurred to delay them. The snow has made it impossible
travel. More than likely they put up at an inn to wait out t
weather. I wouldn't worry, Julian will take good care
Caroline. She probably thinks she's having a great adventur
even if she didn't want to come here in the first place."

"I confess I'm surprised. I never would have expected La
Arabella to send her errant daughter here, of all places."

Brie slanted a glance at her companion. "Honestly, Kati
you make it sound as if Caroline has committed some crime a
that Greenwood is a den of iniquity. She may be silly, but she
young yet. It was more than luck on my aunt's part th
allowed her to discover Caroline's plans and prevent a
elopement. Aunt Arabella has always watched her daughte
with the eyes of a hawk."

Katherine raised an eyebrow. "So she sends Caroline
you?"

Not liking the implication, Brie stiffened. "Katherine, sin

y aunt devised this plan herself, I must be in her good graces
nce again. But I don't appreciate your subtle reminders of my
ast mistakes. All that happened a long time ago. It was a
ifficult lesson for me, but I *did* learn it. I imagine Aunt
rabella thinks I will be sympathetic to my cousin's plight,
nce Caroline seems to be repeating my history. And as little as
wish to have the girl foisted upon me, sending her to the
ountry is the ideal solution. I expect Caroline will see it as
ufficient punishment, since it takes her away from London.
esides, who better than a spinster cousin to show her the
rror of her ways?"

"Well, you haven't taken to wearing caps yet," Katherine
etorted. "I consider you far too young to have charge of a girl
ke that. Of course, the situation would be different if you
ere married."

Hearing the introduction of the familiar subject, Brie
inced. Her refusal to marry was a frequent point of conten-
ion between them. Over the years, there had been any number
f highly respectable suitors who had properly applied for her
and, but since her one disastrous experience with love, she
ad been determined to keep her heart closely guarded. She
idn't think she could stand listening to Katherine lecturing
er on the subject of marriage this morning, though. It had
een bad enough being reminded of her own aborted
lopement.

She drained her cup, then rose, bracing herself for the scold
hat was sure to come. She was wearing buckskin breeches and
coat of faded blue broadcloth that hid the curves of her
lender figure. The shapeless outfit, along with her woolen
eggings and scuffed leather boots, gave her the appearance of a
easant, and only a close inspection would have revealed that
he wasn't the young man she resembled.

Katherine frowned as Brie pulled a peaked cap from her
ocket. "Must you go out dressed as a ragamuffin, Gabrielle?"
he demanded, addressing Brie by her given name as she always
id when she was displeased with her charge.

Trying hard not to lose her temper, Brie deftly twisted h⟩
hair on top of her head and stuffed it under the cap. "I ha⟩
work to do, Katherine. I'm taking Julian's new gelding to t⟩
south field this morning." She tucked a few errant curls out ⟩
sight and turned up the collar of her jacket, then picked up h⟩
riding quirt and leather gloves. Forcing a smile, she bent to ki⟩
Katherine's wrinkled cheek. "Why don't you go upstairs ar⟩
rest? I should be home for lunch, but don't wait for me." Sh⟩
heard Katherine sigh as she left the room.

She was used to such sighs, for Katherine rarely approved ⟩
anything she did. Her unconventional mode of dress ⟩
particular was the focus of a running battle between them. F⟩
that matter, her father's sister had never approved of h⟩
behavior either. Lady Arabella had been shocked by Brie⟩
decision to continue to operate Greenwood as a traini⟩
stable—considering it just short of scandalous.

Those years had not been easy for Brie. Managing such a⟩
enterprise would have been difficult enough for a man, but f⟩
a woman, it had been almost a Herculean task. Even Brie⟩
wealth and position as Sir William Carringdon's daught⟩
hadn't helped her, since very few men were willing to d⟩
business with a female.

Fortunately, she had been able to rely on John Simms. Upo⟩
Sir William's death, John had taken on the responsibility ⟩
dealing with the clients, while Brie had handled the traini⟩
programs for the horses. They had reversed their rol⟩
gradually over time, so that now many of the clients dea⟩
directly with her. John had been offered numerous positior⟩
elsewhere with the lure of sizable increases in salary, bu⟩
nothing had been able to entice him to leave Greenwood ⟩
shake his devotion to Brie.

Brie's spirits lifted a little when she reached the stables. Th⟩
anticipation of a brisk ride on a glorious winter's day alway⟩
held excitement for her, but the smile on John's grizzled face a⟩
he saddled her mount made her recall the duke's letter and h⟩
promise of patronage. John had worked as hard as she for th⟩

moment, Brie reminded herself. She returned his smile, determined not to let her low mood spoil his triumph.

Her costume had been his idea. While boy's clothes might be eccentric on a woman, they were both practical and sensible for the work Brie undertook. And by now most of her neighbors had grown used to her unusual attire. That the slim country lad who sported an ill-fitting blue jacket and rode spirited Thoroughbreds with the abandon of a wild Indian was, in truth, Miss Carringdon of Greenwood was even a source of pride.

Her clothes served her well this morning for they insulated her from the cold. It was still quite chilly. Great curls of steam rose from her horse's nostrils as Brie rode out of the courtyard. The cold air stung her lungs and tinged her cheeks with color, but she breathed deeply, enjoying the fresh scent of snow.

Her mount, the Court Jester, was a young Irish hunter belonging to Julian. At Julian's request, Brie had undertaken to school the horse for the field, for while the bay's action was superb, he was far too excitable when confronting the sights and sounds of the hunt. In the quiet of the winter morning, however, Jester was relaxed and responsive. He cantered easily along the lane, his footing solid in the melting snow and mud. When Brie put him at a low hedge, he took it effortlessly.

She held the horse to a canter, even though his strong pull on the reins indicated his eagerness. Leaving the lane, they bounded over a low stone border and followed a path through the woods to the south field. There were few tracks in the snow, and the only sound disturbing the silence was the muffled beat of Jester's hooves.

The path narrowed at its end. Brie ducked to avoid the low-hanging branches as they whipped by her, but not before the tip of a limb caught her shoulder, loosening a shower of snow. Laughing as a wet clump hit the back of her neck, Brie brought the horse to a halt. Jester snorted impatiently, pawing the ground, but she spoke softly to the animal, calming him as she shielded her eyes against the bright glare and surveyed the lovely scene.

A snow-covered meadow stretched invitingly before her, the sunlight reflecting off its crystalline surface, creating shimmer of silver and gold. Beyond, the barren browns and grays of the surrounding woods contrasted sharply with the pristine white. Above, the sky sparkled a clear, watery blue.

Brie completely missed seeing the dark horseman who blended into the shadows of the opposite trees. Unaware of his scrutiny, she stood in the saddle and tossed her head back, laughing in sheer delight.

The musical sound carried across the snow to capture Dominic's attention. He had no trouble recognizing Brie, for while a stranger to this particular part of Britain might have mistaken her for a lad, Dominic had held her in his arms and knew quite well the extent of her feminine charms. He laid soothing hand on the neck of his own restless mount, and from the cover of a thicket, watched.

The field was laid out in the shape of an L, with the two sections separated by a stream. A dozen or so obstacles of varying shapes and sizes had been set up to form a training course. Brie rode Jester in a large circle as she prepared for the first jump, gradually increasing the bay's speed to a steady canter. They took the first fence soaring, while Dominic caught his breath at the unexpected beauty of their winged flight.

Jester settled into a rhythmic stride. Jumping the swollen stream with ease, he cleared the sloping, snow-covered bank with room to spare, before Brie urged him on to the next obstacle. They swept around the bend of the meadow, hugging close to the dense wood, and at the end, turned, making their way upfield again at a steady gallop.

They were approaching the stream when Jester caught sight of the rider in the distance. His ears shot up, then he shied violently, swerving and throwing Brie off balance.

Seeing the icy banks stretching wide before them, Brie tried desperately to regain her seat, but she was still clinging recariously to the horse's neck when they left the ground. 'he bay cleared the water, but on the far bank, he slipped and tumbled. Giving a mighty lunge, he scrambled up the reacherous slope, while Brie lost her grip entirely. Feeling erself falling, she threw her weight to one side, free of the lailing hooves.

She tucked her body into a tight ball, and the snow softened he impact of her fall, but still she was dazed and breathless by he time she rolled to a stop. She lay there a moment, curled on er side, aware of a painful throb in her shoulder and a loud lrumming in her head. When she recognized the sound as pproaching hoofbeats, she shifted slowly onto her back, vincing as the bright glare of the sun hurt her eyes. Then she linked.

For an instant, the dark image of a horse and rider was tched vividly against the sky. The horse was a giant black tallion, its coat a glossy shade of midnight rippling with blue lighlights. Brie had seen that horse before at the Lodge stables, ut it was Dominic who arrested her attention. He seemed to be n extension of the beautiful animal he sat so effortlessly. He vas hatless, and his ebony hair, nearly the same shade as his lorse, glinted in the early morning sunlight. The black coat he wore made his broad shoulders seem even more powerfully uilt and gave him an aura of strength that was almost tangible o Brie's dazed senses.

The image shattered as he dismounted. Above the ringing in her ears, Brie heard him ask if she were injured. She shook her lead to clear it and slowly raised herself up on her elbows.

"Are you hurt?" Dominic repeated, his piercing gaze sweeping over her body.

Brie frowned as she looked up at him. She was cold and wet and her shoulder was throbbing abominably, but she wasn't about to admit it to him. "No, I'm not hurt!" she muttered rritably, her denial sounding more like an accusation.

Her annoyance mounted when she realized Dominic was subjecting her to another of his brazen perusals. His dark eyes

79

traveled the length of her slender frame, gliding slowly upwar
again to pause measuringly on the curves of her breasts. Th
warmth of his gaze seemed to penetrate her garments. Sh
wondered if he would say anything about her choice of attire—
and he did.

"Interesting," Dominic remarked mildly. "Can't you
protector afford to clothe you in anything better?"

"What are you doing here?" Brie demanded, ignoring hi
question.

His eyes returned at last to meet her own, but he seeme
undaunted by the fierce glare she was leveling at him. A
annoying little smile hovered around the corners of his mouth
"You didn't say goodbye, ma belle. I was beginning to thin
that I had frightened you away."

"You did no such thing," Brie replied with a toss of he
head. The gesture sent her cap flying and her hair tumblin
down around her shoulders.

A lazy, mocking smile spread across Dominic's lips, showin
strong white teeth. His grin unsettled Brie's composure. Sh
felt at a distinct disadvantage with him towering over her
When he bent to help her up, she refused his outstretche
hand and scrambled to her feet, unassisted.

Dominic's grin deepened appreciatively as his eyes took i
the curves displayed by her breeches, but Brie tried to ignor
him. Pressing her lips together and swallowing the hot word
that were forming on her tongue, she brushed impatiently a
the snow that clung tenaciously to her clothes and went afte
her horse.

Jester had not gone far. He stood quietly as Brie approached
allowing her to pick up the reins that trailed the ground. Sh
led the gelding at a slow walk, looking for signs of injury.

Dominic came up beside her. "He's favoring his right fore
Probably strained a tendon."

Brie didn't need the advice, nor did she appreciate Stanton'
interference. She raised a glare of annoyance to his bronze
visage.

It disturbed her to find his gray eyes upon her, watching her closely. His persistent regard was unsettling, but before she could comment, his gaze shifted back to the horse.

Dominic casually removed his gloves, then bent beside the bay and ran a careful hand down the animal's leg. When he nodded his dark head, as if confirming his own opinion, his calm assumption of authority ignited Brie's glowing spark of ire. She rounded on him as he straightened. "I'll thank you, Lord Stanton, to leave the horse to me. In fact, I'll thank you to leave! You are on private property."

One of his dark brows shot up. "I was not aware—"

"I can certainly believe that! You seem to be aware of very little. Indeed, your lack of intelligence astonishes me. What did you mean, riding out of the woods like that, appearing like an apparition without any warning? If I had been a less accomplished rider, Jester could have ended with a broken leg and I with a broken neck!"

A look of sardonic amusement crept into Dominic's eyes as he contemplated her. "You have my profound admiration, mademoiselle, for your daring display of horsemanship. I have rarely seen such magnificent riding, certainly not from a woman. At least your skill matches your boastfulness." The corner of his mouth lifted slowly in a smile. "Tell me, does your master know you have taken that beast from his stable?"

Brie digested his statements with a certain amount of amazement. His words, rather than the contrite apology she expected, were little more than taunts. A warning spark flashed in her eyes, turning them a deep, sparkling green. "I do not boast," she ground out. "I am perfectly capable of handling any horse I care to ride—without your assistance. Besides, what I do with Jester is no business of yours. And my . . . master, as you phrased it, would not have stood for your interference for an instant. He would have had you shot for trespassing and frightening his horse, and asked questions later. I generally don't support such drastic measures, but I am beginning to. Now, will you leave, my lord? I have work to do."

He didn't comply. Instead, he raised a mocking brow and indicated her horse with a slight movement of his head. "You won't be able to ride him for a day or so."

"I realize that!" she snapped.

She was totally dumbfounded when Dominic reached out to lift a lock of her hair from where it lay curled on her breast. "You look a little absurd, standing there all covered with snow," he murmured. "Perhaps you have aspirations to become a snow fairy?" He let the curl drop, watching with a speculative gleam as it caught the fire of the sun.

Brie resisted the urge to slap his handsome face. She was suddenly uncomfortable with his closeness, with the way his penetrating glance lingered on the swell of her breasts. She turned from him abruptly, looking for her lost cap. Adopting her haughtiest tone, she flung over her shoulder, "You, Lord Stanton, are also guilty of a breach of manners. A gentleman does not argue with a lady, nor does he call her absurd."

Dominic's slow chuckle rumbled deep in his chest. "Lady?" he repeated, his voice heavy with satire. "Is that what you are, cherie?"

Brie's cheeks flushed with hot anger, but she continued searching through the snow until she heard Dominic ask if she were perhaps looking for something. When she saw that he held her cap and was waving it gently in the air, she silently voiced an oath and marched up to him, bristling with fury.

Tauntingly, Dominic held the cap out of her range. "Oh no, my lady. You must allow me the honor of rendering such a small service."

Brie glared, her soft mouth set mutinously, but she remained silent, thinking he would put the hat on her head and be done with it. He bewildered her by commanding her to turn around. "I beg your pardon?" she asked, knitting her brows.

"I said turn," Dominic ordered, an odd gleam of amusement warming his eyes.

Brie stared at him uncertainly. But when he grasped her by the elbow, her resentment flared. "Damn you, unhand me!"

Giving a jerk, she tried to free herself, but she found she had miscalculated Dominic's strength. She stumbled and would have fallen but for the supporting arm he wrapped around her waist. Startled by the sudden contact with his hard body, she reacted instinctively and drew back her hand to deliver a stinging blow.

Dominic caught her wrist easily, holding it in an iron grip. "I wouldn't do that if I were you, cherie. You would not like the consequences."

His tone was deadly calm, and when Brie's flashing eyes clashed with his chilling gaze, her words of protest at his barbaric treatment lodged in her throat. Her frozen breath mingled with Dominic's as she stared up at him. Curiously, she could feel her defiance retreating under the hard intensity of his gaze.

Her ebbing anger quickly turned to dismay when Dominic shifted his position and captured both her wrists in one hand. His eyes were half hidden by bold, black lashes, but Brie could see charcoal flecks floating in the gray depths, plus a smoldering gleam that was both predatory and sensual. Reading his look, she attempted to pull away. But his grip merely tightened. When his gaze settled on her mouth, her heartbeat quickened in panic.

Frightened, Brie began to fight him, kicking furiously at his shins since her hands were imprisoned in his grasp. Only Dominic's lightning reactions saved him from her vicious resistance. When her booted foot harmlessly flailed air, Brie exerted all her might in a frenzied attack.

She fought wildly, to no avail. Dominic's strong arms wrapped about her, catching her close against his broad, hard chest. "Be still, my little wildcat," he murmured as she squirmed in his embrace. "I was only attempting to brush the snow from your hair."

Realizing she had no hope of winning against Dominic's superior strength, Brie ceased her struggle. She stood trembling in his arms, her breath coming in deep gasps, her heart beating in slow, painful strokes. Tears of anger and humiliation stung her eyes as she cursed her own stupidity. She was alone with Stanton, miles from any form of help, and she had lashed out at him without considering the consequences. Brie bit her lip, wondering what he planned to do with her.

He didn't seem to be in any hurry. He was stroking her hair and speaking to her softly, as if calming a frightened animal, telling her that she had nothing to fear from him.

Her trembling gradually lessened under the soothing influence of his voice and hands. It was odd, she reflected, but being held in his encircling warmth somehow made her feel cherished and protected. She almost cried out loud when Dominic drew away and his warmth was replaced by cold, empty air.

He did not release her completely, but held one wrist captive while his free hand reached out to cup her chin with gentle forcefulness, tilting her face up to his. Once more Brie tried to pull away without success, but his gray eyes caught her blue-green ones. He looked searchingly at her for a long moment, his expression an unreadable mask. Then he bent his head.

When their mouths met, Brie caught her breath in a gasp, for even though Dominic's lips only brushed hers gently before drawing away, she felt their impact more as a glancing blow. She stood completely still, her eyes shut tightly as she tried to will away the treacherous warmth that was suddenly flooding through her. No other man had ever made her feel such melting desire. Once she had felt something remotely similar for her fiance—but yielding to it had been the greatest mistake of her life. Brie lamely shook her head in protest.

The choice was taken from her, however, as Dominic's arms encircled her once more. He pulled her against him, his hand moving to cradle the back of her head, his fingers twisting in the silken tresses of her hair. Brie glimpsed the darkened passion in his eyes as he lowered his mouth again.

There was no gentleness in his kiss this time. The invading

warmth of his tongue plundered the depths of her mouth, making her senses reel. But his hunger found a responsive chord deep within Brie. She pressed closer, unconsciously molding her slender body to Dominic's larger frame. Alternating waves of hot and cold swept through her, making her shiver.

Dominic kissed her with feverish intensity, then let his lips skim lightly across Brie's face, searing her skin. Wanting more of her, he tilted her head back, giving his mouth access to the softness of her throat. He savored the taste of her skin, while his stroking hands slowly swept down her back, caressing her with a circular, sensual motion. Moving lower, he cupped her soft buttocks in his hands, drawing her slender hips intimately against his steel-muscled thighs.

Brie was vaguely shocked to feel the swell of his throbbing hardness through their layers of clothing. She opened her mouth to protest, but Dominic's hoarsely voiced plea forestalled her. "Come back to the Lodge with me, Brie. Now, this moment. Let me make love to you the way I've wanted to since I first saw you."

His hard mouth claimed hers then, robbing her of breath, and for a moment, her world careened in a wild, hot spiral. But then his hand slid intimately between her legs, stroking her gently.

Brie went rigid, realizing where his attempted seduction was leading. And she was responding to him! She was behaving no better than she had two nights ago. Dear God, she had to get away from him before she surrendered to him completely.

In desperation, Brie tore her mouth away. She wished she had a weapon to use against him, for struggling, as he had decisively proved, would gain her nothing. "No . . . don't," she pleaded, her breath coming in short, ragged gasps.

"Don't what, ma belle? You mean this?" His lips slid across her cheek to her ear. Taking the lobe between her teeth, he teased it with his tongue, stirring those erotic sensations in her again.

85

"Please . . . , stop."

"You don't want me to let you go," Dominic murmured huskily. "You want me as much as I want you. Your body says so."

His allegation was too close to the truth. Furious at herself and at him, Brie pushed frantically at his chest. But he only kissed her again, ignoring her resistance. It was then that Brie remembered the riding quirt tucked inside her boot. With trembling fingers, she groped for it, but Dominic's crushing embrace prevented her from bending enough to reach it.

When his hold at last loosened a little, Brie seized upon her small advantage with frantic speed. She broke away, taking a step backward at the same time her hand closed around her whip. Raising her arm, she swung at Dominic with all the strength at her command. She had not been aiming for his face, but the blow glanced off his shoulder and struck him fully across his left cheek.

Her unexpected action caught Dominic unaware, and for a moment he didn't move. He only watched Brie, his eyes glinting dangerously. Brie stared back at him, watching in horrified fascination as a thin red line appeared on his cheek to mar his dark complexion. She couldn't help noticing how cold and threatening his gray eyes had become. When Dominic brought a hand up to his face to touch the red welt, she backed away nervously. He looked as dangerous as a snarling jungle cat.

There was also ice in his voice when he spoke. "That was not very wise, cherie," Dominic said softly. "Some men kill when they are given such provocation."

Brie shuddered, knowing her own eyes betrayed her fear. "No doubt you're the same," she replied shakily. "And no doubt you take pleasure in raping defenseless women!"

Dominic's laugh was harsh, slashing across the void between them. "For rape, one must be unwilling. You will forgive me, of course, if I failed to detect any reluctance in your response."

Reminded of her wanton behavior, Brie flushed. But she

kept her attention fixed on Dominic. He was moving toward her slowly, his cold, penetrating gaze boring into her.

"I could have had you," he pointed out in that same menacing tone, "a dozen times in the past few days, had I wanted to resort to force. Generally I don't care to use violence with women, but you, mademoiselle, tempt me to overlook my scruples. I vow it would be a great pleasure to teach you to curb that temper of yours. I expect I could think of a fitting punishment for a teasing wench who doesn't know her own mind—that crop across your lovely backside, for a start."

Brie retreated with faltering steps as he stalked her, while her heart beat in a wild, erratic rhythm. She raised the quirt defensively, although she knew she would never be able to catch Dominic off guard again. The implacable determination she saw in his eyes told her she wouldn't be given a second chance to escape.

Dominic was but a yard away from his frightened quarry when he paused, swearing softly under his breath. Seeing him looking over her shoulder, Brie glanced behind her. Her eyes widened when she saw the approaching horseman at the edge of the meadow. She let out her breath in relief, knowing that an audience would prevent Stanton from carrying out his threats.

Hearing her soft gasp, Dominic smiled sardonically. She thought she had escaped him, but he wasn't finished with her yet—by any means. He waited impatiently as Jacques came riding up.

The Frenchman's tone was apologetic but urgent. "Monsieur, a messenger has arrived. You are wanted in London."

Dominic's brows drew together. "Manning?" he asked, already knowing the answer. When Jacques nodded, Dominic pressed his lips together in irritation, but he turned and whistled to his stallion. The black horse came trotting up to him immediately.

Brie watched in amazement as Dominic gathered the stallion's reins and swung into the saddle. She could hardly believe that he would allow their confrontation to end like that. She was right. Dominic urged his horse nearer and looked down at her. "Forgive me, cherie, for leaving you so abruptly. But we will meet again. You can depend on it."

Even if she hadn't heard the soft threat in his tone, Brie could read the determination in his eyes and knew he wouldn't forget what had happened between them. But then neither would she forget.

She stood there, completely motionless, as Dominic turned his mount and spurred him to a gallop. The two horsemen were long out of sight before Brie relaxed her clenched fists and threw her riding whip to the ground. Giving an angry, frustrated cry, she sank to her knees in the cold snow and pressed her hands tightly over her ears.

In her mind, she could still hear the echo of Dominic's promise. He was an arrogant, insufferable devil! Yet she could still see his aristocratic face, still feel the strength in his hard body, the sensuous touch of his lips on hers. No, she wouldn't forget him. If she lived a hundred years, she would never forget him.

Chapter Four

Dominic shifted his weight slowly so as not to disturb the peacefully slumbering woman at his side. Reaching up, he drew aside the velvet hangings of the enormous four-poster bed, preferring the acrid aroma of smoke wafting from the chimney to the more overpowering scent of Denise's perfume. Her heavy scent brought to mind other nights, in wild tropical places far removed from this elegant London residence where outside a winter storm spent its fury.

Generally Dominic welcomed such diversions. Tonight, however, he found the musky scent of Denise's body sweet and cloying and oppressive. Mentally he underlined the word oppressive.

He lay back against the satin pillows and crossed his hands behind his head, a ghost of a smile curling his lip. What had he expected when he had sought Denise out this evening? A shy young maiden blooming with the innocence of spring? Denise had certainly never been that, in all the years he had known her. And he had once known her quite well. She had been his mistress, in fact, although after that affair had ended, he had rarely thought of her. The widow of the late Baron Grayson had done quite well for herself, Dominic noted with cynical amusement as his gaze wandered around the room with its gilt furnishings, velvet hangings, and thick carpets. Yes, definitely oppressive.

Silently he rose and went to the window, throwing aside th[e] heavy draperies to expose the storm to his view. He could se[e] snowflakes churning in the darkness, buffeted by great gusts [of] wind. Oddly, they mirrored his frame of mind. The restlessnes[s] that had driven him to seek Denise's companionship had n[ot] left him. If anything, it was stronger.

He stood at the window, oblivious to the seeping cold on hi[s] bare bronzed skin, his gray eyes piercing the darkness. [If] Manning's sources could be relied upon—and Dominic had n[o] cause to doubt them—his greatest foe had returned to Englan[d] after an absence of nearly four years. Charles Germain was ou[t] there, somewhere in the city.

Germain's reappearance had upset Manning, upset hi[m] enough to make him forgo his customary secrecy; he had sen[t] one of his efficient bloodhounds to the country to trac[k] Dominic down. An unusual event, certainly. Manning neve[r] contacted him directly unless the matter was extremel[y] urgent. Dominic had responded to the summons by setting ou[t] for London at once.

Although it had been late when his coach reached th[e] outskirts of the city, he had gone directly to Lord Manning['s] home in Albermarle Street. He had found his portly superior i[n] the study, busily pouring over a thick set of official-lookin[g] documents.

Manning offered him refreshments, then began withou[t] further ceremony. "My appreciation for coming so quickl[y,] Dominic. I want your opinion on this business. You hav[e] heard, I suppose, that Charles Germain is back in th[e] country?" When Dominic raised an eyebrow, Mannin[g] frowned and adjusted his spectacles higher on the bridge of hi[s] nose. "You may well look surprised. I was, I can assure you. [I] had thought him in India."

Dominic settled back in his chair, swirling the brandy in h[is] glass. "You are certain it is Germain?"

"Quite certain. He was spotted in Folkestone last week an[d] again here in London two days ago. But as yet I have no idea as to his purpose."

"And you want me to discover it?"

"I thought perhaps you might already have knowledge of it."

Dominic coolly returned the older man's gaze. "I am sorry to disappoint you, sir, but I would probably be the last person to whom Germain would divulge his plans. The last time we met I ordered him out of the country, you will recall."

With a sigh, Manning turned back to his desk to ruffle through some papers. He picked one up, staring at it for a long moment. "I remember. You threatened Germain with exposure as a double spy, although you had no proof."

Dominic's expression remained emotionless. "No, I had no proof. Charles liked to be sure there were never any witnesses to his dealings."

"A young French lad was involved, I believe. The boy died while in Germain's custody." Manning tapped his forefinger on the desk. "So," he mused, "Charles Germain was one of us and yet he sold information to the French."

"Yes."

"Do you not think he would do so again?"

Dominic shook his head. "It's highly unlikely. The war has been over for four years, and any information Charles might obtain would be of little value—even if he could be believed. You know better than I that once a man becomes suspect, his credibility vanishes."

Manning, in a weary gesture, removed his spectacles and carefully massaged his temples. "I must be getting old, to be jumping at shadows. Very well, Dominic, so he is not spying. Still . . ." He paused, directing a penetrating glance at his guest. "Still, he must have a reason for his return. A man like Germain does not act without purpose. I have a feeling—a feeling, mind you—that you will be involved in this business somehow. And that it will not be pleasant. Had Germain returned in a less furtive manner, we might assume he had

91

grown bored with his exile and merely wanted to return to his homeland. But . . ." The unspoken words, implying danger, hung suspended between the two men. Dominic, although politely attentive, remained silent.

His reaction was obviously not one Manning felt was warranted. The older man snorted. "Nerves of steel. I had forgotten. Well, perhaps you will be considerate of an old man's ravings and have a care for yourself."

Dominic's lips twisted into a wry grin, his teeth flashing white. "But of course, my lord."

"Bah," Manning said as he waved an impatient hand. "You always were one to go courting danger, as if it were a personal challenge. One of these days, Dominic . . ." He shrugged. "Ah, well. My people are trying to locate Germain. If they find him, I will send you word. Do you stay in London?"

"For a time," Dominic said, rising. "Perhaps Germain will show himself if I make myself conspicuous. I'll let you know where to reach me if I decide to leave."

"Very well. But take care."

It was past midnight when Dominic reached his own townhouse in Berkeley Square. His valet, Farley, showed no surprise when he called for a bath and evening clothes to be laid out. A short time later, Dominic was once again travelling through the streets of London, his destination, but not his intent, as specific as before. He had chosen an invitation at random from the stack set aside for his perusal—one for a ball of no particular distinction.

His arrival created quite a stir, just as he had expected. The Sixth Earl of Stanton was rarely seen at such events, but the title Dominic had inherited from his grandfather, as well as his wealth, assured his welcome.

Dominic surveyed the crowded ballroom with a cynical smile. What better way to make his presence known to Germain than to appear at a glittering social function? If, as Manning suspected, Germain was interested. But Manning's intuition was seldom wrong; it had served Dominic well.

number of times in the past. Of course, he thought with a regretful sigh, the timing could have been better. Because of Germain's arrival, he would have to reformulate his plans. Instead of availing himself of Julian's hospitality, he would have to stay in London to flush Germain out of hiding. But if Charles Germain wanted to find the Earl of Stanton, then find him he would.

The ball had proved to be flatly insipid, with two exceptions, both old acquaintances. The first was his closest friend, Jason Stuart, the Marquess of Effing. Jason was in the process of taking his leave when Dominic arrived, but he delayed his departure long enough to exchange a few words and extend an invitation to dinner the following evening. The second exception was Dominic's ex-mistress, Denise, Lady Grayson.

Dominic had strolled out of the cardrooms after an hour of play and spotted her amid a court of admirers. She was hard to miss. Her blond beauty stood out like a cool candleflame, and tonight it was accentuated by a vivid, rose-colored gown. So why had he been reminded of russet tresses and flashing blue-green eyes?

As he stood watching Denise, his shoulder propped against a pillar, he had found himself unconsciously comparing the memory of Brie's slender, supple body and sweet, warm lips to the elegant vision before him. Oddly, Denise came out the loser. Her hair was far too pale, her figure too voluptuous, her mouth too artificial. She lacked a certain vitality, a freshness that the country beauty had in abundance. But then Denise was also missing the fiery temper.

Dominic had been startled out of his comparison by her approach. Denise smiled coyly, extending a slender white hand for him to kiss. "Darling, for these past five minutes and more, you have been looking at me as a wolf looks at his supper. Am I the lamb?"

Forcibly repressing the memory of his vixen, Dominic bowed over her hand. "No lamb," he said gallantly, "but certainly a delectable morsel." His lips lingeringly brushed the tips of her fingers, eliciting the response he expected: Denise shivered.

"Dominic, it has been so long," she said huskily, desire written plainly on her features, an invitation in her eyes.

He had accepted wordlessly, easily slipping into the old patterns. There had been one major advantage to their past relationship, aside from the obvious. Denise was a woman who knew how to keep silent. He had escorted her to her home, dismissing his coachman with instructions to return in the morning. Within moments of reaching her bedroom, Denise had wound her scented arms about his neck. But while his body had automatically responded to her touch, in his mind a memory had warred with the present.

Now, standing at the window, the cold attacking his bare skin, Dominic's mocking smile was for himself. An imagination run riot was unique in his experience. He had behaved like a veritable schoolboy. While making love to Denise, he had shut his eyes to the writhing creature beneath him and let a memory invade his whole being. The ripe luscious body became younger, firmer, while the blond tresses darkened to burnished auburn. The mouth he plundered so ruthlessly became Brie's, and she had responded to his kisses with a sensuousness that left him hungrily demanding more. She was a wench made for loving, with flaming hair and eyes like the ocean. A sweet fire exploded in him. . . .

Slowly the image had faded, leaving him shaken and spent. Thankfully, Denise had rolled away and gone immediately to sleep. She had not even stirred when he left her bed, seeking escape from the odor of her heavy perfume. Brie's scent had been heather and sunshine, the freshness of spring. . . .

Frowning, Dominic banished the thought. He was making the little termagant into a perfect paragon of loveliness. With a swift motion of his hand, he opened the window, inviting in a blast of snow-sweetened air.

The February weather was as capricious as a woman, Dominic thought cynically. Only a few days ago he had been caught in another storm, one far more serious. He and Jacques had been lucky to reach Julian's hunting box. Dominic had only gone there on a whim. He had been to Ireland in search of stock for his latest venture—a racing stud—but he hadn't wanted to return to London just yet. He had detoured through Leicester, even though he had doubted the change in location would be sufficient to dispel the boredom he had been feeling lately. He had been pleasantly surprised to find Brie. The challenge of pursuing her had made his visit far more enjoyable than he had expected. Too bad his sport had been interrupted by Manning's messenger.

The journey to London had seemed longer than usual. Dominic had spent the better part of it in deep speculation, with Brie at the center of his thoughts. What an enigma, a spitting vixen one moment, a warm passionate creature the next. Dominic smiled to himself as he remembered how she had fought him when he had tried to brush the snow from her hair. She had cut a ridiculous figure in her common boy's garb—but God, what a beauty! Even dressed as a common stablehand, the wench had aroused him. Her protector, if there were one, was wise to keep his beautiful possession hidden deep in the country.

Staring out at the night without seeing, Dominic recalled her stormy eyes and the way they sparkled with tears when she had found herself his prisoner. How vulnerable she had looked, with her long fringe of lashes brushing her wet cheeks, her soft red lips quivering with dismay. How he had wanted to kiss away her tears, to soothe the fear in her eyes.

He had not meant to frighten her in the first place. He had only intended to tease her, to depress the pretentious haughtiness she had adopted with him. But when he had tasted the sweetness of her mouth and felt her lithe, slender body respond to his lovemaking with that curious mixture of innocence and desire, he had wanted her in a way he had not wanted any woman in a long while. She was refreshingly natural, like a wild creature of the forest. She seemed unbound by the conventions that made either prudes or whores of othe women.

Once more Dominic found himself contemplating he station. Her cultured voice indicated that she was not commoner, while her bearing and authoritative manner wer too pronounced for a servant, even a lady's maid. But no self respecting lady of his acquaintance would be caught dead i the faded gown Brie had worn, let alone a pair of men' breeches. Perhaps she was the by-blow of some loca landowner. That would explain her proud but wild conduct. I might also explain why she had had to resort to becoming som elderly gentleman's mistress.

Dominic frowned. The thought of Brie belonging to anothe man was decidedly disturbing. But he would rectify that a soon as he returned to the country. Seducing her might prov to be a delicate task, of course. First he would have to lure he away from whichever gentleman had the pleasure of keepin her, and then he would have to tame the little wildcat. Excep that it was not just a matter of taming, Dominic reminde himself. He would have to overcome her reservations as well He wanted her willing, not flinching with apprehension. H wanted to have her warm body arching eagerly against his, t have those taut, provocative breasts burning against hi chest. . . .

Dominic's eyes glinted as he imagined the enticing sensatio of Brie lying naked in his arms, her silken limbs entwined wit his, her pleasure matching his own. He could half feel he slender hips thrusting sweetly against his loins.

No, he had not expected to find anything quite like Bri when he had accepted Julian's invitation to the quie countryside. Dominic slowly traced the thin red welt on hi cheek where her riding crop had bitten his skin, and then h laughed softly. The willful beauty would not escape him s easily at their next meeting. She would pay for her rashness—a price of his choosing. The wildcat would learn to sheath he claws and purr at his slightest touch.

So vowing Dominic firmly relegated the images of Brie to the far recesses of his mind and shut the window. As he turned away to dress, he spared a glance at Denise wrapped in her warm cocoon.

He regretted the impulse that had led to his renewed involvement with her. It had been a mistake, of course. Old affairs, like sleeping dogs, were best left undisturbed. Indeed, he had only taken advantage of Denise's availability in an effort to dispel a frustrated desire for a stormy-eyed temptress.

Unbidden, the vision of Brie returned and Dominic felt a swift tightening of groin muscles as his body tensed in anticipation. Brie held out her arms to him, beckoning, teasing, taunting, her glorious hair spilling down to hide her slender, womanly curves. . . .

Yes, most definitely he would return. He would find her, track her down if need be. And, yes, punish her for kindling this painful desire that threatened his rational mind. Soon, Dominic told himself as he silently let himself from the room. This business with Germain must be dealt with swiftly, and then he would be free to pursue his vixen.

During the following week, the Earl of Stanton was seen frequently about town in the company of various females, although Denise was not among their number. Dominic made little progress in his search for Germain, however, and by the time he met Jason at White's club on St. James Street a sennight later, he was beginning to lose patience.

The two men settled in one of the reading rooms where they could talk in private. Dominic stood before the fireplace, gazing intently into the flames, while Jason relaxed on a plush leather sofa.

Dominic's friendship with Jason Stuart, Lord Effing, was of long standing—having begun when they were at Eton together. Although they both possessed keen intelligences and virile, muscular bodies, they differed in many respects. Jason was several inches taller and had a heavier build. He was also fair where Dominic was dark, and his features were less harsh. His blue eyes danced with laughter, manifesting none of the chill that often filled Dominic's gray ones.

When Dominic seemed disinclined to speak, Jason broached the subject of Charles Germain. "I take it the search has been futile so far?" he said, tilting his tawny head to one side as he scrutinized his friend.

"Entirely," Dominic responded. "Germain was seen once this past week, but Manning's agent lost him. I think tomorrow I'll begin making my own inquiries. This waiting is growing intolerable. I want to get back to Julian's place as soon as may be."

Jason raised an eyebrow. "A woman?" When Dominic slanted a piercing glance over his shoulder, he chuckled. "Come now, Dom. The shooting cannot be very good this time of the year, and you've never been anxious to bury yourself in the country. There must be another attraction besides Denville's company."

"There is," Dominic said softly, taking a sip of brandy.

"Another conquest to add to your string?"

Unconsciously, Dominic raised a hand to his cheek. "This one won't be so easy. She's a little wildcat who forgets she is female. I was about to teach her a well-deserved lesson when Manning's bloodhound interrupted us."

"Don't tell me she slapped you?"

Dominic's smile did not reach his eyes. "On the contrary, she struck me with her riding whip."

"Good God, it's a wonder you left her with her skin intact. She sounds troublesome. Why bother with her? You have more than enough beauties hanging on your sleeve as it is. What about the Opera dancer all our friends are raving about—Miss Crowell? You were seen with her at least once this past week. I would have thought a woman with her charms could hold you for a time."

Dominic shrugged. "I didn't bother to find out. I only

wanted Cassandra to draw Germain's attention, and she suited my purpose for the evening. Her charms, as you put it, were adequate, but she liked the color of my money too well for me to contemplate anything further. A trifle too grasping. But then, aren't all women? Except Lauren, of course," Dominic added, knowing Jason's love for his wife.

Jason laughed. "Not all, my friend—although many are, I suppose. At least Cassandra Crowell won't expect marriage. I hear Lady Denise has been thinking along those lines. Rumor has it that you have her in keeping again. There's even been speculation that she's holding out for the greater prize of becoming your countess."

"Denise knows me better than that."

"Perhaps, but the odds in the betting books went up when the lady suddenly acquired an exquisite ruby bracelet."

"Merely a parting gift," Dominic acknowledged with a frown. "Do you know, all this talk about women and marriage is beginning to bore me. What do you say we adjourn to the cardrooms?"

"Thanks, but I'll have to decline. I don't like to leave Lauren for too long. She tires easily in her condition. Incidentally, she asked me to remind you of your promise to stand godfather when our child is born."

"I remember. You can assure her I'll be in town for the christening."

They talked for a while longer before Jason took his leave, and afterward Dominic made a leisurely stroll through the card rooms in search of some worthy sport. He had his choice of Hazard, Commerce, Vingt-Un, or Faro, but none of the stakes were as high as he liked. He joined the play at the Faro table for a time, but the game didn't hold his interest for long. A few hours later he was shrugging into his greatcoat and accepting his hat and gloves from a footman. Meaning to walk, he directed the doorman to send his carriage home and stepped into the night.

An icy wind whipped around him as he strode down St.

James Street. The gusts played havoc with the recently installed gas lamps, but the freezing temperatures at least succeeded in reducing the putrid smell of the London streets. Dominic hunched his shoulders against the chill and buried his hands deeper in the pockets of his greatcoat. The silence of the night was sometimes broken by the clatter of a passing hackney, although Dominic hardly noticed as he pondered how to solve his current dilemma.

The situation was indeed puzzling. He had seldom been frustrated by circumstances as he was now, but the mere fact that he was anxious to be done with the problem of Germain was odd. Normally he welcomed such diversions.

When he had succeeded to the title and inherited his grandfather's vast fortune, Dominic had had the means to indulge almost any desire he cared to name. He had given up a life of leisure, however, for the challenge of pitting his skills against the formidable agents of Napoleon's government. During the war, he had had to depend on his wits and his superb physical condition merely to survive. Even with Napoleon imprisoned on Elba, his skills had been needed, since several factions in France and England were busy planning the Corsican's escape while trying to drum up support for his return to power.

Dominic had worked for Edward Manning in the Foreign Office for nearly six years before Waterloo had put an end to his spying activities. At loose ends again, his fortune diminished by inflation and heavy wartime losses, he had set about rebuilding his holdings. He had spent a great deal of time at his country seat in Kent, plowing the income back into the land and making it thrive again.

When his satisfaction with that endeavor had lessened, he had begun to travel a great deal. The lifestyle suited him, although it offered him few challenges. Moving about the great capitals of the world, however, he was at least able to ease the gnawing restlessness that filled him after too long a stay in one place.

His most recent travels had taken him to America where he had enjoyed the untamed wilderness of that vast country for nearly a year before moving on to the West Indies. But the urge to return to a familiar way of life at last had driven him home. Since then, however, he had been oddly discontent with his life. And now he felt trapped where he normally experienced only boredom.

He knew quite well what was causing his present vexation of spirit, though. Brie. He had been unable to forget her. There were constant reminders of her. The glowing coals of a fire, a heated conversation, a passionate embrace, the tang of snow in the air.

Even Jason's wife Lauren had reminded him of Brie. Earlier in the week when he had dined with the Effings, the sparkling green of Lauren's eyes had mesmerized him for a moment, even though they were a different shade from Brie's, with too little blue, and none of the stormy clouds.

Dominic grimaced. He was allowing Brie's memory to affect him far more than was wise. She was naught but a country wench he had known for a short time. Still, he would have to conquer his growing obsession before it got out of hand.

Forcibly, Dominic turned his thoughts aside. When he reached his townhouse in Berkeley Square, he let himself in quietly. Of the skeleton staff he employed to maintain the residence, only Farley, his manservant, generally stayed awake till the wee hours to await his return. It was still early and Dominic was not expected, but Farley appeared in the foyer as if by magic. Dominic relinquished his outer garments and turned to mount the stairs.

"My lord?"

Dominic paused, glancing impatiently over his shoulder. Farley cleared his throat. "Pardon m'lord, but a . . . er . . . lady called a short time ago. She insisted that she be allowed to await your return. I informed her you would not be home till late."

Dominic's lips twitched at the accusation in his servant's

tone, but his curiosity was piqued. In spite of his rakish habits, women seldom appeared on his doorstep uninvited.

"Well, who is it, man?" he asked when Farley hesitated.

"A Miss Crowell, my lord. I have put her in the small parlor."

Surprised and a little puzzled, Dominic bounded up the stairs. Cassandra Crowell was a well-known figure among London Cyprians. A beautiful woman with raven hair and a voluptuous figure, she possessed an allure—as well as a reputation for having a charming bedside manner—that had attracted half the men in town to her side at one time or another. Dominic had escorted her to the theater earlier in the week, but nothing more. Even though Cassandra had pouted and become angry, he had not been interested enough to take what she so willingly offered.

He entered the parlor without knocking and let his gaze sweep the small room. It was quite empty.

Farley, who had followed, exclaimed in bewilderment. "But she was here but a moment ago! I brought her a tray. See, the tea is still warm."

"Perhaps she grew tired of waiting and left."

"Oh no, my lord. I would have heard her."

"Then," Dominic said slowly, "she must still be in the house. Search the ground floor, Farley, while I take this one. And go quietly. If she has a weapon, it would not do to startle her."

Farley swallowed. "A weapon, did you say?"

"Never mind. Just stay out of range and call out if you find her. Now move, man," he ordered as Farley continued to stand there staring.

Dominic began his search along the upper hall, his footsteps making no sound on the carpet as he carefully opened each door.

He wasn't sure what to expect from Cassandra when he found her. His first thought, when he had realized she was in his house, had been that she was still anxious to ply her trade.

But her disappearance had fostered a suspicion that Germain had hired her as an assassin of sorts. It would not be the first time Charles had used a female to further his own ends.

Dominic found Cassandra in his bedroom. She was making no attempt to cover the sounds of her movements as she rummaged through his personal belongings, so it was easy for him to quietly enter the room and observe her hurried search. He could tell she was unarmed. The gown she was wearing was designed to expose as much flesh as possible and could not possibly have concealed a weapon.

Dominic was puzzled. His jewel case containing some diamond stickpins and such was lying open, the items in plain view, but he saw enough to convince him it was no treasure hunt Cassandra had in mind.

"Had I known you were so hungry for me, cherie, I would not have kept you waiting."

A pistol shot could not have startled her more than Dominic's sardonic drawl did. Giving a gasp, Cassandra whirled to face him, hastily crossing one hand over her breasts while hiding the other behind her skirts. "My . . . my lord," she croaked. "I was not expecting you so soon."

Dominic's eyes glittered like cool diamonds. His gaze flicked around the room, then returned to her pale face and heaving breasts. "I can see you weren't," he remarked acidly, closing the door with his heel. He moved toward her unhurriedly, a panther stalking his prey. Cassandra retreated, shrinking from his tall, menacing form, but Dominic prevented her from moving by clamping his hands over her shoulders.

Reaching down, he wrenched her hands from behind her back. An object dropped from her grasp, making a dull thud on the thick carpet. Dominic recognized it immediately—a heavy gold seal ring that had once belonged to his father.

His eyes narrowed to mere slits. "I think that you will tell me why you are here, cherie," he said, his tone deadly.

Cassandra whimpered, then began to plead as his hand tightened around her wrist in warning, but Dominic only

103

increased the pressure on her wrist, twisting slowly.

"All right!" she cried.

"Well?"

"I . . . I was looking for the deed to your property in France."

"Why?"

"I don't know why! I only was supposed to find it."

Dominic studied her face, ignoring the tears that were streaming down her cheeks. His left hand slid upwards, his long fingers winding around her throat. "You have a lovely neck, ma belle," he murmured, "but I doubt it would retain its perfect form when stretched by a rope. Who sent you?"

Cassandra clawed at his hand as his fingers tightened their grip on her throat. "Please, you are killing me!"

"Who sent you?" Dominic repeated, his voice low and savage. "Was it Germain?" When Cassandra nodded, Dominic abruptly released his hold. He watched without pity as she sank limply to the floor. "Where can I find him?"

Cassandra shook her head, sobbing brokenly as she cradled her arm. When Dominic took a step closer, she cringed. "I swear I don't know! He . . . he came to my rooms two days ago. I don't know where he is now."

"How much did he pay you?"

"Two hundred guineas. He was to meet me again on Friday."

A muscle in Dominic's jaw clenched. "Where?"

"My . . . my rooms."

"You will not be there." He walked across the room and gave the bellpull a vicious tug. Turning, he cast a contemptuous glance at Cassandra. "You will leave London tonight, I don't care how. Don't count on Germain for protection if you disobey me, for no power on earth could stop me from killing you if I so much as set eyes on you again." When Farley burst into the room a moment later, Dominic indicated Cassandra with an impatient wave of his hand. "Get her out of my sight."

Familiar with his employer's black moods, Farley quickly bundled up the sobbing woman and half carried her over the

104

threshold, closing the door behind him.

When they were gone, Dominic spun around and sent his balled fist crashing into the nearest wall. Since that brought no satisfaction, he threw himself in the chair beside the bed and sat perfectly still, slowly clenching and unclenching his fists until he felt able to control his rage.

A deep frown curled his mouth as he brooded on the puzzle. For the life of him, he couldn't guess what Germain was planning. He could think of no possible reason why the man would be interested in papers showing his ownership of the land in France, or even why Charles would probe into his personal life. Dominic ran his fingers through his dark hair, swearing savagely.

Before the Revolution the property had belonged to his father, but at the comte's death, the land had been confiscated by the French government. Part of it had been divided among the serfs of the estate; and later, sections had been given as rewards to supporters of Napoleon.

The fall of Napoleon's empire had changed matters, though, and when the war had ended, Dominic had gone to Paris and commissioned an agent to purchase back the estate that was his rightful heritage. It had taken years and had cost a princely sum in bribes and inflated prices to secure the lands and old chateau. Dominic hadn't even visited the estate yet, for only recently had the agent succeeded in converting the parcels to a whole and arranged for a deed to be drawn up. The agent had also reported that while the chateau still stood, it had suffered heavy damages, and that neglect and lack of management had rendered the vineyards and farmlands completely unproductive. So why would Charles be interested in the deed? Dominic asked himself again.

Feeling hatred and anger knotting his stomach, he pulled himself out of the chair and began to pace the room like a wild animal whose cage was far too confining.

Cassandra was no problem, Dominic decided. She was merely Germain's tool. Her connection would be useful, however, since Charles had already arranged to meet her. And of course Cassandra wouldn't be attending the meeting. It would be Dominic himself who made the scheduled appointment.

As it turned out, Dominic never went to Cassandra's rooms to find Charles Germain. Germain came to him.

Early the next morning Dominic was wakened by Farley with the news that a gentleman waited below. Dominic shrugged into a crimson dressing gown and went downstairs to attend his visitor.

The morning caller was definitely Charles Germain. A tall, fair-haired man with hooded eyes and a light complexion, Germain had a slender build and a vapid expression that made him appear harmless. Dominic had long ago learned not to underestimate the man, however. Germain's slight frame enabled him to move with a dancer's grace, and his expert agility was backed by a cunning brain. A formidable opponent by any standards, Dominic reflected as he met his enemy's gaze for the first time in almost four years.

Charles was about forty now, Dominic guessed, but the years under the hot Indian sun had not been kind to him. His complexion was flushed a deep red, indicating permanent skin damage, and there were new lines about his eyes and mouth.

Dominic paused in the doorway of the salon and raised a dark eyebrow. "Such a surprise, Charles. Where have you been hiding all these years?"

Germain's mouth tightened. "Don't play the fool with me, Dominic. Unless Manning's spies have bungled it, you have known for some time of my return."

A dark gleam appeared in Dominic's gray eyes. "I have. But I expected you much sooner—and certainly not in broad daylight. What kept you? I made it easy enough for you to find me."

"Quite easy. I could have killed you several times over."

106

"You could have tried. So why did you not? I confess that has me puzzled."

Charles appeared to consider his words carefully. "You have something I want."

"Ah yes, the deed," Dominic said, thrusting his hands deep in the pockets of his dressing gown. "I'll wager you were disappointed in Cassandra. I could have warned you she didn't have the intelligence to carry out your work. But why do you want the deed?"

Germain's smile resembled a sneer. "It is not for me. It is for . . . a client, let us say. Someone who is extremely interested in your future. I am to receive a large bonus if I can obtain the property in addition to killing you." When Dominic merely raised an eyebrow, Germain waved his hand impatiently. "Last night you were lucky enough to find out about the deed, but now that you've been warned, it should prove difficult for me to get my hands on it. So I have a proposition for you. You get the name of my client in exchange for the property."

Dominic was genuinely amused. "Your wits have gone begging, Charles, if you expect me to turn over a valuable estate to you just for a name."

"What if I were to tell you that my client profited from your father's death?"

Dominic gave him a piercing look but made no comment. Charles shrugged. "Very well, then. We will make it an affair of honor, with the winner's claim either the deed or the information. I doubt you would refuse a duel."

Dominic kept his expression inscrutable as he considered the proposal. Dueling was illegal but he and Charles would come to blows sooner or later. It was inevitable. Charles had revived their past contretemps the moment he set foot on English soil, and it would only be resolved when one of them achieved a clear victory. Besides, a duel would be better than finding himself in a dark alley some evening with Germain waiting to plunge a knife in his back. Even so, Charles Germain was not the kind of man to act without a trump up his sleeve, particularly when the stakes were high. If he were proposing a duel, that meant he planned to win—by fair means or foul.

Dominic was convinced of his suspicions when he accepted the challenge, for the gleam of triumph in Germain's eyes was unmistakable. The smirk disappeared, however, when Dominic added casually, "I believe the choice of weapons is mine? Then let us use foils. I haven't tested my blade in some time. You have kept in practice, haven't you Charles?" He could see Germain hesitate and weigh the disadvantages. "Come now, don't you consider your bonus worth the risk?"

Charles flushed an angry, darker red, but he nodded and suggested a time and place.

"I believe it is common practice to have our seconds agree to the particulars," Dominic observed mildly—with the satisfying result that Germain lost his temper.

"Damn it, man! Where in the bloody blazes am I to get a second? I don't know anyone in London any longer, thanks to you!"

Dominic regarded him coolly. "You may do as you please, Charles, but I prefer to have witnesses. I value my skin, you know."

His remark only fueled Germain's rancor. Balling his fists, Charles strode across the room and turned back at the door to point a commanding finger at Dominic. "Tomorrow morning, Stanton! Bacon's field at dawn. Be there, or your skin won't be worth a farthing when I've finished with you."

An answering spark of fury showed in Dominic's gray eyes, but he made no move to stop his guest's departure.

An hour later, he drove his curricle to the Effing mansion in Grosvenor Square. He found Jason alone, for Lauren was still upstairs resting. When he was invited to partake of breakfast, Dominic declined anything except coffee.

"So what brings you here at this hour?" Jason asked when the footmen had been dismissed.

"I want you to act as my second."

Jason blandly continued to butter a muffin. "Another duel? Do I know the fellow?"

"No, but I've mentioned him. He's Charles Germain."

Looking up, Jason grinned. "However did you manage that? Germain must be mad to have agreed—or a complete fool."

"Actually he challenged me." Dominic proceeded to tell Jason about Cassandra's attempted theft and about the property in France. "Germain showed up on my doorstep this morning trying to get his hands on the deed," Dominic added. "He even admitted that he had been hired by someone to kill me. The estate was to be part of the bargain."

Jason eyed him with suspicion. "You aren't in your cups this morning, by any chance?"

"I thank you for your faith in me," Dominic said acerbically. "But even were I drunk, do you think I would make up a story like that? I'm completely serious. The deed is being held by my solicitor, but I have no idea how Charles found out about it, or why someone would want it. Actually, I was planning to visit France this summer—I wanted to take a look at the land to see what it would take to make it profitable again. But now it seems I will have to move up the trip. I suppose I should be thankful for Germain's greed. He was so anxious to collect his fee that he proposed a duel. The details have already been arranged. Tomorrow at dawn, Bacon's field. We're to use foils. I wouldn't trust him with a pistol."

"But isn't Germain a fair swordsman?"

"Yes, but I don't intend to lose. Regretfully, I can't kill Charles if I want to find out who hired him."

"And then you go to France?"

Dominic grinned. "Not yet. I still plan to take Julian up on his invitation. Unfinished business. I leave tomorrow."

Chuckling, Jason shook his head. "Ah yes, the wench who struck you. One of these days, Dominic—"

"Then I may count on you?"

"Of course. I shall have to tell Lauren, though, or she will wonder where I've gone."

"Thanks, Jase. I had better go for I left my horses standing," he said, rising. "I'll see you in the morning."

Jason waved a hand in dismissal. "I'll bring a surgeon, although I trust it will be Germain who needs his services."

Dominic laughed. "Let us hope so, my friend. My future godchild will be sorely disappointed if you have to find a substitute for me."

Dominic spent the rest of the day putting his other affairs in order, and, after visiting his banker and attorney, he called on Manning to explain the recent development with Germain. He spent the evening gambling with friends, winning and losing large sums. He also drank heavily—so much, in fact, that the aid of his coachman as well as that of a disgruntled Farley was required to put him to bed.

He woke the next morning with a hangover, but except for his slightly bloodshot eyes, Dominic looked the picture of a fashionable gentleman when he left the house. He was elegantly attired in tight-fitting fawn breeches, gleaming top boots, a striped silk waistcoat, and a blue coat set off by a ruffled shirt front.

It was still dark and a thick fog blanketed the city, but the coach was waiting for him. Jacques was sitting in the box, keeping a grip on the reins, while two footmen held the bridles of the lead horses. Two large trunks had been strapped to the roof of the coach, and Dominic's black stallion Diablo had been tied loosely to the rear. The stallion stood proudly motionless, even though the four matched bays stamped and snorted, protesting the coldness of the foggy morning.

Dominic was still not in the best of moods, but he was able to return his coachman's mocking grin with one of his own. "Move over," he ordered, climbing into the box beside the Frenchman. "I need to work off some of the ache in my bones." When Jacques chuckled, Dominic slanted him a fulminating glare. "Stubble it, will you? You try my patience with your infernal giggling."

At his command, the footmen released the leaders and the

110

four powerful bays sprang forward. Jacques leaned back in his seat, closed his eyes, and pulled his hat low over his forehead. He was still grinning, but he wisely kept his thoughts to himself.

It was barely dawn when they neared the appointed meeting place and Dominic turned the carriage off the main road. The swirling mist that shrouded the countryside churned beneath the galloping hooves of the horses as they swept onto a wide field. Beyond stood a clearing encircled by enormous elms, looking like a ghostly gladiator's arena in the gloom.

Jason's carriage was already waiting, but there was no sign of Germain. Dominic brought the coach to a halt and handed the reins to Jacques as he leapt down from the box. Shedding his greatcoat and tossing it into the coach, he took a deep breath, feeling the cold dawn air sting his lungs. The chill silence that surrounded the place matched his grim mood.

Jason introduced the short, bespectacled man as a surgeon, but none of them were inclined toward conversation. For a time the quiet was broken only by the occasional creak of a carriage harness or the muffled jingle of a bit as a horse tossed its head.

Finally, however, they heard the faint drumming of hooves in the distance. "At last," Dominic remarked as Germain and another man approached on horseback. "I was beginning to wonder if I had asked you here for naught."

When Germain rode up, Dominic responded to his curt greeting with a thin smile. While Jason retrieved a long slim case containing a set of matched foils from the coach, Dominic stripped off his coat and cravat. Immediately the cold dampness penetrated the fine linen of his shirt, but he set his teeth against the chill, trying to ignore it.

Charles Germain dismounted and made the same preparations, not bothering to introduce his friend, a heavyset man whose face sported a crooked nose. Charles appeared calm as he inspected the gleaming rapiers Jason presented, but the tight lines around his mouth betrayed his tension. He selected

111

one of the foils and tested its weight in his hand.

Dominic accepted the other, making a quick pass in the air, cutting it with a hiss. The quality of the blade was unmistakable—light and flexible, yet made of the strongest steel.

He moved to the center of the clearing and stood waiting with the razor tip pointed at the ground. When Germain had taken a place opposite, Jason quietly outlined the rules, then retreated a few yards to stand with the others and observe the contest.

"It seems you are a fool after all," Charles sneered, attempting to ruffle his opponent's cool composure.

Dominic's eyes glittered dangerously. With his shirt front unbuttoned, exposing the dark hair on his chest, he bore more resemblance to a Spanish pirate than a fashionable English lord. He grinned wickedly, his white teeth flashing against dark skin. "We are evenly matched, I would say. A fool and a coward. En garde!"

Dominic's challenge rang out, and the gleaming rapiers came together with a clash. In the first engagement, Germain lunged deftly, but Dominic parried his thrust with a finely executed volt. Next Dominic advanced with a series of neat slashes, testing the quickness of his opponent's reaction. When his foil suddenly flashed wide, Germain caught his blade handily. Dominic had to admire the adroit manner in which Charles fended off the attack. The man had improved, it seemed; he fought less conservatively and with a great deal more finesse.

The two of them moved as if in a graceful dance, circling each other, weapons carefully poised. Then their blades met again, crackling and hissing.

When Germain feinted and returned an unexpected thrust, Dominic drew back, deflecting the rapier point with a supple wrist. Whirling about, he launched another flurry. His attack nearly threw Charles off balance, but the man escaped with a

112

nimble leap. There was another silence as the two contestants danced in opposite circles, warily regarding each other. Then they engaged again, steel clashing against steel.

They fought for some time, neither seeming to be able to gain the advantage. Finally, though, Germain began to lose patience. Darting forward, he thrust viciously, and his slashing blade almost succeeded in slipping through Dominic's guard. Dominic bore his hand upward at the last instant, however, and his foil slid nearly halfway up the other blade. With a snarl, Germain leapt back, then attacked with a forced flurry, his blade ringing against tempered steel as it cut swiftly through the air.

Dominic could sense Germain's growing frustration. Both of them were breathing hard from the exertion, but it was obvious that Charles was tiring more quickly; a thin sheen of sweat covered his face and his movements were slower, less refined than at the start. Dominic parried his next strike easily with a powerful flick of his wrist. Then judging the time as ripe, he bore down with fierce determination, keeping his eyes trained on his opponent's face.

In response, Charles became more reckless. He lunged, wildly brandishing the slender rapier. Dominic sidestepped lightly, narrowly avoiding the point of Germain's blade, and continued to give ground as he waited for the right moment. At the next desperate thrust, he caught Germain's blade in a parry. The foils locked at their base, and Dominic flashed a mocking smile as he disengaged. Then he went on a driving offensive, forcing his opponent backwards, his powerful thigh muscles bulging as he advanced with agile steps.

Suddenly Dominic changed tactics. After slowing his onslaught to control the encounter, he retreated, lowering his guard in a deliberate invitation. As he had expected, Germain made a rapid lunge. Too rapid. Charles lost his balance momentarily, and Dominic slashed downward to the right, making a short arc and then an upward extension. The tip sank

113

deeply into Germain's side.

There was a hushed silence as Charles stared down at the bright crimson stain spreading on his shirt front. His face wore a look of dumbfounded dismay before his eyes lifted to clash with Dominic's. For an instant, his features contorted with hatred. Then his expression became altogether blank as his knees slowly buckled.

He pitched forward, clutching his ribs, but Dominic caught him before he fell. Gently lowering Charles to the frozen ground, Dominic rolled him over so that he was lying on his back. Then kneeling, he withdrew the sword from Charles' side and loosened his shirt to expose the wound.

When he saw the damage he had done, Dominic swore a silent oath. His blade had penetrated deeply into Charles' ribcage and blood was welling freely from the small hole located a few inches below and to one side of the right breast. Dominic didn't need to be told that such a wound could prove fatal. Grim-faced, he drew back to allow the surgeon his examination.

"Not good," the doctor muttered. "Not good at all. But he may live." From his bag the doctor pulled a wad of cloth and formed a thick pad, pressing it against the wound to staunch the flow of blood. "Blade missed the lung, but barely," he announced. "Unconscious. Always happens. He'll have a fever—at least a week, maybe two. If he survives that, he should recover."

"Your expenses plus a hundred guineas if he lives," Dominic said in a fierce undertone. "And keep this quiet."

"I will do my best, m'lord, but I beg you not to expect miracles."

Dominic stood up slowly, his eyes on Germain's face. He suddenly felt extremely weary. "I'll have to depend on you, Jason," he said, pulling his friend aside. "Manning knows of a place where Charles can be held."

Jason nodded, his mood far lighter with Dominic the victor.

114

"Never fear. I'll see Germain receives the best of care."

Dominic glanced down at the unconscious man and swore again, clenching his fists. "Bloody hell! Even if he lives, he won't be able to talk for some time."

"Cheer up, Dom. At least you aren't the one they are carting away. That was quite a demonstration, by the way."

They both watched as Charles was carried to Jason's coach. Then they slowly followed. "I take it you don't care to stop Germain's friend?" Jason remarked as the heavyset man mounted his horse and galloped off. "He doesn't seem interested in staying around to see what happens."

"I doubt if he knows anything," Dominic replied grimly. "Germain probably picked him up for insurance. No, I just want to know who is behind all this. *Someone* hired Charles to put a period to my existence."

Jason chuckled. "Unfortunately, until Germain recovers and you can question him, all you have to do is be wary of everyone you meet."

Dominic's answering smile was devoid of humor. "I'll leave it to you, Jason, to see that Charles doesn't escape the good doctor's care. You will send me word of his progress? I can return to London before going to France."

"I'll let you know the moment Germain can talk."

When they reached the waiting carriages, the two men took leave of one another. "Take care of yourself, Dom," Jason said as he gripped Dominic's hand. "I want you to survive to suffer the slings of matrimony yourself."

"So I can sit at home and play nursemaid?" Dominic retorted. "No thank you, Jase. Your milk-pudding existence is too tame for me."

"All the same, I don't much care for this situation."

"I should be safe enough with Charles laid up. Save your worries for your wife, and let me know when my godchild arrives." Dominic climbed into his coach and leaned his head out the window. "By the way, Jase, thanks for covering for me on this one."

Jason grinned. "Any time, my friend. Good hunting."

Dominic returned his mock salute, then rapped on the ceiling. When Jacques flicked the reins, the spirited horses moved briskly forward. A moment later the coach swung around, heading for the open road.

Chapter Five

"Whatever is taking you so long?" Katherine asked at the door to Brie's dressing room. "Luncheon has been ready an age and Caroline is waiting for you."

Brie had spent nearly ten minutes searching through the walnut armoire for something to wear, but she still hadn't changed out of her riding habit. She broke off her search to sigh in frustration. "I'm not hungry, Katherine. Why don't you tell Caroline to begin without me?"

Katherine's mouth tightened in disapproval. "Well, then, Miss Gabrielle, perhaps your highness would deign to come to the sewing room for a fitting."

"I didn't deserve that, Katherine!" Yanking a long-sleeved merino dress from the armoire, Brie flung it across a chair.

Katherine hesitated, noting her flushed cheeks. "Brie, is something wrong? You haven't seemed yourself for the past two weeks or more. Perhaps you are coming down with a bit of a fever?"

"Nothing is wrong!" When Brie saw the genuine concern in her companion's eyes, though, she felt ashamed. "I'm sorry, Katie. But I just don't think I can stand another minute of Caroline's moods. Her depression is becoming contagious."

"You might try for some understanding. I know she has done nothing but mope, but your cousin is just a green girl

117

getting over her first infatuation. She needs someone to listen to her."

"I hardly think I'm fitted for the role of confidant."

"Well, you were the one who approved her visit, remember? I thought at the time that you were taking the situation far too lightly. Lady Langley sent her daughter to you, hoping you would provide a positive influence on the girl, yet so far you've all but ignored her."

"Very well," Brie muttered. "I'll spend more time with Caroline. But please don't expect me to entertain her. I would be at a complete loss."

"She would be better off with some company. Perhaps you could introduce her to some of the young gentlemen in the neighborhood."

Brie shrugged, but then a mischievous gleam began to sparkle in her eyes. "Would Rupert Umstead suffice?" Rupert was the local squire's eldest son. His flowery speeches and general inanities always drove Brie to distraction, but she suddenly realized that she could pawn Rupert off on her mopish cousin and be rid of two problems.

Katherine didn't seem to approve of the idea, however. Seeing her frown, Brie laughed. "How you do like to manage other people's lives, Katie! Very well, I will dress and be down in a moment. Do you still want me for a fitting?"

Katherine shook her head in exasperation. "Brie Carringdon, I will never understand you as long as I live. But yes, I need you. Two of your evening gowns are almost finished and I want to pin the bodice of the amber walking dress. I will expect you in an hour."

Brie smiled in agreement, yet as soon as she was alone again, her smile disappeared. Katherine's comments had been too accurate and pointed for comfort.

It was true, Brie reflected as she began to undress, that she had paid little attention to her cousin. Caroline had been nothing but an irritating nuisance since her arrival. In all fairness, though, the girl wasn't totally at fault. For over a

118

fortnight, Brie herself had been overstrung and restless, and more than once she had snapped at her cousin for some imagined fault. The denial she had given Katherine had been just short of an outright lie, however. Brie knew well the cause of her own ill temper. The problem was she couldn't forget a certain dark-haired lord or what had happened between them. He plagued her thoughts constantly and caused her to start at shadows.

Brie's spirits plummeted as she recalled her last confrontation with Stanton. Even being attacked by her fiance hadn't frightened her as thoroughly as that look on Dominic's face. Brie shivered, remembering the ruthlessness she had seen in those unforgiving gray eyes. She almost hoped she would never see him again.

She had stayed close to home since that day, just in case he decided to return, and the self-imposed confinement had worn on her nerves. But even more disturbing was the bewildering discontentment she had been experiencing for the past two weeks. The feeling had started when Dominic first kissed her, but the burning restlessness had soon spread, leaving her soul smoldering in its wake.

Wondering if her encounters with Dominic Serrault had left any mark, Brie found herself glancing in the cheval glass. There was no outward sign that she could tell. Her face, with its high cheekbones and forehead, was perfectly composed.

Critically, she studied her other features. Men called her beautiful, but she could see nothing remarkable about the slim nose, the coral mouth, or the pointed chin. The eyes were an unusual shade, though. They looked large and luminous in her face, framed as they were by long, thick lashes. Her complexion was smooth, a pale cream tinged with ripe apricot, but she knew her skin would be unfashionably tanned in summer. Her dark hair was her most noticeable feature. Neither strictly brown nor red, it flowed down her back in thick waves, curling at the ends and glowing with a life all its own. More than one man had expressed a wish to touch the silky locks. Dominic's long, lean fingers had played in her hair, twisting and stroking. . . .

Brie flushed, realizing that her mind had again wandered to that evening he had tried to seduce her. He hadn't been the first man to attempt it, but no one besides he had ever made her the victim of such turbulent emotions. His searing lips and invading tongue had made her experience sensations she had never felt before. His passion had almost overwhelmed her for that brief instant of touching and tasting and feeling . . . but at the last moment she had drawn back, frightened of her own abandon and of him.

Almost wistfully, Brie wondered if she would ever meet anyone who could stir her blood the way Dominic had. Someone who could make her feel desire without making her lose herself so completely.

Stripping off the rest of her clothes, Brie stood before the mirror and curiously studied her naked reflection. Her height was about average for a woman, but there was none of the stylish plumpness in her face or figure that had been the fashion for years. Her breasts were high and pointed, but the narrow waist and gently flaring hips made her slender frame look almost boyish. Her slim, tapering legs made her seem tall when she wasn't.

Her figure wasn't voluptuous enough to appeal to most men, Brie thought with a sigh. But what did it matter, anyway? She did not expect to marry. She had passed her twenty-third birthday and had not as yet found any man with whom she wanted to spend the rest of her life.

Giving herself a mental shake, Brie reached for her chemise. She had been a fool for responding to Stanton's advances—and she was still one for not being able to dismiss that arrogant, insolent man from her mind. In that respect, she was no better than her cousin, letting a man she hardly knew affect her so.

When she was dressed, Brie sat down at her dressing table and pinned up her hair, leaving a few loose curls framing her face. Katherine was right, she decided. She needed a new focus. And her cousin Caroline needed a friend. Perhaps taking the younger girl under her wing would help dissipate her own restlessness. If so, they would both benefit.

Determined to find her former sense of equanimity, Brie added the finishing touches to her appearance and then made her way downstairs to the dining room. She found her cousin staring gloomily at her plate.

Caroline Langley was a pretty girl with brown curls and eyes, and a round, rosy face. Normally her disposition was lively and animated, but her expression today was as glum as it had been for the past two weeks. Brie wanted to shake her.

"Good morning," she made herself say instead.

Caroline looked suspicious of her show of warmth. "It is afternoon, not morning."

"So it is. I must have let the time get away from me." She served herself from the sideboard, then took a seat at the table. "Did you find something to occupy your time while I was riding?"

Caroline relaxed somewhat. "Actually I did. I've been exploring the attics. I came across this." She pulled an object from her pocket, dangling it between two fingers.

"Mama's pendant," Brie said, recognizing the chain with its gold medallion. "I thought it had been lost. Wherever did you find it?"

"In one of the trunks. Katherine remembered seeing a fichu of blond lace among Aunt Suzanne's clothes and asked me to look for it. I found this caught in the lace. It has an inscription on the back, but my French isn't very good. Can you read it?"

She passed the necklace to Brie who studied it carefully. The gold disk was encircled by delicate filigree and one side was engraved with tiny letters. "I had forgotten," Brie remarked. "I used to be fascinated by this as a child, but Mama would never let me wear it. Not even when I had been a very good little girl."

"Which, to hear Katherine talk, wasn't often," Caroline interjected.

Brie ignored her teasing and translated. "'Eschewing weakness, abandon to dust this heinous flesh.'"

"How morbid. Why would anyone want such a thing?"

"I believe it was a gift from her mother."

"And?"

Brie shrugged. "And nothing. I don't know anything more about it. Mama's parents died before I was born. She rarely spoke of them, though she did tell me once that I resemble her mother."

"Perhaps there was a deep, dark secret in Aunt Suzanne's past," Caroline intoned with relish. "Here, let me have the necklace and I'll put it away in your jewel case."

"Your imagination is becoming excessive, Caroline," Brie said as she handed the pendant back. "I expect you've been reading too many gothics."

"I have not! Mama won't let me read gothics. I have to sneak them into the house. And you needn't laugh, Brie. You don't know what it's like, living with Mama. I'm eighteen and she still treats me like a child. And now she has sent me away from all my friends. Banished to the country!"

With effort, Brie kept her expression sober. "Your mother was only concerned for your reputation, Caroline. Eloping with a half-pay officer is hardly the thing, you know. And besides, I understand perfectly what it is like to live with your mother. *And* how it feels to incur her wrath. Aunt Arabella sent me home in disgrace my first season, remember?"

When Caroline merely pouted, Brie regarded her with exasperation. "For Heaven's sake, will you quit feeling sorry for yourself? You only have to stay here for a few weeks. Soon you'll be back in London and everyone will have forgotten all about the scandal. I'll take you home myself. We'll go to the theater, if you like, and I hear there is a new opera—"

"But what do I do in the meantime? It is so boring here."

"Perhaps we could do some shopping in the village. The milliner in Oakham is quite talented. And Julian has invited us to join him for tea at the inn this afternoon."

122

Caroline brightened perceptively, but then her face fell again. "I don't think Julian likes me. He was beastly to me the whole time we were stuck in that ghastly inn. You would have thought I caused all that snow. It wasn't my fault his coach lost a wheel or that my maid contracted a cough and had to be treated as an invalid."

"Of course not," Brie soothed. "I'm sure Julian doesn't blame you for that unfortunate storm. Indeed, it rather surprises me that he took his ill humor out on you. Julian is always the perfect gentleman."

"Well, he was forever reading me a scold." Caroline paused in her denunciation in order to glance speculatively at Brie. "He is handsome, isn't he?"

"Julian?" she asked, wary of the question. "Yes, I suppose he is."

"Mama thinks you should have married him."

"Your mother and I disagree quite often, Caroline. Julian and I are good friends, but we argue like siblings. I think even he is beginning to realize how lucky he is not to be saddled with me for a wife. I would drive him to distraction in the space of a month."

"Surely not. You aren't that bad, Brie."

"Why, thank you," she said wryly. "Well, would you like to come?"

"Yes. But must we ride? I'm not very fond of horses, you know. Couldn't we take the gig?"

Brie repressed her smile. "Of course, if you wish. But that may interfere with Katherine's plans. She usually uses the gig in the afternoons to visit our tenants. And you will disappoint John Simms. He has been saving Fanny especially for you."

Caroline sighed in resignation. "All right, I'll try. But I don't promise to like it. Every horse I try to ride either bites me or tries to throw me."

"I don't think you'll have any trouble with Fanny. Besides, even good riders fall now and then. I did myself when I was schooling one of Julian's horses the other day."

"Oh, were you hurt?" Caroline said in dismay.

Brie's eyes kindled as she remembered that incident in the meadow. "Only bruised and shaken a bit," she replied. Then she banished the unpleasant memory and smiled at her cousin. "Perhaps you will even want to hunt next week. Squire Umstead is allowing novices to join us on Monday and John has volunteered to ride with you so you wouldn't have to keep up with the others."

"I suppose I could," Caroline said doubtfully. "Will Julian be there?"

Brie laughed. "Julian miss a chance to hunt? He would far rather break a leg."

They discussed the upcoming hunt for the remainder of the meal, then Brie rose from the table. "I promised Katherine I would try on the new dresses she has been making for my stay in London," she said. "If you like, you may watch her stick me with pins."

Caroline nodded eagerly. "Oh yes, please. I always love to see your gowns, they are so beautiful. Does Katherine make them all?"

"Nearly all. She doesn't trust me to stay in fashion. She says that were I left to my own devices, I would wear breeches all the time. Actually, though, Katherine enjoys sewing now that she doesn't have to earn her living at it. She was a seamstress before she became a companion."

"How romantic!"

"Good heavens, whatever makes you think that straining one's eyes in poor light for fourteen hours a day with raw, bleeding fingers could possibly be romantic?"

"I never thought of that."

"No, I don't suppose you did," Brie murmured as a smile touched her lips. Her cousin was proving to be more diverting than she had expected.

After the fitting, Brie and Caroline changed into riding habits and warm cloaks, then made their way to the stables. John spent some time instructing Caroline on how to handle

124

the small gray mare he had chosen for her, but shortly the two cousins were cantering along the lane to the village, a groom trailing unobtrusively behind.

Brie critically observed her cousin at first, but she soon relaxed. Caroline was in no danger of falling off, and while she didn't seem particularly delighted to be riding, at least she was no longer complaining.

Brie's own mount, another gray, was more spirited and required more attention, particularly once they reached the village of Oakham. They made their way slowly along the cobbled streets, avoiding the square where crowds of people, attracted by market day, shopped and mingled and exchanged gossip.

They stopped first to buy some lace of a particular shade for Katherine, before going on to the milliner's. Caroline exclaimed joyfully over the profusion of bonnets on display in the shop and spent her money freely, and by the time they left the shop, she was all smiles. She was chattering to Brie about her new bonnets, not minding where she was going, when she literally ran into the gangling young dandy who happened to be passing.

"I say!" he protested, trying to untangle himself.

Brie winced when she recognized the high-pitched voice, for it belonged to Rupert Umstead. As usual, Rupert was dressed in an outlandish fashion. His cravat and shirt-points were so high that he had difficulty turning his head, and the bright colors he wore made him resemble a strutting peacock. Brie had considered pawning Rupert off on cousin, but seeing him now, she was no longer certain Caroline deserved such an ill turn.

Rupert was obviously delighted to see Brie, however, for he exclaimed over seeing her, acting as if her presence in town was a unique occurrence. Brie ground her teeth at his inanities, but when he turned and made Caroline an abject apology, she had no choice except to present her cousin.

Rupert made Caroline a sweeping bow. "I am honored to

meet such a beautiful creature," he said solemnly. "I am at your feet, my dear lady—"

"There is no need for that, Rupert," Brie responded. "You can grovel at her feet some other day. For now, I'm afraid you must excuse us. We have another engagement." She firmly refused Rupert's offer to escort them and escaped with her cousin in tow.

Caroline said nothing until they had walked some distance down the street. "What was that all about?" she asked.

Brie smiled, her eyes sparkling. "I've repented."

"What?"

"Never mind. You don't want to know Mr. Umstead, believe me. He would have spoiled our tea and probably invited himself to dinner as well. The man is an utter fool. Come, Julian will be expecting us."

Caroline was unconvinced, for she had enjoyed being called a beautiful creature, but she decided not to argue.

The Viscount Denville had indeed already arrived, they discovered when they entered The Blue Fox Inn. Brie and Caroline were led upstairs to a private parlor where he was waiting for them.

A handsome man, Julian was a few years older and a good deal taller than Brie. He had blue eyes, blond hair, and a ready smile, and his friendly open charm made him extremely likable. Dressed as he was in a dark brown coat and buff leather breeches, he looked every inch the sporting gentleman.

He rose when Brie and Caroline entered. "You are both looking beautiful today," he said pleasantly as he bowed over Brie's hand.

Caroline blushed at the compliment, but Brie laughed. "It sounds far more pleasing coming from you, Julian. Rupert Umstead just said the same thing, only he positively drooled."

Julian clasped his hand to his breast in mock horror. "Brie, you have wounded me mortally. How dare you compare me to that oaf?"

When they were all seated at the table, enjoying the delicate finger sandwiches and dainty iced cakes the inn had provided, Julian asked Caroline how she was enjoying her stay. He listened politely when she described the shopping she had done, but his eyebrows rose when he learned she had ridden into town. "You rode? I thought you didn't care for horses."

"Oh, I didn't," Caroline stammered, "but I do." She blushed at Julian's grin, but then her expression became quite serious. "No one has ever taught me before, like Mr. Simms and Brie did. What to do and say, I mean. And I rode the nicest little mare. Fanny was wonderful."

Julian laughed. "Take care, Caroline. If your cousin has you talking to horses, you'll soon be eating oats. Speaking of horses," he said, turning to Brie, "I've been meaning to ask about your progress with Jester. What do you think? Is there hope for the beast?"

It was Brie's turn to color. "Some," she replied, trying to sound composed. "He still has a tendency to shy at unfamiliar sights and sounds, even though we've kept him around activity as much as possible. But I'm not willing to give up on him yet. Will you let me hunt him next week?"

"If you think it best, of course. By the way, I have a friend who is looking for some broodmares to expand his stable. Do you suppose John might be interested in parting with one or two of your Arabians?"

"He might," Brie said cautiously. "It would depend on the buyer."

"I can vouch for Stanton. He knows about horses and wouldn't mistreat them. I expect you will be green with envy when you see his stallion. A huge animal, black as coal. Spanish, I think."

Brie hardly heard his praise of the stallion. At the mention of Dominic, she paled visibly.

"What is it, Brie?" Julian asked when she threw a darting glance over her shoulder.

"Nothing," she prevaricated. "Tell me, is your friend here now?"

"No, but I expect him any day now. He was at the Lodge a few weeks ago during that fierce storm we had, but he was called away before I arrived. So then, do I have your permission to speak with John about the mares?"

The conversation turned to other subjects and Brie tried to keep up the appearance of enjoying herself, but she found it difficult since she wanted to run and hide. Dominic had been so very angry when she had hit him. If he returned, he would certainly seek her out. But perhaps when he discovered she was the owner of Greenwood, he would see that she merited the respect due a lady. And as Julian's guest, he would surely behave like a gentleman.

In spite of her rationalizations, however, Brie's nervousness did not diminish. When they had finished their tea, she rose and absently gathered up her belongings, hardly realizing when Julian draped her cloak over her shoulders. When he asked if she still wanted a fencing lesson on the morrow, she only nodded.

Caroline had been listening and was shocked. "With swords?" she exclaimed, her brown eyes wide with concern. "Brie, you don't mean to fence with him, do you? Why, you could be killed!"

Julian smiled down at Caroline. "There is no danger," he said gently. "The points of the foils are covered, and we are very careful. Your cousin has been working to develop her coordination and reflexes. In fact she is getting to be quite a good match for me." He threw a teasing look at Brie. "I get the feeling that Brie aspires to manhood. She already rides and shoots like a Cavalryman. I expect her next to try her hand at fisticuffs."

His remark jolted Brie out of her abstracted mood, and she scowled at him. "Julian Blake, that was a wicked thing to say. If you don't wish me to come, you only have to tell me. Fisticuffs, indeed! I ought to give your blasted horse back and let you suffer."

Surprised by her cousin's sudden outburst, Caroline glanced

Julian. She had seen the effect Brie's occasional flashes of temper had on men before, and she wondered how he would react. But either Julian had more self-command or he was accustomed to Brie's sharp repartee, for he laughed and held up his hands. "Truce, truce. Calm down, Brie. Caroline will think we fight like this all the time."

"We do," Brie retorted. "But one of these days I shall best you, and you will be at my mercy."

"I already am, m'dear," he replied, grinning.

Brie was in no mood to be teased, though. Pulling on her gloves, she curtly thanked Julian for the tea, then marched from the room.

Julian followed her retreating figure with his gaze. The odd look that crossed his face was gone in an instant, but Caroline saw it. Realizing he was still half in love with her cousin, she felt an urge to comfort him. "I think something is bothering Brie," she said quietly. "She argued with Katherine this morning, too."

Julian shook himself, then smiled down at Caroline. "Well," he said, gallantly offering her his arm, "if you are interested in seeing an exhibition in swordplay, you may come tomorrow with your cousin."

Dimpling, Caroline wrinkled her nose. "I expect I will find the sport a bit too arduous for my taste, but I should like to watch." When they reached the innyard, Brie was already mounted. Julian assisted Caroline onto her horse, but he barely had time to say farewell before Brie turned and rode out of the yard. Caroline had to spur her mare into a canter to keep from being left behind.

"Brie, are you sure you're all right?" she asked when she caught up.

Brie laughed shakily. "Why is everyone suddenly so concerned with my health? I am perfectly well, I assure you."

"Well, you look pale, like you've just seen a ghost."

Brie shook her head. Stanton was only a man, after all, not a specter. But she couldn't prevent her own silent thoughts from surfacing. "No, not a ghost, dear cousin," she murmured to herself. "Just my own, private devil come to haunt me."

It was early afternoon when Dominic arrived at the Lodge. Homer Dawson was obviously pleased to see him, for the elderly man beamed and bobbed as he accepted Dominic's beaver hat and greatcoat.

Dominic was in the process of asking about Mattie's recovery when he heard the sounds of clashing steel and feminine laughter issuing from the vicinity of the drawing room. When Homer explained that a fencing lesson was in progress, Dominic's curiosity was aroused. He followed the sounds to the drawing room, pausing at the door to survey the scene.

The furniture had been pushed to one side to clear a space on the floor, while near the door, a pink-cheeked young lady was perched on the edge of a chair, trying to stifle a nervous giggle as she watched the action. In the center of the room, Julian was dancing across the carpet in his stockinged feet, gaily wielding a foil. But it was his opponent, a slender, auburn-haired woman, who captured Dominic's complete attention.

His gray eyes narrowed as he studied Brie. She was dressed in breeches again, her hair tied back with a ribbon, her face flushed with excitement. Dominic's most immediate thought was that the image branded upon his memory did not do justice to her beauty. The delicate features were even lovelier than he recalled. He let his eyes roam freely over the shapely figure in male attire. She had been wearing a heavy coat that day in the meadow, but without it, her feminine curves were far more pronounced. Dominic's gaze swept downward, gliding over the provocative breasts, the narrow waist, the slim hips. Not voluptuous, certainly, but as enticing as any man could wish.

He watched as she moved gracefully across the floor, realizing with surprise that she was responding skillfully to Julian's every action. Seeing the brilliant smile she bestowed n her opponent as she managed a particularly fine riposte, Dominic knew a moment of sheer envy. Julian was obviously well acquainted with her. Perhaps he was the one who was enjoying the vixen's charms, after all. It was obvious that he took pleasure in their relationship, whatever that might be.

Dominic folded his arms across his chest and leaned against the doorjamb, prepared to wait for the contest to end. It was only a moment before Brie succeeded in disarming Julian with a rapid wrist action, sending his foil flying.

Her exclamation of delight was met with praise from her opponent. "Brava!" Julian cried. "I couldn't have done it better myself." As he bent to retrieve his sword, he noticed his guest for the first time. "Dominic!" he said cheerfully. "Welcome! Come in, and allow me to introduce you to my neighbors."

In the excitement of the match, Brie hadn't noticed Dominic's arrival, but at Julian's greeting she whirled. When her startled eyes locked with the gray ones she remembered so well, the jolt she received was so unexpected that she dropped her foil. Staring at Dominic, Brie could feel the color drain from her cheeks. He was just as striking as she remembered, with his black hair and dark, aristocratic features, but the piercing intentness of his gaze was unnerving. Only with great difficulty was she able to control a shudder. As she mechanically bent to pick up her fallen weapon, she vaguely heard Julian performing introductions.

"Brie, Caroline, may I present my very good friend, Dominic Serrault, Lord Stanton. Dom, this is one of my neighbors, Brie Carringdon, and her cousin, Miss Caroline Langley. Caroline is visiting from London."

Brie couldn't bring herself to speak. She could only stand there, staring dumbly as Dominic strode into the room. Caroline was not so stricken. Rather embarrassed by her cousin's rudeness, in fact, she rose and curtsied, politely offering her hand.

Dominic bowed over it, then turned to Brie, one dark brow

raised in question. He thought he understood the wary loo
she was giving him—she feared his retaliation. And no doub
she was worried he would reveal their prior acquaintance. Bu
since she had gone to such trouble to conceal her identity fro
him earlier, he decided to play along with her for the tim
being.

His eyes boldly swept her figure, lingering on the curve
revealed by the close-fitting breeches. "*Lady* Carringdon?" h
asked innocently, giving her a sardonic smile.

Brie clutched her foil close to her body as if to shield herse
against his mockery, but she met his deliberate stare withou
flinching. "*Miss* Carringdon, my lord," she replied cooll
inclining her head a fraction.

"Not a lady? Forgive me for the mistake." The verbal thrus
drew an immediate response from her, and Dominic wa
unaccountably pleased to see the sparks that flashed in he
eyes. He smiled down at her lazily.

Brie pressed her own lips together in annoyance, unde
standing his insinuation perfectly. But even if her behavio
had been lacking, her antecedents were perfectly acceptable
"My father was Sir William Carringdon," she said, her voic
edged with anger. "Perhaps you were acquanted with him, m
lord?" Her disclosure did not have the effect she was hopin
for, for there was no change in Dominic's expression.

He was surprised, though. Brie had the bearing and beaut
of a princess, but from her style of dress and the passionate wa
she had responded to his advances, he never would hav
guessed that she was a gently-bred lady of no mean socia
standing. She was an enigma, certainly. He wanted to know
about her, a great deal more.

But he had to be patient, Dominic told himself. "I had th
pleasure of meeting your father some years ago," he sai
mildly. "I didn't know him well, but I was acquainted with hi
reputation. He was an excellent horseman, was he not?"

"Many people thought so," Brie replied, lifting her chin.

"And you, mademoiselle, are attempting to follow in hi
footsteps."

It was a statement, not a question, and the accompanying grin that twisted Dominic's lips infuriated Brie. He might not have given her away, but he was still an arrogant, insufferable devil. She refused to respond to his taunt, however. Instead she glared at him in silent challenge.

It was a challenge Dominic could not ignore. Realizing her status had not lessened his desire for her, although he had seen immediately the need to revise his strategy for seducing the haughty beauty. But how to turn this situation to his advantage escaped him at the moment. He studied her speculatively, noting the angry flush that stained her cheeks. The stubborn set of her jaw could not disguise the delicacy of its line, and he knew that if he stroked the creamy skin there, he could get her to relax those tight muscles. But he would have to get close to her first.

Deliberately, he let his eyes drop to the swelling fullness of her breasts as they strained against the fine lawn of her shirt. She wore a chemise beneath, but he could faintly detect the coral outline of her nipples. He found himself hungering for the taste of those sweet buds. . . .

Brie was a little shocked by Dominic's blatant perusal. Her skin seemed to burn where his gaze touched her, and she could feel her nipples hardening, just as if he were pressing his hot lips against her. When Dominic raised a smile to her glare, Brie opened her mouth to give him a scathing set-down.

Julian spoke first. He had been growing uncomfortable with the flagging conversation, and now he stepped unwittingly into the silent battle. "I've been instructing Brie in the art of fencing, Dominic. In fact we were just wrapping up a match. She is proving to be a formidable opponent. Would you care to test her skill with a bout?"

"No!" Brie gasped. Seeing Julian give her a puzzled look, she realized her refusal had been too vehement and felt compelled to offer an explanation. "We really must be going, Julian. I have taken enough of your time this morning as it is."

The excuse sounded weak even to her own ears, and she wasn't surprised when Julian told her not to be absurd. "I

133

enjoyed the exercise," he insisted. "Besides, you need the experience of trying your hand with other opponents. It will be an excellent opportunity for you to practice." Julian handed his foil to Dominic, then stepped back to watch the contest, grinning encouragingly at Brie. "Just relax and remember what you've learned. Dominic won't take advantage of you.'"

"I wouldn't be too sure of that," she muttered under her breath. When she gave Dominic a sidelong glance, though, she flushed. His mocking half-smile told her that he had caught her words, and the low bow he made to her was the epitome of insolence. Brie lowered her eyelashes to hide her frustration. How she longed to wipe the smirk from his handsome face! Yet he owed her something for that day in the meadow when she had struck him with her whip, and she supposed it would be better to take her punishment here with witnesses present, rather than wait till later when she was alone with him.

For a moment she stood in indecision, while Dominic awaited her with amused patience, enjoying the irony of the situation. Then she reluctantly prepared her stance. They engaged foils, and soon the room resounded with ringing steel.

Brie did not expect to be victorious. She merely wanted to make a good showing. But from the start, there was no question of her doing anything more than preventing a rout. Dominic's superiority was evident in every feint and thrust he made. Brie was amazed at his strength. She was breathing hard after three minutes and sweat had started to blind her, but Dominic seemed as cool as if he were taking an evening stroll. There was no need even for him to exert himself. Brie was infuriated by the way he played with her, first letting her have the upper hand, then relentlessly advancing, his powerful arm driving her to retreat. She felt like a mouse caught by a jungle cat. He was toying with her now, she knew, but any moment he would pounce and make a meal of her.

Dominic's cool gray eyes told her nothing of his surprised appreciation of her skill. She was obviously a novice, but she had been well rehearsed in technique. Her smaller stature was a definite disadvantage, but what she lacked in power and reach, she almost made up in agility and determination. Dominic had to concentrate to prevent her quick thrusts from reaching their mark.

Brie tired quickly. She was at the point of willingly admitting defeat when Dominic asked with a provoking grin what prize the victor was to be awarded. His taunt goaded her into renewing her efforts. She began to fight with violent determination, feeling suddenly as if her very life depended on this one battle. She didn't hear or heed Julian's warning cry that the button had come off her foil and that the tip was unguarded. She was only aware that she had to defend herself against the dire threat her devilish opponent presented.

She was unprepared for the fury of Dominic's response. He attacked with deadly precision, forcing her to make a desperate retreat. A moment later, her sword was torn expertly from her grasp.

Her momentum was still carrying her backward, and when the backs of her knees hit the sofa, Brie went sprawling, the cushions breaking her fall. She was stunned to find herself looking up into Dominic's thunderous face, his blade pressed against her throat.

For an endless moment, the room was completely silent. Brie could feel her heart slamming against her ribs, but she didn't even dare breathe with the tip of Dominic's foil in the vulnerable hollow of her throat. Petrified, she stared up at him. His eyes were glittering shards of ice, impaling her as his rapier might do at any moment.

When Dominic finally moved, it was to raise his weapon only a few inches. Then with the point of his foil, he slowly, deliberately traced a line on Brie's cheek, reminding her of the welt she had raised on his own skin. "The score grows more uneven, my blood-thirsty vixen," he warned in a harsh whisper. "It must be settled."

He let the tip trail downward till it rested between her heaving breasts. "Soon," Dominic added softly. His eyes

135

flicked over the soft curves, then dropped lower to her spread thighs. His jaw tightened. Suddenly, without another word, Dominic tossed the foil away, making Brie flinch. Then he spun on his heel and strode from the room.

Both Julian and Caroline stared after him speechlessly. During the entire match, Caroline had been sitting with her hand pressed to her mouth, but now that the danger had passed, she jumped up and went to Brie's side. "Darling, are you alright? Did he hurt you?" she asked, helping Brie to sit up.

Silently Brie shook her head, her hand going automatically to her cheek where Dominic's foil had caressed it. "I think I have had enough lessons for one day," she said shakily. "Julian, would you be kind enough to hand me my boots and call for our horses?"

The look Julian gave her was incredulous. "Lord, Brie, you can't just leave it at that! I could wring your neck. Why the devil didn't you hold up when I told you your point was exposed? Didn't you hear me?"

"No, I did not," Brie replied stonily. "I am sorry to have disgraced you, Julian, but you may be assured I don't plan a repeat performance. I should have known better than to cross swords with that insufferable tyrant in the first place."

Perplexed, Julian stared at Brie. "Do you know Dominic?"

Brie hesitated. If she had been alone with Julian, she would have told him about being stranded at his house with his friend. But Caroline was listening, and a confession about Lord Stanton's attempted seduction was hardly appropriate for the ears of an impressionable eighteen-year-old girl. "I met him when he was here two weeks ago," Brie said finally.

"Two weeks—Damn it, Brie! Dominic was only here for a few days. What the hell did you do to provoke him so?"

"I! Why do you assume I did anything?"

"Because," Julian said with exaggerated patience as he handed Brie her leather boots, "I have never seen Dominic act so irrationally. He looked like he wanted to kill you."

136

"He probably did," she muttered. When Julian continued to frown at her, she raised her hands in exasperation. "All right! I hit him with my whip. I was out riding one day and he tried to bully me. I was frightened, so I hit him."

"And that's all?"

Brie ground her teeth as she began to pull on her boots. "Yes! His servant came along and then he left."

Pursing his lips, Julian let out a low whistle. "Well, you're lucky to have survived with your skin still intact. At least that explains—" Julian broke off. He had been about to say that he better understood the electrifying tension he had sensed between the two of them, but he decided there would be no point in stating the obvious. "I'm sorry now that I made you fight Dominic. I doubt after this he will forgive you."

"I don't want his forgiveness! Who does he think he is, anyway? Besides, it wasn't your fault, so don't apologize." When Julian started to object, Brie raised a hand. "I know Lord Stanton is your friend, Julian," she said in a fractionally calmer voice, "but it does not mean I must like him. You would be doing me a great favor if you would just keep him out of my sight."

"I can try, Brie, but I doubt you can avoid him for a full month."

"A month! Must you suffer his company for so long?"

"I won't be suffering. I plan to enjoy his visit. He came here to indulge in a bit of sport."

Brie gave Julian a look that clearly labeled him a traitor as she stood up. "Come, Caroline," she said, squaring her shoulders.

When she marched from the room, Caroline flashed Julian an apologetic glance, then tagged meekly behind her angry cousin. Julian followed, still frowning.

When he had seen the cousins safely away, he went directly in search of his guest. He found Dominic in the gun room, seated at a table, carefully cleaning the breech of a fowling piece.

137

"I have servants who are paid to keep my weapons in prime condition," Julian said testily. "They can see to yours as well."

"I prefer to care for my own firearms," Dominic replied without looking up.

Julian pulled out a chair and straddled it, crossing his arms over the back. "Well?" he said impatiently.

Dominic raised an eyebrow. "Well, what?"

"You know what I mean. Did you have to be so hard on her? Brie is only a novice with foils, and she didn't realize—"

"You would defend her?" Dominic asked, his tone as smooth and hard as steel. "Your Miss Carringdon may be a novice, my friend, but hardly an innocent. She had fire in her eyes. She knew very well what she was about."

"I think you are mistaken, Dom. You frightened her quite badly, at any rate."

An imitation of a smile twisted Dominic's mouth. He was not proud of his conduct, knowing that he had responded far too emotionally to Brie's blind attack. He should never have allowed his anger to get so out of hand, particularly since terrifying Brie had *not* been his intention. She had deserved some form of punishment, certainly, but it was not part of his plan to frighten her away.

One glimpse of her fear-widened eyes and ashen cheeks had made him realize how greatly he had overreacted. And as he had stood looking down at Brie, at her breasts rising and falling beneath his rapier, at her thighs parted in open invitation, the quickening heat in his loins had abruptly outstripped the heat of his anger. At that moment, the desire to plunge the sword of his masculinity deep inside her had been almost overpowering. It had far outweighed the urge for revenge with his blade of steel. If he had been alone with her, he doubted that he could have prevented himself from savagely taking her then and there, no matter how unwilling she might have been. He had deserted the scene of battle before his control could be put to the test.

138

And now Julian was frowning at him. "You didn't tell me you had met Brie," Julian remarked.

"Should I have?" Dominic replied, wondering just what Brie had told his host. "What did she say?"

"Only that you two had some kind of confrontation while she was out riding."

Dominic gave a casual shrug of his shoulders. "I came across Miss Carringdon unexpectedly while I was exploring. The bay she was on shied and she took a hard fall. I suppose you might say she misinterpreted my intentions when I came to her aid."

Hearing the reasonable explanation, Julian visibly relaxed. He would not have enjoyed challenging Dominic. "A bay?" he mused. "She must have been riding my new hunter. A few months ago I unwisely bought a gelding from a friend in Ireland, sight unseen, and he turned out to be as green as they come—spooks at his own shadow. Absolutely worthless on the field. Brie agreed to take him for a few weeks, primarily as a favor to me. I sent him to her for training."

"Training?"

"Brie runs the stables her father started. It's called Greenwood. I'm sure you've heard of it, since you've ridden with the Quorn."

Impressed in spite of himself, Dominic glanced up from his work. "I've heard of it. I'll bet a quarter of the Quorn's members have mounts that were either bred or trained at Greenwood."

"I suspect that's true of the Cottesmore and Belvoir hunts as well. Greenwood is close enough to Melton Mowbray to be convenient, and it's known for turning out quality horseflesh. It is quite an operation. They have a few racers, but they specialize in hunters. A fellow by the name of John Simms is the head trainer. Brie spends most of her time managing the place, although she sometimes works with the more difficult horses."

Dominic's mouth twisted in a grin. "Perhaps that explains why she tried to take my head off. I ridiculed her horsemanship. My comments probably stung her pride as much as did her fall."

"I think you did more than hurt her pride. I've never seen her so livid."

"She seems to me to be somewhat headstrong, not to mention foolish," Dominic said, inspecting the bore of his weapon.

Julian shook his head. "Brie may be stubborn and have a temper, Dom, but she is far from foolish. She happens to be the most intelligent woman I know."

"That isn't saying much," Dominic returned cynically. "But I will agree that Miss Carringdon is definitely unique, traipsing around in her breeches. I've seen street urchins who were better dressed. I expect more than a few of my acquaintances would appreciate her unusual style of fashion though—all male, of course."

"She doesn't dress like that all the time."

"I should hope not. How did you come to know her, anyway?"

Julian shifted uncomfortably, avoiding his friend's penetrating gaze. "Do you remember when I first met you in Vienna a few years ago? I told you I was suffering from a broken heart. You laughed in my face, I recall."

"Some girl in London, I believe? Ahh, Brie Carringdon?" When Julian nodded, Dominic once again experienced a surge of irrational envy. "Is she your mistress?" he asked, trying to keep his tone bland.

Julian looked up with a start. "Brie? Good God, no! She's a lady."

"Ladies have been known to overstep the bonds of propriety before, my friend."

"Well, she is not my mistress. I wanted to marry her, but she wouldn't have me."

"Why not? Your fortune not large enough?"

Julian stared hard at Dominic for a moment, not liking his implication or his sardonic tone. Then suddenly he laughed.

140

"Dom, Brie inherited everything from her father. Her fortune is more than adequate and she certainly doesn't need mine. No, she didn't love me."

"I see," Dominic drawled.

"No, you don't see. Damn it, I tell you you're wrong about her. She could have any man she wanted. She's beautiful and kind and honest—"

"Spare me a catalogue of her virtues," Dominic interjected, rubbing his cheek. "I've already sampled her kindness."

Julian grinned. "Brie told me about hitting you."

"She did, did she? What else did she say?"

"Nothing, other than to call you an insufferable tyrant. Completely justified, if your behavior today was any indication of how you treated her then." Julian chuckled. "I would have given a monkey to see the look on your face after—"

"I assume she was the reason you found Rutland so fascinating," Dominic interjected, wanting to know more about his friend's relationship with Brie.

"In part. When I returned to England, I saw Brie again in London and we became friends. I came up here last year with her aunt and uncle when they were visiting. I liked the area, so I bought this place. You might know Brie's uncle, Sir Miles Langley. His wife Arabella was Carringdon's sister."

"I know him," Dominic said with a twisted smile. "And I pity the poor bastard. Lady Arabella is a veritable dragon."

Julian laughed. "Quite. And that's precisely what Brie calls her."

"Umm, perhaps your Miss Carringdon has more sense that I credited her with. Are you over your infatuation with her then?"

Julian gave a thoughtful frown. "I suppose so."

"You suppose?" Dominic said dryly. "Don't you know?"

Shrugging, Julian drew an imaginary pattern on the table top with a forefinger. "You know, I've asked Brie to marry me a dozen times, but she only laughs as if I am joking and says we wouldn't suit. I still love her, but I'm beginning to believe she is right about a marriage between us. She is . . . difficult to handle when she's in one of her tempers."

"You could always turn her over your knee," Dominic suggested, finding some pleasure in the idea.

"You must be joking. That would be the last way to win her affection. She wouldn't stand for it anyway." Seeing the gleam in Dominic's gray eyes. Julian eyed him suspiciously. "You aren't thinking of doing something like that, are you?"

"Not unless she means to use me again as a target for her various weapons. It is unfortunate that she dislikes me so much. I was looking forward to some pleasant entertainment during my stay."

"Dominic, Brie is no lightskirt. If you're planning anything, you had better be serious. But I'll tell you now, she isn't your type. Besides," Julian added with a grin, "Brie is the tiniest bit angry with you at the moment."

Dominic raised a mocking brow. "I'll be damned, I do believe you are warning me away. I find that novel, coming from you. Like the pot and the kettle, isn't it?"

"If it were any other woman I wouldn't object, but you hurt Brie and I'll carve your liver out."

Both of them knew his threat wasn't to be taken literally. In the first place, Julian was far too civilized to carve out anyone's liver, and in the second, he didn't have Dominic's prowess with pistols or swords, even if he was quite a skilled sportsman. But he wouldn't hesitate to defend Brie if she were threatened— not even against his closest friends.

Dominic clearly understood Julian's position, but in spite of the warning he didn't mean to relinquish his pursuit. He hadn't had a challenge like Brie since the war, and he wasn't about to give it up now. And there was still the mystery of why she was so afraid of him.

Dominic smiled blandly. "My dear Julian, I have absolutely no intention of harming the lady. I shall be perfectly charming. In fact, I'll wager that by the time I leave, she will have no reason to fear me."

His reply was not particularly reassuring, but Julian decided not to press the point. Instead he exerted himself to make his guest feel welcome, beginning by telling Dominic what he had planned for their entertainment.

Dominic listened with only half an ear, for his thoughts were centered on Brie. He hadn't liked the fact that she had lied to him about her identity, and he still wasn't sure why she had done so. Some women, given similar circumstances, would have tried to force his hand. Society expected a gentleman to marry a young woman he had compromised—and being stranded in a hunting lodge, with a man of his reputation and without a proper chaperon, certainly qualified as a compromising situation. Not that he would ever have bowed to that kind of pressure. But Brie would have had the perfect opportunity to attempt it.

Of course she might truly be uninterested in marriage or in landing a title for herself. But Julian had to be mistaken about her level of sophistication, Dominic decided. *No* woman that beautiful could be as chaste and innocent as Julian had made her out to be. Besides, he knew from personal experience that Brie was no innocent. She might not be some elderly gentleman's mistress and she might not be particularly expert at lovemaking, but her response to him had been far from virginal.

Dominic's lips curved in a smile as he remembered the feel of that lithe, feminine body in his arms. She has responded to his kisses with her own brand of passion, very sensual and very desirable. He wanted her, despite her hot temper and sharp tongue. And he would have her, he didn't doubt. Very few women had been able to resist Dominic Serrault when he chose to be charming and persuasive.

Not even the haughtiest and most reluctant.

Chapter Six

"What do you plan to do, Brie?" Caroline at last ventured.

They had ridden home without speaking a word, and when they reached Greenwood, Brie had gone straight to her room and flung herself face down on her bed. Caroline had followed, appropriating a corner of the bed while she waited for Brie's misery to diminish.

At the question, Brie rolled over on her back and flung an arm up to cover her eyes. "I don't know," she said bleakly.

"I expect you are too upset now to reflect on the situation calmly, but in my opinion, you have only one choice."

"Murder is a capital crime, cousin. I don't think the satisfaction I would get would be worth hanging for."

Caroline smiled, pleased to see Brie's spirits reviving. "That isn't what I had in mind. I think you should apologize to Lord Stanton."

Brie opened her eyes to stare at her cousin. "He wouldn't forgive me, especially not after what I did to him two weeks ago. He thinks I knew my point was unguarded and that I purposely attacked him."

"I declare, Brie, one would think you were a child. How can you know so little about the male ego? I suppose it comes from living for so long away from society and not having the opportunity to watch your sisters grow up like I've had. *Of course* he would forgive you. In fact, I doubt if anything could make his lordship feel more wretched than a sweetly worded, humble apology."

Brie considered the advice, but then shook her head. "I couldn't do it."

"It might hurt your pride a bit, but believe me, it would be effective. You cannot keep fighting him the way you have, on his terms."

"What do you mean?" she asked curiously.

"Merely that you aren't using what advantages you have. Men hate it when a female challenges their masculinity—and most particularly when one competes in what they consider their natural domain. I had never met Lord Stanton before today, but I'd heard rumors about him. He's credited with being a rake, the kind who always has a string of mistresses in keeping. So, play the game Lord Stanton understands. You're a very beautiful woman, but dressed as you are now, in breeches and top boots, you can hardly hope to attract a man like him."

"But I have no intention of trying to attract him!"

A twinkle lit Caroline's brown eyes. "Antagonizing Lord Stanton further would not be very wise on your part."

Brie gave her cousin a reluctant smile. "I'm well aware of that. But what do you suggest? I've never been able to act the coy young maiden, and I wouldn't know the first thing about playing the coquette to a philanderer."

Caroline laughed. "You don't have to be completely wicked. If you go about it the right way, you will soon have Lord Stanton wondering how he could ever have treated you in such a boorish manner. You have only to be charming and civil to render him harmless. But you'll have to remember not to fly into a pet if he teases you or makes you angry. You must accept his provoking remarks with equanimity and grace, smiling sweetly at him to show he hasn't the power to affect you."

"He will think I am flirting with him."

"Of course he will, goose! That is part of the game. But what harm will it do? Your purpose is merely to convince Lord

Stanton that his way of riding roughshod over you is abominable and entirely undeserved. I think a little flirtation will suffice admirably."

Caroline's smile was so innocent that Brie couldn't help laughing. "You are incorrigible, cousin. Not to mention devious. I hope you're around to advise me if your little plot goes awry. Stanton doesn't strike me as the type to allow some designing female to practice her arts on him. But I suppose I can at least humble myself enough to make an apology. I owe it to Julian to be civil to his guest, at any rate. We could always leave a little earlier for London if I find myself in a scrape."

"Well, it was just a misunderstanding, after all. Stanton is sure to let it pass. Actually he rather surprised me, getting so angry at you. When he first arrived, I thought he looked quite like he wanted to kiss you."

"He wouldn't dare try that again," Brie muttered.

Caroline's eyes widened. "Do you mean he already has?"

Brie shot her cousin a quelling glance. "I assure you, Caroline, I do not go around hitting perfect strangers without some provocation."

"There is no need to be nasty, Brie. I only want to help. And my plan will work, you'll see. Now come, I want to see your wardrobe. We have to choose your most becoming gowns in case Lord Stanton should call."

Brie reluctantly allowed Caroline to take the lead, but it was several days before she had an opportunity to speak to Stanton, and then it was under circumstances Caroline would not have approved.

The weather took a dreary turn and it rained incessantly. During that time, Brie dutifully obeyed Caroline's strictures, dressing her part to perfection and even allowing her cousin's maid to tend her hair. But her meek acceptance was not destined to last. On the first day that rain no longer poured from the skies, she rebelled against her confinement, leaving the house early to avoid her cousin's watchful eye.

It was a miserable morning, for even though the rain had

ceased, dark clouds obscured the sun, wrapping the country-side in a bone-chilling gloom. The ground had frozen hard, and even the puddles in the rutted roads were glazed with ice.

Brie rode one of her favorite hunters, but a long gallop did little to lift her spirits. When she returned to the stables, she ordered Julian's bay saddled, deciding to brave the south field for the first time since her disastrous encounter with Stanton.

She was relieved when she met no one along the way. The expedition, however, brought a return of memories she would rather have forgotten. And for some reason, she couldn't dispel the notion of being watched by hidden eyes. The prickling sensation running down her spine made her glance frequently over her shoulder as she was making her way home. When she heard the distant staccato of hoofbeats, she drew up abruptly, her heartbeat quickening.

Although chiding herself for being a coward, Brie urged the bay off the road behind a bordering yew hedge which, in its overgrown state, sheltered her from view. She had no idea how long she sat waiting for the rider to pass, but she could feel her heart pounding against her ribcage. Jester also sensed the tension in her body and pricked his ears forward in nervous anticipation, his muscles quivering. When a huge black stallion suddenly materialized through the hedge, he shied in terror.

Brie caught a glimpse of the stallion, but she was too busy clinging to Jester's neck and trying to control the frightened horse to wonder at this seeming piece of witchcraft. When the bay at last came to a trembling halt, she looked up to find Dominic observing her.

The first thing she noticed was the elegant cloak and fashionable beaver hat he wore. The second was the deadly-looking pistol he had trained on her. Brie froze when she saw the pistol, while her throat constricted in fear, preventing her from uttering a sound.

The silence mounted, making the air between them vibrate. Dominic watched her intently, his gray eyes cold and alert, and

148

several uncomfortable moments passed before he slowly slipped the gun back into his belt.

Brie let out her breath in a rush, but when she found her voice, it sounded weak and trembling, even to her own ears. "I would count the score even, my lord, for I am unarmed. I was not planning to attack you, whatever you might be thinking. I was trying to avoid you."

Dominic merely sat there regarding her, one hand loosely holding the reins, the other resting on his thigh. "Is that what you were doing, lurking behind the bushes?" he said finally.

Brie couldn't tell whether it was amusement or annoyance she heard in his voice, but his question made her bristle. "I wasn't lurking! Devil take you! You gave me the fright of my life. Did you truly mean to shoot me?"

"The thought had crossed my mind, Miss Carringdon." The words were said with a hint of sarcasm, but his lips twitched as if he were repressing a smile.

Brie stared at his handsome, enigmatic face, trying to guess what was going on behind those cool gray eyes. Then she remembered the odd sensation that had disturbed her earlier. "Have you been following me?" she asked suspiciously.

Dominic's lips twisted in a smile. "No. Did you wish me to?"

"Of course not! I just—" She broke off, realizing he would think her imaginings foolish. He was already grinning at her in that mocking way that made her want to slap him.

"You just . . . what, mademoiselle?" Dominic prompted. When Brie refused to answer, he urged his stallion nearer, till he was directly beside her. "I had thought this road was public domain, but perhaps I should have asked your permission before making use of it."

Brie's anger was rising rapidly. "Certainly you don't need my permission, my lord—though I doubt that would have made the least difference to you. It was just that you frightened me."

"I must beg your pardon, then. It was not my intention to frighten you or to make you avoid my company."

149

Brie eyed him warily, wondering at his sudden amiableness. She couldn't tell if Stanton were sincere or if this were merely another of his taunts. Then Dominic suddenly smiled one of his sweet, angelic smiles. It surprised Brie greatly, making her blink.

"I would not quite call it even between us," he said smoothly, "but it might be wise if we agreed to start over. I am willing to forget our previous encounters if you are."

That her enemy was the first to offer the olive branch did not ease Brie's conscience. She hesitated, chewing on her lip. "But I cannot forget, my lord," she said at last. "I still owe you an apology. Please let me say that I am truly sorry for what happened. In all honesty, though, I didn't realize the condition of my blade. I . . . I suppose I got too caught up in the heat of the moment. I hope you will believe that I didn't really mean to harm you," she concluded lamely. She lowered her eyes then, for Dominic's gaze had suddenly become quite piercing.

"Very prettily said," he remarked.

"Well, if you don't choose to accept my apology . . ." She started to turn her horse around, but he edged his closer.

"Ah, but I do choose." Catching Brie's hand, he lifted it to his lips.

Brie was startled by his intimate gesture. Her fingers tingled with warmth where Dominic's lips brushed her skin, and her breathing quickened. She withdrew her hand as quickly as possible, but her eyes were held by his gray gaze.

He smiled at her again, making her feel that strange, melting sensation. "How could I possibly refuse such a charming apology?" he said softly.

His tone was low and caressing and highly unnerving. Brie felt a quiver run up her spine. "Well, I know you were angry," she said nervously, "but I don't think you were ever in any real danger, with me as your opponent."

"Au contraire, mademoiselle, I was quite impressed with your skill."

She gave him a tentative smile. "Thank you, my lord, but I

150

was not expecting compliments. You were far better than I—and what's more, you knew it. You are just saying that to be kind."

"I am seldom kind, Miss Carringdon."

Unable to tell if he spoke in jest, Brie glanced at Dominic uncertainly. "Then it was mere flattery," she said, trying to dismiss the subject. "But at any rate, it makes no difference. I have vowed to give up fencing."

Dominic grinned, his teeth flashing. "You relieve my mind."

Hearing the dry note in his voice, Brie laughed. "I agree," she retorted. "You are not kind." When Dominic's stallion snorted and began shaking his head up and down as if he concurred, she laughed again.

Jester took exception to all the movement, however, and began prancing nervously. Brie spent a moment calming him, then found herself responding to Dominic's suggestion that they move on.

She was surprised to learn Dominic meant to escort her home, but she accepted his company politely, objecting only when he asked why a groom had not accompanied her. "Your concern is misplaced, my lord," she said loftily. "I am riding on my own land and do not feel the need for a groom."

"I would have thought you had learned the need for caution in these secluded spots. It can be dangerous for you to ride alone."

She slanted a glance at him. "It is extremely ungallant of you to remind me after you said we could forget that particular incident. I have never needed protection before . . . before you."

The corner of Dominic's mouth lifted in a smile. "I was not speaking of myself."

"No?" Brie asked skeptically. "Is it not your habit to go about assaulting every woman you meet?"

"Merely the ones who interest me."

Brie felt her pulse quicken. "Am I to assume I interest you

151

then?" she asked, trying to sound indifferent. "How flattering! But I am not sure I care for your way of showing it. You have already threatened to beat me and run me through with your sword."

"I was given extreme provocation, you will recall. And you could have prevented it, had you told me who you were. Why didn't you?"

Seeing him regard her curiously, Brie felt a blush warm her cheeks. "I was merely trying to protect my reputation. I thought that if you didn't know my name, you couldn't brag to your London friends about finding me alone without a chaperon."

Dominic's eyebrow rose. "I assure you I am far more discreet than that."

Brie suspected there was a double meaning to his words, but she chose not to find out. "I know that now," she said meekly.

"You certainly were convincing. You even had me believing that tale about your elderly protector."

"Well, even if he was imaginary, he did 'protect' me. At least a little."

Dominic grinned. "I suppose he did at that. Should I apologize for making you an indecent proposal?"

Brie felt her blush deepening. "That isn't necessary. I would rather forget about it entirely."

"I expect there are a few things I won't be able to forget," he murmured.

When she remained silent, Dominic let his eyes skim down her figure, noting the disreputable clothes she wore. It was a shame to cover such lovely charms that way, he found himself thinking. A wood sprite ought not be dressed in rags. She needed a gossamer wisp of forest green to drape around her lithe body—if she needed anything at all. When his mind conjured up just such a vivid image, Dominic shifted uncomfortably in the saddle. "Tell me, Miss Carringdon," he said to distract his thoughts, "do you always ride astride?"

Very aware of his scrutiny, Brie was glad for the change of

subject, even if it meant having to defend her eccentricities. "You don't approve of my breeches, I suppose. But you can have no notion of how uncomfortable it is to ride sidesaddle, encumbered by a long skirt and endless petticoats."

Dominic chuckled. "No, and I have no wish to find out. I quail at the thought of sitting in one of those contraptions." Seeing Brie smile, he shook his head. "The look in your eye is daring me to try, but I assure you, Miss Carringdon, I don't intend to take up that particular challenge."

"I don't expect you to, my lord, but neither do I expect your censure. I don't wear breeches to flout convention—merely because they are practical and comfortable. But," Brie added defiantly, "I don't know why I am defending myself to you, Lord Stanton. You probably do exactly as you please without regard to anyone else's opinion."

When Dominic only smiled enigmatically, Brie switched to a more appropriate topic of conversation and asked him about the beautiful animal he rode. Dominic told her that the horse was indeed Spanish and had been named Diablo by his previous owners. It was on the tip of Brie's tongue to ask if the stallion were used for breeding purposes, but she refrained, deciding that such an unladylike question would only give him more reason to disapprove of her. Remembering her cousin's warnings about competing with men, she frowned.

She didn't realize how long she had been silent, until Dominic asked in a somewhat sardonic tone if he had somehow displeased her. Brie looked at him blankly, then silently laughed at herself. What did it matter what Stanton thought of her? He had already seen her at her worst. "I beg your pardon," she replied, shaking her head. "I fear I am guilty of coveting your stallion."

Amusement warmed his gray eyes. "Do you think you could handle him?"

"I should love to try."

"Then by all means, you must do so." He reined in his horse and dismounted before Brie could answer.

153

When he came around to help her down, Brie swung her leg over her horse's neck. "You would trust me with him?" she asked skeptically.

Dominic grasped her waist and easily lifted her down, but he didn't release her at once. When Brie looked up at him, her breath unexpectedly caught in her throat. It was desire she saw in Dominic's eyes, pure and simple. She was shaken by that look, but she stood motionless, caught by his gaze. His hands remained about her waist, exerting the slightest pressure, while his well-shaped mouth moved slowly toward hers. . . .

"Is there any reason I shouldn't trust you?" she heard him murmur, not imagining the huskiness of his voice. She tensed, anticipating the feel of his mouth, of his hard body pressing against her.

But nothing happened. Dominic merely stepped back, breaking the spell.

Leading her to Diablo, he tossed Brie into the saddle, then turned to mount the bay. Brie stared at him a moment, before her attention was claimed by her new mount. Unaccustomed to having such a light weight on his back, the stallion quite deliberately tried to unseat her, rearing and dancing in circles. Brie merely tightened the grip of her legs and kept a strong hold of the reins.

Dominic watched the battle for supremacy with amusement. It was an interesting contest, the beautiful girl and the giant black horse, both spirited and strong willed. But he never doubted who would win. He sat calmly waiting, his hands resting on the bay's neck.

Diablo finally submitted to Brie's control. Pleased by her triumph, she paused to catch her breath, but at Dominic's soft laughter, she looked up sharply. When she realized that the gleam in his gray eyes was approval, though, her defiant glare faded, and she even found herself responding to Dominic's engaging grin.

"May I try his paces over a fence or two?" she asked, edging the stallion closer. When Dominic raised a doubtful eyebrow,

154

Brie laughed. "Come now, my lord, you said you trusted me to ride him. In fact, it might be more appropriate for me to ask if you can handle Julian's gelding. I give you fair warning that he shies. You won't care much for his habits, but you may follow—if you can."

The challenge was flung over her shoulder as she wheeled the stallion around and dug her heels into his flanks, spurring him into a gallop.

She set a fast pace, taking any obstacle in her path, but Dominic was hard on her heels. The bay gave him more difficulty than he had expected, even after Brie's warning, but he enjoyed the chase.

When they at last pulled up after a long run, the horses were breathing heavily. They exchanged mounts once more, much to Brie's disappointment, and turned toward Greenwood.

"Diablo is magnificent!" she exclaimed, trying to forget the discomfitting feel of Dominic's hands around her waist.

He acknowledged her praise with a bow. "And so is your skill," he remarked quite honestly.

"How can one not be good on such an animal?" Brie replied, laughing. "I don't suppose you would consider selling him?"

Dominic gave Brie a speculative glance. Her cheeks were flushed and her eyes were lit with a becoming sparkle, seeming more blue than green in her present mood. Even in her boy's garb, she was undeniably desirable. And when she was laughing, as she was now, she was not only beautiful, she was enchanting.

"I might be persuaded," he replied enigmatically. More than that he refused to say. He was determined not to introduce terms before she was ready to accept them.

Instead, he directed her attention to the approaching storm. He had been keeping a watchful eye on the darkening sky, and now, as his eyes scanned the horizon, he could make out the edge of a swiftly racing squall line.

Brie followed his gaze to where a great black mass of clouds was rolling across the heavens. The flash of lightning in the distance was accompanied by the ominous rumble of thunder, and the raw, wintry wind, which had been gaining force during their long ride, whirled about them now in biting gusts.

Brie returned a worried frown to Dominic's unspoken question. Normally, a bit of rain or even a drenching didn't bother her. But the tempest that seemed to be brewing was menacing enough for concern. In unison, Brie and Dominic urged their mounts to greater speed to escape the imminent deluge.

The first pelting drops began when they were still several miles from Greenwood. Brie started to suggest that they seek shelter somewhere, but the words were whipped away by a blast of wind and rain. When she glanced at Dominic, he flashed her a grin that seemed to dare her to cry craven, so she pressed her lips together and rode on through the downpour.

Her coat was completely soaked through in a matter of minutes. Water sluiced her face and soaked her hair so that it dangled in dripping rats' tails down her back, while icy rivulets found a path down her back, making her shudder.

She soon forgot her own discomfort, however, as she fought for control of her skittish mount. The bay's footing was none too certain, and he slipped more than once, almost tumbling Brie into the mud.

They had just slid down a slope into a narrow hollow when lightning suddenly streaked across the sky. The flash startled Jester, making him rear, and the resultant clap of thunder sent him bolting into a frantic gallop.

That seemed to be the signal for the frenzied sky to unleash its fury. Icy sheets of rain slashed at Brie's face, blinding her as she tried to check her horse's speed. She couldn't see the great stallion racing beside her, but she felt Jester swerve when Dominic reached out to catch hold of his bridle. The bay reared again, just as a strong arm swept Brie from the saddle.

Brie struggled instinctively against Dominic's hold, but he tightened his grip and managed to set her before him. "Be still, you little wildcat," he shouted in her ear. "You could never make it home on that beast. We passed a cottage that should provide shelter."

Brie could only nod in agreement, for an icy blast stole her breath away. When she shivered, Dominic drew the edges of his cloak about her, then wheeled the stallion about.

The driving rain obscured all but skeletal shapes from view, but they made their way unerringly through the storm. Brie was no longer worried. The great stallion's footing was solid and the arms that held her were strong and secure. When shards of sleet began to sting her cheeks, she turned her face against Dominic's broad chest, grateful for his warmth.

After what seemed like hours, they came to halt before a small cottage. Brie recognized it, and when Dominic set her down before the door, she lifted the latch without knocking and dashed inside out of the icy rain.

Dominic was not far behind her. "Not the Royal Palace," he said looking around, "but it will do."

"It belongs to Bennet Johnson," Brie informed him through chattering teeth. "I had heard he was away visiting his son."

The cottage was little more than a hut actually, boasting only one room. The interior was dark, for the shuttered window allowed only the tiniest bit of light to filter through its chinks. Brie could barely identify the few pieces of furniture. At one end was a pitted wooden table and three rickety chairs, and at the other, near the fireplace, was a cupboard that probably contained cooking utensils. A cot rested against the far wall, and in one corner stood a small storage chest.

It wasn't much of a haven, Brie thought with disappointment; even though it provided protection against the rain, it wasn't much warmer than outside. She could see the curling puffs her breath made as she stood dripping on the wooden floor. Shivering with cold, she wrapped her arms tightly around her.

Dominic's gaze swept Brie's trembling figure. "See if you can find some blankets and some dry kindling while I take care of the horses," he ordered. "I'll start a fire when I return.

And take off those wet garments before you freeze to death."

When Brie turned to stare at him, he met her look of indignant astonishment with a mixture of tenderness and amusement. "That wasn't a proposition, cherie," he said with a grin. "I prefer a more appropriate setting when I make love to a woman." He was gone before Brie recovered enough to respond.

She stared at the door, vaguely hearing the hollow sound of rain pounding against the roof. Then giving herself a shake, she groped her way to the window. Throwing back the shutter did little to illuminate the room, however, for the leaded pane was encrusted with grime. Fortunately, there was a tinderbox and two candles on the mantle. She lit them with shaking hands and began to search through the chest.

She found only one blanket. Tossing it on the cot, she rummaged a bit more and came up with two scraps of rough cloth that could be used for towels. Pleased, Brie turned her attention to the wood box by the hearth. The results were more disappointing. There was only a tiny amount of kindling and one small log with which to make a fire.

Brie was too cold to wait for Dominic to return, so she piled the kindling carefully in the fireplace and struck a spark. She held her freezing hands over the tiny blaze, but it did little to ease her misery. Her wet clothes still felt like ice against her skin, and her teeth were chattering so badly that even clamping her lips shut didn't help.

Determinedly, Brie dragged two of the wooden chairs across the floor and placed them on either side of the hearth, then removed her sodden coat and draped it over a chair to dry. She was rubbing her arms, trying to generate some warmth, when Dominic entered carrying an armful of firewood. The icy gust of wind that accompanied him nearly took her breath away.

Dominic slammed the door shut with his heel and strod across the room, dropping his load beside the hearth. As he removed his hat and cloak, he raised an eyebrow at Brie, as if expecting an explanation of her disobedience.

Brie resisted the urge to squirm under that penetrating gray gaze, telling herself that he had no right to give her orders. "There is only one blanket," she said stiffly, indicating the one on the cot.

He flashed her an amused grin. "Then we will have to share, won't we?"

"Of course not! I don't plan to share a blanket with you, now or ever."

"You would rather freeze?"

When Brie didn't answer, Dominic eyed her in a way that made her want to hit him. There was a dancing gleam in his eyes that showed very plainly he was deriving a perverse kind of pleasure from their predicament. Smoldering, Brie planted her hands on her hips. "I think you are enjoying this! In fact I didn't know better, I would say you planned for us to be stranded here."

Dominic laughed. "Even I have not such powers over the heavens, my lady."

The husky sound of his laughter sent an odd shiver up her spine, but she pretended not to notice. "I will not share a blanket with you," she said adamantly. "And I will not undress."

Dominic took off his jacket and waistcoat and laid them across the chair. "Yes, you will," he replied evenly. "I don't intend to let you catch pneumonia."

Hearing the soft assurance in his voice, Brie glared at him. But when Dominic stripped off his shirt, she caught herself staring in fascination. She knew she shouldn't be watching him undress, but she found she couldn't look away. Dominic's bronzed skin was sleek and wet, and it glistened in the candlelight. Dark hair furred the wide expanse of his chest, tapering at the waistband of his tight-fitting breeches. His shoulders were broad and well-muscled, and as he turned and bent down to feed the fire, Brie could see powerful sinews flexing in his back. She swallowed, feeling a curling sensation somewhere below her stomach.

"Why the sudden reserve?" Dominic said casually as he prodded the logs. "I've already seen you without your clothes on."

Brie felt a blush start at the roots of her hair and flood her face. For a moment, she gazed at him in mute embarrassment. Then angrily she turned her back to him, silently cursing Dominic for being an overbearing, arrogant tyrant. Crossing her arms, she stood staring at the wall.

She stiffened when he came up behind her, but when he grasped her shoulder, she didn't struggle. She knew from experience she would be unable to break away. She fumed in silence as Dominic removed the pins from her hair.

He pulled the heavy mass down, combing it with his fingers. When he had wrung some of the moisture from the ends, he bent to whisper in her ear. "I don't plan to ravish your lovely body just yet, ma belle. Now take off your clothes or I shall do it for you." Disregarding her gasp of outrage, he picked up one of the cloths and leisurely began to towel his upper torso dry.

Brie wanted to tell him to go to the devil, but she realized it would be wiser to capitulate. He was perfectly capable of forcibly undressing her if she didn't comply. "Very well," she muttered at last. "But you don't have to look."

"Your modesty overwhelms me," Dominic replied sardonically.

Brie sat in one of the chairs to pull off her riding boots, and when she heard the cot creak, she knew Dominic was doing the same. Deciding it best to ignore him as much as possible, she tried not to notice when he carried his boots to the hearth to dry, but even so, she began to feel uncomfortable. He was clad only in breeches that hugged his muscular legs like a second skin. When he began to remove these as well, Brie gave a gasp and froze. But then he moved away, out of her range of vision. Shakily, she shrugged out of her own breeches and shirt and then stood there shivering in her thin chemise, wondering what to do next.

A scraping noise behind her made her jump. When Dominic

dragged the cot in front of the fire, Brie quickly scurried out of his way. At least he was not totally naked, she thought with relief, seeing that he had wrapped the towel around his narrow hips. It did little to conceal the magnificence of his body, however, and Brie could feel her cheeks becoming heated as she watched him spread the blanket over the straw mattress.

When he had arranged the cot, Dominic picked up the other towel and turned to Brie, intending to help her dry off. He took only two steps, though, before he halted abruptly, sucking in his breath. Brie made an alluring sight, with her damp hair hanging about her shoulders in curling tendrils, her skin gleaming like pale gold in the candlelight. The wisp of linen she was wearing left little to the imagination. The shift covered her buttocks, but every curve of her body was provocatively revealed by the wet fabric. Dominic's eyes darkened as he took in the fetching sight. Her coral nipples were clearly visible as they strained against the delicate fabric, and when she wrapped her arms about her to ward off the cold, her thrusting breasts threatened to spill over the meager bodice. Dominic's gaze roamed lower, touching on the gently rounded hips and slender legs. Then it lifted again, locking with Brie's.

She met his heated glance and shuddered violently, although her reaction had nothing to do with the cold. The lust she saw in Dominic's gray eyes frightened her. Her fiancé had looked at her that way just before he had attacked her. Alarmed, Brie took a step backwards, her hand stealing to her throat.

Dominic could see her sudden fear. Even though he wasn't sure what caused it, he knew better than to make any abrupt movements. Clamping down on his primitive urges, he gave Brie a soft smile that was meant to convey reassurance and moved toward her slowly.

Brie waited, trembling, unable to move. It was only when Dominic began rubbing her arms briskly with the towel that she realized he didn't mean to harm her. Brie stood quite still under his ministrations, more in nervous relief than in

161

obedience. Yet she was very much aware of Dominic'
nearness, and conscious of how bronzed and muscular his arm
looked next to her smooth white limbs.

He bent to dry the backs of her legs, running the clot
quickly over her slender thighs and calves. When h
commanded her to turn, Brie obeyed mechanically. She felt hi
hands move up her legs, then pause when they reached he
inner thigh. Brie looked down, experiencing a shock when sh
saw his ebony head so close. Realizing he was staring at th
dark triangle between her legs, she flushed a bright crimson

The same shock affected Dominic. Feeling himself break ou
in a cold sweat, he stood up and flicked the hem of Brie'
chemise. "This is wet," he said in a strained voice. "Yo
should take it off as well."

Hot with embarrassment, Brie shook her head. Sh
remained mute until Dominic started to wipe her face. The
she snatched the towel away and hastily began blotting at th
front of her damp shift. "I can dry myself, thank you," sh
muttered.

Pretending indifference, Dominic shrugged and turne
away. When he had stretched himself out on the cot and pulle
the woolen blanket up to his chest, he propped his head up wit
his hand and watched Brie as if he were prepared to treat he
stubbornness with undeserved patience. Brie glared back a
him, determined to freeze before she yielded to him. With
movement that was very much like a flounce, she went to si
before the fire.

She was dismayed to see how feeble the flames were. Th
damp wood had not caught well yet and smoke spiraled up th
chimney in spasmodic spurts. Shivering, Brie drew her knee
up under her chin and wrapped her arms around her bare leg
as she stared angrily at the struggling fire. If only the wrath
that burned in her breast or the scorching gleam in Dominic'
gray eyes could heat her chilled body. Then she would be mor
than warm enough.

Behind her, Dominic studied her proud, slender back, tryin

162

trying not to notice that her chemise barely covered her hips and how the damp fabric molded to her slim curves. He was truly puzzled by Brie's fear of him. In spite of his reputation, Dominic had always been particularly selective of the women he made love to. Few, if any, had rejected his advances or refused what he offered. Certainly none had ever been afraid of him, at least not in bed. He had not expected Brie to fall willingly into his arms, of course, not after their singular beginning. But neither had he foreseen that his attempts to charm her would be so unsuccessful.

She had dealt his pride a severe blow, Dominic admitted with a grimace of self-mockery. He was supposed to be an expert at dalliance, a master of the game. But Brie wasn't adhering to the prescribed rituals. Far from acting as if she enjoyed such games, she seemed not even to understand the rules. He knew her to be somewhat experienced, though, and her pretense of offended innocence was starting to wear on his patience.

He watched Brie as she sat there huddled before the hearth, wondering if she were playing some deep game of her own. He had never claimed to understand the singular workings of a woman's mind; he had never even made the effort except in the line of duty. But then he had been dealing with creatures who were tediously predictable. Brie was quite different. She kept him off balance with her outspokenness and fiery temper, and he never quite knew what she would do next. She had a uniqueness that was intriguing, even exciting. But something had bridled the passionate nature that he had so tantalizingly glimpsed. Her fear had been quite genuine, he would have staked his life on it.

Seeing her uncontrollable shudders, he was conscious of an odd feeling of protectiveness, a feeling that was distinctly disturbing. He was not in the habit of experiencing such tender emotions, nor did he care to examine them too closely. Protectiveness was not the only thing he felt, either; he was also growing angry with her continued defiance. "For God's sake, come here, you foolish girl," he said cajolingly. "You're trem-

163

bling enough to shake the roof down."

"I am not foolish," Brie replied stiffly, her teeth chattering. She felt almost numb with cold, but her pride wouldn't allow her to give in to him.

"I've already told you that you have no reason to fear me."

"I'm not afraid of you. I just don't like to be humiliated, as you are so fond of doing."

"I promise to stop," he said in exasperation. "Now come here before you catch your death."

Brie cast an uncertain glance over her shoulder. Sharing a bed with her tormentor was the last thing she wanted, but the promise of warmth was tempting. Her hands and feet were aching with cold, and she could feel her lips turning blue. It did seem rather idiotic to be sitting there, half frozen, when she could be sharing the blanket. But could she trust Stanton not to take advantage of the situation?

Brie searched Dominic's face for any sign of passionate intent, but she could find none. His grave expression held only concern.

She gave a last look at the fire. The blaze, though braver than before, still sparked and sputtered. With a small sigh, Brie gave up her frozen throne by the hearth and went to Dominic, crawling in beside him when he held the blanket up invitingly.

They were both grateful for her decision—Brie for the searing warmth that enveloped her as soon as Dominic pulled her, unresisting, into his arms, and Dominic for governing his impatience. In another moment he would have damned his decision not to force her and dragged her physically to the narrow cot.

Turning her so that her back was against his chest, Dominic drew his leg up to cover hers. "Your skin is like ice," he murmured as he roughly massaged her chilled arms.

Brie submitted wordlessly to his stroking hands. Too cold to be embarrassed by the intimate contact, she lay there with her head cradled on Dominic's arm, savoring the vibrant heat from his body.

She thawed out gradually, and her trembles finally subsided. When feeling began to flow in her limbs once more, she suddenly became very aware of Dominic's hard length molded against her back and the heaviness of his iron-thewed thigh as it rested on her bare legs. She could even feel his breath stirring the soft hairs on the top of her head.

When his hand moved to rest lightly on the curve of her hip, Brie tensed. His knuckles brushed her hip, then slid down to stroke her bare thigh. But it was an idle caress. There was no urgency in his movements.

Brie relaxed against him, beginning to enjoy the solid strength of his embrace. It seemed natural somehow for her to be in his arms. She lay there, lazily watching the fire and feeling oddly content as she listened to the rain pound against the roof. The flames in the hearth began to courageously attack the stubborn tinder until gradually the fire grew into a crackling blaze. The warmth made Brie drowsy, and after a while, she closed her eyes.

Dominic was lost in his own thoughts, but when a log broke apart in the grate sometime later, he snapped out of his reverie. Lifting his head, he gazed down at Brie. She had fallen asleep, he realized with a rueful grin.

Obviously she couldn't be too worried, for she was slumbering with the confidence of a child. Her soft lips were parted slightly and her breathing was quiet and rhythmic. She looked so lovely with her long lashes fanning her cheeks like dark crescents. Cautiously, Dominic reached up to brush aside a damp curl from her brow. Her skin felt like velvet beneath his fingertips, and he ached to do more than touch her.

Lifting a silken tress of her hair, he watched it gleam richly in the firelight as it curled around his fingers. The beguiling fragrance stirred his blood, and Dominic closed his eyes, almost groaning out loud. Having Brie's slender body pressed so intimately against him was an exquisite torment. He wanted to take her there and then, while she slept. . . . But remembering her fear, Dominic told himself that he had to move slowly.

Brie required careful cultivation; she ws far too tempting a morsel for him to risk with precipitate action. Exercising patience would be difficult, though. Already his arousal was painful.

He was grateful when the fire began to die down, for at least it gave him something else to occupy his thoughts. Slowly he eased his arm from beneath Brie's head. She stirred, but didn't waken, and he quietly rose from the cot and went to the fireplace. After throwing another log on the fire, he knelt to stir the coals, staying there for a time, staring thoughtfully at the flames.

It wasn't long before Brie started to shiver. She tried to bury herself more deeply beneath the blanket, missing Dominic's warmth, but when she couldn't find it, she opened her eyes. Seeing Dominic, Brie decided she must be dreaming. A towel no longer draped his hips and his entire body was exposed to her fascinated view. His body looked lean and hard, with long sinewy muscles rippling beneath the bronzed skin. And he was so very dark. He was tanned all over, even his powerful flanks.

"So dark," Brie whispered. She didn't realize she had spoken the words out loud until Dominic responded.

"I like to swim," he said as if in answer to her question.

"You swim *naked?*" When she heard Dominic's soft chuckle, Brie felt a fiery blush flood her face. She was grateful that his attention remained on the fire.

"I do when the sun is hot enough," he replied, sounding amused. "I have a small plantation in the West Indies with a private beach. I was there until a few months ago and my tan hasn't left me yet. Perhaps some day I might take you there."

He rose then, and turned to look at her, cocking his head at an angle and regarding her with a quizzical expression.

Brie stared at him, shocked by his boldness. Beneath Dominic's hard, flat belly was full proof of his masculinity, standing proud and erect. She was amazed that he could be so casual about his nudity, but oddly she felt longing as well as fear curl in the pit of her stomach.

166

Hastily averting her gaze from that enormous swelling, Brie buried her face in the mattress. "Have you no decency?" she exclaimed, her words sounding muffled.

Dominic's mouth twisted sardonically. "I am only human, cherie. I cannot control my body, even if I can manage to keep my desires in check. You do have a certain effect on a man."

Not answering, Brie held herself rigidly still, hoping he would go away. But Dominic only moved closer. She felt the cot sag as he sat beside her. Brie tensed, feeling his hand gently brush aside her hair, exposing the nape of her neck.

His warm fingers began massaging the sensitive area. Then he bent to whisper in her ear, his voice holding a hint of steel. "Your pretense of virginal innocence, cherie, is not very believable. This is not the first time you have been with a man."

Brie was startled that he could have learned her deepest secret. Dismayed, she turned to look up at him. "How did you know?"

Dominic was conscious of a sharp twinge of jealously. "No woman kisses a man as you did, my sweet, without having had some experience. Have there been many others besides me?"

Brie stared at him speechlessly, his insinuation making her furious. She had only had that one experience—and that had been when she was a foolish, love-stricken girl. She hadn't given Stanton any reason to think she would be receptive to his advances, either. Or perhaps she had, Brie amended, remembering that night at the lodge. But just because she had almost fallen for his seduction, didn't mean she would let it happen again, or that he could say such insulting things to her.

She was so angry that her words sounded strangled. "How dare you?" she sputtered. "I am not a . . . a common doxy. There was only one man and it happened but once!"

"Only once?" Dominic murmured. His doubtful gaze held Brie's as his fingers toyed absently with a russet curl. "Well, whoever he was, he must have been a fool to let you get away."

Brie's eyes flashed fire. "He was more than a fool! He was a blackguard and a knave."

Dominic smiled lazily, drawing a finger along her cheekbone. "A knave, is it? Would that he were here so that I could run him through with my sword."

Brie ground her teeth. "You mock me, my lord, but I assure you he was a scoundrel. I found being with him a perfectly horrid experience."

So that was it, Dominic thought. Someone had hurt her. That explained why she cringed in fright whenever he got too close. Feeling a surge of anger toward the unknown man who had laid claim to her body and branded her with his harsh usage, Dominic shook his head. "I do not mock you, my fiery vixen. I think it a pity that your initiation should have been so unpleasant. He could not have been much of a man. I would not have been so careless with the privilege, nor would I have neglected your enjoyment."

Brie arched a scornful brow. "Are you such an expert then?" she asked unwisely.

Dominic shrugged. "I know how to please a woman." His long fingers slowly traced the line of her chin, moving down the curve of her neck and along the delicate collarbone. "You would not have come away from me ignorant of love's delights."

"Of all the arrogant, conceited boasts I have ever heard—"

A smile played on his lips. "You think my words empty?" Shall I show you they are not?"

Brie turned her head, not wanting to endure his mockery. "No, thank you. I don't care to be shown any more than I already know."

His fingers gripped her chin insistently, forcing her to look at him. All trace of amusement was gone from his expression. "I think, mademoiselle," Dominic said slowly, "that you deserve at least a demonstration." His hand moved behind her head, twisting in her hair and holding her captive.

When she realized his intent, Brie's heart went to her throat. "No!" she gasped. But her fervent protest was smothered beneath Dominic's lips. She tried to struggle, but her arms were pinned beneath the blanket and were useless in fending him off. It made no difference, though. Dominic was determined to conquer her fear.

His mouth moved over hers in a deliberate attack on her senses, drawing the very breath from her. His lips were hot and searing, his plunging tongue merciless in its thoroughness. The sultry, penetrating kiss seemed to go on forever, and before long, Brie's resistance began to melt like a snowflake under a hot desert sun.

Dominic could sense her defenses weakening, but he steeled his body against his own urgent need. Tasting the sweetness of her mouth had only increased his hunger, but he knew he had to win her with patience. Slowly, he slid his naked length beneath the blanket and gathered her in his arms.

When he tried to kiss her again, though, Brie gave a start. His heated loins were pressing against her bare thigh, making her intensely aware of his arousal. Frantically, she pushed against his chest, trying to escape the alien hardness. "No!" she cried. "No, please!"

Feeling her struggle, Dominic threw a leg over her thighs to hold her still and raised his head to stare into her eyes. The blue-green pools were as deep as tropical lagoons and filled with fear.

But she wanted him, he could feel it. And it wasn't as if she still had her virtue to preserve. By her own admission, she had known at least one lover.

His mouth sought out her trembling lips once more. She was close to panic, but his soft kisses and caressing voice brought her back from the edge. "Brie, my sweet Brie," he whispered against her lips. "I won't hurt you. You have nothing to fear." Taking her hand, he gently guided her to his engorged manhood. "Feel my flesh, Brie. Touch me . . . yes. Ahh, God, how I want you."

He gave her no choice but to obey him, but when she held him in her hand, Brie experienced a jolt of surprise. This was what she had been afraid of? His shaft was hard, yes, but warm and vibrant, too. It didn't seem to be an instrument of pain, of degradation, of violence. Perhaps she had been laboring under some misconceptions about men. She regarded Dominic in wonder, making no protest when he pushed the woolen blanket down around her hips.

Dominic pressed his small advantage, wrapping an arm around her narrow waist. Lifting her slowly, he drew Brie closer, then bent to press light, feverish kisses down the slim column of her throat. When he reached the swelling curve of her breasts, he kissed each one gently, letting his tongue flick over the cloth-covered peaks.

Brie gasped at the sensation he was creating. The soft lawn rasping against her nipples felt erotic and unbelievably stimulating. She arched instinctively against him, letting her head fall back.

His fingers brushed boldly against her breasts as he freed them from their imprisoning fabric. Then cupping a thrusting mound in his hand, Dominic let his thumb swirl in languid circles over the taut peak. Brie moaned as a sweeping pleasure flooded her body. She clutched at him, digging her fingers into the hard muscles of Dominic's shoulders.

When he bent his head and let his mouth settle hot and moist upon her breast, Brie felt a sudden rush of liquid heat, the force of which made her reel. She clung to him, gasping, her fingers tangling in the thick softness of his hair.

"So beautiful," Dominic whispered seductively, drawing the rigid nipple further into his mouth, teasing the sensitive bud with his tongue.

Brie couldn't think of a reply. All she could do was feel. His hand was caressing her body freely, wantonly, while he suckled her breasts. Then he began kissing her elsewhere, tracing a molten path upward along her throat.

Her lips parted easily beneath his this time as his tongue plunged into her mouth, and she responded to him, kissing him back. She could feel his hand move slowly over her, stroking

170

her in a slow rhythm as it glided over the silken skin of her abdomen, then claimed the softness between her thighs. Shocked by his intimate touch, Brie drew in a sharp breath. But she didn't pull away. A strange warmth was starting to build inside her.

"Your other lover," Dominic whispered against her lips, "did he touch you here? Was he excited by your sweet passion, as I am?"

His whispered words only half penetrated Brie's dazed senses. She gazed down at him, noticing that his dark hair looked like rippling black sable against her pale skin. How could he speak of other lovers? There had been no others.

But she forgot her thoughts as Dominic's exploring fingers parted the soft curls that hid her womanhood. When he softly stroked the tender flesh, Brie moaned low in her throat, feeling a hot wetness flowing between her thighs. Unconsciously, she arched her back and pushed her hips forward, trying to get closer to him, trying to find release for the yearning ache he was stirring in her.

Her eagerness nearly made Dominic lose control. With desire burning through him, he urgently lowered Brie to the mattress, pushing her shoulders down as he parted her thighs and prepared to thrust himself into her.

The sudden mounting pressure of his entry made Brie gasp, but Dominic's reaction was even more abrupt. He froze in sudden confusion as he met the thin wall of resistant flesh. Then his eyes snapped open and he stared at her lovely face with shock. By God, she had lied to him. He was bedding a damned virgin!

He would have withdrawn in sheer astonishment except that Brie clung to him tightly. She knew full well what she was giving him, Dominic realized as he saw the trust shining in her eyes. And he was too fiercely aroused to stop himself from taking it. He felt his heart twist in his chest as he gazed down at her. "Little fool," he whispered against her mouth, lessening the sting of his words by kissing her long and lovingly.

He thrust quickly then, imbedding his flesh deeply inside her, smothering her cry of pain with his lips as his shaft split the fragile barrier of her womanhood.

He lay perfectly still, raining tender kisses on Brie's lips and face, tasting the salt of her tears as he brushed them away with his tongue. Dominic began to move slowly then, forcibly restraining himself from plunging too deeply into the tight sheath that inflamed his passion. Brie felt like silken fire beneath him, but he tried to control the tempo in deference to her untutored body.

She was too tempting, though, too warm and responsive in his arms for him to keep his passion in check for long. And no power on earth could slow the explosive shudders that ran through him as he spent his seed. Delirious bursts of pleasure rippled through his body, making his breath come in harsh gasps. When the last violent tremor had passed, Dominic buried his face in the silken mass of her hair.

Later, when his breathing slowed, when he could once again think clearly, Dominic slowly rolled onto his side, pulling Brie with him. They lay facing each other, not speaking.

Brie gazed at Dominic uncertainly, wondering if she had pleased him, while Dominic returned her gaze, watching the color of her eyes shift like quicksilver. For the first time in his life, he was completely at a loss for words. Inexplicably, he was glad she had been a virgin, yet he could hardly believe she had given him such a priceless gift, or that she had had it to give.

With a gentle finger he traced the outline of her mouth, swollen a little from his bruising kisses. "Did I hurt you?" he asked softly, brushing an auburn curl from her damp brow.

Brie lowered her eyes from his penetrating gray gaze. "Not much," she answered hesitantly. That was certainly true. She had felt only the slightest stab of pain—and that only for an instant, and the present uncomfortable throbbing between her legs was beginning to fade. Indeed, the experience had been nothing like what she had expected, either in pain or pleasure. She had liked the heavy feel of Dominic's body and the hardness of his muscular thighs against hers . . . but she was also conscious of a vague feeling of disappointment. She had been on the brink of a great revelation, but his caresses had ended before she could discover what it meant. Now she only felt strangely frustrated. Her body was still tight with feverish anticipation, still hungering for something she couldn't even name.

Dominic watched her brows knit in fierce concentration and wondered what thoughts were going on behind those beautiful eyes. Shaking his head, he pressed a soft kiss on her brow and rose from the bed, returning with a towel which he used to gently wash away the proof of her virginity.

Embarrassed by such intimacy, Brie tried to protest, but Dominic would have none of her modesty. He brushed her hands away and in a voice filled with tender amusement, told her to be still.

When he had finished, Brie buried her flaming face in the mattress. Dominic sat beside her, his fingers lightly roaming the satin skin of her back. "I thought you told me you had had a lover before," he murmured.

"I . . . he didn't . . . we weren't . . ."

Taking her disjointed stammerings to mean what he had already surmised, Dominic sighed. "I'm sorry," he said very gently.

Brie lifted her head to stare at him. *"Sorry?"* She didn't know whether to feel ashamed or indignant.

Dominic repressed a smile. "Don't misunderstand me. I enjoyed making love to you, more than you could know. It's just that I'm not in the habit of seducing virgins."

"I suppose you prefer to seduce women with experience?"

His brow shot up as he gave her a teasing glance. But when Brie flushed and averted her gaze, Dominic felt a surge of tenderness for her he found difficult to ignore. Placing a finger under her chin, he forced her to look at him again. "Believe it or not, ma belle, I much prefer you. You lack practice, but the instinct is certainly there."

173

When she made no reply, Dominic gave her a soft smile. "Do you need reassurance? Here, feel me. Does this give you any indication of how much I want you?"

Brie gasped as he guided her hand to the dark, curling hair below his abdomen, realizing that his shaft was once again stiff and throbbing. Dominic chuckled at her response, although he himself wondered at the speed of his arousal. When she tried to pull away, he shook his head. "Oh, no, my sweet vixen," he said, his gray eyes warm with laughter. "I intend to make very sure you understand completely what goes on between a man and woman. Just so you never again mistake a boor's drunken pawing for the act of making love. Your lover must have been remarkably inept."

Brie glared at him. "I did not *mistake* anything. And it wasn't 'making love', it was rape. Or at least attempted rape. The only reason he didn't succeed was because I managed to hit him over the head with a fire iron."

"Good God. How fortunate for me there wasn't one available the first time I tried to seduce you."

"There was! I only wish now I had had the nerve to use it on you." When Dominic threw back his head and laughed, Brie clenched her teeth. "I never told you I wasn't a virgin."

His eyes sparkled wickedly. "Oh, no. You merely spun me a tale about an aging protector who couldn't afford the price of a new gown, and a lover who disgusted you with his fumbling attempts to steal your virtue. And that was after I found you alone in a bachelor's hunting box, wearing less than a statue of Venus. Forgive me for casting aspersions on your innocence."

There was some justice in what he said, Brie thought ruefully. And even though Dominic had spoken in his usual dry tone, she could tell he wasn't laughing at *her*. His teasing smile was warm and intimate, inviting her to share his humor. Brie felt her anger melting away. A smile tugged at the corners of her mouth, and in spite of herself, she laughed. "All right, you have a point. But the story about the lover really was true." What was strange, she added to herself, was that she could laugh about that episode in her life as if it were no more than a bad joke.

"Well," Dominic said lazily, "I obviously misconstrued what you said. If I had known the truth, I would never have touched you, believe me. But the damage is done now. I suppose," he said, giving her a speculative glance, "it wouldn't hurt to show you just what you've been missing."

He was no longer laughing, Brie noticed. And his eyes had started to smolder in a way that made her feel highly desirable and more than a little wanton. She was suddenly aware of his nearness, of the heat of his body and the fluttering of her stomach. The air between them seemed suddenly charged with electric current.

Wanting to break the tension, Brie opened her mouth to say something, anything, but Dominic pressed a finger to her lips. "Hush, cherie," he said huskily. "Lie back and don't fight me. I assure you this will be pleasant. It won't hurt this time, I promise."

Pressing her back against the pillows, he captured her face between his open palms. "So lovely," he murmured before lowering his lips to hers.

Any possibility of rational thought fled when Brie felt the touch of his lips. His kiss was like nothing she had known before—gentle and wild, fragile and intense, soothing and provocative. And his hands . . . his hands stroked her gently, arousing a response in her that seemed to come from her very depths.

He caressed her until her slender body was pliant and yielding. And when at last he parted her legs and carefully entered her, she was nearly breathless. She clung to him, her breasts rising and falling rapidly, her head thrashing from side to side. He seemed to fill her, to become part of her.

He began to move slowly then, building the tempo into a tantalizing rhythm. Brie instinctively began to answer him, her hips rising to meet his deep thrusts, her nails feverishly raking his back. And when a glowing spark ignited at the very center

175

of her being, she whimpered. It felt as if every nerve of her body had gathered there.

Dominic could sense when she reached the edge of panic. "Yes, my passionate beauty," he whispered hoarsely against her mouth. "Let me fill you. Let it come." Raising his head, he watched the startled expression on her face change to blind passion.

Brie wondered if she were dying. Her senses seemed to slowly erupt with a wet, white heat . . . And then she was falling, falling. She surged against Dominic, crying out something unintelligible as she reached a shattering climax. She was hardly aware when Dominic's body suddenly went rigid, but she clung to him helplessly as he spent his final passion.

Some moments later, he eased himself away, but it was a great while before Brie could even think to open her eyes. She found Dominic gazing down at her with an expression that was difficult to read. The firelight cast shadows over the harsh planes of his face, but his eyes seemed to hold a tenderness that warmed her all over.

"Is it . . . always like that?" Brie whispered, returning his gaze.

Dominic smiled. "So intense, you mean? Not often."

Brie let her eyes fall shut again. "I didn't think so," she murmured. "Otherwise how would anyone survive?"

Dominic chuckled, gently brushing a curl from her cheek. He studied Brie for a moment longer, before raising his gaze to the window. "The storm seems to have blown over," he said idly.

The warm glow surrounding Brie dissipated at once as reality came rushing back with a vengeance. Feeling acutely self-conscious, she turned her head away, trying not to contemplate the fact that she had just allowed herself to be seduced by a handsome rake. When Dominic bent to kiss her bare shoulder, she flinched.

Watching her, Dominic frowned. He couldn't blame her if

she felt awkward and uncertain—he was feeling something similar himself. But he didn't like to see her so meek and passive. He would rather see her spitting fire, even if it were at him. He knew just how to bring her spirit back, though.

With one finger, he traced a path between Brie's pale, gleaming breasts, letting his hand rest over her heart where he could feel the beat against his palm. "This cabin leaves much to be desired," he observed casually. "Next time I suggest we choose somewhere more congenial to meet."

Brie's eyes flew to his face. "There won't be a next time."

"Are you so sure of that, Brie? Somehow I got the impression you enjoyed my lovemaking."

"Perhaps I did, but I have no intention of allowing it to happen again."

A smile teased the corners of Dominic's mouth. "Well, if you change your mind, you know where to find me. But for now," he added as he pointedly lowered his gaze to her bare breasts, "we really should be going. Unless, of course, you would rather spend the rest of the day in bed."

He could feel Brie stiffen with anger. "No?" he asked innocently when she brushed his hand away. "Then you had better get dressed. I won't be held responsible for my actions if you insist on displaying your charms in such a provocative manner."

Giving Brie a playful slap on her thigh, Dominic stood up and stretched. He watched as she fumbled with the bodice of her chemise, knowing it might be some time before he had another chance to feast his eyes on her beauty.

Furious at him now, Brie snatched the blanket up and gave Dominic a glare that would have pierced him had it been a sword. Dominic merely grinned at her, admiring the flashing green sparks in her eyes. "What a pity no one thought to enlist your services during the war," he remarked provokingly. "One look like that from your beautiful eyes would have routed the enemy without resort to cannon. I imagine you could have intimidated Napoleon himself."

Brie clenched her teeth. "You are beyond all doubt the most uncivil, boorish, arrogant, conceited, odious man I have ever had the misfortune to meet! Why don't you just go away and leave me here? I can find my way home without your help."

Dominic went to the fireplace and began sorting through their various apparel. "I told you before," he replied, tossing Brie's clothes to her. "It isn't safe. I don't want you wandering these woods alone."

"*You* don't want—well, really!" Brie exclaimed, her voice heavy with satire. "What more could possibly happen to me?"

Dominic slanted an amused glance at her. "You're asking *me* that?" Fortunately for him, he was able to avoid the boot she threw at his head.

Chapter Seven

The arrival of an earl in their quiet neighborhood, especially one of Dominic's stamp, was cause for awe and excitement. Brie tried to ignore the furor—indeed, she would have preferred to forget that Dominic existed altogether—but no one would allow her to do so.

John Simms in particular had taken an immediate liking to Dominic. John had been waiting for Brie in the stableyard when Dominic had escorted her home after the storm. Fortunately, he had been too interested in Dominic's stallion to ask many questions about where she had spent the past few hours. When the two men fell to discussing horses and bloodlines, Brie made her escape. She found out afterward that Dominic had promised to return at a later date to inspect several of Greenwood's Arabian mares. John was in such alt over the prospect of breeding the mares to the stallion that for days he could talk of little else.

Caroline, too, spoke of Dominic frequently, for she had seen him accompany Brie back to the house. She had nagged until Brie was forced to give a much abbreviated account of what had happened at the cottage, and then she had asked so many questions that Brie didn't know whether to scream or throttle her cousin first.

As far as Brie could tell, though, not even Caroline guessed

179

that she had been far more intimate with Dominic than was proper. Oddly enough, she trusted Dominic's assurances that he would say nothing of what had occurred between them. And she was no longer concerned that he would ruin her reputation with a careless word. But whatever she remembered letting him make love to her, she felt hot with shame.

She couldn't understand how it had happened. He had aroused a traitorous desire in her when properly she should have felt fear and revulsion. The feel of his hard body had been exciting, and what he had done to her own body had set her on fire. When he had kissed her with such passion, she had surrendered to him like a common hussy. Brie was disgusted with herself, particularly since she still harbored a strong attraction for Dominic.

About a week later, however, Brie was given something else to worry about. Her steward, Mr. Tyler, reported that there had been several thefts in the neighborhood, two of them on Greenwood land. Brie decided to pay a visit to Squire Umstead to see what was being done to apprehend the thieves, since the squire frequently handled such matters.

Brie took her cousin along and shortly regretted the impulse. When they arrived, they found Squire Umstead out with a shooting party, but his wife was at home and she insisted on meeting Caroline. Brie could hardly refuse an invitation to stay for tea, but she cringed inwardly when Mrs. Umstead sent a footman after her son Rupert.

Enduring half an hour of Rupert's company set Brie's nerves on edge. She was relieved when the squire at last returned home, even though her plan of speaking to him in private was forestalled because Viscount Denville and Lord Stanton were with him.

Brie felt intensely self-conscious, meeting Dominic again, for it was the first time since their intimate interlude in the cottage. Seeing him enter the room, she was again struck by his extreme masculinity. He looked impossibly attractive in a claret-colored shooting jacket and buff breeches. The collar of his shirt was opened comfortably at the throat, while a silk scarf was tied loosely about his neck. Brie found the casual touch strangely appealing, but it was his sheer maleness that made her stomach flutter. She knew first hand that his muscular body was every bit as lean and hard as it appeared.

Trying not to remember how it had felt pressed against her, Brie lifted her gaze to his and caught the amused gleam in his gray eyes. Realizing then how intently she had been studying him, she blushed.

She introduced her cousin to the squire, but when the conversation momentarily turned to travel, she found herself being drawn aside from the others by Dominic. When he complimented her on her becoming appearance, she glanced up at Dominic suspiciously. She knew her empire-waist gown of pale peach muslin was stylish and flattering to her figure, but his words seemed to imply something more.

Dominic smiled at her obvious mistrust. "Come now, Miss Carringdon. That was not meant as a criticism. I was growing accustomed to your unique mode of dressing. But I must confess I prefer to see a beautiful woman looking like one, rather than a man.

Brie arched a disdainful eyebrow. "Must you? I expect it is fortunate then that I don't require your approval."

"Ah," he said, shaking his head ruefully, "I can see that I have offended your sensibilities once more."

"Nonsense," Brie snapped. "I find it pleasant to have my femininity questioned by a gentleman who is noted to be an expert."

His laughter was maddening, and so was the way his gaze slowly swept her figure. "I never doubted that you are a woman, cherie," he drawled in a low voice. When his eyes met hers in an intimate, caressing glance, Brie felt a shiver run down her spine. Unable even to think of a reply, she turned away to join the others.

For the remainder of the visit, Brie tried to behave as she normally would, but she was far too conscious of Dominic.

181

She couldn't help stealing a glance at him from time to time as they all sat drinking tea and eating finger sandwiches. Not by so much as a flicker of an eyelid was he revealing the boredom that he surely must feel in such unsophisticated company. In fact, he seemed to be putting himself out to please, conversing easily with everyone, including Rupert, and displaying a considerable amount of charm with the ladies. Not that that surprised her. She knew to her cost exactly how charming Dominic could be when he wished. But his infuriating mockery was far less pronounced today.

And that in itself was irksome. She realized now that she had overreacted to his comment about her appearance. He had simply been being polite, but she had taken offense where none was offered. What was it about Dominic Serrault that made her behave like a shrew? She didn't exactly possess an even disposition, but she had never been so churlish with any other man. She couldn't seem to curb her temper or her tongue whenever she was near him, even when he wasn't behaving outrageously or being deliberately provoking.

Brie's thoughts were so occupied with Dominic that she paid little attention to the flirtation her cousin was waging with Julian. It also was some time before she recalled the purpose of her visit and could capture the squire's attention to request an audience.

She would have preferred to do so quietly, not wanting to attract Dominic's notice or advertise the fact that she had something so unfeminine as business to discuss, but she wasn't successful. Squire Umstead—a short, stocky man with a florid face and balding head—was blessed with a good deal more sense than his son, but he was not big on subtleties. He loudly and cheerfully agreed to discuss the thieves with Brie in the library, and invited Julian as well. As they left the room, Brie saw Dominic's raised eyebrow, for the squire was already talking about how one of his dogs had been killed.

Their conversation didn't last long. Immediately afterward, Brie collected Caroline and made her excuses, not caring to be

182

subjected to Dominic's penetrating gaze any longer.

Shortly, Julian and Dominic also called for their horses. As they rode back to the Lodge, he satisfied Dominic's curiosity as to the subject of the discussion.

"It seems there has been some trouble in the area," he explained. "Evidences of poaching, a tool shed broken into— that sort of thing. The squire thinks it is probably some wandering gypsies, although he hasn't been able to catch the culprits. One of his tenants had a gun stolen. I've offered to help join in the search."

Dominic frowned. "This all just started a few days ago?"

"Yes, how did you know?"

"Jacques listens well. Not much escapes his attention."

"Your coachman?" Julian asked in surprise. "I realize he used to aid you in your nefarious activities across the Channel, Dom, but why the devil is this any of his business?"

"I told him to keep an eye out."

Julian grinned. "So you've set him to spying. What does he do, give you a daily report?"

Dominic returned a cool glance. "Jacques seemed to think the incidents unique enough to concern me—and I have a feeling he may be right."

"Well, he's always seemed a shady character to me, but I know the trust you put in the fellow."

"I do, and I would appreciate it if you would let me handle this, Julian, in my own way."

Julian eyed Dominic curiously, then shook his head. "Oh, no, you don't, my friend. I won't be fobbed off with this talk of appreciation. I would think by now you would trust me enough to give me some sort of explanation, preferably the truth."

"It would probably bore you."

"Unlikely. I know that closed-oyster look of yours. I have no doubt you're hiding a secret that would make any adventure of mine look tame in comparison."

Dominic's mouth twisted wryly. "Very well, but it's a long

183

story and this is not the proper place."

Assuming a wary expression, Julian peered suspiciously at the trees beside the lane. "No one listening that I can see. But perhaps you require a dark alley on a moonless night?" When he received a sharp glance from Dominic, Julian held up a hand and grinned. "A poor joke, I know. All right, a cognac and a fire in the library will do just as well."

Julian bridled his curiosity, but it was much later before he had an opportunity to ask Dominic any questions. He had invited several of his friends to the Lodge for supper and cards, and the game lasted long into the night. It was only a few hours before dawn when Julian showed his guests to the door.

Returing to the drawing room, he added another log to the fire and refilled his wineglass, then settled in a comfortable chair and stretched his legs out before him, just as Dominic was doing. Both men watched the flickering flames in the hearth as Dominic proceeded to tell in clipped tones about Germain's return and the duel they had fought.

"I always thought one day your past would catch up to you," Julian said at the conclusion. "You made enough enemies among the French government to staff an army." He chuckled, remembering some of the stories he had heard about Le Poignard—Dominic's alias. "The Dagger," he translated. "The very name struck terror in the hearts of men. No, seriously, Dom, you were outstanding as a spy. I've heard both Castlereagh and Wellington sing your praises. But this man who hired Germain to kill you—surely he couldn't be connected with your spying activities. The war has been over for years. It seems unlikely he would have waited until now."

Dominic sipped his brandy, his thoughts seeming far away. "Did I say man? It could be a woman, for all I know. But you're right. It makes no sense, either way. Why would someone want the deed to the estate my father owned before his death? Whoever employed Germain knew about the deed and wanted it badly. It must have been even more important than killing me, otherwise Germain would never have resorted to showing his hand. Interesting, isn't it?"

Julian pursed his lips thoughtfully. "And you think these incidences of theft and poaching are related to what happened in London?"

"They could mean nothing, but then again, I've learned to be cautious. Germain is my prisoner for the time being. According to the message I received from Jason yesterday, Charles is still delirious with fever, but the chances of his recovering are improving. Until I can question him, I don't expect to learn much, but it is still possible that whoever hired him has one or two more ideas up his sleeve, including sending one of his assassins after me. Jacques tells me the rumors don't put the blame on anyone local."

"So you want Jacques to investigate."

Dominic sighed. "I want, my friend, to give him some time to find out whether this trouble is in anyway connected to me. He won't be able to if the whole neighborhood is alerted to his activities."

Julian nodded. "Very well, I won't interfere. But we'll have to have some reason for delaying a search. I doubt if the squire would mind having the problem taken off his hands and he would probably swallow a good story, but you won't find Brie so gullible. You had better tell her the truth."

"Not a chance. The fewer people who know about this, the better. Besides, I don't like having women involved. Even if they can be trusted, they only get in the way. I'll think of some other way to handle the lady."

Julian grinned. "I'd like to see it."

Dominic slanted him a glance. "I suggest you concern yourself with her cousin. Now there's a scheming female for you."

"Caroline? You must be joking."

Dominic's smile didn't reach his eyes. "Not a joke, my friend. A warning. She has quite an advantage over an unsuspecting fellow such as yourself. How does marriage appeal to you? For, if I'm not mistaken, that is Miss Langley's aim. And you, Julian, will be fool enough to let her tie you hand and foot and lead you to the altar before you realize you've been trapped."

"Lord, Dominic, Caroline is just a girl. I've known her for years."

Dominic smothered a yawn with his hand. "They teach them young these days. How old is she anyway, seventeen, eighteen? Old enough to marry, at any rate. I would imagine that right now, pretty little Caroline is having pleasant dreams of becoming a countess and planning how she will spend your fortune before you even inherit it."

Anger lit Julian's blue eyes, but he kept his voice even. "If Caroline seemed friendlier than usual today, it's merely because she's recovering her normal high spirits. But, however did we manage to get on this subject? If I had to guess, I'd say your jaundiced view stems from Denise Grayson's arrival this afternoon. You're aware, of course, that she chose to honor the Scofields with her presence?"

Dominic's lips twisted in a frown. "Fully aware. I received a note from Denise informing me of the fact. I can't say that I'm pleased. Did you know she intended to visit?"

"I? Not at all." Julian grinned at him. "You do seem to have a large following, Dom. First assassins and now your ex-mistress. Your visit is proving to be extremely interesting. Of course it's nothing to me if Lady Grayson decides to try her hand with you again, but I wonder what the rest of the world will make of it. People will probably think she's here at your invitation."

When Dominic scowled into his glass, saying nothing, Julian rose. "Well, it's late," he said, stretching, "and I for one am going to retire." He crossed the room, but turned back at the door. "You know, Dom," Julian said quietly, "I cannot agree with your opinion of Caroline. And I didn't care for your remarks about her."

Dominic's eyes narrowed as he looked up. "The warning still stands."

186

"Don't you have enough to concern you without adding my troubles to your list? I believe I can be counted on not to play the fool."

Dominic's mouth twisted in a cynical smile. "Can you? Perhaps you don't remember what condition you were in when we first met in Vienna. You were so blinded by Brie Carringdon's charms that you couldn't see your hand in front of your face."

Noting the cold gleam in his friend's gray eyes, Julian realized it was pointless to argue. Dominic believed that love was a mental illness. "I'll not deny that I loved Brie," Julian replied, "but that was quite another matter." Then, as he turned away, he added softly, "I pity the woman who finally engages your affections, Dominic. I expect you will make her life hell."

Julian's words seemed to linger in the air, even after he had gone, but Dominic's mind wasn't on what his friend had said. He finished his brandy, hardly noticing the warmth of the liquor on his tongue, not even seeing the glowing coals he was watching so intently. His thoughts were wrapped around a flaming haired vixen, just as they had been countless times during the past few weeks.

He knew if he were wise, he would stay away from Brie. Indeed, he should never have gotten involved with her at all. But making love to her once had only whetted his appetite for more, and he seriously doubted he would give up his pursuit of her.

It wouldn't be easy to succeed with her, especially since Brie seemed determined to avoid him. But given time, her proud defiance would crumble. His biggest difficulty would be keeping a leisurely pace for her taming. He had never found it so hard to curb his impatience. Dominic smiled wryly. It would be much simpler if he owned a castle in the wild where he could hold Brie captive, for he could have her then, with or without her consent. Unfortunately he lived in a more modern time, and he was civilized enough to want his women willing.

Yet, now he had additional complications to deal with. Brie had chosen, however unwittingly, to become involved in a situation she did not understand. He would have to insure that she became uninvolved.

And then there was Denise Grayson. Denise could not have appeared at a more inopportune time, Dominic thought sardonically. He quite sincerely wished her in Hades, but he knew he was at fault for bringing about the situation. When they had parted in London, he had seen no reason to tell Denise he merely had taken advantage of her availability. He hadn't expected her to follow him—although he might have foreseen it. Denise was always a woman with an eye out for an opportunity. She had probably deluded herself into thinking there was a chance to renew their old affair. Well, Denise would just have to be disillusioned—before she could cause trouble for him.

Wondering how Brie would react to the presence of his former mistress, Dominic grimaced. She would probably be grievously insulted, and it would be twice as hard for him even to get near her.

The clock on the mantle chimed then, reminding Dominic of his need for sleep. Putting his problems aside, he rose and banked the fire before following Julian's example and retiring for what was left of the night.

But his desire for Brie did not leave him. Dominic lay alone in his bed, staring at the ceiling, remembering what it was like to have her, warm and willing, in his arms. Predictably, the throbbing ache his memory inspired only made it more difficult for him to fall asleep.

The next morning Dominic went to see John Simms, ostensibly to select one or two Arabian mares for his racing stable. While his was there, John showed him around the premises.

Dominic was impressed, for Greenwood was obviously well

run. The yard and schooling rings bustled with activity, and Dominic's experienced eye noted the excellent quality of horseflesh in the adjoining paddocks, as well as the quiet efficiency of the ostlers and grooms as they went about their work. The vast sprawl of barns had been superbly maintained, and the fences were in good repair. Even the house, an ivy-covered mansion of Ketton stone separated from the stables by a line of elms, seemed to blend in as part of the prospering enterprise.

After inspecting the mares, Dominic followed John to a small office where they discussed terms of purchase. Only then did he mention the recent thefts in the neighborhood. When the trainer had related all he knew about the incidents, Dominic offered to handle the matter. He knew the appropriate people to notify, he said, and in the meantime he would have his own men take up the search. His coachman had had some experience in apprehending vagrants.

"I have no objections, m'lord," John replied to his offer. "Actually it will be a big relief. My lads have their duties and they know nothing about thief-catching."

Dominic was sitting across from John's desk in one of the hard-backed chairs that furnished the office. Leaning back in his seat, he flicked at an imaginary speck of dust on his sleeve. "I'm sure you can see," he said casually, "why I hesitate to mention this to Miss Carringdon. I understand she prefers to be involved in everything relating to Greenwood. She might be offended, were I to suggest she wasn't capable of dealing with this problem."

John regarded his visitor thoughtfully. He had been surprised by the proposal, but he was pleased to see Lord Stanton showing an interest in Brie's affairs. In his opinion, Brie could do far worse than to ally herself with such a man. Stanton was just the sort to be able to curb her independent headstrong ways, and he seemed to understand her. John stroked his chin absently. Perhaps he would let this commanding nobleman have his way for a time and see where things led. It went against his principles to withhold confidences from his young mistress, but then Brie really wasn't qualified to handle thieves.

Adding a silent prayer that she would forgive him, John nodded his approval. "You are right, m'lord. It's best not to tell Miss Brie. She wouldn't take it well if an outsider assumed responsibility for Greenwood's problems. Nor would she care to be indebted to you, if you will pardon my saying so."

Dominic smiled pleasantly. "Of course. But this way is best. If your people do happen to stumble across something, you can have them report directly to me."

"Aye, and I'll have a word with Tyler, as well. He's steward here and has charge of the farms. I think I can convince him to go along." Hearing light footsteps in the corridor just then, John looked up as the door opened.

"John, I forgot to ask—" Brie broke off in confusion upon seeing Dominic. "I beg your pardon," she stammered as both men quickly rose to their feet. "I didn't know you were occupied, John. I can return some other time."

She turned to leave, but Dominic caught her arm. He had been admiring the lovely picture she made, standing there framed in the doorway. Her velvet pelisse, trimmed with sable, was the color of sapphires, and the deep hue made her wide eyes appear very blue.

He gently drew her back into the office. "There is no need for you to leave, Miss Carringdon. We have just concluded our business. John was telling me something of Greenwood's history earlier, and I am much impressed. You are both to be congratulated."

Brie could tell his praise was sincerely meant, and she was pleased. She was extremely proud of her heritage, but she was also aware Dominic's own estates had to be immense and that Greenwood must suffer in comparison. She smiled up at Dominic and thanked him. He smiled back, making her quite conscious of how devastatingly attractive he was.

Before she could say much else, however, one of the

stableboys came to the door and requested John's assistance. The trainer glanced at Brie.

"Please, go ahead, John," she said. "My matter can wait."

Muttering an apology, he thanked Dominic for his interest in the stables, then followd the boy from the room. Brie was left alone with Dominic.

She eyed him uncertainly, wondering about the intent look she had just seen pass between the two men. Tilting her head to one side, she arched a delicate eyebrow. "Secrets, my lord?"

After an almost imperceptible pause, Dominic replied smoothly. "Do I detect a note of concern? I assure you it was nothing. We were discussing . . . some horses I intend to run at Newmarket in the spring. Simms was advising me on the best strategy for training." When Brie continued to regard him suspiciously, Dominic's mouth twisted in a wry smile. "Don't look so accusing, Brie. I couldn't steal your trainer away, even if I wanted to. His loyalty to you is admirable."

Brie was surprised at his perceptiveness, since that was exactly what she had been thinking. But she wasn't entirely satisfied with his reply. The look the two men had shared had hinted at some kind of mutual agreement.

Plunging her fingers more deeply into her sable muff, she searched Dominic's face. She could read nothing in his enigmatic expression. "I've never had cause to question John's loyalty," she said finally, "but you wouldn't be the first to try and lure him away."

Grinning, Dominic held up his hands in surrender. "I'm innocent, I swear. At least of that charge."

Deciding that she must have been mistaken, Brie relented. "Oh, very well," she said good-naturedly. "I believe you. I take it then that you discussed the mares."

Dominic told her about the arrangements he had made for buying two of the Arabians, adding that they would be a welcome addition to his stables since he was after endurance as well as speed.

"You should be pleased," Brie replied with a smile, "since

191

you chose the best. It is I who am disappointed. I was hoping John might have convinced you to part with your stallion. You did say you might be persuaded."

Dominic's gray eyes filled with warm light. "So I did. But I was thinking more along the lines of *you* doing the persuading, rather than your trainer."

Not knowing how to respond to his suggestive remark, Brie tried to match his bantering tone. "That might be beyond my capabilities, my lord, but I am willing to try. Perhaps you would stay to dine with us and allow me the opportunity."

He shook his head regretfully. "I should like to, but unfortunately I must return to the Lodge. Julian has invited some of his colleagues over for the afternoon, and I am already late."

Brie was conscious of disappointment, but she extended her hand politely. "Very well, some other time then. I wouldn't want to interfere with a gentleman's sport."

"Will I have the honor of seeing you tomorrow?" Dominic asked, taking her hand.

"At the hunt? But of course. I wouldn't miss a meet so near the end of the season."

"No, certainly not. And I would guess you are set on riding Julian's nag. You are very courageous."

At the hint of mockery in his tone, Brie's chin came up. "Or foolish, you mean? Jester is not so very bad, my lord. In fact, I've grown rather fond of him. He is a . . . a special challenge."

Dominic looked at her thoughtfully. "An apt phrase. Does it apply to men as well?"

Brie wasn't as disconcerted by the question as she was by the fiery pulse that ran up her arm when Dominic raised her hand to his lips and lightly kissed her fingers. She knew he must have felt a similar sensation, for she saw desire flicker in his eyes.

For a moment, she stood looking up at him, mesmerized by the burning intensity of his gaze. When he turned her hand over, gently pressing his warm mouth against the inside of her

rist, she quivered. The touch of his lips made her vividly
call the last time he held her in his arms.

She could tell by the glowing flame in his eyes that Dominic
as remembering, too. His gaze slid downward, stripping her
re of clothing, leaving her feeling exposed and vulnerable.
/hen he said her name softly, his voice dropping to a caress,
rie's heart began to race. For a fleeting moment, she allowed
erself to recall what it was like to experience Dominic's total
assion, to have his warm lips following the searing trail that
is eyes made, for his mouth to linger hotly on her breasts
hile his hands slowly swept lower to torment her body—

Brie gave an abrupt start at the disquieting fantasies going
rough her head. Realizing that Dominic was still holding her
and, she drew it from his grasp. "Apply . . . apply to men?"
e repeated, trying unsuccessfully to keep her tone light.
You couldn't be speaking of yourself, my lord. You must
now I wouldn't dare presume to challenge you."

Dominic hesitated for a moment, as if he might press for a
ifferent response. Then he sighed, his mouth twisting wryly.
I know nothing of the kind, cherie. You have challenged me
n several occasions, if I recall. But I promised not to speak of
e past."

Turning away, he threw his greatcoat over his shoulders,
en picked up his gloves and hat and crossed to the door.
Until tomorrow, then?" he said, giving Brie one of those
evastatingly sweet smiles that never failed to make her heart
urn over.

Brie nodded, not trusting herself to speak. She watched as
e door shut softly behind him, then stood there, listening to
ominic's retreating footsteps. When he was gone, Brie sank
to the empty chair, feeling unaccountably weak. Hugging her
able muff to her stomach, she rested her forehead on her
nees.

The words had remained unspoken, but Dominic had made
explicitly clear that he still wanted her. And now she could
o longer deny that she wanted him, too. The attraction she

felt for him was too strong to dismiss. His virile masculinity was like a powerful magnet, drawing her to him. Whenever he touched her, she felt a treacherous warmth steal over her.

At least he hadn't kissed her this time. Usually he wound up doing that and more. But the look he had given her. . . . Brie trembled, recalling the flame in his eyes. It had made her feel so . . . so desirable, so completely a woman. He had aroused physical yearning within her that was almost tangible.

A soft moan escaped Brie's lips as she buried her face into the thick sable of her muff. Dominic Serrault was a man she hardly knew, a man who had frightened and taunted her. And yet, he had easily stripped away her defenses, exposing passion she had thought deeply buried.

Faith, she must be mad! She had learned from her disastrous experience six years ago that she was far too gullible when men were concerned. She had given her heart too easily then, and now she was in danger of succumbing again to the determined seduction of an expert. She couldn't even delude herself that Dominic was interested in anything but her body. There had been nothing more than desire in his eyes. She was the target for his lust, nothing more.

Absently, Brie rubbed her cheek against the sable. The rich fur felt like cool satin against her flushed skin, and she could detect a lingering trace of Dominic's masculine scent.

She could not yield to him, of course. She would be too likely to give in to him completely, and that hard, cynical man would not want her heart.

Brie closed her eyes, wondering why the thought should make her so very miserable.

She slept fitfully that night, dreaming of being chased by a devil on a great black horse. A strange white field surrounded her, and no matter how hard she ran, she couldn't reach the edge. Just as the specter caught her, the nightmarish image changed and she recognized Dominic's dark features. He gave

er a mocking smile, then swept her into his strong arms and
issed her ruthlessly. When she tried to fight him, his harsh
aughter filled her ears. . . .

Brie woke with a start. For a moment she lay there, listening
o the fading echoes and trying to control her trembling. She
ad obviously been in the throes of a nightmare, for the
edclothes were entangled with her bare legs and her
ightgown had ridden up above her hips. And she felt so very
trange. A thin film of perspiration covered her body, but her
kin was feverish, while her breasts felt full and ultrasensitive.
There was also a hot ache between her thighs that throbbed
vith a sort of pleasurable pain.

Shakily, Brie pulled the covers up to her chin and lay there
taring at the darkness. It was a long while before the tension in
er body unwound and she at last fell asleep.

When next she awakened, light was filtering through her
edroom curtains and someone was tapping on her door. When
Caroline's maid peered into the room, Brie suddenly realized
he lateness of the hour. She rose at once, not wanting to miss
ny part of the fox hunt.

She washed while her riding habit was being laid out, then
llowed the maid to arrange her hair into a smooth knot at her
1ape. When she was dressed, Brie gave herself a final glance in
he mirror. She was pleased to see her eyes didn't have the deep
circles under them she had expected. In fact, she thought she
ooked quite well. The severely tailored jacket and flowing skirt
of emerald green velvet hugged her figure, accentuating the
curve of her waist, while her shako hat of the same shade set off
he glowing color of hair. Not even Stanton would be able to
criticize her attire, Brie thought defiantly.

When she had pinched her pale cheeks to add a bit of color,
she was satisfied with her appearance. She picked up her tan
eather gloves and riding crop, and went in search of Caroline.

It was a beautiful morning for a hunt. The weather was crisp
and cool, and the ground forgiving but not sloppy. Brie could
feel her spirits rise in anticipation, and even Caroline looked

forward to the hunt with enthusiasm. The assembly was to meet on Squire Umstead's front lawn. After Brie had bolted down a hasty breakfast and John had brought their mounts around, the three of them set off down the drive.

Jester behaved well during the quiet ride, but he started to prance when he picked up the distant baying of the foxhounds. Caroline, too, became a bit nervous when they arrived upon the chaotic scene. There were people and animals everywhere. Nearly thirty Belvoir foxhounds—named after the nearby castle—were running in circles, eagerly sniffing at the ground and throwing back their heads to loudly voice their impatience. Spirited horses whinnied and snorted and pawed at the ground while their riders and grooms attempted to control them. Adding to the chaos were keepers caring for the hounds, servants attending their masters, waiters passing mugs of hot mulled wine, and horsemen laughing and calling to each other in loud, excited voices. Caroline stared wide-eyed at the ordered confusion, silently blessing her own gentle mare who stood calmly ignoring the commotion.

Brie had a difficult time with Jester, but she was glad to be occupied. She was determined not to let herself search for Dominic. Even so, her heart gave an odd little lurch when she spotted Julian threading his way toward them, for she knew Dominic would be somewhere nearby.

Julian greeted them cheerfully as he trotted up. "Perfect day, isn't it? Dom will be along in a moment. His horse threw a shoe. It seems that his usual luck is deserting him. So, Caroline, you are riding this morning?"

His tone sounded so dubious that Caroline raised her pert nose in the air. "Isn't that what one is supposed to do in the country?"

Julian flashed her a boyish grin. "Well, see that you don't fall off. I don't want to be obliged to carry you home."

"I certainly hope it doesn't come to that! John plans to ride with me, though, so Fanny and I should muddle through well enough."

Brie listened to their conversation with half an ear as her eyes wandered over the crowd. Seeing a flash of color amid a cluster of riders, she paused to study a lovely blonde lady dressed in a vivid shade of orange.

The woman was a stranger to Brie, but Caroline obviously recognized her; when the blonde broke away from her companions and rode toward them, Caroline gasped.

The woman addressed Julian first, a cold smile fastened on her lips. "Lord Denville, how pleasant. When I accepted Lady Scofield's invitation for a few weeks in the country, I had no idea so many of my acquaintances would be in the neighborhood." Her gaze swept measuringly over Brie, then Caroline. "My word—Miss Langley, isn't it? I had heard you had to leave London for a period. And how are you enjoying your stay?"

Caroline looked anything but pleased, but she managed a stiff answer. "Quite well, thank you. I don't believe you have met my cousin, Miss Carringdon. Brie, this is Lady Denise Grayson."

Lady Denise acknowledged Brie with a slight inclination of her head. "Of course," she said patronizingly. "The country cousin. You must let me have the name of your dressmaker, dear. That is such a quaint riding costume you are wearing."

Brie was so taken aback by the woman's rudeness that she made no reply. Denise smiled frostily, then returned her attention to Julian. "But where is Dominic? Does he not intend to join the hunt?"

Looking uncomfortable, Julian murmured some reply about Dominic being along in a moment. When Denise finally turned her mount and made her way back to her own party, he let out a sigh of relief.

Caroline, on the other hand, was irate. "Of all the nerve! Did you know she was going to be here, Julian?"

He was still staring after the retreating figure of Lady Denise. "Here?" he replied, frowning. "No, of course not. And I doubt Dominic did either," he added under his breath.

"How dare she criticize Brie's habit! Especially when her own shows such shockingly bad taste. All those frogs and epaulettes! And that color. I wouldn't be at all surprised if she gets mistaken for the fox, although a *cat* would be more like it. I have no idea what men see in a woman like that. Then again, I suppose it is obvious." She let the words hang, watching as Dominic's arrival was neatly intercepted by Lady Denise.

"Hold your tongue, Caroline," Julian said, giving her a disapproving frown.

"Well, you may condone her escapades, but I certainly don't!"

"And what would you know of her escapades, young lady?"

"Good heavens, Julian! I'm not a complete innocent. All London knows she used to be his mistress."

The choking sound Julian made was drowned out by the blare of the huntsman's horn. When he glanced at Brie, he was startled to see the stricken look in her eyes. She had the reins clenched tightly in her hands as she watched the little drama being enacted by Dominic and his ex-mistress.

Julian scowled at Caroline, but she only tossed her head and urged her horse over to where John waited for her. "I hope Simms prevents her from breaking her little neck," Julian muttered. "Then I can have the pleasure."

The baying of the hounds grew louder then, and the pack began to move off. "Come, Brie," he said gently. "I'll give you a lead over so that fool animal you are riding will have some idea how to go on."

Brie tore her gaze away from Dominic, only to stare blindly down at her hands. When she didn't respond, Julian swore under his breath, "For God's sake, smile, will you? You've told me often enough not to wear my heart on my sleeve."

That made her head snap up, and she glared furiously at him. "I am not! I couldn't care less what that insufferable man does! Or what paramours he keeps!"

Julian grinned. "Then I'll lay you a wager. A pair of foils against a new saddle says I'll be the first up at the finish."

"Agreed!" Brie retorted, accepting the challenge. She dug her heels in Jester's flanks and the bay leapt forward. Shaking his head, Julian followed.

For the most part they stayed well to the fore, directly behind the huntsman and whippers-in. The pace was slow at first, and the morning was well advanced before a fox broke cover and the entire field took off at a gallop. The wild chase ended only when the baying hounds lost the scent.

An hour later the hunt was riding through a thickly wooded area belonging to Julian. The path was so narrow and twisting that the riders were forced to go single file. Brie ducked to avoid a low branch that hung out over the trail, but when Jester bolted the next instant, she was almost swept from the saddle. She managed to maintain her seat and bring the bay under control before he ran her into a tree or careened into the horses in front, but after that, she slowed her pace, allowing the leaders to widen the distance.

She had no further trouble for a time. When the trail turned again, she urged the bay into a canter to clear the trunk of an oak that had fallen across the path. They landed easily on the other side, but then she happened to glance to her right. Catching sight of a dark figure in the woods, she gave an involuntary cry and pulled her mount to a dead stop.

Julian was following closely behind her and was forced to check sharply to avoid a collision. He let out an oath as he fought to control his rearing mount, then rounded on Brie. "That was a damned foolish stunt! What in blazes were you doing—trying to kill us?"

Brie ignored him, her eyes searching the underbrush for the man she had spotted. He had been some thirty yards away, on foot, and from that distance he had appeared to be roughly dressed, wearing dark clothing and a wide-brimmed hat pulled low over his eyes. At Brie's cry, he had turned away and hid himself in the underbrush. There was no sign of him now.

"Did you see him, Julian?" Brie said over her shoulder. "I would swear he was carrying a gun!"

"What gun? What are you talking about?" Julian demanded. "Damn it, Brie, have you suddenly lost all your senses?" He broke off scolding when a cool voice spoke behind him.

"Might I suggest," Dominic said, "that you two carry on your conversation elsewhere? At the moment, you stand in danger of being ridden down by those behind me."

Brie whirled her horse to face him. "But there was someone in those woods!"

Dominic's eyes narrowd. "I can see no one, Miss Carringdon. Perhaps you imagined a ghost or goblin. It might even be that the wood is haunted."

His sarcasm stung Brie, making her bristle with anger. She started to retort, wanting to say something just as nasty to him, but when she saw more riders coming up behind him, she realized that she couldn't stay there to argue. She contented herself with directing a scathing glance at Dominic before turning her mount and cantering down the path.

The two men followed at a more leisurely pace, and when the path opened into a field, they spread out to ride side by side. Dominic followed Brie's retreating figure with his gaze, noting her stiff shoulders and her proud, straight back. A gleam of amusement crept into his eyes. Seeing it, Julian demanded to know the cause of his humor.

Dominic grinned. "The lady has sharp eyes. She was able to catch Jacques in the act of searching your woods."

"You mean to tell me Brie did see a man? That he was your coachman?"

Dominic nodded, then chuckled. "I honestly believe she would have gone after him if I hadn't stopped her. Perhaps I was too hasty, though. I would have loved to see Jacques' face when he was exposed by a mere woman."

"Brie is not a 'mere woman'," Julian declared.

Dominic smiled at his own private thoughts. "I'm beginning to discover that for myself," he said softly. He slanted a glance at Julian. "I imagine she'll have some questions for you. See what you can do to pacify her and turn her attention away from Jacques, will you? I don't believe she is favoring me with her confidences at the moment."

Julian raised his eyes heavenward. "Well, what did you expect with your accusations of ghost-chasing? She wasn't happy with that one whit. In fact, she'd probably be pleased to see the last of you, particularly since Denise was showing her cat's claws earlier and flaunting her so very obvious association with you."

Seeing Dominic arch an eyebrow, Julian sighed. "It would be far better to tell Brie what is going on, but since you started this charade, I'll do what I can to see it through. Later, though—after Brie cools off. It would be more than my life is worth to speak to her now. Come to think of it, when are you going to start exercising that famous charm of yours?"

Dominic's lips twisted wryly. "I have tried, my friend, but you can see for yourself it isn't working."

Julian grinned. "I didn't think it would."

Chapter Eight

Lady Denise's presence in the neighborhood affected Brie more than she cared to admit. There was a good deal of speculation and gossip about the beautiful blond widow, and her name was quite frequently linked to Lord Stanton's in spite of the fact that they were rarely seen together.

When Brie received invitations to a ball being held in Lady Denise's honor, she considered declining. Dominic was sure to be there and she wanted to avoid both him and his paramour. But Caroline needed a chaperon in order to attend, and since Katherine didn't mean to go, the task fell to Brie.

Feeling a strong need to bolster her courage, she dressed with care. Her ballgown, a satin slip of sea green under a filmy overskirt shot with gold threads, was in the height of fashion and complemented her coloring. The low-cut bodice emphasized the fullness of her breasts, while the soft material clung to her slender figure, accentuating the curves of her waist and hips. Around her throat she wore a delicate diamond and emerald necklace, from her ears dangled matching earrings, and in her burnished, elegantly coiffed curls were tiny sprays of the glittering gems.

In contrast, her cousin was dressed demurely in white with a simple string of pearls around her throat. Caroline, however, did not mind that Brie's beauty outshone hers, for she had high hopes that Brie could capture the elusive Lord Stanton. She was quite certain Brie's alluring elegance would dazzle the most hardened rake.

When the Carringdon coach drew up before the Scofields' brightly lit mansion, Brie told herself for the hundredth time that she was foolish to allow the prospect of seeing Dominic again to daunt her. It should be simple for a woman of her years and experience to maintain an attitude of cool disdain toward him. She was very much afraid, however, that she would not be up to it.

After entering the brightly lit hall and surrendering their cloaks, the two cousins were shown into a large drawing room. More than a dozen of the guests who had been invited to dinner before the ball were already gathered there, seated or standing in small groups. Brie breathed a sigh of relief when she glanced around the room and noted that Dominic and Julian had not yet arrived, and she was able to greet her host and hostess with a warm smile.

Lady Scofield, a tall, overweight woman dressed becomingly in dark rose silk, spoke with Brie and Caroline a moment, before her attention was caught by some new arrivals. "There is Denville," she suddenly remarked. "And that handsome Lord Stanton. They say he is a dreadful rake but I think he is perfectly charming. Excuse me, my dears, while I go stop Henry from talking horses to him all evening. Stanton is buying one of our mares, you know, and I simply won't allow business to interfere with my party." Giving the two cousins a gracious smile, she left them in order to greet her new guests.

At the mention of Dominic, Brie had forcibly managed to keep her gaze from being drawn toward the door. Determined to avoid him, she urged Caroline toward some other of the guests and began making introductions. She left her cousin chatting happily with Lady Scofield's daughter Elizabeth and moved away to join Squire Umstead and his wife.

She had just began to relax when she heard the sound of Dominic's resonant laughter from somewhere behind her.

Involuntarily, she turned to glance at him, stiffening when she saw him standing beside Lady Grayson.

The ravishing blond was draped, Greek-style, in a diaphanous white muslin gown that left one arm bare and little to the imagination. Her pale beauty presented the perfect foil to Dominic, for with his raven hair and dark, aristocratic features, he exuded raw male attraction. Like many of the other gentlemen present, he wore a formal black coat and knee-breeches, a silk flowered waistcoat, and a neckcloth tied in a plain style, but the effect on Dominic was striking. The white linen at his neck made his bronzed skin seem darker, almost savage, and the well-tailored coat and snug breeches added a sleek elegance to his lean figure. He wore no jewelry other than a gold ring and watch, and the starkness of his attire made other men look flaccid and foppish in comparison.

Seeing him smiling down so warmly at Lady Denise, Brie ground her teeth. For some unaccountable reason, the sight infuriated her. Just then, Dominic glanced up and caught her frank stare, and when his eyes locked with hers, Brie felt herself blushing furiously. His look of amusement told her clearly that he knew what she was thinking. Angrily, Brie pressed her lips together and turned away.

She would have been even more angry had she heard Lady Grayson's next remark, for Denise's sharp eyes had missed none of the interchange. "I see now why you have been avoiding me, darling," she observed to Dominic. "You have already found a new *amour*. She is very beautiful, but hardly your type, I should think. Now if you had me . . ." Denise left the sentence unfinished and smiled provocatively up at him.

Dominic grinned and flicked her chin with a forefinger. "But I've already had you, cherie. And you know what they say about greener pastures."

Denise forced a gay little laugh. Having been Dominic's mistress once, she knew him too well to misunderstand him. She had held the position longer than most, but when she had begun to spend his money a bit too freely and then unwisely pressed him about marriage, he had terminated their relationship.

That had been several years ago. Now, looking at his tall, very masculine body, Denise very much regretted letting Dominic slip through her fingers. He had been an exciting lover and a stimulating companion, taking her with him sometimes on his frequent travels to the Continent. She wanted him back, even if she had long given up the hope of trapping him in marriage. She had followed him to the country with the express purpose of luring him into her bed again.

It hadn't taken her long to realize that Dominic had no interest in resuming their previous relationship, but she wasn't about to give up easily. "Darling," she said, keeping her voice low and husky. "Surely you remember the wonderful times we shared. I certainly have not forgotten. But perhaps you no longer find me attractive?"

"Fishing for compliments, Denise?"

Her lips curved in a pout. "Of course not, darling. But you could at least pretend you are glad to see me. To think that I travelled all this way just to be near you, and you aren't even grateful."

Dominic raised a mocking eyebrow. "I don't imagine that you will lack company for very long, my sweet. You'll soon have a dozen admirers vying for your attention. Now, if you will excuse me? My new *'amour'*, as you put it, is no doubt growing impatient with my lack of attention." Dominic turned away, leaving Denise with a frown marring her beautiful features.

A moment later, Brie was startled to hear Dominic's voice in her ear. "I missed you this past week, cherie," he murmured. "You haven't been avoiding me, by any chance?"

Brie turned to give him a quelling glance, but catching the curious looks of the other guests, she made herself smile sweetly. "Indeed, I have, Lord Stanton. I want nothing further to do with you. *Ever*."

He held his hand over his heart with a mock grimace. "I am

desolated. But I'm afraid you'll have to suffer my company for a few hours at least. It seems I am to take you in to dinner. Don't look so dismayed, my girl. Our hostess thinks she is doing you an honor."

Brie made no move to accept the arm he held out to her. "I would have thought Lady Grayson would be your partner."

Dominic's grin flashed charm along with white teeth. "Harcourt won out—his title ranks higher than mine. Come now," he chided, his eyes showing amusement. "These charming people will begin to wonder if there isn't something between us. They might be interested to learn just what happened in a particular cottage during a particular rain-storm. . . ."

"You wouldn't dare!"

He laughed and drew her arm through his, then bent to whisper in her ear. "Never, cherie. I told you I intend to be discreet."

Brie clenched her teeth, not deigning to reply, but as he led her into the dining room, she wondered despairingly how she would ever survive the evening.

Dinner turned out to be even worse than she had expected. She found herself seated between Dominic on her left and an elderly gentleman on her right, with Rupert Umstead directly opposite. As usual, Rupert was determined to make a fool of himself, and before the soup was even served, he had leaned across the table and loudly dedicated a toast to Brie's beauty. Acutely aware that Dominic was observing her discomfort, Brie managed a polite smile. But by the time second course was brought in, she was finding it hard not to grimace.

It was obvious Rupert had been drinking too much for he slurred his words as he recited a poem about the cruelty of the fairer sex. He might have continued indefinitely had not Dominic quietly signaled a footman to remove the boy's wine and directed a soft but curt remark across the table that caused Brie to blush. His intervention had the desired effect, though; Rupert sputtered a bit, turned quite red, and was silent. Brie couldn't help but give Dominic a grateful look, but when she saw the warm lights dancing in his eyes, she quickly turned her attention back to her plate.

The rest of the dinner progressed in comparative harmony, at least outwardly. Inwardly, Brie was far too aware of Dominic's presence. Once, when he was speaking to her, he rested his hand on the back of her chair, his fingers just brushing the bare skin of her shoulder, and Brie was dismayed to feel the tingling current that just this brief contact elicited. She was extremely glad to escape his close proximity at the conclusion of the meal.

After dinner, the ladies removed to the drawing room, leaving the gentlemen to their port. Since the dancing would not begin for another hour when the rest of the guests were to arrive, the ladies amused themselves by entertaining each other on the pianoforte. Brie was beginning to feel the onset of a headache, so when the tea tray arrived, she took her cup and went to sit on a sofa, as far away as possible from the chattering women but where she could still keep on eye on her cousin.

She had only just settled herself when Denise Grayson took the seat beside her. "I hope you do not mind the interruption, Miss Carringdon," Denise said airily, "but I wished to speak to you. And you did look a little forlorn, sitting here by yourself. Now why could that be?"

Brie was taken aback by the malicious gleam in the woman's blue eyes. She murmured a polite reply about having a headache, which brought a cold smile to Lady Denise's lips. "That excuse will serve as well as any, I suppose, even if it is untrue. He is handsome, is he not?"

Not caring at all for the woman's tone, Brie arched an eyebrow. "I beg your pardon?"

"Why Dominic, of course. Do you not find yourself attracted to him?"

"Whatever makes you think that?"

Denise's smile turned brittle. "Of course you wouldn't care to admit it. But I understand perfectly, my dear. Few woman can resist Dominic when he puts himself out to be charming."

"You are mistaken, my lady. I have not found Lord Stanton to be irresistible. In fact, I think him odious and overbearing—" Brie broke off, realizing she was protesting far to vehemently. "But I fail to see how it concerns you."

Denise leaned toward Brie, assuming a confidential air. "I am relieved to hear you say that, my dear. For although Dominic is quite handsome and charming, he sometimes is not very . . . nice in his actions. Or perhaps honorable would be a better word. I only seek to warn you. Surely you are not offended?"

Brie wanted to tell Lady Grayson to go to the devil, but she bit her tongue instead. "He means nothing to me, I assure you."

"I am extremely glad for you. Alas, it is not the same with me. You see, Dominic and I were once very close. By an unkind twist of fate, we were separated, but I have hopes that—"

"You will not break my heart, Lady Denise," Brie interjected. "Indeed, you have my best wishes."

Having attained her goal, Denise gave a satisfied smile and left Brie to herself. Brie watched her retreat, telling herself firmly that the sharp twinge in her heart was not jealousy. The blond witch was no less than Dominic deserved!

The gentlemen entered the drawing room shortly afterward, accompanied by the faint strains of music as the musicians prepared for their night's work. Inexplicably Brie was piqued when Dominic made no move to approach her, since her hand was solicited for a dance by any number of other gentlemen. His neglect seemed blatantly pronounced after his previous attentions toward her. She tried to ignore her infuriating disappointment, however, and focused instead on seeing that her cousin would be suitably partnered during the evening.

When the remaining guests began to arrive, the company filed into the ballroom, and the orchestra struck up for the first dance. Brie had awarded the set to a tall officer who was a friend of Lady Scofield's son. She allowed him to lead her into the cotillion, determined to forget about handsome, dark-haired lords who were too accustomed to having their way with women.

During the next set, however, her glance involuntarily went to the sidelines where Dominic stood with Lady Denise. He was frowning, but she was wearing the contented look of a well-fed cat. Brie wondered what Lady Denise could be saying to him, particularly when Dominic turned to meet her own gaze with narrowed gray eyes. She was glad when the set ended.

Julian claimed her hand for the next dance, and when he turned her over to another partner, her eyes once again went to the sidelines. Realizing then that she was unconsciously searching for Dominic, Brie chided herself for being foolish. She gave her new partner a brilliant smile and let him whirl her away.

She would have found Dominic had she looked in one of the smaller salons. After his highly unsatisfactory clash with Denise in the ballroom, he had joined the guests who preferred cards to dancing.

He played aggressively, but not even intense concentration could make him forget his urge to throttle his beautiful blond ex-mistress or their heated exchange of words. Denise had pleaded with him to return to their previous relationship, and when Dominic had firmly refused, she had become vicious. He had responded in kind.

"Come now, cherie," he had drawled. "Surely you don't expect me to welcome you with open arms. Your escapades of the past year have been a little too rich, even for my jaded tastes."

The smile froze on Denise's lips, while her blue eyes narrowed. "My escapades! Why mine are nothing compared to yours, darling. Or don't you know about the rumors? They say you almost killed that poor Mr. Germain. I hear he is faring so poorly that he may yet die. Perhaps it would have been wiser for you to leave England altogether," she added with a smirk.

Her smug expression changed at once when Dominic's

fingers closed about her wrist, and she gave a pained gasp. "Dear God, Dominic! You are hurting me. It isn't common knowledge, I swear it. I had it from one of your servants."

Hearing the panic in her voice, Dominic relaxed his grip. "How much did you pay for your information?"

There was steel beneath his silken tone, which Denise recognized. "I didn't bribe anyone, if that's what you are thinking," she answered sullenly. "Your man Farley just is no match for me. How else do you think I discovered that you were in this godforsaken place?"

"And yet you wish to take up with me again, knowing I might not be available to you for long?"

She bit her lip as she slanted a glance up at him. "You know as well as I that the authorities wouldn't move against someone of your rank without positive proof that you intended murder, even if the man were to die. And you are too clever for that, aren't you, darling?"

When he made no reply, Denise let her voice drop to a husky whisper. "I am merely concerned for you, Dominic. You must be lonely without a woman to comfort you. And I don't think you would be foolish enough to pursue her," Denise nodded in Brie's direction. "For one thing if you succeeded in seducing her, you would most certainly have to marry her. I understand she has some high-powered friends, not to mention a family of strait-laced relatives. And what's more, she isn't responding to your charm. That must hurt your pride—you whom most women are mad for. But don't worry, darling. Even though she is made of ice, I am not—as you well know. You might as well take me back," Denise summarized, giving him an arch smile.

Dominic glanced across the room to where the auburn-haired beauty was dancing with a red-coated officer. He met Brie's eyes for a moment, before turning back to Denise and eyeing her with distaste. "Your logic leaves much to be desired, Denise. True, you are warm, beautiful, passionate. . . ." Dominic said in a voice that both thrilled her and made her wary. "But I believe I would prefer a snake's venom

211

to your particular brand of poison. Although I admit a snake would not be nearly so comforting in bed."

"Why you—" Denise exclaimed in a shrill voice, before Dominic put a finger to her lips.

"Hush, my sweet. You are a guest here, remember?"

Denise did lower her voice a fraction. "You would prefer that . . . that frozen bitch to me?" she hissed.

"Careful, Denise. Who knows, you may be speaking of my future countess."

He had spoken to spite her, but his words had the desired effect: Denise gaped at him in astonishment. Taking advantage of her stunned silence, Dominic led her to a chair and procured a glass of champagne for her, then left her in order to seek out the cardrooms. He regretted allowing Denise's waspishness to provoke his temper, but perhaps his savage response had ended any hopes she had of resuming their long-ago affair.

Even without Denise to contend with, however, things were not going at all the way he had planned. Dominic grimaced as he recalled the frustration of the past week. The search he and Jacques had conducted had yielded little results; they had not even come close to apprehending the men they sought.

Nor was his relationship with Brie progressing as he would have liked. He had meant to spend the evening pursuing her and trying to get back in her good graces, but she had been too busy glaring daggers at him to be receptive to any overtures he made. Denise's interference hadn't helped matters, of course, but he had teased and mocked Brie when soft words would far better have served him. Now he would have to exercise every bit of charm he could muster if he wanted her back in his arms. Yet, he meant to attempt it—just as soon as his temper cooled sufficiently.

It was several hours before Dominic returned to the ballroom and spied Brie dancing with the squire's son. She seemed to be having a rough time, for Rupert Umstead was weaving through the steps, nearly tripping each time he stepped on her satin slippers.

She managed to extricate herself from her drunken partner when the music ended, but then Dominic stepped directly in the path of her escape. "My dance, mademoiselle?" he said with a conciliatory smile.

Brie looked up at him uncertainly, torn between her smarting pride and a traitorous desire to be held in his arms again. Pride won out. "I think not, my lord," she replied coolly. "I find I am quite fatigued."

"No doubt, after holding that young puppy up half the time. But I promise not to tread on your toes." As the strains of a waltz filled the room, Dominic captured Brie's hand and pulled her, resisting, into his arms. Brie gasped at his audacity, but not wanting to create a spectacle, she capitulated.

She treated Dominic to an icy silence as they whirled around the floor, but she found it difficult to maintain her distance with the music swelling gently around them. They danced together, perfectly in tune.

Against her better judgment, Brie felt herself relaxing in his arms. When she ventured to look up at her tall partner, the dark glitter in Dominic's eyes held her entranced, and she found herself unable to tear her gaze away.

One by one, the other couples seemed to fade away, till only she and Dominic were dancing together in the enormous ballroom. His arm tightened about her waist, drawing her closer, and Brie caught her breath as her breasts brushed the hard wall of his chest. She trembled, watching as his lips came closer and closer. . . .

Fortunately, the music ended. Yet, Dominic continued to stare down at her, his arms locked about her waist. When he made no move to release her, Brie dazedly looked around and saw that the other couples were separating. "M-my lord," she stammered, twisting out of his embrace.

Recollecting himself, Dominic shook his head as he tried to recover his equilibrium. He had been about to kiss Brie in the middle of a crowded ballroom, for Christ's sake! What kind of strange spell had she cast over him?

More shaken by his encounter with this bewitching beauty than he would ever admit, Dominic took refuge in sarcasm. "You seem to be forever running from me," he said acidly.

His derisiveness stemmed more from a desire to protect himself than any wish to hurt her, but it completely shattered the spell for Brie. She stared up at him for a long moment. Then feeling tears sting her eyes, she turned and fled.

Dominic let her go. He had not meant to snap at her like that, but to pursue her now in order to apologize would only exacerbate the situation and perhaps cause a scandal as well. He would have to give her time to recover before he tried to make amends.

Brie threaded her way blindly through the crowd, wanting to escape the oppressive heat and noise of the ballroom. When a waiter passed bearing a tray of champagne, she seized a glass and drank its contents in one long draught, but it did little to calm her agitation. Seeing that one of the French windows had been thrown open to combat the heat of the chandeliers, Brie slipped through the doors and found herself out on the terrace.

The late winter air was cold and biting against her bare shoulders, but she welcomed the chill. Leaning on the stone balustrade for support, she took several ragged breaths, trying to purge the conflicting emotions that warred inside her. Then after a moment she made her way down the flight of steps to the garden and soothing darkness.

Dominic had seen her leave the ballroom and was debating whether to follow her when Squire Umstead clapped him on the shoulder and began telling him about the sow that had won first prize at last year's fair. Dominic listened with one ear as he kept his gaze trained on the French doors. His eyes narrowed when he saw Rupert Umstead wander out onto the terrace.

The squire followed Dominic's gaze and broke off his story to swear heartily. "There's that damned cub of mine, and I'll wager a pint of my best stout that he's up to no good. Brie Carringdon went out that door not two minutes ago. I had better go after him. He'll only disgrace himself."

Dominic laid a hand on the squire's sleeve. "Perhaps you would allow me. I expect it's my fault Miss Carringdon is out there."

The squire eyed him quizzically. "Quarreled, did you?"

"Something like that."

"It isn't Brie I'm worried about. She can take care of herself. My boy's the one who concerns me. He's liable to get hurt if he gets her dander up. Wouldn't want him challenging a man like you, either. Might get his fool head blown off."

The corner of Dominic's mouth twisted in a grin. "I promise it won't come to that. Accepting challenges from callow youths is not something I relish. They're too likely to get off a lucky shot."

Having seen Dominic's skill with firearms, Squire Umstead chuckled. "Very well, then, go to it, man. I suppose Brie would rather have you save her anyway."

"Perhaps," Dominic remarked dryly, before making his way across the ballroom.

Once on the terrace, he paused to let his eyes grow accustomed to the darkness as he searched the shadows below. Although the golden light filtering out from the ballroom stopped short of the garden, the moonlight was bright enough to illuminate the bare foliage.

Dominic could see no trace of Brie, but as he started down the steps, he heard a woman's cry followed by the sounds of a scuffle, then a slap and a loud grunt. Disquieted, Dominic leapt down the remaining steps and broke into a run.

When he rounded a hedge, though, he stopped short. The shadowy scene before him was not what he had expected. Rupert Umstead lay sprawled on the ground, groaning as he clutched at his groin, while Brie stood over him, hands on hips, fairly spitting in her fury. Dominic found it difficult to repress his laughter as she raged at the unfortunate boy.

"If you think I *like* being pawed, Rupert, you are much mistaken! Go lavish your drunken attentions on someone else. I will not stand for it, do you hear?" Her tirade was accompanied by a stamp of her foot for emphasis.

Still moaning, Rupert pulled himself up to a sitting position, trying to regain his lost dignity. "But I want to marry you," he protested.

"Well, I do not want to marry you! I would sooner marry—" Brie hesitated and Dominic knew she was trying to think of an appropriately vile comparison. He was surprised by the one she chose. "I'd sooner marry that odious Stanton!"

The Umstead boy sniffed indignantly. "I should say so. An earl. Who could compete with a fellow of his rank?"

"Oh . . . , just go away, Rupert. Go away this instant, before I decide to tell your father how badly you have behaved!"

Stamping her foot again with obvious impatience, she pointed in the direction of the house. Dominic stepped back into the concealing shadows as she waited for Rupert to slink away.

When her would-be lover had gone, Brie attempted to smooth her hair and straighten her clothes. Realizing then that the bodice of her gown had been torn by Rupert's lecherous hands, she let out an oath that would have done credit to any of the stableboys in her employ and gave a vicious kick to the trunk of the oak tree nearest her, bruising her foot in the process. When the pain had subsided, Brie collapsed against the oak and buried her head in her arms. It was too much, she thought with a groan. She would find Caroline and leave at once.

She shivered with revulsion as she remembered the feel of Rupert's hands on her breasts. She had not been afraid of him; his drunken pawing had disgusted rather than frightened her. But she hadn't liked him touching her. His hands had been cold and clutching, not at all like Dominic's hands. But at least Rupert's fumbling attempts at lovemaking had proved that she hadn't suddenly become a wanton. It was only Dominic's touch that had the power to arouse her. . . .

When she heard footsteps behind her, Brie thought Rupert had returned to accost her again. She whirled, raising one fist while clutching at her bodice with the other. But the man

216

before her was too tall to be Rupert. Too tall, too dark, and too broad-shouldered. "You!" she exclaimed, backing nervously against the trunk of the tree.

Dominic laughed softly, although he kept a wary eye on her upraised fist. "Yes, my little wildcat. 'Tis the 'odious Stanton' in the flesh. You shall never marry, you know. Not if you treat all your suitors with such violence. Do all your swains receive a similar taste of your temper?"

Not enjoying his humor, Brie tried to slip past him. She would have succeeded but for Dominic's restraining hold on her arm. "Why do you run? I shan't distress you with a repetition of the boy's marriage proposal, not even with the encouragement of knowing you prefer me to him."

Brie was too upset even to retort. "Please, let me go."

Dominic stepped closer, his expression suddenly becoming serious as he bent his head to murmur in her ear. "Mille pardons, ma belle. I don't mean to tease you or treat you harshly. You needn't fear me, either."

His warm breath lightly fanned her cheek, before his warm lips pressed against the side of her throat. Brie shut her eyes, swaying dizzily. "Are you mad?" she asked in a pained whisper. "Or merely intent on making me so?"

"Yes, mad," Dominic murmured, letting his lips roam over her fragrant skin. "Mad with desire. I want you, Brie, more than any woman I've ever known."

Trying to control the overwhelming sensations that were sweeping through her, Brie gave a brittle laugh. "I suppose I should be honored."

Dominic turned her face up to his and touched her smooth cheek. "'Tis I who am honored, cherie," he said softly. "And I most humbly beg your forgiveness for provoking you."

Brie stared up at him as he slowly drew a finger over her lips. It was unfair how he could make her want him, she railed silently. His touch almost melted her determination not to give in. But she knew she couldn't let herself be deceived by his methods. She had to harden her heart against his charm.

Shaking her arm from his grasp, she took a step backward. "I do not intend to be included in your harem, my lord. You already have a mistress who seems more than willing to share her favors. Isn't that enough?"

"Brie," Dominic said patiently, "Denise isn't my mistress. We had such an arrangement once, but that was years ago." Advancing, he successfully cornered Brie against the oak, blocking her escape by placing his hands to either side of her. "Did Denise say something spiteful to you? I assure you she is only jealous."

Wanting to believe him, Brie tried to read his expression. The darkness hid all but the dark gleam in his eyes. "But Lady Denise is eager for you," she pointed out. "I am not."

"Are you sure?" he said huskily, raining light kisses upon her face when she avoided his searching lips.

"Yes, I loathe you," Brie declared, her muffled words carrying little conviction.

Triumphant laughter rumbled deep in his throat. "Show me, Brie," Dominic taunted softly. "Show me how very much you loathe my kisses."

Brie caught the glitter of raw desire in his eyes before his mouth clamped down on hers. She briefly considered struggling—but only until his arms came around her. Then she was conscious of the aching need he was deliberately arousing in her.

This was what she wanted, she realized as his muscular thighs pressed against hers and pinned her against the tree. His chest felt like granite against her tingling breasts, while his lips were hot and insistent, demanding a response. Brie let her arms glide upward to encircle his neck as she opened her mouth more fully to his searching tongue.

Slowly his kisses became more urgent, almost savage. With a harsh groan, Dominic wrapped his arms more tightly about Brie's waist, pulling her against him, as if he wanted her to become part of him. Her senses spinning, Brie surrendered passionately to his embrace.

She was bewildered when a moment later Dominic's hands tightened on her shoulders and he tore his mouth away. He held Brie at arm's length, staring down at her, his own breathing as ragged as hers. Brie shivered as the night air enveloped her. She wanted the warmth of his encircling arms, but when she tried to move closer, Dominic prevented her.

There was a hard edge to his voice when he spoke. "Your reputation will suffer if you are seen kissing in the garden, Miss Carringdon. You had best go inside."

Brie stared at Dominic, not comprehending. She had no idea why he had suddenly become so cold or what she had done to make him look at her with such dislike. She had been willing to submit to him, to give him what he wanted. But then perhaps she didn't know what he wanted. Perhaps he had only intended to humiliate her. Perhaps he had only meant to prove how easily he could bend her to his will.

The pain she felt was more devastating than Brie would have thought possible. Wanting to hurt him in return, she raised her hand to strike him. She nearly managed to slap his face before he caught her wrist in an iron grip.

"Your gown is torn," Dominic said curtly, ignoring her attack. "I advise you go upstairs first and repair it."

Her breasts heaving, Brie stared up at him. Was he deliberately trying to be cruel? "Your concern for my reputation amazes me, my lord," she observed, taking refuge in sarcasm to keep her voice from breaking. "You have never before been so particular."

"Brie, I . . ."

She waited, holding her breath while Dominic seemed to struggle with himself. But then he released her and stepped away abruptly. "I suggest you use the servant's entrance in the rear," he said quietly.

Brie bit down hard on her lip to keep back the sob that was welling in her throat. She gave Dominic one last anguished glance before she turned and fled.

Watching her run blindly down the path, Dominic swore

viciously. He wanted to call her back, to explain. But then what would he say? Sorry, my sweet, but when you so obligingly returned my kisses, you scared the hell out of me?

He hardly understood what had happened himself. He had lost control when Brie had responded so passionately to his embrace. For a moment he had been overwhelmed by a force strong enough to make him tremble. He had felt like a man drowning in a sea of fire—and he had used the only means he knew to douse the flames she had ignited. In his entire life, nothing like it had ever happened to him before.

Brie Carringdon was a witch! A beautiful, damnable witch. He had meant to use her for his own pleasure, but she had turned the tables on him, catching him in her own silken web. Indeed, he was probably only one of countless men who had fallen for her wiles. No doubt she had picked him out long ago as her next victim.

Her next victim?

Needing to cool his fevered brain, Dominic began to pace the garden path. Who was he trying to fool? He knew perfectly well Brie hadn't deliberately tried to inflame his senses. He had been caught for a moment, yes, but she wasn't to blame. Hell, she didn't care what she looked like half the time, dressing like the veriest ragamuffin in boy's clothes. She hadn't the faintest notion what her slender beauty could do to a man.

He was aware of it, though. Devastatingly aware. His loins still burned for her.

Dominic swore again. He should have taken her here in the garden, regardless of the strange feelings she aroused in him, for having Brie once more would be the only way to put out the smoldering fires in his body. She would have known pleasure in his lovemaking, he would have seen to that. And she hadn't been afraid of him this time, he was certain. He had not had to force her responses. She had been his for the asking, willing to give herself completely. . . . But then he had driven her away.

Next time, Dominic promised himself, he would not let her go. Next time he would be better prepared. Now that he was warned, he would be able to guard himself against her bewitching spells.

But what then? he asked himself uneasily. When he had quenched his desire for Brie, would he then be free of her? Afterward, could he more easily deny the fierce attraction he had for her?

A long, long time passed before Dominic slowly followed the path Brie had taken to the house.

Chapter Nine

Brie rose early the next morning and flung herself into a frenzy of activity, seeking to bury her frustration and anger in physical exhaustion. She was determined to banish all thoughts of Dominic from her mind. She rode with the stable hands when they went out at dawn's first light to exercise the horses, then coerced John into accompanying her when she rode out again. When she was suitably numb, Brie returned to the house where she attacked estate accounts till sums whirled in her head.

She spent the afternoon with the estate steward, Mr. Tyler, paying some long-overdue visits to several of her tenants. She had been invited along with Caroline to take tea with Elizabeth Scofield, but she refused to go, having no wish to encounter Lady Denise again.

It was nearly dusk by the time Brie returned to Greenwood. When she was informed by the butler Garby that Lord Stanton awaited her in the drawing room, Brie was astonished. She had not expected even Dominic would have the audacity to face her after his rejection of her the previous evening.

Her first impulse was to flee, but she knew she wouldn't be able to avoid Dominic forever, not if he were truly determined to speak to her. And she would be far safer meeting him in her own home with a houseful of staunchly loyal servants to protect her. Brie took as long as possible to remove her gloves and bonnet and smooth the folds of her blue pelisse. Then, reluctantly, she climbed the stairs to attend her visitor.

She paused at the door, trying to bolster her failing courage. She had a good view of Dominic's back, for he was standing at the window, looking out at the front lawn. Her pulse started beating erratically at just the sight of his tall, well-muscled form. He was dressed impeccably in gray trousers and a matching frock coat. He must have heard her, for he turned as she entered.

Brie decided her best defense was a direct attack. "To what do I owe this unwelcome visit, my lord?" she demanded, keeping a wide distance between them. "I warn you that if you have come to provoke me, I shall call a footman and have you thrown out of the house."

Dominic met her defiant glare with a melting smile—that same fallen-angel smile whose sweetness never failed to affect her. "I don't intend to provoke you, Brie. Just the opposite, in fact. I have come to apologize."

"I expect you are referring to your behavior last night. Well, you may save yourself the trouble. I don't mean to listen to your explanations."

Dominic crossed the room toward her. "I'm not apologizing for kissing you. I enjoyed it too much to regret it. But for everything else I am truly sorry."

"Stay away from me!" Alarmed to see Dominic advancing, Brie took a hasty step backward. She had no faith in her ability to withstand him, should he try to take her in his arms.

When Dominic halted, Brie eyed him warily. "Why do you not visit Lady Grayson? I'm sure she would welcome your attentions."

She had no trouble recognizing the amusement that flashed in his eyes. "Perhaps," he replied amiably. "But Denise isn't available. She left this morning for London. Besides, I prefer your charming company."

"But I do not prefer yours," Brie returned, not admitting

224

her relief that Lady Grayson was no longer in the neighborhood.

She never learned how her sparring match with Dominic would have ended, for their conversation was interrupted just then by Garby's entrance. The butler had an urgent summons from John Simms. "He requests that you come to the stables at once, Miss Brie," he said with an apologetic glance for her noble visitor. "There is a problem with one of the horses."

Brie was grateful for the reprieve. She asked Dominic to excuse her and waited only for his polite agreement before making her escape. She was being a coward, she knew. Then again, John never requested her presence unless it was important.

When she reached the stableyard, she understood at once why John had summoned her. He and several of his men were frantically trying to control a struggling broodmare. The horse was rearing and lashing out with her hooves while the men pulled ineffectually on the lead rope tied around her neck.

Brie was puzzled, for normally Firefly was docile and even tempered. But then she saw the long, vicious slashes covering the horse's body and realized the sleek coat was wet with blood. Brie stared in horror, wondering who would have dared beat a defenseless animal, especially a mare in foal.

Clamping down on her anger, she reached for the rope. "Send everyone away, John," she said quietly.

John sent the grooms scurrying, knowing few people could calm a horse as Brie could, but he stood by as she slackened the rope. She talked softly, till at last the mare ceased fighting and stood trembling under her soothing hand.

"What happened, John?" Brie asked in an outraged whisper. "She's dripping in blood."

He gave a tight-lipped nod. "Aye, she is. The lads found her like that in the north pasture. They had no trouble catching her—she was tied to the fence with that rope. I don't know what stupid fool is responsible, but he must have been mad to do that to a fine animal. The lads had the devil of a time bringing her here."

The mare was obviously in pain, for she kept throwing her head down. John went up to her and gently ran his hands under her belly. "Looks like she's going to foal," he observed. "We'd best take her to a stall so we can watch her. There may be trouble. Can you hold her?"

When Brie nodded, John disappeared inside a small barn—an isolated building that was used to house broodmares and horses recuperating from various ailments. There were only ten stalls, most of which were occupied, but they were spacious and immaculate.

John lit a lantern and spread fresh straw on the floor of the stall, while Brie slowly lead the nervous mare down the aisle. Firefly balked at the door, causing the other horses to snort and whicker at the disturbance, but together Brie and John managed to coax Firefly into the box. They stood silently watching as the mare began to move restlessly in circles. Brie hardly noticed when Dominic quietly joined them.

Seeing the mare kick at her swollen belly, John frowned. "Aye, she's going to have trouble," he predicted. "It's too early for a normal birth. I'll wager the foal's twisted inside her, poor beast. Cleaning the wounds can wait, but she won't have that colt on her own."

"I'll get one of the men," Brie offered, realizing she wasn't skilled enough or strong enough to assist at a difficult birth.

"There's no need," Dominic said. "I've some experience, and more observers would just frighten the mare." Even as he spoke, he was shedding his elegant coat and cravat.

John eyed him skeptically, but then he nodded. "Very well. You're bigger than most of my lads."

He entered the stall and caught the mare, then eased a rope halter over her head. Dominic followed after directing Brie to bring another lantern, some rags, and a sharp knife. She obeyed instantly, returning in time to see the two men wrestle the mare to the floor.

Dominic held Firefly's head while John probed gently for

226

the foal. Shortly, John rocked back on his heels and grunted. "I think we can save it, but it's got to be turned. The forelegs are jammed up tight." Nodding, Dominic told Brie to take his place at the mare's head.

She was glad to be of use. Quickly hanging the lantern on a peg so that light flooded the stall, she sank down in the straw beside Dominic. He must have sensed her anxiety, for he flashed her a reassuring grin as she handed him the knife. Brie gave him a shaky smile in return, before bending over the mare to secure a good grip on the halter.

It was nearly an hour later before the men were able to turn the foal, but to Brie it seemed like an eternity. Her shoulders and back were aching, and in spite of the chill, she could feel perspiration trickling down her forehead and between her breasts. She was a bit queasy as well, for the operation was bloody and extremely messy. She felt a surge of exultation, however, when two spindly front legs finally appeared.

The two men worked frantically to pull the foal from its mother's body. Then Dominic used the knife to cut the cord tangled around its neck before it died of strangulation. When the small body had been safely deposited on the straw, John worked on the mare while Dominic gently wiped the foal clean.

Brie could have cried for joy when the little filly blinked and looked around curiously at her new surroundings, but several times during the next half hour, Brie laughed at the filly's wobbling attempts to stand up.

The mare, although limp from pain and weariness, finally struggled to her feet to accept her new offspring's suckling, while John watched proudly. Brie turned to Dominic to express her thanks, giving him a smile of such brilliant warmth that he was dazzled. It took him a moment, in fact, to understand why John had suddenly shouted in alarm.

When the trainer rushed past him into the corridor, Dominic recognized the ominous crackling sound and the nervous snorting of frightened horses. He leapt to his feet, telling Brie to stay put.

227

As he watched John scurry back down the loft ladder, he swore under his breath. Floating wisps of burning straw and hay followed John's descent, while smoke poured through the open trap door. The loft was on fire, Dominic noted grimly. And the doors at the end of the barn leading to the courtyard were shut tightly when they had been wide open an hour ago. Instinctively he knew they would be locked.

When he applied his shoulder to the doors, he realized they had been deliberately jammed shut. Meeting John's worried gaze, he told the trainer to find an implement to pry the doors open, then turned and quickly made his way back through the gathering smoke to Brie.

She was staring up at the flaming loft. Dominic pushed her back in the stall, sweeping up his discarded coat and cravat as he went. "Take off your pelisse," he commanded, dipping his own coat in the horse's water bucket. Doing the same to Brie's, he handed her his dripping cravat. "Now cover your head with this and stay here until I say differently." Lifting the half-filled bucket, he left her again.

Brie obeyed without protest, for the situation was far too serious even to consider arguing. Already the acrid smoke was making her eyes burn, and she could hear the frightened neighs of the horses above the growing roar of the flames. As a landowner, she well knew the danger of fire. She knew also that it was probably too late to save the barn. The fire had spread so rapidly that it must caught hold of the timbers by now. She only hoped they would be able to save the horses and perhaps the adjacent barns.

She donned her wet pelisse and wrapped the cravat around her head to cover her abundant tresses, then cautiously peered from the stall. The haze was far worse in the corridor. Dominic had closed the loft trap door, but smoke was still seeping through the cracks and flaming sparks were raining down from above. By straining, Brie could see that the two men were still trying to open the huge doors. She bit her lip, wondering if they would all die in a blazing inferno.

A moment later she felt a rush of wind against her face. Realizing the doors had finally given way, Brie closed her eyes and offered up a silent prayer of thanks. When she heard Dominic shout her name, she turned and gathered the new little filly in her arms, then started back down the corridor with her awkward burden.

She was amazed by how intense the heat was. She could hardly breathe, the air was so thick. She coughed, her lungs feeling as if they were on fire as she fought her way blindly through the smoke, following the sound of Dominic's voice.

He saw her first. Grasping her by the elbow, he threw a wet blanket around her shoulders and led her through the open doors into the courtyard. Then leaving her with Jacques, Dominic disappeared into the burning barn again.

Brie stumbled into the coachman's arms, drinking in great gulps of fresh air. She wouldn't relinquish the filly to him, though, and when she had recovered her breath, she carried her precious burden well away from the burning building, depositing the foal on a patch of grass.

She would have returned to the barn then, but she was forcibly detained by Jacques. He captured her arm, telling her very apologetically that his lordship had entrusted him to see to her safety. Brie pleaded, insisted, and even shouted at the Frenchman, but Jacques remained adamant. When she at last realized that he wouldn't let her go, Brie clenched her fists in frustration and turned helplessly to watch the fire.

The household servants had entered the fight to save the main barns. Men and even women were scurrying frantically to and fro, carrying buckets and wetting down blankets. Some had formed lines, passing the buckets up the ladders to the men on the roofs and back again, while others were dousing the walls of the nearest buildings, trying to prevent the flying sparks from taking hold. Only a hundred feet or so of cobblestone separated the burning barn from the rest of the stables. The entire yard was lit with a harsh yellow glow, and Brie could feel the tremendous heat even from where she stood.

Her attention never wavered from the flames. Desperately worried, she bit her knuckles each time a fear-crazed horse came racing through the doors of the burning structure. Both John and Dominic had braved the thick smoke in order to rescue the horses, but she could see no sign of either man.

The roof of the small barn was a blazing inferno when John at last stumbled out. Brie gave a hoarse cry and broke away from Jacques, determined to help. The elderly trainer was coughing so badly that he could hardly stand. Putting an arm around his waist, Brie half dragged him across the courtyard, away from the flames.

"Too . . . much . . . smoke," he rasped between fits of coughing. "Too . . . late. Stanton tried . . . to save . . . Firefly. . . . Couldn't get her out."

Brie felt her heart stop. Dear God, Dominic was still trapped inside the burning building! Knowing she had to try and save him, she began to run toward the fire.

John made a desperate lunge, grabbing hold of her arm and preventing her from moving. "No! 'Tis too late!"

"But he's still in there!" she sobbed, trying to wrench her arm free.

But as John had warned, it was too late. One of the main roof timbers of the barn came crashing down.

Brie screamed, watching in horror as flames filled the doorway. She couldn't believe what she was seeing. Dominic could not have been trapped beneath the flaming wreckage. Not him. Not when she loved him.

The heat of the fire was too intense to allow anyone near, and Brie could only wait, praying desperately that any moment Dominic would appear through the wall of flames. But the fire continued to burn, and there was no sign of him.

At last the entire roof gave way. The resulting explosion was deafening, the flames shooting upward to light up the night sky.

Brie stared in shock at the blazing wreckage. When she

realized that Dominic could not have possibly escaped alive, she sank to her knees, too stunned even to cry. A terrible emptiness burned in the pit of her stomach, and there was a scorching ache in her throat that had nothing to do with the acrid smoke still choking the air.

She hardly noticed when Katherine placed a comforting hand on her shoulder. "You mustn't be upset, Brie," Katherine said gently. "You can build a new barn. Why don't you come inside? Cook has prepared food for everyone, and Garby and Caroline are tending the injured in the hall. No one was hurt badly, thank the Lord, although there were a few burns. You should come into the house and change out of those filthy clothes."

Numbly, Brie looked down at her wet, soot-streaked pelisse. Then she shook her head. Katherine obviously didn't know what had happened to Dominic. Brie couldn't tell her, though. She couldn't put the horrible truth into words. "Please, Katie," she whispered, "I want to stay here. Will you just see to John?"

She was grateful when Katherine left her alone. Still kneeling on the cobblestones, she bowed her head.

After a time, the rain came. It was only a light drizzle, but it was greeted by shouts of triumph by the firefighters, for even though the small barn would continue to burn, the danger to the other buildings had passed. Men would watch through the night, and in the morning they would begin to clear away the charred rubble.

Brie couldn't share their joy. She was too numb to care about what happened to the barns. She couldn't feel the rain either. Icy streams ran down her face and soaked her skin, making her shiver, but she wasn't aware of it. After a while she began to cry, softly at first, then in racking sobs.

How ironic, she thought. Dominic's death had made her realize how much she loved him. In spite of her efforts to resist him, the magnetic attraction she had always felt for him had developed into something stronger, something more vital. But

231

even loving him was ironic. He probably would have laughed to see her crying for him, mocking her pain as he had everything else.

Tears were still streaming down her cheeks when a tall figure loomed before her. It looked so much like Dominic that Brie covered her face with her hands, thinking she must be seeing a ghost.

But the hard hands that gripped her shoulders were real enough, and the familiar masculine voice was Dominic's. "Are you hurt?" he asked urgently, pulling Brie to her feet.

Brie stared up at him, not comprehending. Dominic looked worse than a London chimney sweep. His clothes were torn and filthy, and he was covered with grime as black as his hair. But even with his face streaked with soot and his dark hair plastered down by rain, Brie had never seen a more beautiful sight.

When Dominic sharply repeated his question, she shook her head. "I . . . I thought . . . you were dead," she said in a hoarse whisper.

Dominic laughed and pulled her into his arms. "Almost, but I'm hard to kill."

Relief flooded through her. He was alive! He hadn't died in the fire. Brie clung to him, burying her face against his wet shoulder. It was a long moment before the old suspicions came rushing back, and then she drew away, her eyes flashing. "You beast! You let me think you were dead!"

Giving her a smile so tender that Brie felt her heart melt, Dominic drew her back into his arms. "I'm sorry, ma belle," he said soothingly. "I would have come sooner had I been able, but I was unconscious for a while. Jacques said he almost despaired when he couldn't revive me, but the rain finally woke me."

Looking around her, Brie suddenly realized that the Frenchman had disappeared. "But however did you escape?" she asked.

"The far side. Your steward—Tyler, I think his name was—

took an ax to the wall and cleared an opening. I managed to get the mare out just before the loft collapsed. That's the last I remember."

"But you weren't injured?"

"My lungs smart like hell, but I'll recover."

Searching his face, Brie shuddered. "You should not have gone back in there."

"I had to," Dominic said simply. "Otherwise you would have done something idiotic like try to save the horses on your own—foolish girl." Yet he took the sting out of his words by lowering his mouth and brushing her lips gently with his.

When he lifted his head, Brie was trembling again. She gazed up at him wordlessly, loving the sight of his harsh, aristocratic face.

Dominic gave her another of his angelic smiles and pushed a dripping russet curl back from her face. "You know, someone tried to kill us, or me . . ." He broke off, his expression hardening. In all likelihood, the arsonists were the same men who had been following him, but this time Brie and John had been exposed to danger. His unknown enemies meant business, and this latest incident made it imperative to discover who and why.

Swearing silently, Dominic turned to survey the flaming wreckage of the barn. "I called this afternoon to offer my help in apprehending your neighborhood vagrant," he said dryly.

Brie felt suddenly shy. "And I thought you meant to torment me again," she murmured, looking away.

Dominic caught her chin in his hand and turned her face toward him. His eyes searched hers for a long moment, before he bent to capture her mouth with tender savagery.

His kiss lasted only a brief while. Then, as if he had suddenly become aware that he was embracing her in plain view of dozens of curious grooms and household servants, Dominic released her. "You had better get out of this rain," he said curtly, his tone once more holding a mocking edge to it.

"But what about you? You will come inside and get warm,

won't you? Those wet clothes—"

"I've dry ones at the Lodge. I must leave you now. Your servant, mademoiselle." Stepping back, he bowed with exaggerated formality, then turned abruptly on his heel and strode away, leaving her standing there.

Brie stared after him, wondering what had caused such a sudden change in his manner. But as she watched Dominic disappear around the corner of the nearest barn, she smiled to herself. Somehow his brusqueness didn't upset her as it had yesterday. She didn't understand him, true, but he was what he was—and she loved him. Perhaps one day . . . but there would be time enough for that tomorrow.

It was only after Brie had returned to the house that she remembered the hundred questions she had wanted to ask him. Dominic seemed to know more about the fire than he had been willing to share. And what was more, she had let him leave without even thanking him for saving her horses.

The rain continued throughout the night and the fire gradually burnt itself out, but the cold gray light of morning brought little cheer to the inhabitants of Greenwood. A pile of ash and charred timbers lay where the barn had once stood, vividly reminding them all of how close they had come to disaster.

A great deal of work needed to be done before the stable's routine could return to normal. All training exercises were cancelled for the day, but the horses that had escaped the flames had to be found and cared for, and the buckets and blankets used to fight the fire had to be cleared away. And there still were the regular chores of cleaning stalls and feeding the animals.

When these tasks were accomplished, Brie ordered everyone to rest. She herself slept for a few hours, and when she woke shortly before noon, she dressed warmly, wanting to tour the stables before beginning the Herculean task of cleaning up after the fire.

The house was quiet, but Brie stopped by her cousin's room to check on her. Seeing Caroline sleeping soundly, she smiled. The girl had reacted surprisingly well to the events of the previous night, taking charge of the household and organizing the staff while Katherine saw to the needs of the injured. Obviously, Caroline wasn't the empty-headed romantic that everyone believed.

The rain had stopped by the time Brie left the house, but gray clouds hid the sun, making the soot-washed stableyard look desolate. Brie shuddered when she saw what was left of the small barn, remembering how the smoke and cinders swirled about them. How narrowly Dominic had escaped a horrible death! He had played down the danger to keep her from worrying, but she wasn't blind. Someone had tried to murder them, and she intended to find the culprit and see him punished.

She spent the next hour touring the barns and carefully checking each horse for injury. She was pleased to see the new filly eagerly nursing at Firefly's side. Brie had tended the mare's wounds herself that morning, and the whip-marks seemed to be healing. With luck, only the deepest slashes would leave scars.

When Brie finished her inspection, she turned her attention to interviewing Greenwood's large staff, using John's office as a headquarters. She was grateful the office had been spared. Barns could be rebuilt, but that particular room with its old desk and hard wooden chairs held many pleasant memories for her. As a child she had spent innumerable hours there with her father and John, learning the intricacies of running a training stable.

She questioned everyone who had been present during the fire, but when she had finished, she was no closer to finding the arsonist. Her suspicions were partially confirmed, however; a piece of wood had been driven between the doors and the metal latchbar, indicating that someone really had intended to murder them. She also discovered one of the lads had seen two strange men leaving the stableyard shortly before the fire broke out—and they had been carrying guns. The boy had followed them a short distance across a field, but had returned when he saw the light from the fire.

Brie was sitting at the desk, pondering her next step, when John joined her. "You don't appear to have slept much," she chided, noticing the weary slump of his shoulders and the dark circles under his eyes. "You ought to rest after all you did last night."

"I'm all right. Lungs still hurt a bit, but it will pass. Besides, that young lord did most of the work. Fine man, that Lord Stanton." John looked at her closely, and Brie found herself trying not to blush. She felt self-conscious whenever Dominic was mentioned. Changing the subject, she told John what she had learned from her interviews.

He frowned when she had finished. "I don't like seeing you become involved," he remarked. "You shouldn't be concerning yourself."

Brie gave him a puzzled look. "I think you must have taken leave of your senses, John. I am already involved. Someone destroyed part of my stables and tried to kill us. Do you expect me to do nothing?"

"I think you should let Lord Stanton handle the matter," he said stubbornly, not meeting her eyes.

"Stanton? Nonsense! I am perfectly capable of handling the affairs of this estate without his help. The local authorities—"

"He has already spoken with the magistrate."

"I beg your pardon? How do you know what Stanton has or hasn't done?"

John sighed. At times Brie could be too headstrong for her own good. "Lord Stanton was here earlier, while you slept. He informed me of the steps he was taking to apprehend the criminals."

Brie sat back in her chair, challenge written all over her face. "I see. And what else did his lordship tell you? Was I to be kept in total ignorance?"

John shifted uncomfortably in his seat. "He sent for the Bow Street Runners and some of his own people. They should arrive in a few days, but in the meantime, he plans to conduct his own investigation. He said he feels responsible for what happened last night. He intends to pay for the new barn, too. Told me to send the bills to his man in London. He also told me not to let you become involved."

"The devil he did!"

"It makes sense to me, Miss Brie. He doesn't want you to go about unattended, either. Said he doesn't think you are in any danger, but suggested that you carry a weapon whenever you leave the house."

"That," Brie said, rising, "is the first sensible thing I've heard. I will carry a weapon, but I am more likely to use it on him!"

It was very late when Dominic dismounted and turned the nag he had been riding over to an astonished Patrick Dawson. Dominic's rough clothes and his strange flea-bitten horse, were enough to make Patrick scratch his head in puzzlement. Julian's reaction was similar, but he waited until his guest had changed clothes and been served a late supper in the dining room before asking what the devil Dominic was up to.

Dominic sipped his wine, leaving much of the food on his plate untouched as he answered. His voice was tinged with sarcasm, an indication of his weariness and frustration. "I've been searching for the men who set fire to the Greenwood stables. The clothes were a disguise of sorts. I can hardly track down a pair of arsonists dressed in the height of fashion. And, I'm sorry to say, there is now a horse in your stable that doesn't deserve the name."

"Did you find any sign of the culprits?"

"One or two, but the tracks lead nowhere." Dominic's jaw hardened. "Damn it, I know Germain is behind this! I don't have a shred of evidence, but my instincts tell me he planned this in case he lost our duel. He must have arranged for his henchmen to follow me here, and when they realized they weren't going to get the deed, they decided to take what they could get. That fire last night was no accident."

"I know," Julian replied. "Brie told me." The previous evening he had been astonished when Dominic had come home drenched to the skin and looking as if he had been dragged through a char pit. Julian had also been dismayed to learn the Greenwood stable had been set on fire, and had called there twice that day to offer his help. The first time he had been told Brie was resting. The second, he had found her seething with anger.

"So, now what do you do?" he asked, postponing his discussion of Brie.

Dominic gave a weary sigh. "Keep looking until I find them, I suppose. You're aware that a message arrived from Jason today? He says Germain has recovered from his delirium but that he's leaving the pleasure of interrogating Charles to me. By the way, Jason also writes that Lauren was delivered of a healthy baby girl."

Julian was pleased to hear about the child and he said so, but he was more interested in what Dominic planned to do about the attempts on his life. "Do you mean to go to London then?" he asked.

"I haven't decided. I could probably learn more from Germain now that he's well enough to talk, but it would save me some trouble if I could catch his agents here. Besides," Dominic added softly, almost to himself, "I hardly think it appropriate to leave for London now, with the way things are."

Julian wasn't quite sure what Dominic's cryptic remark meant, but he let it pass. Mentioning the call he had paid on Brie, he relayed her message to Dominic. "She was furious with you, Dom. She said in no uncertain terms that you should mind your own affairs and that she would handle the matter herself."

Dominic gave Julian a hard glance. "I credited Brie with more sense. She realizes, I hope, that the men who set fire to her stables will not stop because their first plan went awry."

Seeing Dominic's set expression, Julian sighed. It was inevitable that his two strong-willed friends should clash. Ever since he had introduced them, he had felt undercurrents of tension in their relationship. It was a pity, though. Brie and Dominic could have been made for each other. But Dominic was determined to believe that women were weak and foolish and untrustworthy, and Brie had competed in a man's world too long to accept masculine domination meekly. She bristled like a hawthorn hedge whenever her ability was challenged.

In this case, however, Julian agreed with Dominic. A man, particularly one of Dominic's experience, was better suited to deal with killers. Not that he would share his opinion with Brie, but he was worried she might do something foolish just to prove she didn't have to obey Dominic's orders.

"She knows they are murderers," Julian answered. "But the point is, she thinks you have no right to take charge. She doesn't understand why you are doing what you're doing. I'll say it again—you ought to tell her what's going on."

Dominic pressed his lips together in a tight line. "I don't want her to become involved."

"But isn't it possible that these men might try to hurt Brie in order to get to you?"

"Possibly, but not likely. Brie and John weren't intended to be victims. They just happened to be present."

Julian frowned. "All the same, it concerns me. Brie often rides alone, and if she were to come across those villains, well, they might not hesitate to abduct her or some such thing, especially now that they've shown their cards."

"You're being a bit melodramatic, don't you think?" Dominic replied, refusing to admit that the thought worried him as well.

"I would hardly call murder melodramatic. Besides, whoever they are, they couldn't know that you don't care a whit about Brie's welfare."

Dominic's hand tightened around his wine glass. "I care," he said, his tone curiously flat.

Julian gave an exasperated snort. "Then why the devil don't you tell her what you've told me? Let her know the facts? That's the only way Brie will listen to reason."

Slamming down his glass, Dominic glared at Julian. "Because I haven't the time or the inclination to pamper the pride of a spoiled beauty! One who is foolish enough to become involved in a situation that is well over her head, at that." When Julian remained silent, Dominic stood up abruptly. "Hell, tell her what you like. But whether she agrees or not, I will act as I see fit." With that, he turned on his heel and strode angrily from the room.

Leaning back in his chair, Julian pursed his lips in thought. He found his friend's reaction highly curious. Dominic had never been one to brook interference—and certainly not outright defiance—from a woman. But he rarely let a woman move him to anger. The violence he had shown just now was not in keeping with the cool, impervious cynic Julian knew.

Ah, my noble friend, Julian thought smugly, your actions betray you. In spite of what you pretend, you are taken with Brie. And that rankles, doesn't it? To be attracted to a woman who refuses to fall for your practiced charm? But beware, Dominic, lest you end up presenting your cold heart to her on a platter. After all, are you so different from the rest of us poor mortals?

Dominic had been gone several hours by the time Julian rose the next morning. Still concerned, Julian rode over to Greenwood, intending to give Brie a much needed explanation. When he arrived, however, he was informed by the lad who took his horse that Miss Brie had ridden out early and was not expected back before noon.

"Was she alone?" Julian asked, knitting his brows.

"Yes, milord. She didn't want anyone with her. But she was carrying a pistol. A body had better think twice before bothering her."

Truly worried now, Julian requested to see Caroline and was shown into the breakfast room where she was still eating. "Where is your cousin?" he asked impatiently, not wasting time with polite greetings.

"Why, she is out riding," Caroline responded in surprise. "But any of the servants could have told you that."

"I didn't think Brie would be so foolish. Doesn't she know there are men at large who may very well be killers?"

"Of course she knows! Who could forget it after the fire? Brie said—and I perfectly agree with her—that it would serve no purpose to sit at home cowering while some monster beats her horses and burns down her barns. Indeed, I wouldn't be surprised if Brie has gone in search of them."

"What?" Julian said incredulously. "And you let her go?"

"Well, what, may I ask, did you expect me to do? Lock her in the dungeon? We don't have a dungeon!"

"For God's sake, Caroline, be quiet. I must think." Ignoring her indignant expression, Julian raked a hand through his hair and began to pace the floor. "At least Brie had enough sense to take a weapon. I only hope she won't be afraid to use it. Well," he said, stopping to glower at Caroline. "Don't just sit here staring. Get me some writing materials."

His tone was so serious that she decided not to argue. She returned a moment later with paper, pen, and ink.

Julian hastily scribbled a message and handed it to her with directions to have it delivered personally to Dominic. Then he picked up his hat and strode to the door.

Caroline ran after him. "If you're going to look for Brie, I'm coming with you."

Julian halted in mid stride, nearly causing a collision when he turned. His frown was menacing as he grasped Caroline by the shoulders. "No you won't, young lady. This is no task for a woman. If you so much as budge from this house, I will personally give you a sound thrashing. Do you understand?"

"Y-yes, Julian," she stammered.

He glowered a moment longer, then astonished her by grinning. "I only wish Brie were half so compliant. I'll be back as soon as I find her."

When he had gone, Caroline stood there staring until she suddenly recalled his instructions. Obediently then, she turned to give the bellpull a tug and proceeded to dispatch a footman with Julian's message.

Dominic had just returned to the Lodge when the note was delivered. Recognizing Julian's handwriting, he quickly perused the message, not having to read it a second time to realize that Brie had deliberately ignored his warning not to get involved. It read: *Brie has gone after your quarry. Am going to search for her. Suggest you do the same. At least she knows how to shoot.*

Dominic swore under his breath, calling Brie any manner of uncomplimentary names—the tamest of which was 'idiotic little fool.' Promising himself when he found her he would wring her lovely neck, he lost no time in calling for his stallion. He also enlisted Jacques' aid in the search, ordering the Frenchman to cover the territory south of Greenwood, while he took the north.

Once he was on his way, galloping across the countryside, Dominic found himself growing increasingly anxious. If something should happen to Brie he would have only himself to blame. He had intended to tell her about his suspicions when he had called on her two days previously, but then the fire had made the situation far more serious. Wanting to get on with the search, he had not taken the time to explain.

That had been a mistake, Dominic admitted to himself. He had wanted to keep Brie out of it, but he should have told her his plans, as Julian had first suggested. He could well imagine her angry reaction when she learned he was controlling her servants. She was too proud to meekly accept his orders without reason. But now she had deliberately gone in search of danger, and she could be anywhere within a ten-mile radius.

When Diablo showed signs of laboring under the fast pace, Dominic slowed the sweating horse. He had been heading toward a distant stand of birch trees where he had discovered signs of habitation the previous day. The underbrush not only had been disturbed, but a charred spot indicated where someone had recently set up a campfire. The remains of several rabbits had been buried nearby, suggesting that the poachers had been there for more than one meal. Dominic was inclined to believe that the forest visitors and the men who had ignited the Greenwood fire were one and the same, and he meant to start his search for Brie there.

The morning seemed unusually quiet. Even Diablo's steel-shod hooves made little noise, muffled as they were by the damp earth. In the silence, Dominic had no trouble hearing the shot that rang out, or the woman's scream that followed.

He felt his heart lurch. Whirling the stallion in the direction of the shot, he dug in his heels.

At that moment Brie was wishing she had heeded Dominic's warning. She had not intended to search for anyone. She simply had refused to be confined at home and had gone riding. With half of Greenwood's servants out looking for the arsonist, however, she had expected to be quite safe. Taking her father's pistol had merely been a precaution.

She had ridden a good distance, letting Jester have his head, when she came to a shallow stream. The horse started misbehaving then, balking at the water and refusing to enter the woods on the far side. Brie had difficulty controlling the skittish animal, particularly since she was wearing skirts and riding sidesaddle, and she had further difficulty once they were among the trees. When they finally left the woods behind, Brie was in a fine temper. Seeing a field spread out before her, she urged the bay into a gallop, meaning to work off his fidgets.

They were in full stride when a loud retort sounded from the far end of the meadow. Jester suddenly stumbled, then fell hard, pitching Brie headfirst and startling a cry from her. She landed on her shoulder, doing several violent somersaults before coming to a halt.

The fall jarred her entire body. Dazed, she pushed herself up and shook her head to drive away the ringing echo in her ears. Her left ankle was throbbing, but otherwise she thought she was unhurt.

The man who had fired the shot was moving toward her, but she only had eyes for her injured horse. Jester lay a few yards away where he had fallen, blood streaming from his chest. Brie could tell from his thrashing movements that he was badly wounded, and his feeble efforts to rise brought tears to her eyes. She wiped them away as the gunman approached, however, realizing that this was no time for sentiment.

The man was a stranger to her. He was short and heavyset, and his rather ugly face sported a nose that had been broken at least once. He was grinning broadly, an unpleasant smile that made Brie want to shudder.

Slipping her hand in the pocket of her riding jacket, she felt for her pistol and breathed a sigh of relief when her fingers closed around the smooth handle. She kept it hidden beneath a fold of her skirt, waiting to see what the man would do.

Crooked-nose walked over to the wounded horse and savagely prodded the bay's neck with the butt of his flintlock. Giving a grunt of satisfaction, he turned to Brie. "Too bad about yer horse, ain't it?"

Brie had no difficulty believing this was the man who had beaten Firefly and burned her stable, for she could see the enjoyment he was deriving now from tormenting a wounded animal. Nauseated by his cruelty, Brie inhaled a deep breath. "You obviously don't care for horses, do you? I assume you were the one who tied up my mare and whipped her till she was covered with blood."

244

The man eyed Brie speculatively. "Liken it was me. Then again, it could 'ave been me brother. Martin likes to 'urt things, 'e does. It gets 'im excited." His gaze travelled insolently over her body. "Martin'll be right glad to see you. 'E ain't never 'ad a lady before. Bet you'll scream good an' loud."

Recognizing the lecherous look in his eyes, Brie shuddered. If that leer was any indication, Martin would not be the only one who had his way with her. Crooked-nose would rape her first before turning her over to his brother. Brie began to feel frightened, even knowing she had her pistol for protection. "Who are you?" she asked uneasily. "What do you want with me?"

"Freddy Boulter's the name, but it ain't you I want. I want that Stanton fella. You'll be the one what brings 'im to me. I seen you and 'im riding together—an' I seen you comin' outa that cabin that day. Liken you'd been spreading yer legs for 'im."

Brie felt her cheeks burn, but she tried to ignore Boulter's crudity. "What do you want with Lord Stanton? What has he done?"

"I don't bleedin' know what ee's done, an' don't care, neither. I been paid to do a job. I mean to kill 'im."

Hearing his cold-blooded admission, Brie felt her stomach churn. "I don't expect your employer would approve of your methods," she said shakily. "Locking us in the barn wasn't very clever. And you didn't succeed in killing Lord Stanton."

The man shrugged his heavy shoulders. "'E got lucky. But I mean to try again. I'll bet 'e'll come along right fast when 'e finds out we got you."

He took a step toward Brie. "Now, little lady, jest you 'old yer tongue. Yer be coming with me."

Brie abruptly drew the pistol and aimed it at Boulter. "I wouldn't be too sure of that, Mr. Boulter," she replied quietly. "I think you will be the one coming with me—straight to the local magistrate. Any number of people will be pleased to see you in prison."

Seeing the elegant, highly polished weapon in her hand, Boulter froze in his tracks. Brie tightened her grip on the pistol. She was tempted to put a bullet through this horrible man, but she didn't think she could stomach actually shooting him.

"Put down your gun, Mr. Boulter," she indicated the flintlock he was still holding. "It won't do you much good in any case, since you didn't reload."

Boulter hesitated, regarding Brie in indecision. He had seen women who were handy with a knife before, but never a lady with enough nerve to use a gun. This one, however, was far from fainting or having hysterics. Even though her hand was unsteady, she looked as if she meant business. She might very well shoot him. But his alternative wasn't pleasant, either. He would be sent to Newgate where he would hang. He decided to take his chances with the lady.

Swinging the flintlock around, he threw it straight at Brie, then charged her, trying to catch her off guard. Brie was in an awkward position to dodge the weapon, but she managed to deflect it away from her body with her arm. She couldn't do the same with Boulter. He landed directly on top of her, hitting her with the force of a battering ram.

Brie felt the pistol discharge in her hand, felt Boulter's heavy body give a violent jerk. Then lights exploded in her head and she tumbled into oblivion.

Dominic had reached the meadow a few moments before, but when he saw Brie sitting on the ground, conversing with the man who apparently had just shot her horse, he abruptly reined in his mount. She was still alive and he wanted her to stay that way. He would be risking her life if he charged across the meadow, for he could see the gun Boulter was holding and knew it still might be loaded. He also knew he couldn't hope for accuracy with his own pistol at that distance. His only chance to rescue Brie safely would be to circle around the field, using

246

the trees for cover until he could get within shooting range and draw the man's fire. Even as he turned his horse, though, he saw Boulter lunge and heard the gunshot.

Dominic couldn't tell who fired or if Brie had been hit, but dread gnawed at the pit of his stomach as he galloped across the meadow. He reached her in a matter of seconds, leaping from his horse to kneel beside the two still figures.

When he rolled the man's body away and saw all the blood, Dominic thought for one heart-stopping moment that Brie might be dead. The front of her habit was drenched with red, and her face was pale and lifeless. Carefully, Dominic ran his hands over her body, but he found no wounds. Then he noticed the pistol still gripped in her hand and he let out his breath slowly.

A quick inspection of the dead man revealed a ragged hole in his chest where the ball had penetrated. Dominic murmured a silent prayer of thanks and set about the task of reviving Brie.

Loosening her jacket had no effect, so he gently slapped her face. Brie moaned, stirring slightly, then suddenly started to struggle. Dominic had trouble holding her down. "Stop fighting me, damn it! Brie, look at me."

She froze, hearing his voice, then slowly fixed her gaze on his face. Dominic could see fear in the blue-green depths.

She anxiously searched Dominic's face, clutching at his shoulders as she remembered the moment before she had blacked out. "What happened . . . to Boulter?" she whispered hoarsely.

Gently Dominic gathered her in his arms. "If you mean the fellow who was attacking you, he's dead." When her eyes filled with pain and she turned her head away, he cupped her chin and forced her to look at him. "No, Brie, it is better to talk about it. Listen to me. It isn't easy to kill a man, and your feelings are only natural. But you acted in self-defense. Would you have preferred that he kill you instead?" When she took her head, he tenderly brushed a curl back from her face. "Tell me what happened," he urged.

"I . . . I was riding across the field. . . . Jester . . . Jester is dead, isn't he?"

The trembling of her lips wrung his heart. "I haven't had a chance to look at him yet," he said grimly.

"He shot Jester . . . and he admitted setting the fire. Dominic, that man deserved to die."

She gazed up at him, her eyes pleading with him for understanding, and Dominic involuntarily clenched his fists. Wanting to comfort her, he drew Brie more closely against him.

Haltingly then, she recounted her conversation with Boulter, answering all of Dominic's questions. When she had finished, she closed her eyes and buried her face in his shoulder. "I didn't mean to kill him," she said, shuddering.

A surge of tenderness flooded Dominic's heart. He stroked her tumbled hair and murmured meaningless words in her ear, feeling a protectiveness he had never before felt for a woman.

Yet, all the while he was silently scoffing at himself. Brie hadn't needed his protection. She had proved her courage. Indeed, she had been braver than many of his acquaintances would have been in similar circumstances. She was shaking uncontrollably now, but she was only feeling the shock of having taken a human life.

Giving a sigh, Dominic brushed his lips against her hair, then held her away. "Come, ma belle, we had better get you home. Did you break any bones? I hope not, for we have but one horse."

Brie tried to smile. "Nothing . . . is broken, but I'm afraid I must ask for assistance. I'm not quite up to mounting a horse by myself at the moment."

With Dominic's help, Brie got to her feet, but the movement made her dizzy. She swayed once before her knees buckled beneath her.

Dominic caught her as she fainted. Scooping her up in his arms, he carried Brie to his horse, but he was saved the difficulty of mounting while holding her, for Julian rode up just then.

Julian sucked in his breath when he saw Brie's blood-stained clothes. "My God! Is she . . . ?"

"No," Dominic replied tersely. "Only bruised a bit. The blood gave me a fright as well, but it belonged to him." He tossed his head in the direction of the dead man.

"Who's he?"

Dominic gave Julian an impatient frown. "I'll explain everything, but later. Now I just want to get Brie home." When Julian held out his arms to take Brie up with him, Dominic shook his head. "I'll see to her. I got her into this mess. You can take a look at that horse of hers. Perhaps he's not dead and we can save him."

He mounted his stallion, settling Brie securely in front of him, but before he left, Julian asked what should be done with the corpse.

Dominic's mouth curled sardonically. "I don't give a damn what you do with him, so long as that horse is alive when I get back. If Jacques heard the shots, he will be here shortly. He'll know what to do. I'll return as soon as I can."

Turning Diablo then, he urged the stallion forward.

The next few hours were difficult ones for Dominic. When he reached Greenwood, he was greeted with cries of alarm by the entire household. Brie's elderly companion was particularly shocked. Her face turned white when she saw the bloody riding habit.

By the time the doctor had examined Brie and given her a sedative, Dominic was glad to make his escape. He returned to the meadow to find Julian and Jacques hard at work on the wounded horse.

Julian showed Dominic the ball they had extracted from Jester's chest. "It didn't hit any organs, but there's a nasty hole, Dom, and he lost a lot of blood. It would be much easier to put him away. He isn't worth saving anyway."

"I don't expect Brie feels that way," Dominic replied dryly.

"I know. But if infection doesn't set in and kill him, the horse will have to have food and shelter. How do you propose to do all that?"

Dominic's answer was a bit complicated, and several hours later Julian was still shaking his head. It had taken ten men to load the horse on a wagon and carry him to the Lodge stables where Dominic had designed a contraption to keep the injured animal from thrashing about and reopening the wound. A heavy net was suspended from the rafters by a series of ropes, then stretched under Jester's frame, holding him upright and immobile while a special harness supported his head and neck.

Afterward, Dominic and Julian stood watching as Jacques applied a foul-smelling poultice to the raw wound and changed the bandages. Patrick Dawson was also present, for he was to care for the injured horse.

When Dominic had inspected the coachman's handiwork, he drew Julian aside. "That should draw the heat and keep infection down. If the horse can live through the next week, he'll make it. I'd rather you didn't tell Brie about this, though. If it doesn't work, she'll only be disappointed."

Julian slanted an inquiring look at his friend. "Why are you going to all this trouble? I thought you didn't even like Brie."

Dominic became curiously preoccupied with a speck of lint on his sleeve. "Perhaps I've changed my mind."

Julian grinned, saying nothing, but his expression held such amusement that Dominic, for the first time in his life, felt himself close to blushing. He turned and directed a glance at the wounded horse, remembering the agonizing moment when he thought Brie had been shot and his fierce relief afterwards.

"Yes," he said slowly to himself. "Perhaps I have."

Chapter Ten

Struggling up from the depths of a terrifying nightmare, Brie woke, gasping for breath. When she realized she was safe in her own bed at Greenwood, her terror subsided, but the images of blood and death still remained to haunt her. She lay trembling in the darkness, her heart pounding, her skin feeling cold and clammy.

What had happened to her? Her brain felt foggy, her body stiff and sore. And why was her left ankle bound with strips of linen? She remembered falling from her horse, but the rest was a collage of murky images.

As she rubbed her sore ankle, she gradually recalled the events following her fall: her talk with Boulter, the recoil of the pistol in her hand as she fired, Dominic's concern. She had regained consciousness shortly after he had brought her home, and she remembered Dominic carrying her up to her bedroom. Then Caroline had helped her into a nightgown and she had been made to suffer the attentions of the doctor when all she had wanted to do was sleep. As soon as he had gone, though, she had slipped immediately into a deep slumber. Recalling the vivid dreams that had awakened her, Brie shuddered. Her bedroom was so cold. . . .

Sitting up, she saw that the fire in the grate had died to a dull glow. After lighting the candle on the bedside table, she eased herself from the bed and carefully tested her wrapped ankle. She was surprised to find she could move easily, despite her aches and bruises. Her robe was lying at the foot of her bed, and she drew it on. Still shivering, she slowly made her way to the hearth and stirred the coals, letting the warmth from the glowing embers drive the chill from her trembling body.

Once she was warm, she became aware of other discomforts: her throat was parched and she was beginning to feel hunger pangs. The hour was past midnight, Brie realized, glancing at the clock on the mantle. She decided against ringing for a servant, for she didn't want to wake the household when she was capable of finding her way to the kitchens, even in the dark.

But the house wasn't totally dark, Brie discovered as she moved quietly along the hall. A wall sconce had been left burning at the top of the stairway. And not everyone was asleep. Brie was halfway down the stairs when a figure detached itself from the shadows below and moved toward her.

The unexpected sight startled her, the dark presence bringing to mind her horrible encounter with Boulter. She couldn't stifle her cry of alarm, even though she swiftly covered her mouth with her hand. She stood paralyzed in the middle of the stairs, tightly gripping the polished banister, the light from the lamp outlining her night-clad body.

The shadowed figure moved into the light, giving her a clear view of ebony hair and dark, aristocratic features. When she recognized Dominic, Brie let out her breath in a rush. "What are you doing here?" she asked in a rasping voice, relief making her question sound like an accusation.

Dominic was coatless, his white shirt opened at the neck exposing an expanse of hard-muscled chest. He placed one booted foot on the bottom step and looked up at her, a smile playing at the corners of his mouth. "I see your brush with death didn't soften your tongue any," he observed dryly. "But I could ask the same of you. Why aren't you asleep?"

"I was hungry."

He raised a dark brow, then laughed softly. "Go back to bed, I'll bring you something."

When she remained where she was, not obeying, Dominic felt a surge of irrational anger steal over him. Brie looked so damned virginal, standing there with the collar of her white nightgown buttoned up to her throat. The soft woolen wrapper she wore did nothing to hide the curves of her slender body, though, and the golden glow of the lamp behind her cast a flaming halo about her head, setting her mantle of flowing tresses on fire. She was a vision of seductive innocence, one that made his loins ache.

Yet, he knew her appearance of innocence was deceiving. He remembered quite vividly how Brie had responded to him that day in the cabin and then again in the garden. And now, when he finally had another opportunity to make love to her, he found his hands tied. He couldn't take advantage of her now, not after the experience she had gone through with Boulter. He was that much of a gentleman, at least.

But still he felt angry. Dominic bounded up the stairs and swept Brie off her feet, cradling her in his arms. "For once you'll do as you're told," he said gruffly, ignoring her surprised gasp.

The contact only made matters worse for him, and as he carried Brie back to her bedroom, Dominic found himself swearing silently. It was impossible to ignore the feel of her soft body pressed against his chest, and he knew if he held her much longer, he wouldn't be able to let her go. When he reached her room, Dominic set her on the bed none too gently, and roughly disengaged the arms she had wrapped about his neck.

Brie stared up at him in amazement, too surprised even to protest his callous treatment. But she found her tongue when Dominic turned to leave. "Must you always resort to physical violence?" she asked tartly. "Does it give you pleasure to behave so brutally with defenseless women?"

Dominic turned back at the door to give her a piercing look.

His jaw was clenched tightly and his eyes glittered with an emotion Brie found hard to read. But then his mouth twisted in a ghost of a smile. "Since when have you ever been defenseless?" he said softly.

When he had gone, Brie let out her breath slowly. He was wrong, she thought despairingly. She *was* defenseless when it came to him. He only had to touch her and she wanted to melt. She was still quivering from the contact with his hard body. But even though his presence was unsettling, it was reassuring as well. She had no idea what Dominic was doing at Greenwood, but she was glad he was there. She didn't want to be alone with her nightmares.

When Dominic returned a short while later, Brie was sitting up in bed with the covers pulled up to her chin. Her eyes widened when she saw the amount of food he had scavenged from the kitchens: a half loaf of bread, a large slab of cheese, slices of cold ham and pheasant, several pieces of fruit, and a bottle of wine.

He set the tray on the bedside table and silently served her, then poured a glass of wine for himself and left her to eat in peace. Wandering restlessly about the room, he intentionally studied his surroundings in order to keep his thoughts on something besides the beautiful young woman in the bed behind him.

He could have imagined Brie in this setting, Dominic realized without surprise. Her bedroom, done in soft blues and greens, was feminine and fresh but uncluttered. The furnishings seemed appropriate somehow—graceful but not fragile, with a subdued richness that quietly proclaimed wealth and beauty. He felt oddly at ease here.

As he stood before the fire, watching the leaping flames, Dominic felt the tenseness in his muscles begin to relax. He had full control of himself when he at last returned to Brie's side. After refilling both of their glasses, he drew an armchair close to the bed and sat facing her, his long legs stretched before him as he leisurely sipped his wine.

Brie had been watching him surreptitiously, but she looked away when she felt his gaze settle on her. She finished her meal, then drained her glass for courage before repeating her earlier question about why he was here.

"I'm leaving for London tomorrow," Dominic replied. "I thought—"

"So soon?" Brie exclaimed, her eyes fixing to his face. When Dominic's eyebrow shot up, she bit her lip. "I . . . I mean, won't it be dangerous for you?"

"Concerned for my welfare? I'm touched."

His mockery annoyed her less than the gleam of amusement in his eyes. "Of course not!" Brie snapped, her own eyes flashing. "You can go to the devil for all I care."

A slow grin spread across his lips. "Do you know your eyes turn green when you're angry?"

Brie almost choked. He was baiting her again, and obviously enjoying having her at such a disadvantage. "You still haven't explained why you are here, my lord," she said stiffly.

He studied her for a moment before answering. "Your cousin gave me a room for the night," he replied, taking a sip of wine. "I thought you might be in need of moral support when you woke."

Brie frowned. "*Caroline* let you stay? What about Katherine?"

"I suppose you mean the elderly woman who was hovering over you like a broody hen? I imagine it will be tomorrow before she stirs. The doctor gave her a sedative to calm her nerves. She was a bit overwhelmed when she saw the blood on your jacket. Incidentally, I thought it best to tell everyone I killed Boulter. It should spare you some unpleasant questions, not to mention the good opinion of the neighborhood. I've explained to the magistrate that I found Boulter trying to attack you, but that I fired the shot. Otherwise, the story I gave was the truth. I doubt if there will even be an inquest."

"Th-Thank you," Brie stammered, knowing the words were entirely inadequate to express her appreciation. By taking the

255

blame for killing Boulter, Dominic had protected her reputation as well as spared her further drama. It had been very considerate of him.

He flashed her a wry smile. "I'm not so sure I deserve your gratitude. Not only was I too late to help you with Boulter, but I find now that I'm a veritable hero for rescuing you. My praises are being sung all over the district. But I would be obliged if you would let me handle this business from now on."

Brie nodded fervently. Then a shadow darkened her brow and she dropped her gaze. "I . . . I dreamed about him," she whispered. "It was horrible."

"You'll forget it after a time," Dominic said gently. "How do you feel, other than that?"

"A bit weak . . . and my ankle hurts. But you haven't told me about Jester. He's dead, isn't he?" She didn't really expect a contradiction so she wasn't surprised when Dominic remained silent.

He took the empty plate and glass from her and placed them on the tray. "Let me see your ankle," he commanded. Without waiting for permission, he sat beside Brie and pushed the covers aside, exposing her injured foot. He ignored her sharp intake of breath as he grasped her leg and carefully began to unwrap the cloth that bound her ankle.

Brie bit her lip as Dominic examined her injury, experiencing acute agony. But it wasn't her bruised limb that was causing her such discomfort. It was the touch of Dominic's warm fingers on her bare calf. His unintentional caress made her pulse quicken and her skin suddenly feel overheated. Brie shivered with warmth, trying to will the sensations away. When Dominic recommended that she leave off the bandage, the casualness in his voice made her want to hit him. Didn't he notice the unnerving effect he was having on her? Was he totally immune to the hot little flames that were shooting up her leg and making her entire body throb?

Then Dominic looked up and met her gaze, and Brie knew by the dark flames in his eyes that he wasn't as unaffected as he pretended to be. She felt his fingers tighten around her ankle, and as she stared at him, the sound of the crackling fire seemed to fade away.

Returning her gaze, Dominic swallowed hard. She was too damned desirable, sitting there in her prim nightgown, with her hair streaming around her shoulders, reflecting the dancing light of the fire. The covers had slipped to her waist, and he couldn't prevent his eyes from sliding downward to devour the thrusting mounds beneath the soft woolen robe. He ached to take her in his arms, to crush those soft breasts against his chest.

Brie felt the bold caress of his gaze like a physical fondling. She shuddered, and nervously wet her trembling lips with her tongue. Slowly then, hesitantly, she raised a shaking hand and reached out to him.

Dominic jumped as if he had been burnt. He stood up quickly, muttering a brusque goodnight, and turned to leave. He was almost to the door before Brie spoke, her voice a mere whisper. "Dominic . . . don't go. Please . . . I don't want to be alone."

Her plea touched his heart, but he knew if he stayed one moment more, he couldn't refrain from taking her. Torn between common sense and his own desires, he rested his forehead against the wooden panel of the door. A low sound that was half groan, half growl escaped his lips. "I'm not a bloody saint, Brie. I'm a man, with a man's needs. And I want you. But then, you know that, don't you?" He gave a soft, derisive laugh. "And here I stand, like a stupid fool, damning your lovely eyes and wishing that you weren't so desirable." He paused, then added with quiet anguish, "Damn you to hell, you little witch. What kind of spell have you woven around me?"

Not sure how to reply, Brie watched Dominic in silence. He was struggling with himself; that much was obvious from the way he was clenching his fists. But *why?* She didn't think it ws because of any moral principles that he seemed suddenly determined to observe the proprieties. A man of his stamp would not have any qualms about making love to her, not when she had practically issued him an invitation. And he had said he wanted her. So what was stopping him?

Brie bit her lip, wondering what she should do. Dominic's sudden shifts from savage to tender and back again were as confusing as they were frustrating. But he had to care for her a little. He had risked his life for her the night of the fire, and she hadn't imagined the gentleness he had shown her then; or yesterday in the meadow when she had needed him to hold and comfort her. But now he was acting almost as if he were afraid to touch her—

But perhaps he was afraid. Perhaps his rebuffs had not been deliberate cruelty. Perhaps he simply didn't want to be attracted to her, to become attached to her. That she could understand. For years she herself had been afraid to love, afraid to be exposed again to the pain of giving her heart where it wasn't wanted. But it wasn't fear that drove Dominic, Brie surmised. It was something stronger, something far more bitter. Hatred, perhaps?

She was only guessing, but her intuition told her she was right. And there only one response she could give. Slipping out of bed, Brie went to him, her arms encircling his lean waist as she pressed herself against his broad back. Tenderly, she rubbed her cheek against the soft linen of his shirt, feeling the hard muscles beneath. "It is surely a spell, Dominic, but I am caught in it as well. Please," she begged softly, "don't leave me."

Dominic turned slowly, as if not daring to believe what she was saying. Placing a finger under her chin, he tilted her head back so he could look into her eyes. They were soft and liquid and incredibly lovely. Dominic sucked in his breath. "I won't be content with only a kiss or two," he said hoarsely. "And if I stay, it will be for the entire night."

Brie nodded wordlessly. Dominic hesitated a moment longer, searching the fragile features of her face for any sign of the fear she had once shown him. When he found none, he slipped an arm about her waist, catching her close so he could feel her soft breasts against his chest.

As he slowly bent his head, Brie parted her lips in breathless anticipation and braced herself for the impact. But then Dominic's mouth came down upon hers and she lost the ability to think. Desire flowed between them like a warm current, flooding Brie with sensations that left her weak and trembling.

When his tongue slid between her teeth, delving deeply, she clung to him in surrender. She no longer cared that he was an experienced rake who knew how to ply his skills to his own advantage. She no longer cared if he had kissed a hundred other women in exactly this same way. The taste and smell of him was intoxicating, filling her, making her yearn for more of him. She pressed closer, wanting to give herself completely.

She was vaguely aware of Dominic's practiced hands stroking her back, of his husky voice whispering her name as he spread flaming kisses over her face. She could feel the moist heat of his open mouth as he nuzzled at her throat. Moaning softly, she tilted her head back to allow his lips better access.

Her passionate response set him on fire. With shaking fingers, Dominic relieved her of her wrapper, then her nightgown, sliding the garments down over her shoulders and letting them fall to the floor. Stepping back, he let his gaze range her full length. He was tantalized by Brie's naked beauty. Her slender, silken limbs and high, firm breasts were made for a man's caress—*his* caress. Her skin gleamed pale and golden in the candlelight, and he felt a fierce desire to touch and taste every inch of her.

As if he could no longer wait to have her, Dominic swept Brie up in his arms and carried her to the bed. Laying her down gently, he pressed her shoulders back against the soft pillows. Yet now that the moment was at hand, Dominic found he wanted to draw it out, to linger in its sweetness. Taking his time would only heighten the pleasure of making love to her.

He undressed slowly, keeping his eyes on Brie, savoring the view of her lovely body. She was beautiful, with her glorious hair cascading over the pillows, her smoke-darkened eyes heavy-lidded with desire. A sweet ache filled him as he thought of what was to come.

Caught up in similar emotions, Brie wasn't aware how intently she watched as Dominic removed his shirt. She gazed at him hungrily, admiring the magnificence of his shoulders and bronzed chest, thinking how much his movements resembled the sleek, sinuous grace of his stallion.

Her eyes widened perceptively when Dominic slid his breeches down over his narrow hips; the sight of his fully erect manhood made her catch her breath. She knew no fear, though—not even when Dominic stretched his long length out beside her on the bed. She wanted to be in his arms, to feel his hard, muscular body pressed against hers. She wanted to belong to him, to become part of him. She gazed at him expectantly, holding her breath.

Dominic propped himself up on one elbow and drew a finger down the smooth column of her throat to the hollow between her breasts. He could feel the rapid beat of her heart against his palm as he splayed his fingers. With tantalizing slowness, he let his hand wander over the swelling curves, caressing her satin-smooth skin, stroking softly. Brie closed her eyes and shuddered. This delightful torment was not what she had expected, but Dominic showed no inclination of stopping.

He aroused her nipples to diamond-hard points, pinching gently and rolling the aching buds between his fingers until Brie had to bit her lip to keep from moaning out loud. When he bent to kiss the tips of her breasts, she gasped with pleasure, arching wantonly against his hot mouth. His tongue brushed a taut peak, erotically teasing the sensitive flesh and making Brie writhe. Blindly she reached for him, curling her fingers through his dark hair, wondering if she would survive Dominic's tender assault.

He languidly laved each nipple, setting her nerves on fire with each flick of his tongue as he expertly tutored her in the art of love. And when he had stimulated her senses to a feverish pitch, he slowly slid his hand down to caress the insides of her thighs and the softness between. Brie quivered as his fingers gently explored, but she no more wanted to stop him than she wanted to stop breathing. She wanted to be stroked and caressed by that bold hand, wanted him to put an end to the aching need he aroused in her. She was trembling by the time he raised his head, and her skin was flushed with heat.

"Please . . . ," she whispered, pleading with him to continue. Urgently, she wrapped her arms around Dominic's neck, pulling his head down, seeking his lips.

His gray eyes glittered in triumph. Obligingly, he clamped his mouth over Brie's, driving his tongue deeply into her honeyed recesses.

Brie surrendered willingly to the sweet fierceness of his kiss, parting her lips ardently under his. She clung to him, oblivious to everything except his touch and the longing she felt for him.

Hot blood surged through Dominic's veins as he felt her fiery response. His lips twisted hungrily against hers, ravaging, taking, giving back again. When he could no longer resist the urge to possess her, he positioned himself between her parted thighs and entered her carefully, fusing their bodies together.

Brie whimpered as his throbbing maleness filled her. When she arched against him, Dominic nearly lost control, but he savagely clamped down on his body's urges. "Slowly, cherie," he murmured against her mouth. "We have all night." Lowering his lips to her quivering breasts once more, he withdrew from her slowly, then thrust into her again, beginning a rhythm that was calculated to arouse her totally.

Dominic made love to her slowly, exquisitely. Again and again, he stroked her with his hardness, thrusting deeply, then drawing away, deliberately prolonging the ecstatic torture.

His erotic attentions drove Brie into a frenzy. She wrapped her legs around his iron-hewed thighs, grinding her hips against his in an attempt to ease the intense ache that was making her whole body throb. But her efforts brought no relief. Dominic continued his unhurried movements while his mouth made a leisurely meal of her breasts.

Sobbing now, Brie clutched at his shoulders, her hands urging, pleading. But he only captured her wrists and clamped them above her head. She could only writhe helplessly beneath him, waiting for the moment when he chose to end his rapturous torment.

Only when Dominic had driven her to the brink of mindless passion did he raise his head from where he was feasting on her breasts. "Look at me, Brie," he said hoarsely. "I want to see what I do to you." At his command, her eyelids fluttered open, and he could see how dark and slumberous her eyes had become. The pupils were wide and dilated, but the irises were a smokey forest green.

Dominic took her again then, swiftly and fiercely, greedily watching her expression as she began to lose control.

Brie surged against him, clinging to him in desperation. She was drowning; she was falling; she was rocketing to the stars. She cried out Dominic's name, her nails digging into his hard flesh as spasms of delight shot through her body.

Her impassioned cry was captured by Dominic's burning lips, and when he felt her violent tremors, he lost the iron control he had been holding on himself. He groaned, feeling his own muscles grow rigid as a fierce urgent ache suddenly exploded up through his body.

They recovered slowly. Their passion spent, they lay limply entwined, their breathing gradually returning to normal.

Dominic moved first, lifting himself on his elbows to relieve Brie of some of his weight. Brie merely lay where she was, throbbing with warmth, enjoying the heavy feel of him and the warm dampness of his skin.

When she at last floated back to full consciousness, it was to find Dominic gazing down at her with tenderness. Her own eyes were soft and languid as they searched his face. "I . . . I never knew anything could be so wonderful," she murmured.

Laughter rumbled deep in his chest as he brushed a damp curl from her cheek. "Nor I, my vixen," Dominic replied softly. "Nor I."

He delayed his withdrawal to nibble on her ear, then carefully eased his weight from her. Rolling on his side, he pulled Brie against him, nestling her in the curve of his body. When he had drawn the covers up over them, he lay there holding her, wondering at the strange contentment that had stolen over him.

The warmth lulled Brie into a doze, but sleep eluded Dominic. Absently he fingered one of her burnished curls, breathing in the soft fragrance as he tried to make some sense of his feelings.

He was surprised at the intense passion he had aroused in her, but he was more surprised at himself. He had expected his desire to subside once he had satisfied his body's needs, but here he was, holding her tightly, wanting to keep her close always.

Always?

Ridiculous, Dominic told himself—and impossible, besides. Brie had spirit, wit, beauty, everything he could want in a mistress, but while she might have derived as much pleasure from their lovemaking as he had, she would never consent to such an arrangement. She would be offended were he even to suggest it. And what did he want with a little firebrand like Brie anyway? She was an infuriating vixen—beautiful, certainly— but infuriating.

He still wanted her, though. That much was certain. She stirred his blood as no other woman ever had. He would probably grow tired of her after a time . . . but not yet. Dominic smiled to himself, feeling his desire kindle anew.

Brie woke to the pleasant sensation of Dominic's hands caressing her body. Drowsily, she turned and wrapped her arms around his neck, lifting her face for his kiss. When he possessed her mouth, she could sense the urgency of his passion. She parted eagerly for his invading tongue and kissed him back as he had taught her to do—deeply, invitingly.

She was surprised when a moment later Dominic lay back

and pulled her on top of him. Brie looked at him questioningly.

"I know how much you enjoy riding astride," he said, his gray eyes gleaming at her.

Blushing, Brie traced a pattern on his bare chest with her forefinger. "Who could refuse such a fine mount, milord?" she replied with brazen impudence.

Dominic grinned and curled his hand behind her neck, drawing her lips down to meet his, letting her silken hair spill over them both in a rippling mantle.

For a long while no more words were spoken. When the heat of their desire had mounted to a feverish pitch, Dominic's stroking hands slid down Brie's back, over the soft curves of her buttocks. Holding her hips, he lifted her up, positioning her above him.

Brie sucked in her breath when he impaled her on his heated shaft, but she arched her back instinctively, wanting more of him.

He began to move then, thrusting deeply inside her, his rhythm slow but sure. Brie followed, tentatively at first, then with more confidence, and it was only a short while before she was gasping. Her fingers tightened on Dominic's shoulders as a sweet piercing throb began to radiate from her very center. Closing her eyes, she gave a guttural moan that was half sob, half cry.

The primitive sound inflamed Dominic. Grasping her hips, he began a relentless, driving rhythm, watching with hungry satisfaction as Brie's head fell back in surrender. He wanted her to discover the depths of her own passion, wanted her writhing with need.

His sweet-savage movements at last sent her over the edge. He felt the shattering ecstasy that rocked her body, felt her rigid, quivering response. Only then did Dominic allow himself one final fierce thrust that ended in wild, surging pleasure for himself.

Chapter Eleven

He left before the dawn. Unable to sleep, Brie lay in bed, watching the gray morning light banish the night's shadows. She already missed Dominic's warmth, but her expanded knowledge of womanhood had given her something to ponder.

She knew now what the poets meant when they wrote about love and desire. Several times during the night she had tasted passion in the fullest sense, and she had found it a breathtaking experience. Dominic had satisfied her unnamed desires beyond her wildest imaginings. Remembering the feel of his hard, driving male body, the heavy pressure of his loins against hers, Brie felt a warm blush steal over her skin. She hugged her pillow to her stomach, quivering with joy and remembered pleasure. How glorious it had been to be held in Dominic's arms, to surrender to his embrace.

But it was more than just physical desire she felt for him. The longing was in her heart as well. She didn't regret last night. She had been proud that he had wanted her, desired her. Desire—not love. Yet. But perhaps in time Dominic might come to love her.

Determinedly, Brie ignored the thrill of anticipation that thought engendered. She would not let herself dwell too specifically on her future with Dominic. He was leaving today, and although he had promised to call this morning, it would be at least a week before she would see him again in London, if even then. She had learned very little about his plans when they had lain awake last night talking. Dominic had not divulged what he meant to do about the threat on his life, but he had intimated that the business might take him out of the country for a time.

Her own departure for London was planned for the following Friday. Each year at Katherine's insistence, she spent several weeks in town, replenishing her wardrobe and attending the various entertainments the season offered. Katherine would have liked her to choose a husband from among the many gentlemen she met, Brie knew, but she had never found any man who could induce her to risk her heart again. Yet she had often made contacts that benefited her training stables, and that, as much as the enjoyment she derived from the brief visits, kept her going back each year. This trip she would also be taking Caroline home, and since Julian intended to return to his house in town, he would act as their escort.

For a moment, Brie considered moving up the date of her departure, but she quickly discarded the idea. She would place no demands on Dominic, create no ties except those that developed naturally. *And if they didn't develop?* She shied away from the question. It was enough now to savor her new experience, her love. She had never felt so intensely alive or eager to begin a new day.

She needed a bath, though, Brie thought with a wry smile. Dominic's masculine scent still clung faintly to her skin, and her thighs were sticky with the proof of his passion. She also needed to straighten the room. The bedclothes were in a wild tangle and her nightwear was strewn all over the carpet. It was very obvious that something out of the ordinary had happened, and while she herself was not terribly disturbed by her wanton behavior, she knew Katherine would think it scandalous.

When Brie could safely assume the household was stirring, she rang for a maid and ordered hot water for a bath. When she was immersed in the tub, she relaxed back against the rim,

etting the heat soothe her sore muscles. After the emotional
nslaught of the past few days, it was good to dwell on nothing
ut pleasant thoughts. The water felt sensuous against her
kin, evoking memories of Dominic's hands and lips. Brie felt a
remor run up her spine as she remembered his tantalizing
aresses. They had made her gasp with pleasure, while his
urning kisses had left searing trails on her flesh. . . . Brie
rought herself up short. She simply could not let herself dwell
n such things. She would be blushing all day long.

She made herself concentrate on the task of washing her
air, then the rest of her body, and only after the water had
rown quite tepid did she leave her bath. She was drying her
hick tresses before the fire when her tranquility was disturbed
y Katherine's entrance.

Surprisingly, though, her companion's anxious concern
idn't irritate her as it once might have done. She meekly
ubmitted to Katherine's probing inquisition and then
utifully agreed to spend the day doing nothing more
trenuous than reading. After breakfast, she found herself
nsconced in the drawing room with a book and Caroline for
ompany.

Brie quickly discovered that her powers of concentration
ad deserted, her, however. The same printed lines of her book
ept reappearing and her mind kept wandering dreamily.
aroline, too, was a distraction. The girl obviously suspected
what had happened last night, for twice Brie looked up to find
herself being regarded speculatively.

Being the object of such intense scrutiny annoyed her. Her
feelings were too new to be subjected to Caroline's romantic
conjectures. The next time she found herself being watched,
she snapped at her cousin, saying she would prefer solitary
confinement to Caroline's plaguesome presence.

Caroline obligingly turned her attention to her needlework,
but a smile played on her lips. "I beg your pardon, Brie," she
replied serenely, "but I find it odd that you have not turned a
single page in half an hour. Perhaps a light novel would be

more to your liking." Brie started to retort, but just then Garb announced Lord Stanton.

"Show his lordship in, by all means," Caroline ordered with irritating calm, while Brie panicked. What would she say to him? What did a woman say to a man who just a few hours before had shared the intimacies of her bed?

Brie hardly knew where to look when Dominic entered the room, but she was immediately aware of the sheer magnetism that seemed to emanate from him. When she finally found the courage to meet his eyes, her heart did a violent little somersault in her chest, for Dominic was smiling at her—that sweet, melting smile that always turned her limbs to honey. It was all she could do to keep from gazing at him like a moonstruck schoolgirl.

But their meeting really was not as awkward as she had feared. She was at least able to manage an outward show of calm when Dominic greeted her, and his casual attitude when he asked how she was feeling did much to put her at ease. He expressed his regret that he had been called away to London then turned to speak to Caroline, giving Brie time to compose herself.

She wasn't required to contribute much to the conversation either. The banter that ensued between Dominic and her cousin surprised her, though. Caroline seemed to have reached some sort of understanding with him, Brie decided as she listened to the girl's artless chatter.

Dominic stayed only a short while, but when he took his leave, he requested the honor of calling on the two cousins when they arrived in London.

Brie extended her hand to him in farewell, wishing it wouldn't tremble so. "But of course, my lord," she said, trying to keep her voice even. "After the events of the past few weeks life here may seem rather dull without you. Although I fervently hope there will not be quite so much excitement when we next meet."

His warm grin made her heart flutter. "Vixen," Dominic

murmured softly as he brought her hand to his lips. When his tongue lightly brushed her knuckles, Brie was reminded so vividly of the passion they had shared that she gasped.

Hearing her sudden intake of breath, Dominic released her hand, but he stood looking down at her for a long moment before turning and striding from the room. Brie let out her breath slowly. Never before did a week seem like such an eternity.

Brie had known Katherine would be shocked to learn about her affair with Dominic, but Dominic's visit that morning had repercussions even Brie hadn't forseen.

At the same moment Dominic was saying farewell, Katherine was leaving the house. Having satisfied herself that Brie was recuperating, she had planned to call on a tenant's sick child and had ordered the tilbury brought around.

She saw the elegant travelling coach drawn by four magnificent bays standing in the drive, but beyond noting the impressive crest on the side panel, she paid no particular attention to the carriage or its driver. She had almost reached her own vehicle when she heard a man gruffly exclaim in French, "Mon Dieu! Could it be? Madame Briggs!"

Hearing the name she hadn't used in nearly twenty-five years, Katherine turned slowly, afraid of what she might find. The coachman had jumped down and was waving for a groom to hold his horses. When Katherine realized who he was, she took an involuntary step backward, all color draining from her face.

It had been nearly a quarter of a century since she had last seen Jacques, but she had no trouble recognizing the burly Frenchman. He had changed little since then, except perhaps to grow a little broader at the girth. When Katherine had known him, Jacques had been a groom on the Valdois estate, while she had been companion to Lisette Durham and governess to Lisette's daughter Suzanne.

The memories came flooding back, bringing a wave of pain so intense that Katherine might have fallen had not Jacques

grasped her frail shoulders in support. When the faintnes
passed, she realized the coachman was speaking to her in rapi
French. She shook her head, not understanding. "Je ne vou
comprends pas," she managed to say in the language she ha
not spoken for years.

Jacques switched to heavily accented English, surpris
momentarily making him voluble. "To find you here! I coul
not believe my eyes when I saw you! It is fate, non? You worl
here, then? You are in the employ of Mademoiselle Carring
don? Me, I have met her."

Katherine nodded once or twice, letting Jacques talk on
while she recovered from the shock of seeing him again. He
grinned at her, gesticulating with his hands. "Mon Dieu, it ha
been many years, madame. We have grown much gray on the
head since that time. But it makes my heart glad to find tha
you are well. You go away so suddenly from France. But you
are yet Madame Briggs? You have not remarried?"

She shook her head, not having the strength to explain tha
she had resumed her maiden name upon returning to her
homeland and was now known as Katherine Hewitt.

Jacques didn't question her answer, but tapped his broad
chest with his fist. "Me, I never marry," he said proudly. Then
his tone changed so suddenly that Katherine flinched. "But
what of la petite mademoiselle, Suzanne Durham?"

His contempt for Suzanne was apparent, for his face
darkened and his lip curled when he said her name. Katherine
closed her eyes. What should she say? Jacques blamed
Suzanne for the death of the Comte de Valdois, as many did.
But it had all happened so long ago. There would be no point in
protesting that the girl had been innocent, useless to explain
why she and Suzanne had fled France for the safety of England.
Better to leave the past buried, Katherine thought with a
shudder. "Suzanne Durham died several years ago," she
whispered at last.

Jacques nodded solemnly. Then his brows drew together in a
thoughtful frown. "Peut-etre . . . that is why I think I see

ademoiselle Carringdon before. She has the red hair also, the
me as Madame Lisette."

Katherine's age-lined face paled once more. "I expect it is
erely coincidence," she said hurriedly before Jacques could
llow his line of thought. "Tell me, what are you doing here in
ngland?"

Jacques seemed surprised by her question. "Surely you did
ot think I would desert Monsieur Dominic?" It was
atherine's turn to look puzzled. "Monsieur Dominic,"
cques said patiently. "The comte's son. Do you not
member him? He was but a boy then, but his life was in
anger. It was not safe for the *aristos*, you understand? So I
me with him to England, soon after you disappear. He has
own to be a fine man. The comte would have been proud of
is son. Now he has the English title and I am his coachman."

"His coachman," Katherine repeated, her voice faint.

"Mais oui. Ah, Lord Stanton comes now," Jacques said as
is tall, dark-haired employer descended the front steps.
Pardon, but I must leave you. It was good to see you again,
adame—although I think I have brought you unpleasant
emories. But the past is the past," he added with a Gallic
rug. "Au revoir. Perhaps we will see each other again, non?"

He left Katherine standing by the tilbury and resumed his
lace in the box. When Dominic had climbed into the coach,
cques whipped up the bays and skillfully maneuvered the
ehicle around the turn and down the gravel drive.

Katherine stared blindly after the disappearing coach, her
ce chalk white, her arthritic fingers convulsively gripping
er walking cane. The man who had brought Brie home the
revious day was the son of the Comte de Valdois, the son of a
an she had once feared and hated!

Katherine could not remember making her way to her
edroom, but she found herself huddling in front of the fire, as
its warmth could drive away the chill that had invaded her
ged limbs. She was still trembling with the shock of her
iscovery. Philippe Serrault's son was now Lord Stanton—the

same Lord Stanton who had shown such a marked interest in Brie recently.

Katherine stared into the flames, seeing only the ghostly images in her mind. Why had she not felt any premonitions of danger? She had heard the neighborhood gossip about Stanton, but his surname had never been mentioned. Even so, she should have seen the strong resemblance he bore to the comte. Did he even know of the connection between his late father and Brie's family? Perhaps not. He had been a mere boy when the nightmare had ended with the deaths of two people. But now it seemed that history was repeating itself. . . . Indeed, that explained why Brie had been acting so strangely of late. She had been bewitched by the fatal Serrault charm.

Giving a moan, Katherine buried her face in her hands. Surely the fates could not be so cruel. "My poor Lisette," she whispered in anguish. "My poor sweet innocent. I warned you, but you paid no heed. And now your granddaughter . . . with his son. I won't let him hurt her, Lisette. I could not save you, but I will save Brie. She will not suffer your fate. Somehow, I will see to it."

The following week was an extremely trying one for Brie. Never before had she felt such a strong urge to escape her home. Caroline's secretive smiles irritated her, while Katherine's dire warnings of the evils of London nearly drove her to distraction.

The change in Katherine was puzzling. Overnight, she seemed to have aged ten years, a look of pain replacing the usual sadness in her eyes. She had astonished Brie by adamantly refusing to take part in the preparations for the trip to London. But even though Brie could tell something was troubling her elderly companion, no amount of cajoling could make Katherine disclose what it was.

"Why this sudden dislike of London, then?" Brie finally asked in exasperation. "A month ago you were insisting that

272

not miss the season, and now you want me to cancel the trip after I promised to accompany Caroline. There must be a reason." When Katherine refused to answer, Brie stubbornly declared she would go, with or without her companion.

For Dominic was in London, and Brie discovered that his absence only intensified the longing she felt for him. How absurd it was to pine after a man, she thought crossly. And yet, how pleasant to recall the wonderful moments they had shared. Her emotions continually oscillated between despair and excitement. She found herself constantly wondering what Dominic was doing, experiencing a stab of jealousy whenever she pictured him in another woman's arms, and a flash of fear whenever she remembered that someone had been trying to kill him.

She was worried about Katherine's strange behavior, though. Wanting to discuss the matter, Brie went in search of John Simms. She found him at one of the small paddocks, watching Firefly and the new little filly.

John looked up as she approached. "Nothing wrong with that one," he said critically, pointing to the frolicking youngster.

Brie smiled, grateful that John at least hadn't changed. He was still the same quiet-spoken, thoroughly reliable man she had always looked up to like a father. She stood beside him for a time, observing the horses in companionable silence.

"John," she said at length, "do you have any idea what is troubling Katherine? She's upset about something, but I can't get her to talk about it. She just keeps repeating that I shouldn't go to London. Why, I can't imagine, for she has always said I spend too much time buried in the country."

He was silent for so long that Brie thought he might not have heard her. Glancing at him, though, she realized he was considering the question carefully. Finally, he cleared his throat. "Well, Miss Brie, I'm not certain, but I expect she's worried about losing you."

"Losing me? Whatever do you mean?"

John squinted up at the sun, looking embarrassed. "Katie's getting on in years. It would be hard on her if you were to go away."

"But she's coming with me. And it won't be forever. A month at most."

"I'm not talking about your trip to London." He cleared his throat again. "What I mean to say is that a lady is expected to be with her husband, and when you are married—"

"Married! And just who am I supposed to marry?"

He eyed her reprovingly, as he had whenever she had pulled a mischievous prank as a child. "Come now, Miss Brie, I've known you since you were a babe. I can tell when something's afoot. You've been acting like a skittish colt lately, and that young lord hasn't been much better. He's right taken with you. I'd wager a year's salary there's something between you two."

It was Brie's turn to look embarrassed. "That doesn't mean that he wants to marry me," she said in a small voice, her fingers nervously twisting a button of her spencer. "Or that I want to marry him."

John shrugged. "Well, now, he's a fine man, Miss Brie. Reminds me of a horse I once knew. Strong, proud animal. Wild as the devil himself. Wouldn't let anyone near him, till one day, this little girl came along and broke him to the bit, gently as you please. Surprised us all. Remember that, Miss Brie?"

Brie flushed, recalling the incident. When she was ten or so, her father had bought a new stallion that no one dared to ride. Against Sir William's express orders, Brie had climbed on the animal's back and proceeded to tame him. Remembering her father's reaction—rage mingled with pride in her skill—Brie laughed self-consciously. "Surprised? Papa was furious with me for riding him. But you can hardly compare Lord Stanton to a horse."

"I don't know about that," John shook his head slowly. "People aren't so different from horses. They need patience

274

and understanding . . . a firm hand sometimes, a loose rein others. I'd think about it carefully, Miss Brie. Your father would have been proud to have Stanton for a son."

Brie did think about it, but she had none of John's confidence about her future. Nor could she objectively view her relationship with Dominic. She would toss restlessly in her bed each night until she fell asleep, and then she would dream of him. In her dreams, Dominic would take her in his arms and make love to her till she thought she would die of happiness, but once or twice her fantasies turned to nightmares, filled with hatred and fear. Brie would wake, gasping for breath, still feeling the strangling pressure of strong fingers around her throat. It left her with a sense of foreboding that she found hard to understand and even harder to dispel.

Brie's relationship with Dominic was the subject of concern in yet another quarter, for Caroline was still determined to bring her cousin and the rakish Lord Stanton together.

Caroline had never learned precisely what had happened the night Dominic stayed at Greenwood—and she had wisely refrained from asking Brie about it—but she could tell *something* was different. Brie had positively glowed the next morning, and Lord Stanton had smiled at her in a way that was unmistakably intimate, his cool gaze softening whenever he looked at her. Caroline, who was no stranger to courting rituals since she had grown up with three older sisters, had no trouble recognizing the possessive interest in his eyes.

She spent several days contemplating what else could be done to further Brie's cause, but she was still dwelling on the vexing problem at the end of the week—even when she was supposed to be playing chess with Julian.

"The devil take it, Caroline, can't you keep your mind on the game?" Julian demanded as he neatly checkmated her defenseless queen.

Startled, Caroline looked up from the chessboard. "I beg your pardon, Julian. I suppose I am worried about Brie."

"Yes?"

"I . . . I think she is in love with your friend, Lord Stanton."

"That doesn't surprise me. Dominic can charm the birds out of the trees if he puts his mind to it."

Caroline eyed Julian curiously. He didn't seem disturbed to have a rival for Brie's affection, for he was casually rearranging the playing pieces. "But I thought you were in love with Brie," she said doubtfully.

A smile curved his lips. "I was, once. A strong case of calf-love, I've come to realize. Luckily Brie had the good sense to turn me down."

"Then you wouldn't mind if Brie married Lord Stanton?"

Julian shot her a disapproving glance. "This is hardly a suitable subject for us to be discussing, don't you think?"

"I don't see why not. We are her friends, and I for one am concerned for her happiness. Lord Stanton is said to be a rake and a womanizer and—"

"You aren't even supposed to know of such things."

"Well, I do! And I think it's horrid that girls are supposed to be blind to what goes on around them."

Julian tried to repress a grin at her sudden earnestness. "I expect the gossip about Dominic is greatly exaggerated. He just doesn't care what people say about him."

"Then you ought to help me."

"Help you? Help you do what?"

"Why, help me help *them* make a match of it, of course." When Julian laughed out loud, Caroline glared. "I don't see what you find so amusing."

"Caroline," Julian said patiently as he attempted to control his humor, "Dominic wouldn't thank me for interfering in his affairs, or you either for that matter."

"But we must do something!"

"I've already warned him not to trifle with Brie. If I say any more on the subject, I'll have to back up my words with pistols at dawn." When Caroline's eyes widened, Julian leaned back in his chair and crossed his arms over his chest. "Besides, I'm not sure that we would be doing Brie a favor. Dominic has the devil's own temper at times, not to mention a tongue that can let blood faster than a rapier. Before this, I had always thought him too cold-hearted to fall in love."

"Then you think he returns her regard?"

"I don't believe there's any question that he's attracted to Brie, but whether he will marry her is a different matter entirely. He's always had a particular aversion to marriage."

"But why?" Caroline persisted. "I can't believe that he simply hates women, not with all the affairs he is said to have had."

"No, he doesn't hate women. He just won't allow himself to trust them. I suppose it might have something to do with his mother."

"What about his mother?"

"To tell the truth, I'm not really sure. Normally Dom won't talk about her. But as I understand it, she deserted him when he was quite young—just walked out one day, leaving her husband and son behind. Shortly afterward Dominic lost his father, too."

"Oh, how sad! Was it an accident?"

Julian shook his head. "Dominic's father was a French count who owned a large part of Burgundy—Valdois, I think the place was called. The comte was sentenced to death for murdering a woman who lived on the neighboring estate.

"Murder!" Caroline exclaimed in horror. "Was he guilty?"

"Lord, I have no idea. Dom certainly doesn't think so, but he only told me the barest details."

"Surely there had to be proof of some kind."

"Caroline, it happened during that bloody revolution of theirs, when the French beheaded their own king. They delighted in chopping off the heads of anyone with blue blood, most particularly loyal royalists. I doubt if the Comte de Valdois was even accorded a trial. If so, it would have been a farce. Dominic is still bitter about it—and about his mother's

277

desertion. To this day he refuses to see her or speak to her, and he won't acknowledge her existence if they meet in public."

"I can certainly understand why!"

"Well, the whole thing seems a little odd to me. I met Lady Harriet last year, and while I'd never say this to Dominic, I thought her a lovely, kind lady. She didn't strike me as being the type of woman to abandon her family for no reason at all. She's remarried now, and she appeared to be quite content with her husband."

When Caroline chewed thoughtfully at her lower lip, Julian leaned toward her and pulled one of her curls. "What are you thinking now, minx?"

"Lord Stanton simply must marry Brie. She will be miserable without him."

"Well, I warn you, there'll be no use trying to hurry him. Dominic has never been in love before. He'll be very cautious—and slow. He probably doesn't even realize that he's in deep water now."

"But what if he never realizes it?" Caroline asked, gazing up at Julian expectantly.

Julian settled back in his chair. "That is entirely possible. We'll just have to see what happens, won't we?"

It was several days later when they all left for London—Brie, Caroline, Katherine, Julian, and a number of servants. Two carriages were required to accommodate them and their vast array of luggage.

As they pulled away from Greenwood, Brie tried to remain calm, but there were butterflies in her stomach brought on by nervous excitement. Caroline, too, was in high spirits, and Julian could be heard whistling cheerfully as he rode beside the coach.

Only Katherine stared out of the carriage window, not sharing in the general mood of anticipation.

Chapter Twelve

The hour was late when Dominic's coach reached London and pulled up before his townhouse in Berkeley Square, but he lost no time in sending a message to Jason. Some half hour later, the Marquess of Effing was ushered into the library.

Dominic offered his friend a brandy, and when they were both settled before the blazing fire, he raised his glass in salute. "I take it congratulations are in order? You certainly look less hag-ridden than when I last saw you."

Jason laughed. "I tell you, Dom, I've been through some harrowing experiences before, but nothing quite as frightening as childbirth. The doctor assured me Lauren had an easy time, but it scared the devil out of me. I was amazed at how calm she was. The pain she must have suffered! We may dub woman the weaker sex, but courage and determination aren't only male traits."

Dominic shifted restlessly in his chair. Odd, but he had been having similar thoughts of late. Brie had shown . . . but that would have to wait. Driving away thoughts of her, he returned to the subject. "And the babe, a girl, did you say?"

"Yes, a beautiful daughter. No, don't grin at me. She *is* beautiful, and so incredibly small. I expect she'll have Lauren's eyes."

Jason continued in the same vein for several minutes before

he recalled the purpose of his visit. "You have mellowed, old friend," he said with a chuckle. "My raptures have been boring you to flinders and you haven't once interrupted me. You want to know about Germain? Actually there's been no change since I last wrote you. He has recovered enough to talk, but so far he hasn't been inclined to divulge any secrets. I can take you to see him tomorrow, if you wish."

Nodding in agreement, Dominic then told Jason about Boulter and the recent events of the past weeks, though he avoided mention of Brie's part in the affair.

Jason's expression grew grim as he listened to the tale. "It's unfortunate that Boulter is dead," he said at the conclusion. "Did you get any information from him?"

"Only that he and his brother were hired to kill me. My guess is that when Germain failed, they followed me from London."

"And do you still think it has something to do with your activities during the war?"

Dominic nodded slowly. "That's the only explanation I can think of. But why go to so much trouble to make it look like an accident? No doubt Boulter had several opportunities to put a bullet through me. And Germain's challenge was contrived to look natural enough."

"Perhaps they didn't want an investigation if you were killed."

"Or perhaps the deed to the land in France is what stopped them. They can only get the deed from me. It must be important to whoever hired them."

The two men were silent for a time, each thinking his own thoughts. Finally Dominic grinned. "Are you certain you want me to stand as godfather to your daughter?"

Jason's blue eyes danced with humor as he rose to take his leave. "You wouldn't dare think of backing out now, would you? Lauren would never forgive you—or me either, for that matter. We've set the christening date for Saturday next. Surely you can stay alive long enough to attend."

"I'll manage somehow."

"From that look on your face, I'd say Germain may not be so fortunate. I wouldn't care to be in his shoes tomorrow. Although I must admit I am looking forward to seeing what methods you employ to loosen his tongue."

Dominic's mouth twisted sardonically. "Haven't you guessed? I shall simply lock him in a room with you while you expound on the joys of fatherhood. In less than an hour, Germain will be begging for mercy. Nine o'clock tomorrow, then?"

Dominic rose early the next morning and ordered his curricle brought around. When he arrived at Lord Manning's office in Whitehall, he was shown into a tiny room where an elderly clerk greeted him.

"I regret that his lordship is not here at present," the clerk said, rising from behind his desk, "but I have been instructed to aid you. Please be seated. Now where did I put the file? Ah, here it is," he muttered, shuffling through his stack of papers. "Strange case, strange case."

When at last he turned, he found Dominic watching him impatiently. Unnerved by the cool intensity of his visitor's gaze, the clerk cleared his throat. "I have an assistant, my lord, who spends a good deal of time in the local taverns where he gleans bits of information here and there. A few weeks ago he came to me with an interesting story which, only recently, I decided might have some bearing on this case. My man overheard—well, perhaps it would be better if he told you himself. If you could wait one moment please."

He left the office and returned a short time later, followed by a rough-looking character whom he introduced merely as Tom. "Tom, tell Lord Stanton, if you please, what you learned at the Boarshead tavern."

Tom took a moment to look over the dark-haired lord, then broke out in a grin, showing a gaping hole where his front teeth had been. "So yer the one they was after. It ain't no wonder then." His grin disappeared when Dominic's eyes narrowed.

281

"Well, you see," Tom hastened to explain, "I was at the Boarshead when this cove comes in an' starts drinkin'. 'Ee wa drownin' 'is sorrows, like. I didn't give 'im much mind first off till 'ee starts to say something about them Frenchies. So starts to listen."

"This 'cove'," Dominic interjected. "Was he named Boulter, by any chance?"

"Yeh, Freddie Boulter. 'Ow'd you know?" When there wa no reply, Tom decided it best to get on with his story. "Well Boulter was drunk as a fiddler an' 'ee didn't make much sense Seems there was a swell what was to do for you, but 'ee got done for 'imself. So Boulter was cryin' about 'avin' to go off an' finish the job." Tom gave Dominic another gap-toothed grin. "'Ee didn't finish it, did 'ee?"

"Boulter is dead."

It was said so calmly that Tom shifted his feet uncomfortably. "Well, I don't s'pect anyone will miss the likes of 'im."

"What about the reference to France?" Dominic asked.

"Yeh, well, the nob what 'ired Boulter and the swell, 'ee came from France. But I don't think 'ee was a Frog. 'Ee was Hinglish, with a title. Didn't catch it, though. Boulter said the nob was touched in the upper works."

"Do you suppose this 'nob' is still in England?"

"No, 'ee ain't, if 'ee ever came in the first place. You see, Boulter only got part of the brass till the job was done. 'Ee was wonderin' 'ow 'ee was to get the rest, with the nob across the Channel and the swell havin' disappeared, like."

"I will need an address, a location in France. Could you get it for me?"

Tom grinned again. "Boulter won't be needin' it, will 'ee? I'm yer man, gov'nor . . . er . . . milord."

Dominic tossed him a coin. "Watch out for Boulter's brother while you're at it. Martin, I think is his name. I understand he enjoys making people scream." Rising then, Dominic directed the clerk to send any new information to his own address and left the office.

Tom remained where he was, stroking the dark stubble on his chin. "Cor," he said to no one in particular. "Good thing that nob from France didn't 'ire me to do 'is dirty work. I don't think I'd be standin' 'ere now."

When Dominic brought his horses to a halt before the Effing residence, Jason was waiting. He grinned as he climbed into the curricle. "Wouldn't do to let Lauren see you. Not unless you want to spend the next hour admiring our daughter."

It didn't take them long to reach the house where Germain was being held—a small, white structure a few miles north of town. They were greeted by a grim-faced housekeeper. "But you'll be wanting to see Mr. Germain, no doubt," she said, directing them up the stairs. "This way, if you please."

She led them to a closed door at the end of a corridor, where a brawny, dark-featured man was standing guard. Withdrawing a heavy key from her pocket, the housekeeper unlocked the door and stepped aside to admit the gentlemen. Dominic made no comment as he followed Jason into the room, but he noted the elaborate precautions with approval, including the heavy bars on the window.

Germain was lying on the bed, his eyes closed. The thick bandage wrapping his chest, as well as his sickroom pallor, indicated that he was recuperating from a severe injury. He didn't bother to look up when they entered.

"Morning, old man," Jason said cheerfuly. "Lovely day, isn't it?" When Germain gave an indignant grunt, Jason clicked his tongue. "Come now, you can do better than that. I've brought you a surprise."

The injured man opened one eye. Catching sight of Dominic, he sat up abruptly, clutching at his bandage while his color turned a shade more pale.

"Hello, Charles," Dominic said in a dangerously soft voice. When Germain only stared at him warily, Dominic raised an eyebrow. "What is this? Have your manners gone begging, Charles? Are you not going to invite me to be seated?"

"Oh, to be sure," Germain snarled, indicating the chair beside the bed. "After all, I am your prisoner, am I not?"

Turning the chair around, Dominic straddled the seat and casually draping his arms over the back. Then he pursed his lips as if considering a difficult problem. "That depends. I have several alternatives. Would you care to hear them?"

"I expect you plan to tell me, regardless."

Dominic remained unruffled. "My first is to turn you over to the authorities for attempted murder," he said coolly. "You might escape hanging, but a man recovering from a chest wound such as yours would not long survive a London prison."

Germain relaxed back against the pillows, his mouth curling in a sneer. "You won't have me arrested. That would implicate you as well, and you have far too much to lose."

"Did I say anything about a duel? Actually I was referring to the two ruffians you hired to kill me."

Charles was suddenly wary again. "You have no proof."

Dominic's lips twisted in a slow smile. "Ah, but I do. Before he died, your friend Freddie Boulter implicated you in front of a number of witnesses."

"Boulter is dead?" Charles asked, his tone sounding less assured.

"Quite dead. That is my second alternative for you, by the way. You were accosted by highwaymen, so the story goes, and were severely wounded. You were brought here to recover, but alas, you succumbed to a fever. Of course I mean to show profound grief at your death. I'll vow that I did everything in my power to save you. . . . But perhaps I needn't say anything at all. No one knows you are here. As far as the world is concerned, you disappeared three weeks ago. And I'm sure the good man waiting just outside your door could be persuaded to dispose of your body."

Germain said nothing, but there was a look of burning hatred in his eyes. Dominic returned his gaze steadily, his own eyes as hard as flint. "Then there is always torture," he remarked blandly, "but that can be rather distasteful, wouldn't

284

you agree?" Dominic flicked an imaginary speck of dust from his coat sleeve. "The last alternative might be more appealing to you, though I confess I don't care for it much. You can go free."

Seeing the flicker of interest in Germain's eyes, Dominic bent closer, his gray gaze holding Germain's like a moth with pinned wings. "I want the name of the man who hired you to kill me."

Germain licked his suddenly dry lips and involuntarily glanced at Jason for help. The tall marquess stood with his back to the room, looking out the window, ignoring the scene being enacted behind him. Germain returned his gaze to Dominic. "No," he said defiantly, determined to brazen it out.

Dominic stood up slowly. "Don't tell me you have suddenly developed a streak of loyalty, Charles. Remarkable. I never would have thought you capable of it. Jason, are you coming?"

Dominic went to the door and opened it, but then he turned back to address Charles once more. "I believe I neglected to tell you that I already have a good deal of information about your client. I know, for instance, that he is an Englishman currently living in France. And in a few days I shall have his direction. I will find him, even without your help."

Germain's bravado cracked. "All right, damn you! I'll tell you. It's Durham. Sir Charles Durham."

Dominic stiffened visibly, white lines appearing around his mouth. Then suddenly, he turned and walked out.

"Wait!" Germain shouted after him. "Did you hear me? You said I could go free!"

Dominic was already seated in the curricle when Jason joined him. Once glance at his friend's expression convinced Jason to hold his questions, but when Dominic sent his whip cracking over the heads of his pair, Jason stayed his arm. "Wait a minute, Dom. Let me take the reins till you cool down." He received a fulminating glare, but he made the exchange anyway.

As the curricle slowed to a more sedate pace, Dominic sat

back in his seat, clenching his fists in cold fury. *Durham*. The very name was a curse. First the daughter, now the father. Dominic swore violently, venting his rage and frustration in a succession of oaths.

It was some time later when he took note of his surroundings. They were jogging slowly along a quiet road, some distance from the city. "Might I ask if we are going anywhere in particular?" he demanded of Jason.

"Ah, it speaks!" Jason replied. "But for the profanity issuing from its mouth, I would have sworn it had been struck deaf, dumb and blind."

Dominic gave a snort of mirthless laughter. "Blind, certainly. I should have expected something like this. Turn the horses around, Jase."

"Of course, after you tell me what set you off like a firecracker. No, that won't wash, my friend," Jason said when Dominic eyed him coldly. "You forget that I've known you too long for your withering looks to have any effect. And you can't knock me senseless while I'm driving your cattle. Besides, I'm, a new father, remember? That was quite a performance you gave with Germain, incidentally. Very effective. Durham," he mused. "Where have I heard the name before?"

Dominic's lip curled. "Do you recall what I told you about my father's death?"

Jason nodded, remembering the story Dominic had related some years ago when they had both been less than sober. There had been bitter anguish in Dominic's voice when he had spoken of the false arrest. "She accused my father of murder," he said, clenching his fists till the knuckles turned white. "She lied! My father was no more a murderer than you or I, yet he was condemned to die by a vicious bitch for God knows what reason. She even tried to make him believe it was all a mistake. Treachery at its finest." Dominic had closed his eyes and laughed grimly. "How well I remember the look on my father's face when he learned Suzanne Durham was his accuser. She got away with it, though. She fled France and my father lost his

286

head to the Republic. I should have killed her!" When Jason had pointed out that Dominic had been a mere child, his face had become shuttered. He had never again mentioned his father.

"Ah, yes," Jason said, making the connection. "The girl's name was Durham, wasn't it?"

"Suzanne Durham. Sir Charles was her father."

Jason brought the horses to a halt. "And he is the man who wants you dead? But why, after all these years?"

"If I knew that, do you think I'd be sitting here now? But at least one puzzle is solved. Durham must still be living near Valdois. That must be how he knew of the sale of the estate. And the timing is right. I only purchased the deed a few months ago. My guess is that when he learned I had bought the property, he hired Germain to prevent me from assuming control."

"Nice neighbor you have," Jason remarked dryly. "So, what do you intend to do now?"

"Go to France. I'm just the least bit curious about why Durham wants to kill me. Christ! He must be well over seventy by now, though how he ever escaped the Revolution and the war with England I can't imagine. Here, let me drive. I'm calm enough not to land us in a ditch."

When Jason handed over the reins, Dominic turned the curricle around and urged the horses into a brisk trot. "I've been meaning to go to France anyway, to put Valdois in some sort of working order. This business with Durham makes it imperative. If I leave tomorrow, I should be back in a matter of weeks."

Jason glared at him thoughtfully. "I have a better idea. Wait until after the christening and I'll go with you. It won't hurt to have me along when you confront Durham, and I would enjoy the trip."

Dominic hesitated. His first impulse was to say no, for the sooner he set out, the sooner he could solve the puzzle about Sir Charles Durham. Jason's plan would mean a delay of nearly

287

a week, and he had already put off the trip more than once. He had been reluctant to return to Valdois, knowing he would dredge up unwanted memories. But wasn't that why he had bought the damned property in the first place? So he could face the past? So perhaps then his bitterness would leave him? He wanted to rebuild the land, if only to prove . . . prove what? That he could conquer the devils that drove him? Would he then find peace?

When a vision of Brie suddenly floated into his mind, Dominic shook his head. Brie, peaceful? A contradiction in terms, certainly. But he did want to see her again. She would be arriving in London on Friday, the day before the christening. That left Saturday evening. . . . He and Jason could leave the next morning for France. Admittedly, having Jason as a travelling companion would make the journey far more enjoyable, but Dominic couldn't fool himself over why he was willing, even eager, to postpone the trip.

"Well, have you made up your mind?" Jason broke in on his musings.

Dominic gave a curt nod, even while chiding himself for letting Brie influence his plans. "You know you are welcome. But shouldn't you be with your wife at a time like this?"

Jason grinned ruefully. "Frankly, Lauren will be relieved to be rid of me for a while. I'm afraid I've been getting a bit underfoot lately."

Dominic slanted him a mocking glance. "So domestic bliss is not perfect after all. I wondered how long it would take you to discover it."

"I never said it was perfect, my thickheaded friend. But I will say this—I wouldn't trade it for the world."

When they returned to Grosvenor Square, Jason led Dominic to a small sitting room where his wife was sewing a ruffle onto a nightgown for their new daughter. Lauren looked lovelier than ever, Dominic thought as he greeted her. Motherhood had not marred the elegance of her regal figure, or dimmed the luster of her golden hair.

288

She returned his greeting with enthusiasm and pressed him into staying for lunch. "For you have not seen Alexandra yet," she added with a smile, "and I shall not let you leave until you have admired her properly."

Over lunch, Dominic gave an account of his stay with Julian, dwelling mainly on the social aspects of his visit. He managed to hide his surprise when he discovered that Jason and Lauren knew Brie.

"We only met her last year," Lauren explained, "but she truly impressed me. It must have been extremely difficult for her to keep up the training stables her father built. I hadn't realized she and Lord Denville were such close neighbors, or I would have written and told her you were coming."

Dominic smiled at her artless comment. How different his first meeting with Brie would have been, had she been warned of his arrival. How different *all* their meetings would have been.

Realizing his thoughts had drifted, Dominic steered the conversation to safer channels, mentioning his impending journey to France with Jason. Lauren had several questions for her husband about the trip, and they spent the remainder of the meal discussing plans and itineraries.

After lunch, Lauren and Jason took Dominic upstairs to the nursery where baby Alexandra was just waking from a nap. Dominic was surprised when Lauren gently lifted the infant and placed her in his arms, but while he wasn't quite sure what to do with the tiny child, he paid all the proper compliments.

The proud parents fairly beamed with approval, he noted sardonically. Watching them, however, he was conscious of the odd sensation of being an outsider. He could never share the special bond that existed between Lauren and Jason—a bond that had been strengthened by the birth of their daughter. Yet, seeing Jason smile so tenderly at his wife, Dominic actually found himself envious of the unique happiness his friend had found.

Even after he had taken his leave of the couple, the feeling persisted, and later, when he was pondering his strange reaction, he recalled that Jason had once tried to explain his love. "I don't want to live without her, Dom," Jason had insisted. "I *can't* live without her." Dominic remembered laughing at the time.

He had no inclination to laugh now—particularly when he thought of the auburn-haired, hot-tempered beauty he had left in Rutland. It was not a question of being able to live without her, of course. He could. He wanted her, though.

The question was, how much?

Dominic was still asking himself that same question nearly a week later as he sat drinking alone in the comfort of his library. He frowned, staring at the crystal tumbler of brandy in his hand, not really seeing the swirling golden liquid. In a few hours, Brie would arrive in London, and as yet he had reached no conclusions as to what to do about her.

Several times during the past week, he had found himself regretting his decision to delay the journey to France. He had grown bored with waiting and his usual pursuits had afforded him little pleasure. Tonight he had actually turned down an invitation for an evening of cards, preferring instead the solitude of his own company. After a quiet dinner, he had retired to the library where he planned to read, but his book lay unopened on a side table. As he lounged in a large, stuffed-leather chair before the hearth, his long legs stretched before him, his thoughts unavoidably strayed to Brie.

Only one thing was certain: they could not continue their present relationship. Brie's reputation would never survive an affair with him. Dominic had learned the rules at an early age. While it was perfectly acceptable for married women to take lovers and spawn a dozen bastards, young single ladies were strictly forbidden to engage in such activities. There would be rumors a-plenty were he even to call her. And were society to learn that the wicked Earl of Stanton had seduced the lovely

Miss Brie Carringdon, had stolen her innocence and spent a night in her bed, the gossips would have a field day.

Dominic frowned. He wanted Brie for his mistress, but he could see how impossible such a course would be. Even if he could somehow convince her, even if they managed to keep it hidden for a time, sooner or later someone was sure to discover it. She was known in the better circles of town and couldn't be passed off as an actress or young widow. He could easily weather the resulting scandal, of course, but Brie would be badly hurt.

He had been surprised to find himself concerned for her reputation, for he rarely let such considerations influence him. But then, she had been a virgin. He had been her first real lover. Perhaps that explained his current dilemma. He was experiencing a twinge of conscience, to say the least.

The situation was more complex, however, than Brie's loss of innocence, and he damned well knew it. He had become too involved with her, had let his passions interfere with good judgment. He should have left at once for France. Given time, he would forget the russet-haired beauty who had been in his thoughts so often during the past weeks. Or would he?

Dominic shifted in his chair, wondering why the devil he was dwelling on such thoughts. He had never been one to waste time analyzing his own emotions, particularly where women were concerned. He preferred instead to live his life without encumbrances, to act for the moment, not exactly drifting—for he had done quite well at rebuilding his fortunes—but the goals that he set for himself were always tangible challenges, avoiding completely the issues of relationships. His pursuit of Brie had begun as such. . . . So why now, when he had more pressing matters to consider, did he worry about a relationship with a woman he had met only a few weeks ago?

He knew full well why. Because he could picture Brie in his arms, passionate, warm, yielding. Because he could feel her soft, silken body writhing beneath him. . . . Devil take it, his heart started slamming against his ribs whenever he just *thought* about seeing her again. Virgin or no, making love to her had been one of the best experiences he had ever had with a woman—and strangely, the most satisfying. But why the tight constriction in his chest when he considered putting an end to their relationship?

Draining his glass, Dominic dismissed the nagging question. Brie Carringdon was an enchanting witch, impossible to ignore or forget, but he had to stop seeing her. There would be no honorable course other than marriage if he continued his pursuit of her, and not for any woman, no matter how ravishingly beautiful, would he suffer those chains willingly. He would use his trip to France as an excuse to dissolve what they had begun. He would see Brie on the morrow and explain that his departure was unavoidable. And by the time he returned to England, perhaps he would have conquered his fierce attraction for the beautiful little termagant. Indeed, dismissing her from his life should be no more difficult than discarding a favorite coat, Dominic told himself firmly as he raised his glass of brandy to his lips.

He did not, however, think it odd that he was required to drink almost a full bottle of the potent liquor before he believed himself thoroughly convinced.

Dominic was perusing the newspapers over breakfast the next morning—as well as trying to recover from a severe hangover—when Julian arrived, interested in hearing what had happened with Germain. When Dominic briefly recounted the details, Julian let out a slow whistle.

"You know, Dom, you lead a charmed life. I am truly in awe, for nothing like that ever happens to me. After you left last week, the most excitement I had was determining how to protect Brie and Caroline if we should come across any highwaymen. And since we weren't accosted by so much as a scarecrow, the journey turned out to be rather uneventful. I almost wish I were going to France with you. Although . . .

aren't you leaving rather suddenly?"

"It isn't sudden," Dominic replied. "In fact I've already delayed almost a week so I could attend the christening this morning."

"Er, of course. I merely thought that since Brie just arrived in town . . ." Julian hesitated, noting the sudden glitter in his friend's eyes.

"Yes?" Dominic prodded, his soft tone a warning in itself.

"Never mind," Julian replied, deciding not to press the issue. He told Dominic, instead, that Jester seemed to be healing nicely, and it served to turn the conversation.

They talked for a while longer before Julian rose to take his leave. "By the way," he said, keeping his tone casual. "I am escorting Caroline and Brie to the Vauxhall Opera this evening. You are welcome to join us, if you care to."

"Thanks, but I mean to attend the Copely's ball. I suppose I will see you when I return from France."

"Yes . . . , well . . . , good luck then, Dom." His words were warm but his tone was stiff and formal. He turned to go.

"Julian," Dominic called after him.

"Yes?"

"Quit trying to play matchmaker, will you? You are much too obvious."

"Dominic," Julian said with a good-natured grin, "I begin to understand why someone wants to murder you. You know how to thrust where it hurts!"

The christening went smoothly and lasted only a short while. His afternoon free, Dominic drove his curricle to the Langley residence in Russell Square where Brie was staying. He planned to invite her for a drive, wanting a few moments alone with her.

His expectations were short-lived, however, for when he asked to see Brie, he was told that Miss Carringdon was not at home. "I believe she is expected to return shortly," the butler added. "Would my lord care to wait? I would be pleased to inquire if Lady Langley is receiving."

Since Dominic had absolutely no desire to see Brie's aunt, he declined and politely thanked the servant. He was turning to leave when someone called his name. Looking up, he saw Brie's companion standing on the grand staircase, leaning heavily on a cane. She was staring down at him, one hand held at her throat, her age-lined face a ghostly shade. Dominic was puzzled by her expression. The elderly woman looked as distressed now as when he had brought Brie home the day of the shooting.

"Lord Stanton," Katherine said again, her voice unsteady. "I should like a word with you, if you can spare a moment."

"Miss Hewitt, is it not?"

"Yes, my lord. We can use the salon, there, to your left."

Dominic waited as Katherine slowly made her way down the stairs, then allowed her to precede him into the room, curious to hear what she had to say. He expected her to take a seat, but she only turned slowly to face him, eyeing him with that same strange mixture of horror and dread.

Dominic shut the door and moved to stand near the fireplace, letting his glance travel around the room as he waited patiently for Katherine to speak. The salon was done entirely in blue and cream shades, and elegantly furnished with Louis XVI furniture. There were several portraits hanging on the walls, and Dominic noted the one of Lady Arabella with an inward grimace. Brie's august aunt stared stiffly down from the canvas, her likeness evincing the kind of chilling hauteur that shriveled souls.

Her proud look subtly reminded Dominic of Brie, but he knew it would take Brie twenty years of practice before she ever came close to achieving the same degree of rigid imperiousness. Lady Arabella The Terror, Dominic thought with a sardonic grin. She was a petty tyrant, ruling her household and those around her with iron control. Her husband should have taken her in hand from the beginning of their marriage, should have taught her to curb her temper and channel her natural aggressiveness into softer forms of expression. That was what he would do, should Brie become his—

Dominic caught himself abruptly. He had been about to say *wife,* for Christ's sake. Forcibly he turned his thoughts aside, giving his full attention to Brie's companion. "You requested an audience, Miss Hewitt," he prompted gently, wondering why she was looking at him as if he had grown a pair of horns and a tail.

"Yes," she replied, clenching her fingers around the knob of her cane. "I wanted to speak to you . . . about Brie. As her companion, it is my duty to look after her."

"I won't dispute that," Dominic said when Katherine hesitated.

"I am concerned for her."

He raised an eyebrow and waited.

"It cannot be good for her reputation for her to be seen in your company," Katherine continued at last. "This is not Rutland, my lord, where Brie is well known and respected. Her good name could easily be damaged."

If you only knew, Dominic thought wryly. Aloud, he responded with a question. "Are you perhaps suggesting, Miss Hewitt, that I confine my calls to the times Miss Carringdon is well-chaperoned?"

"No, my lord. I would like you to keep away from Brie entirely. You are not the kind of man I could wish for her to know too well."

Dominic's eyes narrowed. It was one thing to decide himself to stop seeing Brie; it was another to be warned away by a woman he hardly knew. He turned away to mask his anger, noticing the miniatures displayed on the mantlepiece as he did so.

His gaze was immediately drawn to a girl with russet hair and sparkling blue-green eyes—obviously a much younger Brie. The artist had executed his work well, Dominic thought as he glanced down at the tiny portrait. She was laughing, looking very much as if she had the world in the palm of her hand, but there was a hint of something in her eyes that suggested fire and passion. Dominic found it hard to tear his gaze away.

"And if I do not choose to comply with your wishes, Miss Hewitt?" he said, almost to himself.

"Then I shall have to take steps to see that you do, my lord. I do not intend to allow Brie to follow the same path as Lisette."

"Who, may I ask, is Lisette?"

"You really do not remember, do you? You should look more closely at the miniatures, my lord. Perhaps you will recognize the one there on the right."

Growing impatient with her cryptic remarks, Dominic directed his attention to the other portraits. To the left of Brie's likeness were miniatures of several children, including a very young Caroline Langley and, Dominic assumed, her brothers and sisters. To the right was a matched set, one of an older man whom Dominic recognized as Brie's father, Sir William, and one of a dark-haired woman who could have been her mother. Dominic picked up the miniature of the woman, his gaze arrested by the look of sadness in her eyes. Staring at her, he felt the stirring of a vague memory. He was certain he had seen that face before. "Should I know her?" he asked, turning to look at Katherine.

"Yes, my lord, you should. That . . . that is Suzanne."

It was at the same moment that the formidable Lady Arabella swept into the room. "Good afternoon, Lord Stanton," she said with rigid politeness, not noticing how very still her guest had become or how his lips had tightened. "Carson informed me that you had called. I understand that you are acquainted with my niece."

Dominic ignored her entirely, his gaze narrowing on Katherine. "Suzanne?" he repeated, his tone soft but unmistakably menacing.

When Katherine made no reply but simply stared at him, white-faced, Lady Arabella broke in. "Whatever is the meaning of this, my lord?" she demanded in chilling accents.

296

"Why are you browbeating this poor woman?"

Dominic turned his glittering gaze on Lady Arabella, indicating the miniature he still held in his hand. "This is a likeness of Suzanne Durham?"

Astonished by the savagery in his tone, Lady Arabella blinked, then focused her gaze on the portrait. "Yes, that is Suzanne."

"How did it come to be here?"

"Why . . . Suzanne was Brie's mother. My brother William married her shortly after she came to London. She was Miss Durham then, and Miss Hewitt was her companion. I did not approve of the match, of course, for Suzanne was destitute. There was some tragedy, I believe. They had to leave France quite suddenly, for it was during the barbarous uprisings there—"

"Do I understand you correctly?" Dominic interrupted softly. "Your niece is the daughter of Suzanne Durham?"

Something in his tone made Lady Arabella want to shiver. "Yes, but where is this leading, my lord? And where are you going?" she demanded as Dominic suddenly strode past her. "I have not dismissed you, and you still owe me an explanation!"

Dominic halted abruptly, then turned slowly to face her. His eyes glittered like shards of ice as they flicked once over Katherine, then settled on Lady Arabella.

"You are mistaken, madam," he said, tossing the miniature at her feet. "I once owed much to Suzanne Durham, and I now owe a great deal to your niece. But to you, I owe nothing."

Chapter Thirteen

"He must hate me, Julian. But I didn't know. I swear I didn't know!"

The pleading note in Brie's voice wrung Julian's heart. He tightened his arm about her shoulders, ignoring what her tears were doing to the front of his striped silk waistcoat. Gently he stroked her hair, offering comfort as he would to a small child.

He had arrived only a short time ago to find the Langley household wrapped in oppressive silence. When Carson had informed him in hushed tones that the ladies would not be attending the opera this evening, Julian had asked to see Brie and was shown into the drawing room. He had been shocked to see her pale face and wide, haunted eyes. When she had blindly reached out to him, he had wrapped his arms about her wordlessly, supporting her while she clung to him. After a time he had led her to a sofa, where he had succeeded in drawing out a faltering explanation.

"Dominic called this afternoon," Brie said in a shaky whisper. "Caroline and I had been shopping and we returned just as he was leaving. He didn't speak to me at all. . . . Julian, the look he gave me." Brie shuddered, recalling the cold fury on Dominic's face. He had seemed to look right through her, the icy contempt in his gray eyes chilling her blood.

Taking a steadying breath, she told Julian about finding her aunt and companion in the salon. "I hadn't the faintest idea what was going on or what I had done to deserve that look Dominic had given me, but Aunt Arabella was in a rage. She said Lord Stanton had behaved with unconscionable rudeness and that he had questioned her about my mother. Katherine wouldn't speak at all, she was so upset. But finally she told me . . . she said that years ago Dominic's father had been arrested and put to death and that my mother's name was on the arrest warrant. That was why Mama left France and came to England to live. But I never knew. Mama never spoke about her family. She said all the Durhams had been killed during the Revolution."

Julian grew quite still, remembering the name he had heard on Dominic's lips but a few hours before. In an odd voice, he asked if the Durhams had been neighbors of the Comte de Valdois.

"I believe so, why? I wanted Katherine to tell me more about it, but she was so distressed that I sent her to bed. But don't you see? Dominic hates me now for what my mother did. He probably thinks I knew about it. But I didn't, Julian! My mother never told me about her past."

Her tone held such anguish that Julian felt his heart wrench "Lord, what a mess," he said, giving a sigh. He held Brie away from him, gazing at her in sympathy. "I'm afraid it is more complicated than that, Brie," he said gently. "Just this week Dominic discovered who has been trying to kill him. The man's name is Sir Charles Durham. Do you know if he might be related to you?"

Brie stared at Julian, her face draining completely of color "Mama's father," she said in a horrified whisper.

"Your grandfather, then. Here," he said, offering his handkerchief. "You could use this."

"I am not crying! I never cry!"

"No, of course not," he murmured soothingly as Brie wiped furiously at her eyes with the back of her sleeve. He drew her into his arms again, resting his chin on the top of her head as

300

he buried her face in his shoulder. "I'm afraid it's true, however. Your grandfather is behind the attempts on Dominic's life. It seems that Sir Charles is still living in France. Dominic plans to seek him out—he leaves tomorrow, in fact."

"Then there is only one course open to us," Caroline said from behind them. She had heard most of the conversation, having come quietly into the room.

Kneeling at Brie's feet, Caroline looked imploringly at Julian. "You must see Lord Stanton, Julian, and make him understand that Brie had nothing whatever to do with any of this."

Julian shifted uncomfortably. "I doubt that Dominic would listen. If he believes Brie knew about her family, then nothing I could say would change his mind. It would be better to wait till Dominic returns to England. By then he may even have discovered the truth on his own."

"But he might not!" Caroline protested. "And that could be weeks, or months. He would never believe her then. No, Julian, you must see him now and explain."

Brie sat up, clenching her fists. "Will you two please stop! I am not a scrap of meat to be divided between you." Lifting her chin, then, she looked at her cousin. "Caroline, you are right. I cannot allow this misunderstanding with Lord Stanton to continue. But neither will I allow Julian to fight my battles for me. I must speak with Dominic myself. However," she said, giving Julian a tremulous smile, "I would appreciate an escort. Dominic has a house in town, doesn't he? Will you take me to him?"

Julian eyed her with a sinking feeling. "Come now, Brie. You cannot expect me to be a party to such a foolhardy scheme." He tried to dissuade her by repeating his earlier arguments, but his efforts were fruitless; Brie had already made up her mind. "And besides," Julian concluded lamely when she would not be swayed, "Dominic isn't at home."

"But you know where to find him," Brie returned. "Please, Julian, I must see him. Perhaps I could discover his direction from his servants, but it would give rise to gossip. You could save me time and trouble by helping me."

"Damn it, Brie. . . ."

An hour later, Julian was handing the cousins into his barouche. He kept his oaths to himself, however, as he watched Brie rest her head wearily against the squabs. She looked breathtakingly beautiful in a crepe gown of pale peach with diamonds sparkling in her hair and at her throat, but she seemed drained of all energy. Julian tore his gaze away and focused his frown on her cousin instead. Caroline had insisted on accompanying them to the Copely's ball. She sat next to Brie, silently staring out of the coach window.

Except for Julian's terse directions to his driver when they alighted from the barouche, none of them spoke a word till they passed through the receiving line where they were forced to respond politely to Lord and Lady Copely's greeting and exchange pleasantries. Brie's smile was visibly strained by the time they were free to move on, and Julian could feel the tension in her slender shoulders as he guided her up the last flight of stairs. As they entered the ballroom, he suggested once more that she wait to speak to Dominic, but she remained adamant. Her eyes feverishly scanned the crowd, searching for the tall, dark-haired lord who owned her heart.

"Fetch her something to drink, Julian," Caroline whispered, seeing how pale Brie was. "Champagne, I think."

Nodding, Julian gently propelled Brie across the room where a line of stiff-backed chairs had been arranged for the guests. Ordering her to sit, he left her in Caroline's charge while he went after something to revive her.

Brie obeyed, only because her courage had suddenly faltered. Clenching her hands tightly in her lap, she stared straight ahead, seeing nothing of the exotic shrubs and potted palms that turned the ballroom into a luxuriant garden. Dancers twirled past her, their gay laughter blending with the music in pleasant harmony, but she saw nothing of them either.

Some of the color returned to her cheeks when she had drunk the brimming glass of champagne that Julian gave her, but she paled again when Julian said he had seen Dominic. Forcing a tremulous smile, Brie rose unsteadily to her feet and asked Julian to lead her to him.

Brie could hear her heart pounding as they made their way through the crowds, but her courage deserted her entirely when she spied Dominic's tall form. His back was to her, and his dark head was bent to catch something his beautiful companion was saying. Recognizing Lady Denise, Brie turned to flee. But then Julian was telling her to buck up her chin and was urging her forward again. Knowing she was too close to give up now, Brie took a deep breath, and allowed herself to be led.

She thought she had braced herself for Dominic's reaction. Earlier, as she was dressing, Caroline had told her about Dominic's estrangement from his mother and how he refused to acknowledge Lady Harriet whenever they chanced to meet in public. But Brie was truly unprepared for the cold fury that flashed in Dominic's eyes when he turned and saw her. The gleaming daggers he directed at her would have impaled her instantly, had they been made of stronger stuff. Brie flinched involuntarily, wishing she were anywhere besides facing this dangerous-looking man who was staring at her with such savage hatred, but she squared her shoulders and forced herself to say a pleasant good evening.

Watching her, Julian silently applauded Brie's spirit, for he was well aware of what it was costing her. Lady Denise, too, could feel the tense undercurrents that had suddenly charged the atmosphere. Wisely, Denise did not protest when Julian drew her aside, giving Brie a chance to speak privately with Dominic.

When Brie asked if she might have a word with him, however, Dominic's lip curled. "Your explanations are unnecessary, Miss Carringdon," he said with chilling formality.

303

He started to turn away, but she placed a hand on his arm. Dominic's grim countenance never changed, although his eyes narrowed even further. Seeing his warning look, Brie removed her trembling hand, but she refused to be intimidated any further. "They are necessary, my lord," she insisted. "But what I have to say is best said in private, not in a crowded ballroom. Five minutes, my lord. I ask but five minutes of your so valuable time."

At her bitter tone, Dominic raised a sardonic brow and regarded her in silence. Brie held her breath as she waited for his reply, but finally Dominic nodded. "Very well," he said curtly. "Five minutes. I believe there is a drawing room on the floor below. I will meet you there shortly." Brie nodded wordlessly, unable to speak for relief.

After some searching, she discovered the drawing room he had mentioned. The room was empty, but the lamps had been lit and a fire burned in the grate, giving off a cheery warmth. Brie stood before the fire, holding out her chilled hands to warm them as she waited with mingled dread and hope for Dominic to appear. He had said he would come, she reasoned. He would give her a chance to explain. Perhaps he would even believe her.

The minutes ticked by slowly, the interminable waiting stretching Brie's overwrought nerves to fine wires. Intent on her own thoughts, she did not hear Dominic enter. The sharp click of the latch as the door closed made Brie start and swing around sharply. Dominic stood there, looking darkly handsome in his formal black evening clothes, yet the hard expression he wore made the rough planes of his face appear even more forbidding than usual. His eyes were as cold and glittery as glaciers. They raked over her as he leaned his shoulders against the doorjamb and folded his arms across his chest. He watched her, waiting, as if daring her to speak, and Brie knew what his verdict would be before she had even voiced her plea.

The words she had so desperately wanted to say died on her

lips as she stared at this cold stranger she had grown to love. She felt only compassion for him, and a despairing sadness. How terrible it must have been for him as a child, Brie thought as she returned Dominic's gaze. First his mother's desertion, then his father's death. They had left scars that had never completely healed—scars she should have seen before now. There had been times, of course, when she had sensed the bitterness and rage simmering just below his polished, cynical exterior. But now that she understood why, now when she might have given him comfort, Dominic had erected a barrier of hatred and misunderstanding between them. He was as unreachable as the most distant star.

"Well, cherie? I granted you five minutes," Dominic reminded her when she was silent. "Four remain."

Brie turned her head away, feeling hot tears sting her eyes. "I am so very sorry, Dominic," she whispered.

"Well, well, what have we here?" Dominic drawled with acid mockery. "A sign of remorse? Regret perhaps? Save your tears, little viper, they are wasted on me."

"They are not for you," Brie retorted, swallowing a sob. "They are for me—for being foolish enough to think you would listen to me. You obviously have made up your mind about me. I stand convicted." Feeling a surge of anger then at his unfairness, Brie whirled to face Dominic again, her hands clenched at her sides. "On what evidence, may I ask? I was not even born when your father died. And until this afternoon, I knew nothing about my mother's relatives."

"I suppose next you will say you had nothing to do with the attempts on my life," he said flatly, his voice devoid of all emotion.

It took Brie a moment to register his words, but the impact of his accusation took her breath away. She stared at Dominic in disbelief, forcing down an hysterical urge to laugh. Dear God, not only did he blame her for her family's actions, but he thought her guilty of conspiring to murder him!

"That is absurd, my lord," Brie said shakily when she found

her voice. "Had I wished your death, I surely could have hit on a better scheme than one which necessitated the destruction of my stables. Even you could not believe me capable of such a foolhardy act."

His arctic expression never changed. "Is that why you killed Boulter? Because his methods were not to your liking? You should be more particular in your choice of servants, cherie."

The futility of their conversation was rapidly becoming apparent to her. She gave a bitter laugh. "That is excellent advice, my lord! I shall consider it carefully when I next try to murder you. Now, however, there is nothing more to say. You have obviously closed your mind." She took a step toward the door, but then halted, realizing Dominic blocked her path. She watched him warily, waiting for him to step inside.

When he responded, though, it was to push himself from the door and walk toward her. He moved with the easy grace of a panther stalking his prey, and it took every ounce of courage she possessed for Brie to stand her ground rather than retreat.

They were but a few inches apart when he stopped and slowly reached up to curl his long fingers about her bare throat. For one panic-stricken moment, Brie wondered if he intended to choke her to death. He might be capable of it, she thought, staring into his smoldering gray eyes. There was something infinitely frightening about his savage expression—although there was also something in his eyes that looked vaguely like . . . regret? Regret mingled with the desire for revenge? Would he feel remorse if he killed her? Brie could hear the blood pounding in her temples as Dominic slowly stroked the vulnerable hollow at her throat.

"One thing still puzzles me," he murmured. "What did you hope to gain by giving yourself to me? Did you think to ensnare me with your lovely charms?"

Brie might have answered him, had not her voice been trapped in her throat. As it was, she could only stare, mesmerized, as his lips slowly descended to hover over hers like a bird of prey.

His warm breath brushing her mouth chilled her as nothing else could have done. Realizing that he intended to kiss her, Brie made a desperate attempt to avert her face, but his hard fingers tightened on her throat, holding her still. Then his mouth crushed down on hers with brutal force.

It was a punishing, ruthless assault, tasting of implacable fury. The eloquence of his merciless kiss showed Brie far better than words how inexorable was his contempt for her, but her own body's response was even more humiliating. She could only cling to him helplessly, her mind reeling, whirling, spinning. She couldn't think, couldn't breath, couldn't feel anything but Dominic's burning lips, his hard body pressed against her.

She wasn't aware when the door to the drawing room was flung open to admit three less-than-sober gentlemen. They were laughing uproariously at something one of them had said but in spite of their inebriated condition, they checked their headlong rush into the room upon seeing Brie in Dominic's arms.

"Whash the meaning of this, Sh-tanton?" one growled, swaying on his feet. "Why d'you want ush to meet you here if you meant to sample the wares firsht?"

A second man whistled through his teeth. "B'god, Percy! Even three sheets to the wind you can see why he was so eager to start without us. I want the wench next, Dominic."

Dominic abruptly ended his assault and raised his head, but a deep frown creased his mouth as he turned to stare at the new arrivals. Brie, still dazed, opened her eyes and managed to focus. Seeing the lascivious grins the men were directing at her, she stiffened in shock. Dominic had planned this! He had invited these drunken boors to join him here in the drawing room. This, then, was his revenge, to humiliate and expose her before his friends. Perhaps he even meant to watch while they had their way with her.

Shock quickly turned to blind fury. Brie struck out at Dominic wildly, a cry of pain and outrage erupting from her

307

throat. Her nails raked the side of his face before he managed to pin her arms at her side.

Voicing an oath, Dominic held Brie's twisting, writhing form in an iron embrace as he tried to explain that he had not asked his friends there. He had not staged their entrance—although he could easily guess who had when he recalled Denise's interest in where he was going.

But Brie was beyond the point of listening. "You bastard!" she sobbed, struggling ineffectively against his superior strength. "I hate you! I wish Boulter had killed you!"

Her angry words struck at his heart. Rage blazed in Dominic's eyes as he jerked Brie against him, clamping her fiercely against his body. Brie was bent back over his arm, her hands twisted behind her, her breasts crushed against his chest.

She could feel his hips grinding painfully into her belly, could see his teeth bared in a primitive snarl only inches from her face. Fear streaked through her at his murderous expression. Dominic truly meant to kill her this time, she realized. A whimper of pain escaped her as she closed her eyes, waiting.

The pitiful little sound penetrated Dominic's blind rage, flaying him with guilt. Swearing violently, he released Brie so abruptly that she went sprawling on the carpet. She lay there, pale and shaking, looking up at Dominic with eyes that were huge with fright.

A savage sneer curled the corner of his mouth as he drew a handkerchief from his coat pocket and pressed it against his bleeding cheek. "Your wishes are quite apparent, cherie," he observed sardonically. Then turning to his astonished acquaintances, he executed a flourishing bow. "Do come in, gentlemen. Perhaps you will have more luck than I in persuading the lady to share her favors." He paused, throwing a contemptuous glance at Brie. "I assure you, it will be worth the effort. She can be temptation enough for any man when she chooses."

Then he spun on his heel and stalked from the room.

Lady Denise knew the instant when Dominic returned, for her eyes were riveted on the ballroom doors. Earlier in the evening, she had been surprised to receive Dominic's note offering to escort her to the Copely's ball. She had not expected to be the recipient of his attentions again since his parting words at their last meeting had seemed quite final, but she hadn't hesitated to accept his invitation, hoping that his interest signaled a willingness to resume their previous relationship.

When he had arrived in his carriage to take her to the ball, however, her hopes had immediately suffered a setback. Dominic's striking features had been shrouded in an enigmatic expression, his manner distant and uncommunicative. He had seemed barely to tolerate her presence once they reached the ball, and it had been nearly impossible to hold his attention and keep him at her side.

Her optimism at her success had taken a plunging dive when Brie Carringdon arrived, and when Dominic had agreed to a private conversation with the auburn-haired beauty, Denise had been infuriated. She had watched him leave, then seized the opportunity to thwart her rival by arranging for Dominic's friends to interrupt his planned tête-à-tête. Awaiting Dominic's return with nervous impatience, she had kept her eyes trained on the doors.

Now he was headed toward her, wearing an expression that boded ill. She knew him well enough to recognize the signs of a savage temper held barely in check.

She forgot her own precarious situation, though, when she saw the deep scratches marring his cheek. "Good heavens!" she was startled into exclaiming. "Whatever happened to your face?"

Dominic appeared to smile. "Use your imagination, my sweet. I doubt you will have any trouble guessing this was the

309

result of the little scene you staged. Come, I intend to take you home. I've already ordered the carriage."

"But . . . we have only just arrived! You can't mean to leave so soon."

He raised an eyebrow and fixed her with his glittering gaze. Denise made no protest, therefore, when he took her arm and steered her toward the wide double doors. She held her tongue as they made their way down two flights of stairs, not wanting to antagonize him further, and with effort she even refrained from staring at the red grooves that furrowed his cheek.

Dominic was draping her fur-lined cloak about her shoulders when someone growled his name. He paused, looking up, while Denise followed his gaze to the top of the wide staircase. Julian Blake stood there, glaring down at them. She heard Dominic give a muttered curse as the viscount bounded down the stairs.

Julian halted barely a foot away, his fists clenched, his usually pleasant countenance twisted with anger. "You go too far, Dominic," he ground out between his teeth.

Dominic appeared not to have heard. Denise watched in amazement as he turned away to accept his evening cape from an attendant footman. She had never before known Dominic to allow anyone to use that tone of voice with him.

"By God, Dominic—"

"This is hardly the place to discuss our differences," he said calmly.

Julian clamped his mouth shut, saying nothing further until they were out on the street and Denise had been handed into Dominic's carriage. Then he repeated his accusation in a voice that was taut with suppressed fury.

Denise had no trouble hearing the exchange through the open carriage door, and by parting the curtains slightly, she could also see. Dominic stood with one foot poised on the carriage step, his expression inscrutable, but when Julian reached out to grasp his arm, a dangerous gleam flashed in his eyes.

At his warning, Julian released his grip, although he retained his belligerent stance. "I'll not let you get away with this, Dominic. Did you think she had no protectors? That I would stand by and let you make a mockery of her honor?"

Dominic's reply was cool, but his voice held a savage undertone. "You are mistaken. Miss Carringdon needs a keeper, not a protector. Now if you will excuse me?"

He turned away, making to enter the coach, but when Julian spoke again to demand satisfaction, Dominic froze. "I will pretend I did not hear that remark, my friend," he said softly.

"You would ignore a challenge?"

"I have no wish to put a bullet through you, Julian—and certainly not because a scheming little witch has you blinded with her beauty. I leave for the Continent tomorrow. I trust that by the time I return, you will have come to your senses." Dominic climbed into the coach, then, slamming the door behind him.

As the carriage pulled away, Denise managed a final glance out the window. Julian stood there, glaring after them, his face white with fury.

Denise hid her triumphant smile as she settled herself comfortably against the cushions. She had no desire to see Dominic engaged in a duel over another woman, particularly Brie Carringdon, but this last exchange convinced her she had nothing to fear. Even if her wide experience with men had not made her a competent judge, one look at Dominic's brooding features would have told her that he held no love for her beautiful rival. For whatever reason, the Carringdon chit had incurred his wrath, and then Julian had added fuel to the fire by defending her.

Wisely, Denise was silent for the short trip to her home. She fully intended to capitalize on Dominic's violent mood, but she knew better than to draw his attention while his fury was still at its peak. His strong profile was barely visible in the darkness as he lounged negligently in his seat, staring out the window, but Denise could sense the unleashed tension in his body. He was like a powerful, savage beast, tightly controlled but primed for attack, awaiting the slightest provocation.

Her pulses leapt when at last Dominic turned to look at her. His eyes were hard and glittering, holding no trace of gentleness. The banked fires of his passions needed a release, she knew, and she hoped he would find it in her body.

When the carriage drew to a halt before her house, she murmured his name and in her husky voice, invited him to come inside. Dominic merely leaned over to push open the door.

"You aren't leaving now!" she exclaimed in bewilderment.

His gray eyes raked her body. "I'm not feeling particularly amorous at the moment, if you hadn't noticed."

"Dominic, about what happened this evening—"

"I don't wish to discuss it, Denise."

When she realized he was serious, Denise flounced down from the carriage and whirled to face him. "Damn you, Dominic! What do you want from me? You practically command me to attend the ball with you this evening, but when we arrive, you completely ignore me. Then you whisk me away while everyone is staring at us, without so much as a by your leave, and *then* you have the temerity to drop me on my doorstep like a piece of unwanted baggage!"

"I've no interest in sharing you with half the men in London, cherie."

"Well! I never expected you of all men to act the prude. You and your little Miss Carringdon are well matched, I must say!"

"Leave her out of this," he said savagely.

Denise's smile was a perfect imitation of Dominic's usual sardonic one. "Did that touch a nerve, milord? She put those scratches on your handsome face, didn't she. *Poor* darling. It must rankle to know that not every woman leaps at the chance to bed the great Lord Stanton!"

Dominic's eyes narrowed, but he said nothing. Denise stood there a moment longer, glaring at him defiantly, but then she bit her lip. "Please forgive me for saying that, darling." Letting tears well in her eyes, she held out her arms to him.

Dominic looked at her with cool contempt. "Enough of your tricks, Denise. I'm not coming in. If you wish, however, I shall stop the first gentleman I pass and send him to you. It would be a pity to let your lovely charms go untasted."

Denise uttered a shriek and tore her reticule from her wrist, intending to throw it in his face, but Dominic closed the door and rapped on the ceiling. The coach pulled away, leaving her to vent her fury on the hapless cobblestones.

Chapter Fourteen

For the first few hours, the Earl of Stanton's well-sprung travelling coach made good time on the road from London to Dover. The coach's occupants travelled in comparative comfort, although there was little conversation to lighten the tedious miles.

Jason, finding Dominic uncommunicative, settled back to watch the passing scenery from the coach window. After a time, though, his thoughts strayed from the rolling Kentish landscape to the ugly rumors that had reached his ears before leaving London that morning. According to the reports, Dominic had behaved outrageously at the Copely's ball and had torn Brie Carringdon's reputation to shreds in the process. Jason would have liked to know just how much truth was in those rumors, but Dominic had refused to discuss the matter.

He didn't appear to be too concerned now, Jason thought with a glance at his friend. Dominic was dozing in the forward seat, his arms folded across his chest, his long legs stretched comfortably before him. Jason shrugged. One could never tell about Dominic. The man had a well-developed talent for keeping his thoughts hidden. His success as a spy had depended on it. It was only because they had known each other for so long that Jason was able to sense the simmering anger behind the enigmatic mask. *Something* definitely had happened yesterday, Jason knew. But he also knew the subject would remain closed until Dominic chose to open it.

Jason was about to follow Dominic's example and get some sleep when the horses suddenly slackened their pace. He could hear the coachman's voice raised in altercation, and when he glanced out the window, he could see a lone, caped horseman riding beside the box.

"I think it would behoove you to wake up, Dom," Jason said as the coach ground to a halt. "I do believe we are being held up."

Dominic raised one eyelid. "Jacques has dealt with highwaymen before. He can be counted on to handle it."

"Is that so?" Jason replied, watching as the rider dismounted. "Then why do you not tell that to our uninvited guest? He appears to be coming this way."

Dominic sat up then, and as a precaution, checked to see that the pistols in the carriage side pockets were primed and loaded. Jason kept an eye out the window, relaxing somewhat when he realized the horseman was but a mere youth. The boy had a slender figure, and although his hat was pulled well down to cover his face, his exposed chin was smooth and beardless. He was hidden from view as he handed his reins to one of the footman, but a moment later the door was flung open. To his astonishment, Jason found himself staring directly into the lovely blue-green eyes of Brie Carringdon.

She seemed surprised to see him as well, but as she took the seat next to Jason, she recovered her poise. "I beg your pardon, Lord Effing," she said with an aplomb that would have done credit to a diplomat. "I did not expect to see you here." With a faint smile, Brie indicated the pistol in her hand. "You needn't worry. I don't intend to shoot *you*. Your friend, however, is another matter entirely. Hello, Dominic."

Jason, knowing Dominic well, expected any number of reactions from him: surprise, scorn, anger, even caution. But neither Jason nor Brie anticipated Dominic's amusement. "Ah, cherie," he said, his gray eyes narrowing with laughter.

"You never cease to amaze me. I thought I had gotten rid of you, yet here you are, pointing a gun at my head after holding up my coach in broad daylight. What will you do next, I wonder?"

Brie shrugged indifferently, keeping a firm rein on her temper. She would never have let Dominic know what it had cost her pride to arrange this meeting. His cruelty last night had hurt her beyond feeling—or so she told herself. "I am sorry to disappoint you, Lord Stanton," she replied, "but I did not hold up your coach. Your coachman recognized me and allowed me to board."

"I did not think Jacques was so lacking in sense. Tell me, dear girl, what do you intend to do now? Kidnap me?"

His tone held the familiar mockery, but Brie had braced herself for it. "Not at all," she replied coolly. "And in any case," she gave Jason a brilliant smile, "I doubt Lord Effing would allow such a thing."

Jason returned her smile with one of his own. "Probably not, Miss Carringdon, but I expect it would depend on your reasons." He leaned back in his seat, beginning to enjoy himself. "Why did you, er, join us in such an unorthodox fashion?"

"I want to know where you are going."

"Why?" The question came from Dominic, and Brie tried not to flinch at his savage tone.

"Yes, why, Miss Carringdon?" Jason asked more gently.

She turned pleading eyes to Jason, finding it easier to look at him than Dominic. "Lord Effing, I assume you have heard by now of the Durhams? Are you also aware of my relationship with that family? Suzanne Durham was my mother. I . . ." Brie faltered, then took a deep breath. "I have several reasons for wishing to accompany you. First, Lord Stanton believes that my mother was responsible for the arrest of his father. I do not. My mother was simply not the kind of person who could send someone to a certain death. I intend to find out what happened."

She paused, her gaze involuntarily returning to Dominic. "Lord Stanton also believes," she said with a trace of bitterness, "that I, in conjunction with my grandfather, plotted his death. Until yesterday, I was unaware that my grandfather was even alive. And while I admit there have been times when Lord Stanton and I have had . . . our differences, I have never wished him dead."

Unable to bear Dominic's chill stare any longer, Brie looked at Jason. "I don't know where my grandfather lives, only that he is somewhere in Burgundy. I have no wish to chase you across several hundred miles of unfamiliar country, however, so if you will only give me Sir Charles' precise location, I will leave you in peace."

"I suppose," Dominic said with acid sarcasm, "you plan to ride through France, dressed as a highwayman and brandishing a pistol."

"I don't have much choice!" Brie snapped, turning to glare at him. "A woman can hardly travel alone without a disguise. Besides, I thought it best to leave London. After last night I dare not even show my face."

Dominic didn't reply. He knew he should explain that he had been innocent of trying to humiliate Brie in front of his friends, but he was still furious for having allowed himself to be so taken in by her lies—and angrier still because he had been unable to suppress the sudden rush of pleasure at seeing her again. She had knocked his equilibrium off balance by stopping his coach. He had known, of course, that she was spirited and stubborn, but never would he have guessed she would try and follow him to France. Just what the hell was she up to?

Moreover, why was she pretending to know nothing about her grandfather? He knew damned well she was lying. He could recall how she had reacted to him that night at the Lodge when they had first met. Brie had recognized his name, he was sure of it. He had seen the flicker of alarm in her eyes when he had introduced himself. And what about her extreme wariness later, and all those stories she had made up to keep her identity a secret? She had claimed it was merely to protect her reputation, but he could see now she had been afraid he would discover her connection with Durham. Dominic clenched his jaw, remembering Brie's fear of him. All that time he had been concerned for her, thinking she had been frightened by a bad experience with a lover.

Watching her now, though, Dominic found it easy to see how he had fallen for her lies. Even dressed as she was in her rough boy's clothes, Brie was beautiful. She was glaring at him fiercely, her eyes flashing with indignation, her cheeks flushed with anger. Feeling his groin muscles tighten, Dominic swore under his breath. Fiend seize it, he was becoming a candidate for Bedlam! After all that had happened, he still wanted her. Brie had lied to him, maybe even tried to kill him, yet he was still attracted by her beauty, by her vibrancy. He couldn't deny that she still had the power to stir him. He wanted to reach out and take her in his arms. . . .

But she had played him for a fool, Dominic reminded himself viciously. And while he found himself wanting to believe she wasn't nearly so treacherous as circumstances indicated, he couldn't allow himself to trust her.

He glanced at Jason, noting that his friend wore a look of grave concern. Damn the little witch! She already had Jason wrapped around her finger. "Jason, you're a fool if you believe half of what she says," Dominic said in disgust. "She knows well enough where to find Durham."

When Jason remained silent, Dominic's raking gaze sliced back to Brie. "My dear Miss Carringdon," he said as if their discussion had become a wearying bore, "I'm afraid I find your reasoning a bit difficult to accept—although certainly it is more plausible than your protestations of innocence. Nothing you may do or say, however, will sway me. I strongly recommend that you give up this foolishness and go home, but of course if you choose to visit your grandfather, that is your affair. I warn you, though, I do not relish being hounded. And

319

now," Dominic added implacably, "do you need assistance mounting your horse?"

For a long moment, Brie stared at him, as if unwilling to accept his answer. Then finally she lowered her gaze and shook her head. She had lost her desperate gamble. Dominic hated her and there was nothing more to be said. When he leaned over to open the door, she gathered up her shredded dignity and climbed down, suddenly feeling very weary.

She gave Dominic one last wistful glance as she tossed her pistol on the seat beside him. "You may need that, my lord. If you are made uncomfortable by my hounding, you may shoot me. But," she added, "take care to check the priming first."

When she had retrieved her horse, the coach at once sprang into motion. Jason waited until they were moving at a steady pace again before speaking. "Miss Carringdon's methods may be a bit unusual, Dominic, but her motives seemed plausible enough."

Dominic's eyes narrowed as he shot an irritated glance at his friend. "What did you want me to do, invite her to come along?"

"What I want doesn't signify. You were a little hard on her, don't you think?"

Dominic turned to stare out the window. "I was hoping to convince her to go home."

Jason leaned across and picked up Brie's pistol. "I wonder if she knows how to use this," he said, examining the weapon.

Dominic snorted. "She knows, alright. I've seen her shoot a man at point blank range and not even hesitate."

Ignoring Jason's raised eyebrow, Dominic settled back to resume his nap, but he was hindered in his attempt to sleep by Jason's slow chuckle. "I fail to see any cause for humor," Dominic growled, prying one eye open to glare.

"You will, my friend, when you look at this pistol. It is unloaded."

Both Dominic's eyes flew open as he sat up. "That witless little fool! When I get my hands on her I'll—" Catching

Jason's curious stare, Dominic clamped his mouth shut.

"Yes, what will you do?"

"Never mind." A grim expression hardened his features as he settled back again and pretended to go to sleep.

Brie did not go home. Dominic's unwillingness to believe her had only made her more determined than ever to prove her innocence—or at the very least, to vindicate her mother.

By the time she reached Dover, however, she was to the point of regretting her decision to follow Dominic. Having had little sleep the night before, she was exhausted from long hours in the saddle, as well as cold and hungry. For the moment she wanted nothing more than a hot bath, a warm meal, and a soft bed. When she halted her hired mount in the busy yard of The George, however, Brie hesitated. The George was a respectable-looking inn that promised to offer all the comforts her weary body craved, but if she were to find transportation across the channel for tomorrow, she knew she ought to book passage tonight. With a regretful glance at the inn, she turned her horse toward the docks.

Dusk was settling over the town as she made her way through the nearly deserted streets. Except for the clattering of her mount's hooves on the cobblestones and the dull murmur of the sea in the distance, the evening was quiet. Brie shivered as a cold wind whipped at her cloak. Hunching her shoulders against the chill, she pulled her hat down further to shield her face.

As she neared the quay, she found another reason for discomfort. Lounging in the doorways and roaming the docks were small groups of fishermen and sailors who looked as if they would enjoy nothing more than a drunken brawl. Cursing herself for a fool and wishing she had kept her pistol, Brie urged her mount into a trot. She had no protection except the anonymity her hat and cloak provided, and that would hardly serve if she were to meet with any kind of trouble.

She was very glad to find the shipping office. Keeping her head well down to hide her face, she dismounted and tethered her horse in front of the building, then entered quickly. The clerk behind the desk gave her an odd look when he realized she was a woman, but he accepted her money without argument when she requested passage to France on the first available packet.

Brie was smiling at his dubious expression as she left the office, but when she reached the street, she halted in confusion. Her horse was nowhere in sight.

Smothering a wave of panic, she forced herself to think. The shipping office would at least be safer than the dimly lit street, she realized. She was about to retrace her steps when she heard footsteps behind her. Whirling, she just managed to evade the rough hands that grabbed at her, but her heart leapt to her throat as she faced four unkempt sailors who reeked strongly of liquor.

"We wants yer purse, cove," one said as all four slowly started to close in on her.

Terrified, Brie took a step backward, then another, watching them warily. She knew they could smell her fear, for she could hear her own heart pounding. She was wondering if she should turn and run when, at a signal from the first man, they all rushed her at once.

Brie struck out wildly, trying hopelessly to evade their grasping hands. Her hat was knocked from her head during the struggle, sending her hair tumbling around her shoulders.

"Bloody 'ell, it's a woman!" the leader exclaimed.

Brie gave a cry of mingled pain and outrage as his hand groped her breast. She brought a knee up hard, contacting his groin and causing him to double over in pain, then looked around desperately for something to use as a weapon.

There was nothing. She caught a glimpse of a dark horseman further down the street just as another of her assailants grabbed her, but when a fist struck her face, she saw stars. She would have fallen but for the rough hands holding her.

Then abruptly, the scene dissolved in a whirl. Brie heard the ring of steel-shod hooves on cobblestone and vaguely realized that the horseman had ridden his mount directly into the fray. There were grunts of surprise from her attackers, then howls of pain as the horseman lifted his arm time and time again to bring his riding quirt down on the shoulders of the men who held her.

When their grasping hands released her, Brie's legs gave way and she sank to the pavement. She knelt there, sobbing and gasping for breath as her attackers fled.

"Did they hurt you?" She recognized the familiar voice—and tone. It was clipped and harsh and implacable. Brie shook her head, not daring to look at her rescuer.

"Then I suggest," Dominic said caustically, "that unless you enjoy being ravished, you seek safer ground. Where is your horse?" At Brie's mumbled reply, Dominic barked the question again.

"I don't know!" she cried, tears coursing down her cheeks as she glared up at him. He sat his horse easily, his whip resting across the saddle. Seeing his casual pose, Brie wanted to scream. She was shaking with fright, her pride was in tatters, and her nerves were frayed almost to the breaking point—and all he could do was berate her in that hateful, sardonic tone. At that moment she firmly believed she hated Dominic. It was bad enough that he should find her such a defenseless position, but his contemptuous tone made her humiliation complete. She bowed her head and started crying in earnest.

Dominic muttered a soft curse as he dismounted and scooped her trembling form into his arms. He ignored her half-hearted struggles, easily thwarting her attempts to break free, and when she at last lay still, he set her on his horse and mounted behind her, wrapping an arm securely around her waist. Brie sagged limply against him and wept, having lost the strength and the will to fight him further.

As they made their way through the dark streets, Dominic found himself wishing he had done more to the men who had attacked her than to have administered a mere beating. Brie's quiet sobs tore at his heart. She was trembling uncontrollably as well, and the feel of her soft body made him recall other times when he had held her in his arms—when she had trembled with passion.

Unable to dispel the disquieting emotions that were warring in his chest, Dominic swore silently. He ought to beat Brie for causing him such anguish. He had hoped his harsh words to her in the carriage would send her scurrying home, but obviously she hadn't listened. Thank God he had told Jacques to keep an eye out for her! Jacques had seen her leaving the inn and followed her to the docks where Dominic was giving his final orders to the captain of his yacht. Dominic had forgotten his anger, had forgotten that Brie might very well have plotted to murder him, and had ridden after her.

Christ, but he had been given a fright when he had seen her struggling against those four ruffians! He had wanted to kill the bastards with his bare hands. And it didn't seem illogical that while he might like to wring her neck himself, he would permit no one else to harm her.

"Foolish girl," Dominic murmured as he brushed his lips against her hair. The gentle fragrance aroused his senses, and he couldn't refrain from turning Brie's face up to him. He kissed her soft lips, determined to comfort her and drive away her fear. When Brie clung to him in response, Dominic could feel her desperate need for reassurance. Tenderness welled in his heart, while a fierce wave of protectiveness surged through him.

Only when they arrived at the inn could he bring himself to pull away. "Come, my sweet," he whispered huskily. "We are causing a spectacle." Brie nodded, but she was too exhausted to care about the gawking stares and grins they drew from the ostlers in the yard.

Dominic hid her face from view as he brushed passed the astonished innkeeper and carried her up to his room. Laying Brie gently on the bed, he quickly divested her of her clothes, leaving her slender body clad only in her shirt which barely covered her hips. He carefully tucked the covers around her, then stood back. Hearing the even sounds of her breathing, Dominic smiled in spite of himself. Brie was already fast asleep. He let himself out of the room quietly.

When he joined Jason in the private dining room, he found two serving maids occupied in laying out a sumptuous meal. Ignoring both their appraising glances and the more subtle scrutiny of his friend, Dominic poured himself a generous glass of claret and drank deeply, and only when the maidservants had left did he take his seat at the table. Absently, he began serving his plate, his mind still on the sleeping woman in his bed.

It was several minutes later before he realized Jason had spoken. "I beg your pardon," Dominic said, looking up from his food. "What did you say?"

Jason smiled wryly. "I asked you twice if your ship will be ready to sail in the morning."

"Yes, with the tide. I found everything in order. Captain Rogers assures me that the weather will be fair and that we can expect an easy crossing." He lapsed into silence once more, frowning as he tried to decide what in hell's name he was to do with Brie.

Jason, too, was silent, but he studied Dominic curiously throughout the meal.

Dominic finally looked up to find himself being watched. "Is something wrong? Did I spill the gravy on my neckcloth?" he asked sarcastically.

"No," Jason replied, leaning back in his chair and taking a sip of wine. "I was merely wondering at the cause of your bad manners. All day you've been as moody as the Caribbean during a hurricane season, and you've spoken a mere three sentences all during dinner. *And* you've hardly touched your food. Your obvious preoccupation wouldn't have anything to do with the fact that you've finally let a woman get to you, would it?"

It seemed to Dominic that the room had suddenly become overly quiet, for his sharp intake of breath was clearly audible. He hadn't been prepared to hear the truth stated so blandly.

He wasn't about to admit to such a weakness, though. He forced himself to release the air in his lungs slowly. "Of course not," he returned, sounding more irritable than he had intended.

Jason grinned, his blue eyes sparkling with amusement. "Then how do you explain your churlish behavior this evening?"

Dominic ran a hand through his hair in a gesture of frustration, knowing he hadn't fooled Jason any more than he had fooled himself. He had allowed himself to become far too involved with that enticing, lovely schemer. But blister it, what red-blooded man wouldn't be attracted to a beauty like Brie Carringdon? Yet he had let his attraction for her threaten his friendships with men he had liked and respected for years. Because of Brie, he had nearly become embroiled in a duel with Julian and now he was taking his ill-temper out on Jason.

"Well, you're right on one account," he said curtly, skirting the issue. "I had no cause to bark at you. I apologize."

Jason's grin widened. After draining his glass, he stood up. "You know what they say, the hardest hearts take the hardest falls. If you ask me, you have fallen."

"I didn't ask you," Dominic returned grimly.

"You should have. I can see it, even if you can't. You, my good friend, are in love."

"No!" His vehemence was accentuated by shattering glass as he swept out an arm and sent his wine goblet flying half the length of the table. He stared morosely at the red stain spreading across the white tablecloth, not willing to face such an impossible dilemma. He couldn't explain the tender feelings he had for Brie, but it wasn't love. It couldn't be.

"There, you see?" Jason said, chuckling. "Why else would a man of otherwise reasonably sound mind behave so violently? Good night, Dominic. Sleep well—if you can."

Having had more than enough of Jason's provoking good humor, Dominic raised his gaze to glare fiercely. "Get out, Jason," he said through clenched teeth. "Get out, before I decide to turn my unreasonable violence on you!"

It was nearly midnight when Brie was awakened by the crash of a slamming door. Startled, she sat up, her eyes anxiously searching the darkness of the unfamiliar room. Her heart leapt wildly when she spied Dominic leaning against the doorjamb, watching her. His face was in the shadow, and the beginnings of a beard on his jaw made him look harsh and dangerous.

Involuntarily, her hand crept to her throat. "You . . . you frightened me," she said hoarsely. Then she caught sight of the empty bottle in his hand and her gaze narrowed in suspicion. "What are you doing here, my lord? I demand you leave this room at once."

Dominic's lips curved in a slow smile. "You demand? But my lady, this is my room, and you are in my bed."

"You are drunk!"

Unsteadily, Dominic bowed. "Yes, my sweet. Drunk with desire for you." He sauntered into the room, keeping his eyes trained on her face.

Brie was more than a little frightened by the feverish glitter in his gaze. As he came nearer, she shrank from him, nervously pulling the covers up to her chin as if for protection. But he didn't touch her. He carefully deposited his bottle on the bedside table. Then giving Brie a casual glance, he began to undress.

"What . . . what do you think you're doing?" Brie asked falteringly, already guessing his intent.

"I, my lovely vixen, plan to collect the payment that is due me. Did I not save you from ravishment this evening?"

"To what purpose? So you could rape me yourself?"

He lifted an eyebrow. "I told you once before—for rape you must be unwilling."

"Well, you won't find me willing!"

Dominic merely shrugged and sent her a leering grin. Moving to the foot of the bed, he tossed his coat and waistcoat over the back of a chair.

Brie remained where she was, staring as Dominic unwound his cravat and removed his shirt. But when he was naked to the waist, she scrambled to her knees. Sweeping up the empty bottle, she brandished it threateningly. "I'll be damned if I will let you touch me, you . . . you drunken libertine!"

Dominic laughed harshly as he sprawled in the chair and began to struggle with his boots. "Methinks the lady doth protest too much. Besides, it's not as if your virgin honor were at stake."

His reactions obviously had not been dulled by the amount of wine he had drunk, for he was able to dodge the bottle that came flying across the room. It missed his head by inches and shattered on the floor.

Dominic glanced at the broken glass, then back at Brie, his eyes narrowing. "That was a mistake, cherie," he said softly. With menacing slowness, he finished pulling off his boots, then stood to remove his breeches.

Brie could only stare at him, suddenly feeling faint. She had experienced this same, nightmarish scene before: a strange inn, a darkened bedroom, a powerful ruthless man who was determined to use her body for his own purposes. She had escaped then, but she knew with certainty the ending this time would be far different. Her fear returned now in full force, threatening to choke her.

She was responding only to the primitive instinct for flight when she bounded from the bed. She raced for the door, having no thought in mind other than escape, but Dominic was faster.

Brie yelped in pain as his hand shot out to catch her hair, and her cry became one of fright as he spun her around. Dominic curled his fingers over the collar of her shirt, and with a single swift motion, rent the garment from the neck down, exposing her slender body to his gaze.

For a moment Brie was too shocked even to scream. She could see the sudden flare of lust in his eyes as they fixed hungrily on the pale globes of her breasts. Panic filled her, and she struck at him blindly, trying to pummel his chest with her fists.

Her feeble efforts were no match for his strength. His arm went around her waist, jerking her to him, while his other hand stripped the shirt from her body and flung it aside. Then, with one fluid motion, Dominic picked Brie up and threw her upon the bed. Before she could scramble away, he fell on her, grasping her wrists and pinning her arms beneath her, rendering her struggles useless. Brie was terrified to feel his hard body, pressing her down. Half swooning, she thrashed her head slowly from side to side, whimpering.

Hearing the pitiful sounds, Dominic realized he had gone too far. The violent rage that had momentarily gripped him drained away. Looking down at Brie, seeing her pale face and wildly tangled hair and feeling the shudders of fear that racked her body, he swore under his breath. He couldn't take her with force, no matter how satisfactory a revenge it would be.

"Hush, cherie," he murmured soothingly. "I won't hurt you." He lay completely still, moving only his lips as he whispered gentle, meaningless words in her ear. When she quieted, he began to press light kisses against her throat, nuzzling her soft, fragrant skin.

It was a long moment before Brie realized she felt no pain. When Dominic raised his head, brushing a tousled curl back from her face, she opened her fear-darkened eyes. His gentleness bewildered her, but as she met Dominic's triumphant gaze, she suddenly understood what he had intended. He had *meant* to make her cower in fright. He had *meant* to reduce her to a quivering mass of jelly.

Immediately Brie's fear dissolved, to be replaced by a heated fury that flashed in her eyes. She glared up at him, her breasts rising and falling with rage. "What are you waiting for?" she demanded, her voice shaking.

"Ah, the fire is back," he taunted, his own voice husky with desire.

"Damn you to hell, Dominic! Why don't you get it over with and be done?"

"My, aren't you an impatient one?" Shifting his weight slightly, Dominic very deliberately, very slowly, began to stroke her body with his hand. "I am waiting, my little wildcat, for you to say you want me."

She stared in shock. His punishment, his revenge, was not complete. Dominic meant to humiliate her further by making her admit her desire.

"Never!" Brie cried, starting to struggle again. But her words of protest were cut off as he covered her mouth with his own.

Ignoring her struggles, he parted her lips with an ease that shamed her. His thrusting tongue probed the depths of her resistance—insistent, demanding—while his fingers continued the slow, insolent exploration of her body.

Brie held herself rigid, willing herself not to respond, but she could feel every muscle, every nerve ending in her body growing taut with desire. And when Dominic began to stroke her breasts, lingering over each nipple until it throbbed, she realized her body was responding to his arousing caresses, despite all her efforts.

Brie quivered with mortification, knowing it was only a matter of time before she gave in to him. Already his passionate kisses were drugging her senses, conquering her will. . . .

His lips left hers then, moving lower, playing a sensuous melody on her skin, pausing to torment the tips of her breasts. Brie shivered as the stubble on his jaw rasped against the sensitive flesh. When his mouth closed over a hardened nipple, she couldn't prevent a gasp of pleasure. She let her head fall back, no longer wanting to stop him. She could feel his roaming hand caressing her thighs, and when he urged them apart, his fingers stroking and exploring, she opened to him in surrender. She no longer cared about her vanquished

330

pride. She was aware of nothing but her intense need for Dominic, of the hot ache in her body that only he could ease.

Only vaguely did she realize when Dominic shifted his position to kneel between her parted legs. He lowered his head once more, pressing featherlight kisses over her smooth abdomen and lower, at the junction of her thighs. Brie jumped in shock when his lips began to nuzzle the soft curls that hid her womanhood, but Dominic's hands gripped her hips, raising her off the bed and forcing her to remain still. His tongue claimed her then, turning what had been mindless fear into mindless pleasure.

His tongue lapped and swirled and stoked and teased, delving into her, making Brie writhe and gasp for breath. Her fingers tangled in the dark waves of his hair, demanding a release from the exquisite torment. But Dominic taunted her to the brink of ecstasy—only to leave her dangling there helplessly.

When he lifted his head to stare down at her flushed face, his eyes were almost black with the force of his emotions. "Say it, my passionate beauty," Dominic demanded. "Say you want me."

"Yes," Brie moaned, her voice hoarse with desire. "Oh, yes! Please, Dominic . . . please. . . ."

He gave a triumphant, gutteral laugh before he took her, plunging into her, swiftly, forcefully. Brie gasped at his deep penetration, but in only a moment she was sobbing with pleasure. His loins were hard and thrusting, filling her, making her forget everything but her own mounting passion.

He drove into her with savage force, needing to control, to possess, to conquer, but Brie wanted his possession. She clasped him fiercely to her, digging her fingers into the flexing, iron-hewed muscles of his shoulders. When he gave a final explosive thrust, she arched against him, yielding him the final victory as he swiftly brought her to a shattering climax. Dominic's own release came at the same instant. His body shuddered convulsively as he held himself, shaking, inside her.

When it was over, when their breaths no longer came in

ragged gasps, Dominic slowly rolled off her. Brie shivered as the night air caressed her sweat-dampened skin, but she didn't move. She merely lay there with her eyes closed, not wanting to face the significance of what had happened.

He had conquered her completely. Dominic had skillfully sharpened her desire to a razor's edge, until she had pleaded for him to take her. He had bent her to his will, demonstrating his contempt by making her beg for his touch.

Feeling hot tears sting her eyes, Brie turned away, clutching her arms to her stomach in a gesture of protectiveness, as if she could ease the pain that sliced through her heart.

Dominic lay beside her, listening to her muted sobs and staring at the ceiling. He was completely sober now—and he felt like a complete cad. But he should have been pleased, he reminded himself savagely. He had succeeded in doing precisely what he had intended. He had wanted to frighten Brie, had wanted to hurt her as well as hold her and make her cry out with passion. But proving his mastery over her body hadn't made him feel any better. And he was still no closer to resolving this damnable situation. He still didn't know if he could trust her.

Swearing in self-disgust, Dominic turned his head to look at her. She was curled on her side, her back to him, but he could see her shoulders shaking. Involuntarily, he reached out a hand to comfort her—but he drew it back almost instantly, knowing if he took her in his arms, he would never be able to crush the tenderness he had begun to feel for her.

He had tried to deny its existence entirely. God knows, he had tried. Sometime during the long evening, while he was purposefully drinking himself into oblivion, he had even hit upon the madly insane idea that he could exorcise the hold Brie had over him by taking her body again.

But it hadn't worked, Dominic thought grimly, realizing his desire for her hadn't diminished in the least. The hell of it was that it hadn't worked.

Chapter Fifteen

When Brie was awakened early the next morning by an insistent tapping at the door, Dominic's side of the bed was empty. She sat up slowly, staring down at the pillow where his dark head had lain. Dominic was gone.

But perhaps it was for the best, Brie reflected, trying to ignore the feeling of desolation that filled her. She could not have faced him this morning.

Remembering what had happened, she winced. Dominic had made love to her in the most degrading a manner possible, simply to prove that she meant nothing to him. He had delighted in humiliating her, in forcing her submission. What a fool she had been, letting herself believe that he could love her! Perhaps, given time, he might have come to care for her, but now she stood no chance. He thought her family a pack of murderers, herself included, and his suspicions had crushed any love he might have felt for her. He hated her and that was the end of it. She would go home to Greenwood and never see him again, and in time, forget him—if she could.

"My lady?"

Brie hadn't noticed the bustling entrance of a young maidservant, but the rosy-cheeked girl was trying to get her attention.

"Begging your pardon, milady, but his lordship bid me to ask you to hurry. 'Tell my wife,' he says to me, 'that the *Falcon* sails within the hour.' I've brought hot water and your clothes."

Bewildered, Brie gave the girl a blank stare. "My . . . my clothes?"

"Yes milady. His lordship explained to me how you were traveling to meet him here, and how you were set upon by ruffians who made off with your coach. Bless me, but the highways aren't safe anymore."

As the maid busied herself lighting a brace of candles, Brie glanced around the bedroom, noting the cheery fire burning in the hearth. The shirt she had been wearing last night was gone, but the pile of broken glass was still on the floor, reminding her of the bottle she had thrown at Dominic. "Er, yes, thank you . . . ?"

"Daisy, ma'am." The girl smiled broadly and bobbed a curtsy. "At your service. Will your ladyship be requiring anything else? I have to run down and get your breakfast."

"No . . . thank you, Daisy. That will be fine."

When the girl had gone, Brie got out of bed, draping a sheet around her naked body, and crossed to the window to pull the curtains aside.

It was barely dawn, she realized with a start. The morning was still gray and gloomy for the sun had not even risen. Then Dominic could not have sailed! And the maid had said—

Not yet daring to draw any conclusions, Brie inspected the items the girl had brought. To her surprise, she found an elegant travelling suit of forest green merino, along with a hooded cloak trimmed with luxurious sable. There were also appropriate accessories to the outfit, including gloves and kid half-boots, and a small dressing case containing toilet articles. Brie found herself blushing at the sheerness of the undergarments and wondering how Dominic had managed to come by them so early in the day, but she was too grateful for his thoughtfulness to be anything but pleased.

Finally conceding that Dominic meant for her to accompany

him, she let relief and elation sweep through her. She didn't understand why he had changed his mind, but whatever his reasons, it didn't matter. She wanted to go with him, wanted to be with him. It seemed that she had no pride or shame where Dominic was concerned. But he had been kind to find a proper outfit for her to wear—and to let the servants think she was his wife. His *wife*, Brie murmured, and then quickly shook her head. She would be a fool to read anything at all in the tale Dominic had fabricated to explain her presence at the inn. But at least he had been considerate of her reputation.

She washed and dressed quickly, finding to her surprise that her new clothing fit superbly. When Daisy returned, Brie asked for help with the more troublesome buttons, then ate a hasty breakfast while her hair was brushed till it shone.

"Cor, you're beautiful, you are, milady," Daisy said as she finished pinning the auburn tresses in a smooth chignon. "His lordship will be mighty pleased, that he will."

Brie wasn't so certain, but she thanked the girl before going downstairs to join her alleged husband.

She found the coach waiting in the yard while Dominic impatiently paced the cobblestones. When he gave her a swift appraising glance, Brie thought she saw approval in his eyes, but her tentative smile was met with cold silence.

He had shaved, she noticed as he handed her into the coach, but the shadows under his eyes suggested he hadn't slept well, and the furrows between his dark brows indicated he was suffering a headache as a result of all the wine he had drunk the night before. Indeed, his expression was so forbidding that Brie decided now was not the time to thank him for providing her clothes. She even held her tongue when Dominic gruffly informed her he would ride in the box, although she couldn't help wondering if he were doing it to spare himself the pleasure of her company. If so, it was hardly a propitious beginning for a journey.

His surliness annoyed her, but during the short drive to the docks, Brie reminded herself just what she owed him. Not only

335

had he rescued her from those horrible men the previous evening, but he had let her come with him this morning, in spite of his obvious reluctance. Perhaps she should make allowances for his foul mood, she decided. It was no more than Dominic deserved if he were feeling the effects of a hangover, but she could repay his kindness by overlooking his churlish behavior.

Her resolve was put to the test almost immediately, for when the coach drew to a halt, Dominic came to the door and told her to remain seated. "Jacques will escort you to the ship," he said brusquely. "He will be along when he has seen to the horses."

Brie stiffened at his tone, but she held back the retort that sprang to her lips. "Very well, if you wish it," she replied meekly.

Dominic's features darkened into a scowl. "The docile lamb hardly suits you, ma belle. I liked you better when you showed some spirit."

Brie's eyes kindled, but before she could reply, Dominic had turned abruptly and was striding away. She stared out the window after him, thinking that it was just as well she had no riding crop with her at the moment.

She was not obliged to wait long, for the burly Jacques appeared almost at once. "If you will come with me, mademoiselle," the coachman said as he took her dressing case. "Monsieur instructed me to show you to your cabin." When Brie hesitated, betraying her indecision, Jacques lowered his voice to a murmur. "Mademoiselle, you must not be distressed. He has a temper, that one, since he was a leetle boy, but he is a fine man. I think you will do him much good."

In spite of the Frenchman's presumptuousness, Brie could not be affronted, for she read only kindness in his intent. She responded with a grateful, albeit doubtful smile.

If Jacques' words had bolstered her flagging courage, the sight of the graceful ship riding in the harbor, with its flashing white sails and elegant lines, made her spirits rise even further. The *Falcon* was Dominic's yacht, Brie was told as Jacques assisted her on board. The two-masted schooner had been built for speed but carried its own cannon, and the captain and crew—some of whom Brie saw as Jacques led her below deck—had been in Lord Stanton's service for many years. Brie was tempted to ask why his lordship felt it necessary to retain such an expense or why they needed cannons on board, but she decided her curiosity might be misconstrued.

When Jacques conducted her to a small cabin which he said had been allotted for her use, Brie was surprised to find it quite comfortable and rather elegant. Going to the porthole, she settled herself in the window seat where she could watch the numerous other vessels in the harbor and listen to the raucous cries of the sea gulls.

She could easily tell when the ship got underway, for the waves slapped against the hull with greater force and the rolling motion of the *Falcon* increased drastically. Although it was not her first time on board a ship, it was her first seafaring experience, and the rocking floor had an unsettling effect on her stomach. Having read somewhere that fresh air helped to cure seasickness, Brie wished she had thought to ask for permission to go up on deck.

She soon had another reason for wanting to leave her cabin; she was used to an active life, and with nothing to occupy her time, she shortly became bored. After nearly an hour of fighting nausea and restlessness, Brie decided to risk Dominic's disapproval and go topside. Retracing her steps along the companionway, she made her way up a steep flight of steps and found herself on the gleaming, well-scrubbed deck. A cold sea breeze stung her cheeks and whipped her skirts around her, but once she was in the open air, her queasiness disappeared. She found an unobtrusive spot on the aft deck where she could watch the receding shores of England shining golden in the early morning sunlight.

No one bothered her, and after a while Brie found herself paying more attention to the fascinating activities of the crew than the scenery. All of the sailors were busy with something—raising and lowering sails, securing lines, calling out signals, or climbing the rigging. Brie's heart jumped to her throat when she saw a young man slip and make a grab at one of the topmast stays, but he didn't fall. The next instant he was scurrying up the ratline like a monkey, as if he hadn't just nearly missed a thirty foot plunge to his death.

Dominic was also on deck, she noticed. He was near the helm, talking to the gray-haired man at the wheel, but he seemed to be ignoring her presence entirely. Brie could not dismiss him as easily. He looked so vitally masculine, standing there with his feet apart, well braced, and his hands stuffed in the pockets of his greatcoat as the wind ruffled his ebony hair. Just looking at him brought a tingle to her skin. His body was superb, muscular and hard to the touch, and he knew so very well how to use it to make a woman . . .

Brie flushed, remembering his fierce lovemaking and the incredible passion he had so easily aroused in her, remembering also how he had shown his contempt by making her plead. She watched him wistfully, wondering if she would ever succeed in getting him to trust her again. She could understand why Dominic would feel hurt and betrayed, why he would want nothing more to do with her, but still she couldn't help wishing she hadn't lost the chance to win his love.

Feeling a sudden, tight ache in her throat, Brie turned abruptly and made her way forward to the bow. The English Channel stretched out before her, the waves catching the rays from the sun and dazzling her eyes with silver splendor. She could see the shoreline of France in the distance, and as she took in the beauty of the magnificent scene before her, she was able to forget for a moment the tension and heartache of the past few days.

The same could not be said for Dominic. In spite of his seeming indifference, he had been aware of Brie's presence from the moment she came up on deck. Indeed, she had never been out of his thoughts since he had woken that morning to a throbbing headache. And no matter how hard he tried, he ouldn't keep his gaze from inadvertently straying to where he stood at the rail.

She looked devastatingly lovely this morning, Dominic thought, seeing her in the cloak he had searched three different shops to find. He had roused two grumbling shopkeepers and a dressmaker from their beds to provide an adequate wardrobe for her, but it had been worth the trouble. The forest green color was stunning on her, just as he had expected it would be, and the way the rich sable framed her face was enchanting.

But it was more than Brie's beauty that kept her at the center of his thoughts, just as it was more than a severe hangover that was the cause of his savage mood. Each time he looked at her he could hear Jason's parting words ringing in his ears.

"You must marry her, Dominic," Jason had said when he learned Brie had spent the night in Dominic's room. "Your honor demands it. You have compromised the lady beyond all bounds."

Infuriated by the thought of being trapped into marriage, Dominic had sworn in response and told his friend to mind his own business. Jason had merely grinned. "I plan to do just that, my friend. My presence here is obviously *de trop*, so I will take myself back to London. I trust the next time we meet, I may wish you happy."

Dominic laughed mirthlessly. "You're more likely to read in the morning papers that my lifeless body has been discovered in some dark alley! Marriage to Brie would be impossible, as you well know."

"You have never been unable to manage a woman, Dom."

"Perhaps, but you are forgetting the circumstances. Would you have me bound to the family which has very nearly destroyed mine?"

"It is possible, of course, that there is a reasonable explanation and that Miss Carringdon is innocent of any involvement."

Dominic's expression hardened. "I can assure you, she will

not find life very pleasant if I discover otherwise."

"Well, then at least refrain from passing sentence until yo[u] learn the true facts. It isn't like you to jump to conclusions. [I] agree that her killing Boulter seems more than just circum[-]stantial, but she could be telling the truth. And I still say you[r] judgment may be clouded by whatever personal feelings yo[u] have for her, whether you admit it or not."

Jason had been right about that, Dominic thought with [a] snort of self-disgust. His judgment was definitely clouded Glancing at Brie again, he felt his fury rise. He was damned [i]f he would let a conniving little jade force him into marriage

Had she really been so devious? Has she really tried t[o] entrap him? She looked so fresh and innocent standing there a[t] the bow of his ship. The hood of her cloak had fallen back, an[d] the sun glinted off her upswept hair, turning the shinin[g] tresses to fire. Dominic felt an urge to unpin those gloriou[s] russet locks and run his fingers through the silken mass—bu[t] he knew if he went near her, he was likely to find his finger[s] wrapped around her throat as he tried to choke the truth out o[f] her.

Fortunately for Brie, his angry thoughts were interrupte[d] when the *Falcon*'s cabin boy came to announce that a luncheo[n] had been laid out in the ship's stateroom. Captain Roger[s] turned the wheel over to the second mate and went below, bu[t] Dominic stayed up on deck. He needed a moment to get hi[s] anger under control, or he knew he would find himself back i[n] England and facing murder charges.

Brie was seated at the table when the captain and three othe[r] of the ship's officers when Dominic at last joined them, and h[e] couldn't help noticing the immediate effect his arrival had o[n] her. One moment she was laughing delightedly at somethin[g] Rogers had said, her eyes bright and sparkling. The next, sh[e] had stiffened visibly and lowered her eyes to the table Dominic had trouble curbing the savage oath that sprang to hi[s] lips.

The meal could not have been called a success. Except for a[n]

occasional attempt at humor by the captain, the atmosphere remained subdued and even strained. Brie escaped as soon as politeness allowed, returning to her position by the rail where she tried to recapture her carefree feeling of a short while ago.

She failed miserably.

Angrily dashing away a tear with the back of her hand, she scolded herself for being an idiotic fool. What had she expected from Dominic? Warmth and affection? That he would come to trust her, perhaps even to love her? How could he when he barely acknowledged her presence? He had made it perfectly obvious that he would have preferred not to have her on board, for he had spoken little during lunch, and then only to the captain. His silence had chilled her, and she had discovered that she could bear his icy detachment no better than his anger. She shivered as she thought of the days ahead.

"Are you cold?"

Startled less by the question than the nearness of his voice, Brie turned to find Dominic standing behind her. He was watching her intently, but his expression was impossible to read. "Do you care?" she countered.

Something flickered for just an instant in his gray eyes, before they became impenetrable once again. "I can have Jacques find something warmer for you to wear," he said evenly.

Brie lifted her chin. "My cloak is quite adequate, thank you. Besides, I would not want to put *Jacques* to any trouble."

If she had hoped to provoke Dominic, she failed. Without replying, he moved to stand beside her at the rail, gazing out over the waves.

They were both silent for a time. Then, because she sensed Dominic would have preferred to remain so, Brie spoke. "I have not yet thanked you for letting me travel with you, my lord."

He shrugged. "I expect you would go to France, regardless. This way I can at least keep an eye on you and see that you don't run into the same trouble I found you in last night."

Brie flushed at his cool reminder of what had happened on the docks. "I haven't seen Lord Effing about," she observed changing the subject. "Is he on board the ship?"

Dominic's mouth twisted wryly as he slanted a glance at her "Jason returned to London this morning. It seems he was under the impression that I might prefer your company to his."

Wincing at his sarcasm, Brie wondered if she had been wise to start this conversation. "Well," she said, determined not to lose her temper before Dominic lost his, "allow me at least to thank you for the clothes you provided for me. It must have been difficult to come by them so early in the day."

"It was nothing."

"I marvel at the excellent fit."

Dominic's gaze swept her slender figure. "I've had a little practice," he replied blandly.

"Choosing garments for your mistresses, no doubt," Brie muttered.

She regretted her remark at once, for Dominic's gray eyes gleamed with sudden amusement. He turned toward her leaning an elbow on the railing. "But of course, mademoiselle I have always been generous to the women under my protection."

"I will not be your mistress!"

Dominic's mouth crooked in a provoking grin. "You haven't been asked yet, cherie," he said mildly. "Besides, I could hardly allow you to travel with me, dressed in those boy's rags you always wear."

Brie glared up at him, wanting to slap him. "How considerate you are, my lord! I suppose it was my ill fortune that your kindness didn't prevent you from forcing yourself upon me last night. Your behavior was despicable—"

Brie's words were abruptly cut off as she found her arm caught in an iron grip, with Dominic's snarling face only inches from hers. Seeing the icy glitter in his eyes, Brie realized that she had finally moved him to anger, but the knowledge

342

idn't give her much satisfaction. In fact, she was suddenly a
ittle afraid of him.

"So your enjoyment was a pretense, was it, Brie?" he said
menacingly. "Then I congratulate you. Your performance was
better than the most desirable whores of my acquaintance."

"How dare you!" she hissed, furious at his insult. Yet her
anger quickly turned to dismay as she was pulled roughly into
Dominic's arms. She pushed frantically against his chest,
trying to reason with him. "Dominic, not here! The sailors—"

"You forget, cherie, that I own this vessel. And while you
are under my protection, you are mine." He kissed her then,
ruthlessly, punishingly, wanting to crush her defiance and
tame her proud spirit.

Unprepared for the violence of his kiss, Brie emerged from
his embrace bruised and trembling and—Heaven help her—
weak with desire. She averted her face, not wanting him to
know how strongly he had affected her. "Your presumptions
are ill founded, Lord Stanton," she whispered hoarsely. "I am
not yours, nor do I enjoy being mauled. Now if you are quite
finished humiliating me, I will return to my cabin."

Dominic, too, was shaken from their encounter, but he had
far more experience hiding his feelings. "Ah, yes," he said
nastily. "Once more the lady whose reputation has been
compromised. Will you now demand marriage as compensa-
tion for your lost honor?"

Brie's eyes flew to his face, but for a moment she was too
stunned even to reply. Then, suddenly, she began to laugh. "I
am sorry, Dominic," she finally gasped, "but it lacked only
that to . . . to put a c-cap on this ridiculous adventure! I know
you think me capable . . . of such ex-extortion, but you may
rest easy. You are s-safe with me. You . . . you have to be the
last man . . . I would ever, ever . . . choose to marry!"

Knowing she sounded hysterical, Brie put a hand over her
mouth, but she was unable to stop laughing. Deciding that she
had better return to her cabin, she turned and made her way
unsteadily across the deck to the hatchway.

Dominic watched her disappear in silence, his fingers tightly gripping the rail. Damn the little witch! How she cut up his peace! His chest ached with the turmoil she stirred in him. Last night when she had turned away from him to weep softly onto her pillow, he had felt guilty as hell. And this morning, when Jason had insisted that marriage was the only course, he had been furious with himself for overlooking such an obvious trap. But even knowing that Brie might have planned to use his weakness for her to her own advantage, he hadn't been able to leave her behind. And now . . . now he only felt a strange aching emptiness.

Could he believe what she had said just now, that marriage wasn't her aim? She had seemed genuinely astonished by the suggestion, before she had started laughing so wildly.

But even that was a minor issue. The real question was could he trust her? Could he believe her when she said that she was merely an innocent victim of circumstances?

Dominic turned to gaze to the French coast. He had crossed the Channel many times in service to the English crown, though generally under the cover of darkness. His missions then he had treated as a game, where the wrong move could perhaps result in his death, but where the prize was the balance of power between European nations. Once again he was involved in a situation that could cost him his life. But what now was the reward for winning? And why did he have this persistent feeling that the elusive prize would be as important to him as life itself?

They docked at Dieppe late in the afternoon, and once the coach was off-loaded, Dominic ordered his small party to press on. Brie wasn't at all surprised when Dominic elected to ride in the box, rather than share the carriage with her, but she staunchly pretended his actions didn't matter. And at least, the arrangement would give her an opportunity to sleep something she couldn't do easily under Dominic's penetrating

344

gaze. Pulling a blanket over her lap, she settled back against the cushions and closed her eyes.

When nightfall approached, she was still asleep. She didn't even wake when the coach pulled into the courtyard of an inn some ten miles outside Rouen, or when Dominic opened the carriage door to hand her down.

Impatient with the delay, Dominic leaned into the carriage, searching the dark interior. Seeing Brie curled up in the far corner asleep, he felt his breath catch in his throat. The picture she presented was one of artless seduction. Her hood had fallen back again, letting a riot of curling tendrils escape their pins, while a ray of lantern light fell upon her face, lending her skin a golden glow. Her dark lashes lay on her cheeks like soft shadows, and her coral lips were slightly parted, seeming to beckon for a kiss.

Her charming dishevelment affected Dominic strangely; the anger that had been simmering inside him for the past two days vanished. He reached out to run a finger over Brie's lower lip, his own mouth curving in a smile. He would find out the truth, he promised himself, one way or another, but until then he would give her the benefit of doubt.

Brie's eyes fluttered open when he gently shook her awake, but the shock of meeting Dominic's gaze held her immobile. His gray eyes were warm and teasing, and he was smiling at her in that half-tender, half-amused way that always set her heart thudding against her ribcage. Brie felt a shiver of excitement run through her, knowing exactly what that look promised.

Dominic's smile widened into a grin as he folded his arms across his chest and leaned a shoulder against the doorframe. "I hate to disturb your nap, cherie, but unless you intend to spend the night in the coach, you had better make yourself presentable. I can't allow you to enter a public inn looking like you've been repeatedly tumbled by an ardent lover. It might give some hot-blooded male the notion to try his own luck."

Brie knew she ought to respond with something appropriately cutting, but she still wasn't fully awake. She contented herself with glaring groggily at Dominic as she sat up and tried to repair her appearance.

Dominic waited as Brie smoothed her rumpled skirts, but when she attempted to subdue her unruly tresses, he grew impatient again. Pushing her clumsy fingers out of the way, he drew her hood up to cover her hair and tucked the remaining tendrils out of sight.

"I can manage without your help," Brie grumbled, uncomfortably aware of Dominic's nearness. "I am not a child, you know."

His eyes dropped the length of her body and he chuckled. "How clever of you, my sweet. You have discovered the one topic with which we are in complete agreement."

Brie didn't deign to reply. She merely gave Dominic a withering glance as he handed her down from the coach and preceded him to the inn.

The innkeeper was a widow—small, sour faced, and thoroughly French in her conviction that the English were not much better than the aristocrats her fellow countrymen had guillotined during the Revolution. Dominic had no difficulty overcoming her prejudices, however.

Brie watched his progress in awe, finding it hard to follow his rapid, colloquial French, but having no trouble seeing the effect his considerable masculine charm had on the widow. When the Frenchwoman actually began to blush and simper, Brie rolled her eyes at the ceiling, wondering if all women behaved like idiots when Dominic merely smiled. But then she remembered that she too had found Dominic fascinating and impossible to resist. She lowered her gaze to the crudely woven carpet and kept it trained there until the proprietress was ready to show them upstairs.

Much to Brie's relief, she and Dominic were given separate bedchambers. The room was also far more cheerful than she had expected. A welcome fire burned in the hearth, and the rather large bed, bare of hangings, looked clean and comfortable. When she spied the big wooden tub in the corner,

346

Brie felt her spirits rise considerably. She asked if she might have a bath before supper, and the Frenchwoman grudgingly agreed to send up some hot water, as well as a tray of food.

While she waited, Brie removed her cloak and gloves and hung the spencer of her travelling suit in the wardrobe. That done, she found herself staring thoughtfully at the bed and wondering why Dominic had decided not to share it with her. She had no desire to repeat the previous night's humiliating scene, but the thought that he might not want her wasn't as comforting as it should have been.

When a knock sounded at the door, Brie hesitated, thinking that it might be Dominic. But it turned out to be a procession of maids carrying cans of hot water. They were followed by two strapping lads who lugged a large trunk into the room and set it beside the bed.

Brie was puzzled by the trunk and curious to find out what it contained. While the tub was being placed in front of the fire and filled, she inspected the contents. To her surprise she discovered more clothing, enough to fill her needs for an extended journey. Brie smiled softly, realizing that Dominic had gone to greater trouble than he had acknowledged.

When the servants had gone, she carefully closed and locked the door. Anticipating the pleasure of a long bath, she undressed quickly and sighed with contentment as she stepped into the tub. When she had scrubbed herself till her skin was pink and glowing, she washed her hair, then relaxed back against the rim, letting her tired limbs relax. The water felt heavenly, and she closed her eyes, willing her mind to shut out the unsettling images that drifted through it.

The peaceful interlude didn't last long. It seemed like only a moment before she heard the barely discernible creak of a floorboard. Realizing that she wasn't alone, Brie gave a start and sat up. She gasped when she saw Dominic standing beside the tub, looking down at her, his eyes glinting roguishly. His shirt was opened to the waist, displaying a broad expanse of dark-furred chest, and he had a towel flung carelessly over one shoulder.

Seeing where his warm gaze was focused, Brie hastily covered her breasts with her arms. "How did you get in here?" she demanded breathlessly, affronted at her lack of privacy.

"There is a door behind that screen which connects our rooms," Dominic replied, a smile playing on his lips. Cocking his head to one side, he gave her a full grin. "Why such modesty, cherie? I am quite familiar with your body by now. There is no need to hide."

Brie ignored his teasing remark and sank lower in the tub. "What do you want?" she asked, watching him warily.

"Can't you guess?" His gray-eyed gaze roamed her bare shoulders and dipped lower, coming to rest again on the glistening hollow between her breasts. Brie felt her stomach muscles tighten.

When she didn't answer, Dominic added softly, "Are you afraid?" His tone was gentle, much like a caress, and hearing it Brie bit her lip. Afraid? Yes, she was afraid. Not of his violence, for she could fight that with anger. But if he touched her with tenderness, she would respond in the same shameless, wanton way she had the night before. And she could tell by the look in his eyes that Dominic knew it, too.

Brie shook her head. She had to steel herself against his charm, his physical attraction. Even if it meant fighting him every step of the way, she couldn't let herself give in to him so easily.

To her dismay, Dominic tossed his towel on the chair that flanked the fireplace and leisurely began to undress. Seeing the flexing muscles of his arms as he removed his shirt, Brie wondered frantically if there were any way she could delay the inevitable. "You'll get wet," she murmured in a faint voice.

Dominic threw back his head and laughed. "But of course, ma belle. That is what one usually does when one bathes. I thought I would share your bath, since it seemed a shame to put our kind hostess to further trouble. I trust the water is still warm?"

When his breeches followed his shirt, Brie averted her eyes from the magnificent sight of Dominic's nakedness and reached for a towel to cover herself. "I don't believe your motives include sparing the servants," she retorted, irritated by his mocking humor. "You are doing this to annoy me. If I were a man, I would—Oh!" Brie yelped as she was suddenly lifted from the tub and set on her feet.

When Dominic's arms wrapped around her waist, pulling her full against him, her heart started to beat so wildly that she was certain he could hear it. The linen towel was still between them, but it was a negligible barrier to Dominic's hard lean body. Brie could feel the heated warmth of his skin as her breasts pressed against his chest, and she couldn't help but be aware of his flagrant masculinity as her thighs molded against his powerful ones. There was no question that he was aroused.

Feeling a hot blush flood her cheeks, Brie focused her gaze on the corded muscles of Dominic's throat, watching the strong beat of his pulse. But when he gripped her chin between his fingers and forced her to meet his gaze, she saw that his grin had faded.

"If you were a man, my sweet," he said grimly, "you would be long since dead. You should be thankful that your body still has its attractions, that you can turn a man's blood to fire."

When she didn't reply, he held her away a little and with a finger, traced a damp path between her breasts. "What is your game, Brie?" he asked, his tone softening. "What secret thoughts are hidden by your bright eyes? Are you a sorceress seeking to bewitch me with your soft lips and seductive curves?"

Brie could only stare at him and wonder at the strange expression in his eyes. Oddly, she could read uncertainty in the gray depths, and she could see anguish flickering there as well.

Then, as if he had said too much, Dominic abruptly released her. Brie shivered as the warmth from his embrace faded. Turning away, she wrapped the towel defensively around her.

When she heard a splash behind her, she knew Dominic had stepped into the tub and that she was safe for the moment. Her voice dropped to almost a whisper. "What colorful images you have of me, my lord. First a murderess, then a marriage-minded whore, and now a witch. You really must make up you mind, for I cannot be all three. It would be illogical for me to wish both to kill and to marry you; and if I truly were a witch, no doubt I could have found a way out of this predicament before now. God, how I wish that I had never laid eyes on you!" She paused, staring at the fire. "But I won't burden you any longer. I will not be leaving with you tomorrow."

"Do you think it that simple, Brie?"

"I beg your pardon?" She turned to find Dominic watching her intently as he rubbed soapy lather over his chest and shoulders.

"I don't intend to let you out of my sight until this is over," he said holding her gaze.

Her eyes widened in amazement. "Do you mean to keep me a prisoner then?"

Dominic was silent for a long moment. "Only until I have seen your grandfather," he responded at length. "Then you may do as you wish."

"You can't bring yourself to trust me, is that it? What do you think I'll do? Run to him and warn him of your arrival?"

Dominic didn't answer. When he reached for a can and poured warm water over his head and torso, Brie spun around and stalked over to the trunk where she rummaged angrily through the contents, searching for a nightgown. Unable to find one, she pulled on a wrapper of green silk and tied the sash with a jerk.

"Why did you follow me, Brie?" she heard him ask softly.

Startled by the question, she turned to look at him. Was he finally giving her a chance to explain? "I told you why," Brie said stubbornly. "I don't believe my mother caused your father's death. How could she when she spent her life helping others? She even died because of her selflessness; she caught a fever while she was nursing a tenant's child. My mother was the most loving person I've ever known. She was gentle and kind, and she never hurt anyone or anything in her life. I don't expect you to understand that," Brie said bitterly, tears sparkling in her eyes, "but I want her name vindicated."

Dominic seemed unmoved by her impassioned declaration. "Then you should have no objection to continuing the journey with me," he observed calmly as he reached for his towel.

"I doubt my preferences would matter to you. You delight in riding rough-shod over people."

"Brie, I . . ." He broke off, scowling as if she had hit a sensitive nerve. When he looked away, she could see a muscle tighten in his jaw.

Brie watched him for a moment, wondering what he had been about to say to her. When he remained silent, she turned her back and began to towel her hair dry. She tensed when she heard Dominic step out of the tub, but he only finished drying himself off and picked up his clothes, leaving the room without a word. Brie breathed a sigh of relief. She had not expected to be let off so easily.

Pulling the armchair before the hearth, she sat down to comb the tangles from her hair. The warmth from the fire helped to dry her long tresses, but they were still curling damply about her shoulders when a knock sounded at her door.

It turned out to be the proprietress again, announcing that supper had been laid out in monsieur's chamber. Incensed by Dominic's blatant disregard for her wishes, Brie marched across the room and flung open the door that connected her room with his. "Perhaps you weren't aware," she said mutinously, "but I requested a tray in my room."

Dominic gave Brie's green-clad figure an appreciative perusal, taking in her flushed cheeks and riotous tresses, but he wisely withheld his comments about her provocative appearance. "So you did," he replied evenly, "but I thought this would be more pleasant."

"Pleasant?" Brie mocked. Her eyes swept the room, finding

351

it a mirror image of her own. The only difference was that instead of a tub, a supper table had been set before the fire. The table was heavily laden with dishes, and the appetizing aroma that filled the room made Brie realize how hungry she was. She hesitated, watching Dominic cautiously as he poured two glasses of wine.

To her chagrin, she found herself distracted by Dominic himself. The full-length dressing gown he wore was black embroidered with silver dragons, and the colors greatly enhanced his dark good looks, making his harsh, aristocratic features seem even more striking. He exuded male attraction, Brie thought with mingled dread and anticipation. It wasn't hard to tell that he was naked beneath the robe, for where it parted at the throat, his muscular chest was bare, and where it belted at the waist, the rich silk molded against his narrow hips and the rippling sinews of his thighs. Brie swallowed hard, wondering if this were part of some plan to lure her into his bed.

"You planned this, didn't you? That's why there was no nightgown with the other clothes you provided."

The corner of his mouth curved upward. "Honestly, I forgot about a nightgown. It isn't high on my list of requirements for the women who share my bed."

"I won't sleep with you!"

"I think you will, Brie."

It was said lightly, and Brie expected to see amusement in Dominic's eyes when he looked up from pouring the wine. But there was no laughter or mockery in his gaze, not even any lust. His expression was completely serious. When he held out a glass, she accepted it, but she went to stand before the hearth, where she wouldn't have to meet his penetrating gaze.

The crackling fire seemed to grow louder as the silence stretched between them. Finally Dominic broke it. "Don't you think it time we put an end to this verbal fencing, Brie? We have been at each other's throats since London, and I for one am heartily sick of it."

Feeling a tight ache in her throat, Brie looked down at her glass. Didn't he know that she hated fighting with him? Didn't he know her heart bled a little with each hurtful exchange that occurred between them? "So am I," she whispered.

Dominic sighed. "I suppose I should start by explaining what happened at the Copely's ball. I didn't stage that scene in the drawing room, Brie."

She turned to stare at him, her eyes widening. "But those men . . . they knew you would be there. If you didn't ask them to meet you, then who did?"

"Denise Grayson, I regret to say. She sent them to find me, intending for them to interrupt our discussion exactly as they did. But I was just as surprised as you were when they barged in."

"You might have told me."

Dominic's mouth twisted wryly. "I tried to at the time, but you gave me little chance to explain. Afterward, I was too angry to stay in the same room with you, much less soothe your outraged virtue." He paused, taking a swallow of wine, then raised his intent gaze to her again. "I don't find it easy to apologize, Brie, but I would like to say I'm sorry for what happened. I had no intention of subjecting you to such ridicule."

Brie was too amazed to reply. Dominic smiled briefly at her silence, then continued. "As for our present situation, perhaps a truce is in order. You have a purpose for coming to France, so do I. I can give you information and protection, whereas you can offer me . . . comfort of a physical nature. A bargain of sorts, struck with reluctance on both sides, but nevertheless one from which we can each profit. On my part, I will refrain from making accusations and questioning your motives. That alone should reduce and friction between us. On your part . . ."

Dominic paused, his eyes searching her face. Then slowly, he moved toward her, till he was near enough for her to feel the heat of his body. Taking her wine glass, he set it on the table along with his own. "I want a woman in my bed, Brie," he said softly. "Not a shrew or a martyr, but a woman who is passionate and willing."

Brie stared up at Dominic, hypnotized by his gaze, by his nearness. The firelight masked his dark features in shadow, but his eyes burned with their own flames. Seeing the desire reflected in the gray depths, Brie was suddenly flooded with a wave of longing so fierce that she trembled. All thought of arguing fled. There was no past, no future, nothing but this moment. She took the final step toward him, closing the distance between them. Slowly reaching up, she encircled Dominic's neck with her arms, letting her body press against his.

His mouth came down on hers then, hard and hot and compelling, branding her with fierce, possessive kisses as he crushed her to him more fully. A low moan sounded in Brie's throat. She could feel Dominic's hands moving feverishly over her body, wanting, needing, taking. . . .

Later, when she lay naked in his arms, her passion spent, Brie couldn't recall how they had come to be in his bed. She remembered Dominic thrusting into her with a fierceness that stopped her breath, even remembered crying out his name as they plummeted from the dizzy, soaring heights of ecstasy together, but she couldn't recall what they had been discussing before that.

Replete, she lay curled against him, her head on his shoulder, drawing dreamy patterns on his flat, hard-muscled stomach while his fingers played lightly in her hair. But she was very much aware when Dominic's arousing hands began to stroke her body again, and she responded with the same wild abandon as before, meeting his ravening need without restraint, surging against him, answering his tormented groans with gasping sobs of pleasure.

Still later, when they were satiated with lovemaking and the fires of passion were merely banked embers, they shared an intimate dinner, acting like lovers, laughing and touching and gazing into each other's eyes. And although the dishes had grown quite cold, no morsel had ever tasted so delectable to Brie, no wine so heady.

The intimate atmosphere vanished when two serving maids came to clear away the remains of their meal. Seeing the frank admiration in the girls' eyes as they shamelessly ogled Dominic, Brie experienced an intense stab of jealousy. Picking up her wine glass, she retreated to a far corner of the room where she no longer had to watch the display of fluttering eyelashes and swaying hips—even though she was still unable to ignore the annoying giggles.

At long last, however, the room became quiet. Brie could hear the scraping of a chair behind her as Dominic rose from the table, then footsteps as he crossed the room to her. She caught her breath as his arms slipped around her waist, wondering how she could experience such a sudden rush of desire at only the touch of his hands.

She felt his breath, warm and tantalizing against her temple, before his lips lowered to nuzzle the bare skin between her neck and shoulder. When his hands moved upward, gliding over the silken material of her wrapper to cup her breasts, Brie leaned weakly against Domonic's hard frame. A drugging heat was stealing over her, sapping the strength from her limbs.

His hands began caressing her breasts then, his thumbs running lightly over the silk-covered nipples, making Brie shudder with longing. "We have a long day ahead of us tomorrow, my sweet," he murmured huskily in her ear. "We had best try to get some sleep."

But it was not sleep that was on Dominic's mind as he led Brie to the bed and divested her of her wrapper. Nor was sleep his prevailing need as he rode again between her soft thighs. He felt only a hungering ache to possess her slim body, to capture the vixen and make her his own; only a fierce need to ease his desire for her—a desire that taunted him to the brink of madness.

Chapter Sixteen

Surprisingly enough, the fragile truce lasted. An easy camaraderie sprang up between Brie and Dominic, while a mellow warmth invaded their still somewhat spirited relationship.

Dominic proved to be an excellent travelling companion, alleviating the boredom of the long hours by describing the history of the places they passed and sharing amusing anecdotes about his past travels. Occasionally he would hire mounts at one of the posting inns, and he and Brie would ride horseback, retiring to the comfort of the coach only when they grew tired of the exercise. Brie soon began to relax in Dominic's company. Sometimes she even felt he was enjoying their private moments as much as she.

She was surprised when Dominic listened with apparent interest to stories of her own life. He seemed particularly intrigued when she told about shooting the stallion that had killed her father in a hunting accident. "But I don't remember it," Brie added hastily, not wanting any sardonic remarks about her predilection for using pistols. "John said that I was in shock and didn't hear him shouting at me. I pulled the trigger before anyone could stop me."

Thinking back to that time of loss, Brie felt her throat tighten. "My father's death affected me more than I would have thought possible," she murmured. "All I remember is feeling this great emptiness inside. Katherine was worried that I would never go back to living a normal life, but I eventually did. I think it was because my father's solicitors tried to convince me I wasn't capable of running Greenwood. They said I should sell and put the money in more experienced hands—meaning a man's hands, of course. But I threatened to take my business elsewhere and they finally gave in."

"You must have found it difficult to run Greenwood, being a woman," Dominic offered gently.

Meeting his eyes, Brie smiled. "Quite difficult. At first I was afraid I had made a mistake, for none of my father's clients would trust their affairs to a woman. But I learned to play the game—their way. I sent John to deal with them while I looked after the stables. They would have been horrified to learn that I was the one training their horses, but they never suspected. I couldn't have succeeded, though, if it hadn't been for John. After a year or two, we were able to change places again, and I even had a few successes of my own. And not just with younger men," Brie had said sharply when Dominic flashed her a suggestive grin.

The weather turned nasty as they left Paris, and that afternoon they were threatened by a terrific storm. They had put up at an inn that was small and crowded, but while Brie had to share a room with Dominic, she didn't mind; she lay warm and protected in his arms as the storm spent its fury overhead.

It was still pouring the next morning. When a sudden change in the wind made the windowpanes rattle, Brie came awake with a start. Seeing the rain lashing against the leaded glass, she shivered, feeling pity for anyone forced to brave the icy torrent. She buried herself deeper into the quilts, wishing Dominic were there to warm her but not having the energy to wonder where he had gone.

She had not been cold the previous evening—far from it. A soft smile curved Brie's lips as she remembered. She had worn one of his lawn shirts to bed, expecting to have it rapidly removed, but Dominic had seemed content merely to hold her, one strong hand stroking her arm, while the other played absently with a lock of her hair. She had been surprised when instead of making love to her, he had merely kissed the tip of her nose and closed his eyes, prepared to sleep.

Already thoroughly aroused herself, Brie felt a spark of irrational anger flare in her. She was so keenly aware of him that she was almost trembling with anticipation, and as she lay there, molded against his hard, warm body, the intensity of her arousal only increased. She could feel her breasts growing fuller, their hardened nipples straining against the thin fabric of her shirt, while the ache between her thighs grew, spreading hot fingers of sensation through her. And still Dominic did nothing to ease her torture.

A fiery blush came to Brie's cheeks as she recalled her wantonness then. Shifting from her comfortable resting place on his shoulder, she had begun kissing Dominic, tentatively at first, her lips nibbling at his throat and then hair-roughened chest. She could feel his stomach muscles tighten as her tongue flicked out to touch him, so she began licking patterns on his skin, deliberately trying to arouse him. He tasted faintly sweet and salty, and she loved it. Emboldened, she let her hand travel downward over his taut abdomen, stroking, caressing, her unpracticed movements tantalizing him with her search to give pleasure.

Brie heard Dominic's sharp intake of breath as her fingers closed around his enlarging member. His manhood felt scaldingly hot, but smooth and hard in her hand, like satin over steel. Daringly, she let her lips move lower, her hair cascading over his body as she knelt above him and found his throbbing shaft.

Dominic stiffened as if in pain when Brie teased him hesitantly with her tongue, but he gave a groan of pure animal pleasure when her mouth totally engulfed him. His hand came down on her head, tangling painfully in her hair, guiding her to a sure rhythm.

His response inflamed Brie. She herself was almost wild with hunger by the time Dominic caught her shoulders and rolled her on her back. His mouth clamped down on hers as he raised her shirt to her waist and grasped her hips. And then his shaft was driving deep within her, fiercely, endlessly, his sweet, savage thrusts igniting her senses in a blinding explosion.

She had fallen asleep, still joined to him.

When the pounding of the rain lessened, Brie heard a faint rustling noise. She rolled over and blinked. She had thought herself alone, but Dominic sat at the table near the cheerily burning fire, studying some papers spread out before him. He had covered himself with a dressing gown, she saw, and he looked more relaxed than she had ever seen him. His profile seemed less harsh than usual, in spite of the faint growth of bristle on his jaw, and his ebony hair, still tousled, made him look younger and more vulnerable.

As if he had sensed her watching, Dominic looked up and met her gaze. Brie's heart did a complete somersault when she saw the warmth in his gray eyes. She smiled at him, loving the softness in his expression. Dominic briefly returned her smile before shifting his gaze back to his papers.

Annoyed that he could forget her so easily, Brie stretched and brushed a strand of hair out of her eyes. "What time is it?" she asked in a voice still husky with sleep.

"A little past ten," he replied absently.

"Good God! Why didn't you wake me? I never sleep so late."

Dominic's lips twitched. "No matter, we won't be travelling today. The storm has made the roads poor going and I don't care to risk an accident in this downpour. You can stay in bed if you like. Would you care for some chocolate or coffee?"

Before Brie could answer, a knock sounded at the door. She barely had time to pull the covers up to her chin before Dominic gave permission to enter. It was his coachman, Jacques. With an apologetic glance at Brie, Jacques handed a rolled-up parchment to his employer, then left again, shutting the door quietly behind him.

Dominic was unfurling the paper when a pillow came flying across the room to hit him squarely in the head. He flinched, letting out an oath, and his narrowed gaze swung to Brie. "What the hell—"

"How dare you?" she demanded furiously, her face scarlet with embarrassment at being seen in Dominic's bed. "How dare you treat me like a . . . a . . . oooh!"

Her cry was one of pure outrage. She looked around wildly for something else to throw, but Dominic decided not to wait till she found something that would hurt. He was on her in an instant, pinning her beneath him, holding her arms by her sides. She fought him furiously. "Let me go, you . . . beast! I will not stand for this!"

After a struggle which left her gasping for breath but no less a captive, she finally quieted and merely glared at Dominic beneath her lashes. "You are hurting me," she said through clenched teeth.

Dominic's grip shifted, but he didn't release her as he returned her glare. "And I'll continue hurting you, until you tell me what in hell's name you're ranting about." His look turned to puzzlement. "Did Jacques say something, do something?"

"Yes! He found me in your bed, damn you! How dare you expose me to your servants in such a fashion?"

Dominic's grin was positively wicked. "Is that all? Jacques has seen women in bed before."

Brie itched to slap that provoking grin off his face. "In *your* bed?" she asked in a dangerous voice.

Dominic pursed his lips thoughtfully. "I don't remember. Shall I call him back so you may ask him?" He was unprepared for the spitting, clawing wildcat his teasing unleashed. It took every ounce of his strength to keep Brie from doing serious damage to his face. At last he wrestled her to a draw by rolling her on her stomach.

Face down, Brie was helpless. Dominic's legs were holding her immobile, while his hands twisted hers behind her back.

Her impotence only increased her rage, though, and the fact that her nose was pressed into the mattress left her positively rigid with fury. The bedlinens still bore traces of Dominic's masculine scent and the musky fragrance of their lovemaking.

"I could kill you!" she cried, her declaration muffled by the pillows.

Dominic's entire body stiffened. His reply, when it came, was low and savage in her ear. "So we are back to that, are we, cherie? How naturally talk of killing me comes to your lips. But I suppose I should thank you for reminding me. I've become so enamored of your charms lately that I stupidly forgot your true character. I warn you, though, were you to touch one hair on my head, Jacques would tie you to the nearest tree and flay your smooth skin from your beautiful body."

He released her abruptly then, as if he could no longer bear touching her. Pushing himself off the bed, he retrieved his clothes and without saying another word, slammed from the room.

Dismayed and shaken, Brie stared at the closed door. She had not meant to destroy the fragile bond between them—but she had, with a few angry words. Oh, when would she ever learn to hold her wretched tongue?

Shortly afterward, a servant brought her breakfast, but Brie found she couldn't eat. Her stomach seemed to be tied in knots. She took a long bath, but even that gave her little enjoyment.

She was sitting in a chair before the fire, slowly brushing her hair, when the bedroom door opened and Dominic walked in. Brie tensed when she met his gaze, for his expression was still arctic. Perversely, he had never seemed more handsome or more appealing. He had shaved and changed clothes, and was dressed casually in buckskin breeches and a full-sleeved white shirt.

Her eyes searched his face for some sign of softening as she waited for him to say something, *anything*. But when he merely shut the door and seated himself at the table before his forgotten papers, Brie resumed her brushing, staring sullenly at the fire. She would not *grovel* for his forgiveness.

She would have been gratified to know just how distracted Dominic was by her presence. Finding it difficult to concentrate on the documents before him, he frowned unknowingly at the parchment in his hand—a map showing what once had been the vast Valdois estates. He owned all the land now, except for a hundred or so acres that his agent had been unable to purchase. No doubt the disputed acreage belonged to Sir Charles since it bordered the Durham lands.

There was also a report on Valdois which gave a detailed account of the condition of the fields and chateau. Dominic's agent had warned him about the neglect and destruction the estate had suffered, but he could see that for himself as he perused the columns of figures. All of the income from the land had been spent elsewhere, not a penny going to increase the yield of what had once been profitable vineyards and farms. It would take years to rebuild the estate, years until it once again was self-supporting.

In spite of his efforts to study the rows of figures, though, Dominic found his mind wandering to Brie. She had finished brushing her hair and with deft fingers was pinning the shining russet locks into a knot. Her sedate appearance made him recall how seductive she had looked that morning, with her hair still tousled from their fierce lovemaking.

Remembering the soft smile Brie had given him when she had awakened, Dominic mentally flogged himself. Her smile had been a priceless jewel, one that had taken his breath away with its quiet brilliance. Afterwards he had found it impossible to concentrate on reports. All he wanted to do was climb back in bed and gather Brie's warm body in his arms.

But then Jacques had delivered the map. Dominic, in spite of his knowledge of women, had not understood Brie's anger and embarrassment. He had mocked her when he should have soothed. He now greatly regretted teasing her like that, almost as much as he regretted his subsequent outburst. Damn it, but he would be glad when this business was finished and he knew

363

the truth about her. The uncertainty was driving him mad.

Brie sighed then, reflecting Dominic's thoughts. Hearing the unhappiness in the soft sound, he watched as she stood and walked to the window. She stared out at the storm for several minutes, then began to pace quietly, while Dominic followed her with his gaze.

Admiring her gently swinging hips, he found himself picturing Brie as she had been the night before, without the elegant bronze silk gown, without the severe upswept hair style—but with her flaming hair streaming wildly over her shoulders, her head thrown back in ecstasy.

How her passion had delighted him! He had sometimes deplored Brie's aggressiveness for being far too masculine, but the previous evening her boldness had pleased him beyond rational thought. Dominic's eyes glinted as he recalled the hungry way she had touched him, had tasted him. She needed no urging from him to make love the way most well-bred woman would find scandalous. He could feel his groin muscles tightening at the mere memory.

Just when he felt he could no longer resist the lure of those shapely curves, though, Brie went to her trunk. Seeing her withdraw a cloak, he was surprised into asking what she meant to do.

Brie stiffened and lifted her chin. "I am going for a walk, if you don't object."

Dominic forced back a smile; Brie's portrayal of the haughty beauty was unequalled. "I'm afraid I must object," he replied, struck now by an irrational whim to keep her near him. "It's raining outside—or hadn't you noticed?"

"Of course I noticed. But I have been in worse weather."

"I'm not disputing your ability to withstand the elements, but the fact is, Jacques can't be spared to escort you at the moment and I personally have no desire to brave the storm." He paused, raising an eyebrow quizzically. "Would you have me accuse you of going to meet someone?"

Brie left off tying the strings of her cloak to stare

incredulously at him. "Just who am I supposed to meet?" she asked finally. "A lover, perhaps? Or your nameless enemies, or maybe even my grandfather? Your imagination astounds me!"

Seeing Dominic's unchanging expression, Brie threw up her hands. "Very well! Just to prove to you that there is no meeting, I will sit here and quietly go mad from boredom!" The low rumble in Dominic's throat sounded suspiciously like a chuckle, and it made Brie bristle. "I am serious, Dominic! I shall go distracted any minute now."

"Can you not sew or embroider or—"

"Is that how you think I occupy my time, *embroidery?*"

This time Dominic didn't hide his laughter. "Nothing so mundane or feminine as stitching for you, little wildcat, is that it?" Still chuckling, he rose and went to his trunk. Brie watched him warily, but Dominic only fished out a leather-bound volume and held it out to her. "You do read, do you not?"

Brie accepted his offering, arching an eyebrow when she saw the title. "Richard III? I didn't think your tastes ran to Shakespeare."

"I enjoy many things, cherie," he said with a grin. He tugged at the ribbons of her cloak, but when he slid the garment from her shoulders, Brie spun away and settled herself on the rug before the fire. She lay on her side, her head propped up with one hand and her feet tucked under her skirts. Watching her, Dominic couldn't help but smile. She was forever unconventional; never would she do the expected. He went back to his work, giving Brie only an occasional glance as he made his plans.

Some time later a discreet knock at the door brought an end to their quiet interlude. Remembering the contretemps of that morning, Dominic went to the door, giving Brie time to adjust her undignified position and smooth her skirts before a maidservant entered with a luncheon tray. The girl spread the dishes on the table and departed with a curtsy, leaving Brie and Dominic to enjoy a savory stew and a bottle of the inn's finest wine.

They ate in silence, a silence Brie felt acutely after the past few days of lively conversation and laughter. At the conclusion of the meal, she carefully set down her fork and launched into the apology she had formulated. "Dominic, I am sorry for what I said this morning. I didn't mean it . . . about killing you. I . . . I suppose I overreacted. Katherine has always said my greastest failing is my temper."

When she wouldn't look at him, Dominic reached out and gently grasped her chin. His eyes were warm and teasing again as they scanned her face. "No matter, vixen. The pleasure you bring me is enough to make me overlook your occasional tantrums."

Brie's eyes flashed at his provoking remark, but she held her temper in check as she twisted her chin from his grasp. "You can be so kind one moment, and yet such a beast the next."

Dominic leaned back in his chair, his expression suddenly hooded. "I never claimed to be kind, Brie. If I am, it is merely because of our agreement."

"I know," she said, looking away.

Feeling more despondent than ever, she rose and went to the window. The rain had almost stopped, but the world outside was still sodden and gray. It looked precisely the way her heart felt: miserable. Dominic wasn't coming to care for her. By his own admission, his cordiality was only a means to his own end—only a way of making the time spent in her company more bearable.

"Brie, come here." When she heard his soft command, she tried not to respond, but then his voice dropped to a caress and he said her name again. Slowly, Brie turned and went to him.

He was startled by the sadness in her eyes. Wanting very much to erase that look, Dominic curved an arm around her waist and gently pulled her down onto his lap. Tilting her face up to his, he stroked the delicate line of her jaw for a moment, then bent his head and kissed her.

His lips were soft and warm at first, moving over hers with

tender possession. But then his tongue began alternately to caress and plunder.

Brie responded with an awakening hunger, raising her hands to his shoulders, involuntarily curling her fingers into his hard muscles. Her tongue warred with his, dueling, caressing in return. When his arms tightened around her, pulling her closer, she felt a treacherous heat begin to build inside her. Dominic's thighs were like flexing granite beneath her, and the feel of his probing hardness through their layers of clothes aroused and excited her.

When his lips left hers to slide hotly across her cheek to her ear, Brie shuddered as a tremulous wave of longing racked her body. She made no protest as Dominic deftly unfastened the buttons at the back of her high-necked gown. He pushed the fabric from her shoulders, freeing her breasts from the confines of her chemise, then bent his head once more.

"Dominic!" Brie gasped as his mouth closed over her nipple. But as a sweeping wave of desire flooded her, she arched her back, shamelessly offering herself to him.

Dominic greedily accepted her offering. He savored the sweetness of her flesh, his tongue curling over the desire-swollen peaks, his teeth nipping at her with gentle fierceness. Brie was aching with need even before his hand found its way beneath her skirts, gliding past silk stockings and lacy garters to stroke a slender satin thigh, then beyond to the recesses of her femininity, already hot and wet with welcome.

Brie whimpered, her body straining against his, begging for release. But Dominic only nuzzled his face deeper into the satin hollow between her breasts, while his fingers continued expertly plying the softness between her thighs.

Finally Brie could stand no more. Her hands fumbled feverishly with the buttons of his breeches, until at last his sex sprang huge and proud from a nest of dark, curling hair. When Brie's fingers closed around him, Dominic sucked in his breath. "God . . . you little witch."

Feeling his control begin to slip, he raised her gown to her waist with savage impatience, baring her fully. Then grasping her hips, Dominic lifted Brie to settle her astride him, onto his powerful shaft. He closed his eyes and groaned as he was sheathed in rippling velvet.

He might have proceeded slowly if Brie hadn't begun to move her hips in a desperate attempt to assuage the aching need he had created in her. Losing all control then, Dominic closed his hands over her buttocks, lifting her up only to bring her down again, and then again, thrusting himself even more deeply inside her each time, his hardness impaling her soft flesh.

Brie loved his fierceness. Sobbing, she threw her head back, mindlessly digging her nails into his muscled back as his body slammed upwards into hers. She felt him shaking and throbbing inside her as she cried out his name. And then came the blinding explosion, an intense burst of pleasure that sent sweet shocks flooding through her and Dominic, as well.

When it was over, Brie collapsed on his chest in breathless exhaustion, her arms still wrapped around his neck, her face buried in his shoulder.

His own breath coming in ragged gasps, Dominic let his head fall back. "I suppose that is one way to end a quarrel," he said with a weak laugh.

"Mmmm."

His hand moved caressingly over her bare shoulders, then upward to stroke her hair. "We shouldn't talk, ma belle. Our bodies say everything that needs to be said."

When she only responded with a feeble nod, Dominic shifted so he could study her face. Her lips were red and glistening and bruised with passion, and her skin was flushed with color. When Brie slowly opened her eyes, Dominic could see they were a deep, languorous green. There was no reproach in those lovely changing eyes, he realized with pleasure. Their coupling had been pure animal lust, but she had wanted it as much as he.

Even as he came to that conclusion, Dominic felt a new

quickening in his loins and shook his head in amazement. Damn, but it was impossible! His desire was starting again. Could he never get enough of her to be satisfied?

He rose with Brie in his arms and carried her to the bed. Then wordlessly he undressed her, taking his time, not bothering to disguise his admiration of her body as he removed his own clothes.

Feeling his eyes move over her with lazy ownership, Brie flushed. But she was less embarrassed by Dominic's casualness than by her own desire to reach out and run her hands over his magnificent, sun-darkened body.

"What must you think of me?" she said ruefully when she was once again lying in Dominic's arms, her head on his chest. "I may have been rash before, but I've never been *abandoned*."

Dominic smiled as he removed the pins from her hair and tossed them, one by one, somewhere in the vicinity of their pile of cast-off clothing. "Ah, yes, abandoned, wanton, depraved. . . ."

"Indeed, I am not!" Brie raised herself up on one elbow to glare at him, before seeing the laughter dancing in his gray eyes. "No more so than you, at any rate," she said, wrinkling her nose at him. When Dominic flashed her a grin, she trailed a finger down his well-muscled chest. "Beware, my lord, or I shall demand payment for my favors."

Dominic sighed heavily. "Then I should be a poor man, cherie. All the gold in the kingdom would not be sufficient payment for one sweet kiss from your lips."

"Very prettily said. But I think I should like you to be poor, Dominic. Perhaps then you would not be so arrogant and beastly."

Dominic laughed, tightening his arm around her. "'Tis not my wealth or lack of it that makes me so."

"No? Then what is it?"

Rolling till she lay beneath him, Dominic stared down into her wide eyes. "You, wench," he said soberly. "You are much too desirable for my peace of mind," He bent briefly to kiss a rosy-tipped breast, then raised his head. "What to do with you?" he asked softly, searching her face as if to find an answer to his problem.

Brie's answer was a mere whisper. "Love me, Dominic, just love me."

His eyes darkened slumbrously. And for a moment, before his mouth descended on hers, before his body merged with hers, Brie believed that the tenderness in his eyes was something more than desire. Dominic's heart belonged to her, if only for a moment.

The moment did not occur again. Brie had no further reason to suppose that Dominic's heart could be touched. And at least on one occasion before their destination was reached, their truce was threatened.

They were riding in the coach one afternoon, discussing the foibles of London society, when Dominic made a particularly cynical comment about women.

Brie stared at him with dawning comprehension. "I think I am beginning to understand you, my lord," she said slowly. "You hold my entire sex in contempt. Women are only useful to you for physical pleasure. Other than that, they need not exist at all. But I suppose I should be comforted to realize you hate all women."

"I don't hate all women," Dominic returned, his features hardening.

"No? It isn't only I who has suffered your ill will. You dislike my cousin Caroline, and you believe the worst of my mother. Why even your own mother—Julian says you haven't spoken to her in years."

"That is quite enough, Brie. I don't deny that I have little regard for females in general, but you know nothing of my mother."

"I know she deserted your father when you were quite young."

"Congratulations."

Brie ignored his sarcasm. "I suppose since you never had the comfort of a mother's knee, you never learned to appreciate a woman's love."

Dominic shrugged. "What is there to appreciate?"

"I might have expected you to say that. You could live to be a hundred and never understand that particular emotion."

He raised a sardonic eyebrow. "And you are such an expert on the subject?"

Brie looked startled. "No, but—"

"Love is a maze that only fools enter willingly. By the time they find their way out—which inevitably happens—they find themselves trapped in a marriage contract, which only serves to perpetuate the race and begin the cycle again."

"I could almost pity you, Dominic, except that you would throw it back in my face."

"How right you are. Now if you are quite finished—"

"I suppose you think women are at the root of all this evil. Tell me, is it the male character which inspires your trust? Are men, in your opinion, the only ones deserving your high regard?"

His eyes narrowed dangerously. "Are you attempting to reform me, Brie?"

"That would be impossible!"

For a moment they glared at each other. But then Dominic leaned back in his seat, looking amused. "There, we have found another topic on which we agree. Incidentally, I seem to recall a number of instances where you have flaunted convention. Your breeches, for instance."

"We were discussing you," Brie retorted.

"No, *you* were discussing me. I was trying to change the subject."

"You are confusing the issue! Conventions have nothing to whatever do with character. And why must you bring my breeches into the conversaton? You are mocking me again, Dominic. I thought we had a bargain."

371

His lips curved into a slow smile, while glowing lights began to dance in his eyes. "Ah, yes, our bargain. Shall I give you an opportunity to fulfill your part, cherie?"

Brie glanced at him in puzzlement when he reached up to draw the curtains across the windows, but she had no trouble comprehending Dominic's purpose when he wrapped a strong arm around her waist and lifted her onto his lap.

"But, Dominic—" she protested halfheartedly as he started to unfasten the buttons of her spencer.

"We won't be disturbed," he assured her before silencing her protests with his lips.

Two mornings later their truce dissolved completely. Brie woke feeling apprehensive, knowing that the day would see them at their journey's end. Already they had penetrated deep into the wine country, having passed through Chalon the day before and turned south toward Lyon.

Brie opened her eyes slowly. The faint gray light filtering into the bedroom promised little in the way of warmth and only served to increase her foreboding. Lifting her head, she peered down at Dominic. She was surprised to see that he was awake. He was lying with one arm flung across his forehead as he stared at the ceiling.

Sensing his withdrawal, Brie felt an inexplicable chill run up her spine. Dominic's gray eyes were arctic, holding no trace of the warmth that had been present the past few days. His expression seemed so forbidding that she edged away from him a little.

"Is it far?" she ventured at last.

"Far?"

"To your home."

"A half-day's ride, no more. Dress warmly. I expect it to rain."

His expressionless tone reminded Brie of icicles in winter, and her heart sank. The wall was between them again. She could almost see it. Her fingers plucked nervously at the blanket. "And when we arrive? What do you intend to do?"

Dominic turned his head to look at her, his eyes narrowing as he studied her face. "That remains to be seen."

Brie's gaze slid away from his. "You still don't trust me. I-I had hoped. . . ."

"What had you hoped? That I would dismiss the possibility of your past involvement? You have a very poor opinion of me, cherie, if you think I so easily confuse business and pleasure. Although I admit it has been a pleasure." He reached over to stroke her cheek, but Brie recoiled in pain and anger.

"Don't touch me!" she cried, leaping from the bed. "Don't you dare touch me." Catching up her wrapper, she threw it about her shoulders. "This 'business' cannot be concluded too rapidly for my taste. A truce, you say. But only so long as it serves your purpose. Well, it appears that I have served your purpose long enough. You can damned well seek your pleasures elsewhere!"

Not wanting Dominic to see the hot tears that filled her eyes, Brie fled to the safety of her own bedchamber, slamming the connecting door behind her. She would see him in hell before she let him see her cry.

Leaning against the door, she clenched her fists in an effort to stem the tears rolling down her cheeks. Stupid, stupid fool! She had fallen in love with a man who wouldn't give tuppence to spare her feelings, had allowed herself to be hurt, time and time again. When would she learn that Dominic didn't care for her, that he never would? She must come to terms with that understanding—before her heart broke into little pieces.

It was quite a while before Brie had control of herself again, but then she poured water in a bowl and splashed some on her flushed face, trying to erase the traces of tears.

Breakfast in the common room of the inn was a solemn affair. Brie ate in stony silence, trying to ignore both Dominic and the bustle around her. She was grateful when at last Jacques came to inform them the carriage was ready.

Once on their way, Brie couldn't help contrasting this leg of their journey with previous ones. She was alone in the coach and there was no spirited banter or pleasant companionship to alleviate the boredom—not even any exercise to relieve the tedious miles. The day was gray and overcast, wrapping the countryside in gloom, and Brie spent so much of the time staring out the window that she grew to hate the dreary landscape with its endless vineyards patterning the hillsides.

They changed horses twice, but neither time when she stepped down to stretch her legs did she see Dominic. During their second stop, she was told by Jacques that Dominic had ridden on ahead.

At last, after what seemed to be an interminable interval, the carriage pulled off the main road. Jacques slowed the horses to a walk, but the lane was in such a sad state of repair that the coach bucked and swayed continually. Each rut and pothole jarred Brie's teeth, and several times she was almost thrown from the seat.

After a quarter mile or so, the lane gave way to a clearing—or at least what once must have been a clearing, Brie thought grimly as she noted the overgrown weeds and unkempt shrubbery. Then the coach crawled around a bend in the drive and the once-magnificent chateau came into view.

Seeing it, Brie gasped involuntarily. She had supposed the manor house might be in poor condition, but she hadn't expected the utter desolation of the place. Although the frame and main walls of the house still stood, great gaping holes took the place of leaded windows, and a section of the roof had collapsed where a limb from a nearby tree had fallen on it. Peeling paint and crumbling mortar completed the picture of abandonment and ruin, while a gray mist hovered around the place, giving the scene an unearthly aura. Brie shuddered at the eerie silence, suddenly not wanting to leave the relative security of the coach.

The soft jingle of a harness was the only sound she heard as she opened the door and stepped down. Jacques was still in the

374

driver's box, she noted, but he was staring grimly at the wreckage of the chateau.

Slowly, as if in a dream, Brie mounted the steps to the house. There was no front door to impede her progress, but she had to duck her head to avoid the cobwebs as she entered. If possible, the inside of the chateau was in worse state than the outside. Holding her skirts high to avoid the debris and rubble, she began a tour of the silent mausoleum.

Bits of crystal from a fallen chandelier crunched under her feet as she moved along the entrance hall. In rooms to her right and left, she could see broken pieces of furniture strewn on the moldering carpets, and all the walls were badly stained and oozing dampness. The once magnificent staircase was missing the banister, and Brie had to step carefully as she made her way upstairs.

On the second floor she discovered what must have been a music room. A discarded harp, its bow snapped in two, lay on a pile of charred wood. Someone had obviously built a fire—not in the fire place as one might expect, but in the middle of the room.

On the third floor Brie opened a door and checked abruptly. Dominic stood at the window with his back to her, his head bowed. He seemed not to have noticed her presence, but as Brie turned to leave, he suddenly spoke. "Welcome to my ancestral home, Miss Carringdon," he said, his voice sounding harsh and bitter.

Brie hesitated, not knowing how to respond. Then, without warning, Dominic suddenly whirled and threw something against the side wall with such force that the plaster cracked. Brie flinched, realizing when the object clattered to the floor that it was a broken toy soldier.

Dominic gave a derisive laugh at her startled expression. "This, by the way, is the nursery," he said in that same bitter tone. "And that," he added, pointing to the pieces of the wooden toy, "was once my favorite plaything. I always wondered what had become of it. I left it here that night, when the soldiers came for my father. I can remember, years later, still feeling uncomfortable at the sight of a uniform, even British."

His gaze returned to Brie, his eyes raking her figure as if daring her to mock him. She had no intention of mocking him, though. She could see the raw pain in his eyes, and her heart went out to him.

"Dominic," she said, searching for the right words. "It does no good to relive the past. Neither you nor I could have prevented what happened. Can you not forget?"

His mouth twisted in the curving sneer she hated so much. "Forget? That is hardly likely, mademoiselle, when your very presence in this house serves to remind me. Your mother used to visit here, did you know? In this very room, while I was at my lessons." He paused, regarding her narrowly. "Come here."

Suddenly wary, Brie hesitated. But when Dominic abruptly repeated his command, she slowly walked across the room to where he stood. He grasped her arm and turned her face to the window that overlooked the front lawns, then stepped behind her. When he placed his hands on her shoulders, Brie tensed, not quite sure of his intentions. But Dominic merely began to speak in a low, faraway voice.

"I have never forgotten that night," he said softly. "I was supposed to be in bed asleep, but instead I was here, playing with my wooden soldiers. When I heard a disturbance, I looked out this window and could see real soldiers—a small troop, actually. There." He pointed to the spot. "The sun had already set, but I could see the men's faces clearly in the light of the torches they carried. When I opened my window so I could peer down, I heard my father's voice demanding an explanation for the intrusion. He received no answer. I saw him walk down the front steps toward the waiting men, and didn't wait any longer but ran out of the nursery. I'm not sure what I intended to do. Save my father, I think, though from what danger I wasn't certain.

"Only years later did I understand why he had left the apparent security of the house. He was protecting *me*. Had he stayed, the revolutionary soldiers would have stormed his home, but as it was, the soldiers forgot me. I believe they were too surprised my father put up no struggle."

Brie closed her eyes, blinking back tears as she pictured the young boy Dominic had described. How frightened and bewildered he must have been to see his beloved father taken away by the soldiers. She wanted to say something to let him know she understood, but he spoke again.

"I raced downstairs, but when I reached the front hall, I came face to face with my tutor who caught me and very effectively ended my headlong rush into the fray. I fought him, to no avail. Then finally I quieted so I could hear what was being said. My father's arms were bound behind him, and he was speaking to their captain, demanding to know why he was being arrested. I almost laughed when I heard the charges, they were so outrageous. Treason and murder! Treason because he was of noble blood—that I could almost understand. As young as I was, I was aware of the mood of the country. I had heard all the gruesome details about what was happening in Paris from a travelling gypsy, and I could realize no nobleman was safe from the trumped-up charge of treason. But murder! He was charged with killing Lady Lisette, your grandmother. And it was your mother Suzanne who accused him."

Brie had been listening intently to Dominic's story, but she interrupted him at this point to deny her mother's involvement. "I don't believe it," she declared. "My mother would never do such a thing."

As if recalling her presence, Dominic dropped his hands from her shoulders and stepped back, putting a distance between them. "I haven't finished the story. The captain had barely gotten the words out of his mouth when your mother appeared on the scene. She threw her arms around my father,

377

protesting her innocence, much as you did just now—although her sobbing added a bit more drama. It was quite a touching scene."

Hearing the hard note in his voice, Brie turned to face Dominic, her eyes searching his face. "And you chose not to believe her?"

Her expression remained enigmatic as he returned her gaze. "It was too much of a coincidence not to. Had Suzanne Durham been innocent, she would not have known of the charges, nor would she have arrived at that particular moment. I don't think my father believed her either, for that matter. The soldiers took him away shortly, and I never saw him or your mother again. My tutor, having a high regard for his own skin—and mine as well, I suppose—bundled me up and whisked me off to England to my mother's family. I was told that my father would be safe once he could clear his name of the charges. It was less than a month later when we received word of his execution."

Brie stared at Dominic, wanting desperately to understand this complex, bitter man she had come to love. "Is that why you sided against the French during the war?" she asked finally. "You wanted revenge?"

Dominic looked away, sighing wearily. "Not precisely. Napoleon had to be stopped at all costs and I merely did my part. But you miss my point. Granted the tide of the revolution was evil, an uncontrollable evil, but it was merely an instrument which Suzanne Durham used to bring about my father's downfall."

"But if the comte really did kill my grandmother, that would explain my mother's action."

"Explain, perhaps, but not excuse. My father did not kill Lisette Durham."

"But how can you be sure?"

Dominic leveled his piercing gaze at Brie once more, and there was a long, pregnant pause before he spoke. "Cherie, you are either very, very naive, or you are a superb actress. You

378

almost had me doubting my father. But perhaps that is your game, after all."

It was all Brie could do to keep from looking away. She had always known Dominic was no more willing to believe her own innocence than her mother's, but his words still hurt. "I am playing no game, Dominic," she murmured, trying to keep the tremor from her voice.

"We shall see," he replied, the warning in his tone apparent. "We shall see."

Chapter Seventeen

Brie buried her hands beneath the folds of her cloak to hide their trembling, but it was a futile gesture. Dominic knew already how nervous and apprehensive she was. Yet how could she be otherwise when the atmosphere in the coach was fraught with tension as she and Dominic approached their final destination?

When they had left the Valdois estates a few hours before, they had gone to the village inn where Dominic ordered rooms and a light repast to be served in the private parlor. Brie had made no pretense of eating, but if Dominic noticed her lack of appetite, he hadn't commented on it. Afterward he had told her to wait in her room until the horses were rested. When they set out once more, Dominic rode with her in the coach. He was silent and preoccupied, and Brie remained just as silent, hoping fervently that the impending confrontation with Sir Charles Durham would provide both a key to the past and a vindication of her own actions.

The coach finally came to a halt before a house which wasn't as large as the Valdois chateau but had been built in a similar style. Dominic handed Brie down from the carriage, then escorted her to the front door.

It was quite a while after his knock that the door was opened a mere crack. A slovenly-looking porter peered out, eying the visitors with undisguised hostility.

"It would seem we are expected," Dominic observed sardonically. When the door started to slam in his face, he forced his way in and roughly grabbed the servant by the collar of his liveried jacket, jerking him up. "Now my good man," Dominic said brusquely in French. "You will tell me where I may find your master before another minute is up, or I will throw you to my coachman. Jacques knows quite well how to deal with your kind. Ah, excellent timing," he added when Jacques entered behind Brie. The burly coachman was brandishing a pistol and looking quite capable of using it.

The porter, finding himself outnumbered, gave a frightened whimper and in a strangled voice, said that Sir Charles could be found in his study. Dominic gave a brief nod. "Jacques, you may take charge of this fellow. See that we aren't interrupted, if you please." Taking hold of Brie's arm then, he guided her down the hall.

When he stopped before a closed door, he spared a glance for her. Her cheeks were rather pale, but she met his eyes bravely. Returning her gaze, Dominic once again doubted his wisdom in bringing her along. If she were innocent, she would be in no little danger when he confronted Durham. On the other hand, if she were a party to her grandfather's plans, then he, Dominic, would have to be doubly on his guard. But he had to know. And it was much too late now to allow his doubts to interfere with his course of action. Quietly, Dominic opened the door and ushered Brie into the study.

A man, grayed and stooped with age, was hunched behind a massive oak desk at the far end of the room. He was richly dressed in brocade and lace, his clothes belonging to an earlier generation. The curling, powdered wig he wore had gone out of style some twenty years ago.

He did not look up, but growled in a feeble voice, "Take it away, you imbecile. How many times have I told you not to bring tea while I am busy?"

"It must be a great trial to you, Sir Charles," Dominic said softly, "to be surrounded by incompetence. You would do better to choose your employees with more care."

At Dominic's first words, Sir Charles had looked up, impatience written on his grizzled countenance. But his impatience quickly turned to puzzlement, then comprehension, and finally fear. "Who the devil are you?" he demanded without conviction.

Dominic shut the door quietly behind him and moved further into the room, drawing Brie with him. At closer range, he could see the unhealthy pallor of Sir Charles' complexion. The old man was obviously an invalid, for his eyes were sunk deep in their sockets, and his thin, spotted hands were trembling.

Disgusted to have a foe so unworthy of his steel, Dominic wondered if he had somehow been misled about Durham's intent to kill him. But then he caught the fiery gleam of hatred in the sunken eyes. "I hardly think introductions are necessary," he replied, "but since you insist, I am Dominic Serrault."

Sir Charles stared malevolently at Dominic before his attention shifted to Brie. Then suddenly his face turned a deathly shade of white, while a strangled gasp erupted from his throat. "Lisette! My God." His claw-like hands gripped the edge of the desk, and he swayed, shutting his eyes. When he opened them again, he was still staring at Brie.

Watching Sir Charles' reaction, Dominic could see his shock was real. It was obvious the old man thought he was seeing the ghost of his dead wife Lisette. Dominic felt such a flood of relief that his knees went numb. Brie hadn't been lying to him. *She hadn't been lying.* A slow, spiraling joy began to wing its way upward from his heart.

But he ruthlessly forced his chaotic thoughts aside in order to concentrate. The shock had disappeared from on Sir Charles' face, to be replaced by suspicion and a rapidly increasing anger.

With a swift motion that belied his years, he pointed an

accusing finger at Brie. "You are not Lisette!" he bellowed, his face becoming mottled with rage. "Who are you? Who are you?"

Brie was startled by his fury. "I am your granddaughter, sir," she answered warily, wondering if Sir Charles possessed an unsound mind.

"That is a lie! I have no granddaughter."

"I assure you it is true. I am Brie Carringdon. Your daughter Suzanne was my mother."

Sir Charles hesitated. "Suzanne? Suzanne, did you say?" He sneered, his eyes becoming more hooded. "So the little slut ran off and found herself a husband. I always wondered what happened to her. Was Carringdon fooled? Did he think you were his child?"

Brie was first astonished, then enraged by the insult. "How dare you!" she said between clenched teeth. "How dare you say such a thing about my mother." She took a step toward him but was restrained by Dominic.

"That is quite enough, Brie," he said quietly. "You may leave the room." When Brie raised a questioning gaze, Dominic gave a curt shake of his head. "This quarrel is not yours, but mine. Go, now. Wait for me in the hall."

The expression on Dominic's face was unreadable, but Brie couldn't ignore the command in those gray eyes. Lifting her skirts, she turned to obey.

Later, she wondered if the outcome would have been different had she not done so, for when she reached the door and opened it, she came face to face with Jacques. The next instant she was flung roughly to the floor as a pistol shot exploded behind her.

The fall stunned Brie, knocking the breath from her body, and she missed seeing Jacques raise his own pistol and fire. But the retort of his weapon was still ringing in her ears as she lay there gasping and trying to recover her senses. When she heard a woman's voice exclaiming in horror, Brie thought she must be imagining things, for it sounded very much like

384

Katherine. Then gentle hands grasped her shoulders and she heard Julian's voice, asking her if she were all right.

Bewildered, Brie looked up to find him kneeling beside her, his concerned blue eyes fixed on her face. "No, I'm not hurt," she insisted, struggling to her feet. "Please . . . help me up. What—"

The question froze on her lips as she caught sight of Sir Charles. He sat slumped in his chair, his head lolling to one side, a bright red stain spreading across his chest and contrasting vividly with the ivory color of his waistcoat. A large pearl-handled dueling pistol lay on the desk, making Brie recall the first pistol shot.

Her shocked gaze swung to Dominic. He had shrugged out of his coat, and Brie saw with horror that his right shirt sleeve was rolled up to expose a bloody gash on his upper arm. Jacques was dabbing at the wound with a handkerchief, trying to stem the welling blood, while Dominic, with one hand, was untying his cravat to use as a bandage. When the coachman began deftly wrapping the injured arm with the neckcloth, Dominic looked up and met her gaze, his gray eyes locking with Brie's blue-gren ones.

His face was devoid of expression, but Brie felt the impact of his gaze as surely as if he had reached out and touched her. She stood there, unable to look away, not even realizing that she was still clinging to Julian's arm.

It was Julian who broke the spell by speaking. "I had best go in search of some brandy," he said quietly. "And perhaps a strong footman to carry Sir Charles to his room. Brie, can you see to Miss Hewitt?"

The question surprised her. She had been vaguely aware that someone was crying, but hadn't even realized it was Katherine. The elderly woman had collapsed in a chair and was sobbing softly into her hands.

Finally comprehending what Julian had said, Brie glanced once more at her grandfather. There was nothing more anyone could do for him. The realization left her feeling sick and shaken, but she made a determined effort to quell her nausea and nodded in answer to Julian's question.

"Good girl," he said, squeezing her hand. "See if you can find a place for her to lie down. I'll just be a moment."

Obediently, Brie went to the weeping woman and put a comforting arm around her shoulders. "Come, Katherine," she urged, aware that Dominic was watching her. She desperately wanted to know what he was thinking, but she couldn't find the courage to ask him, or even to look at him, Involuntarily, her gaze returned to Sir Charles, and she shuddered. It could so easily have been Dominic whose life had ended in that one brief moment.

She led Katherine from the room, conscious all the while of Dominic's eyes following her. Upstairs, she found a small parlor where they could wait in relative comfort. After making Katherine lie down on the sofa, Brie settled in the wing chair opposite and tried to keep her thoughts focused on anything but what had just happened in the study.

Julian joined them about ten minutes later, bringing with him a decanter of cognac and three glasses. "This is quality stuff," he said as he poured the brandy, "but I had the devil of a time finding it. The servants are all in an uproar because of the shooting, though I'll wager they are more concerned for their jobs than for Sir Charles. Here, drink this, Miss Hewitt. You'll feel much better." Helping Katherine sit up, he handed her a full glass, then poured one for Brie. "You too, Brie. You look as if you could use something to settle your nerves."

Brie accepted her glass and obediently took a swallow, gasping as it burned a path from her throat to her stomach. "How . . . how is Dominic?" she ventured to ask.

Julian shot her a quizzical glance as he sat in the chair beside her. "Dominic is fine. The ball passed clear through the flesh of his upper arm. I've sent for a doctor, though, and the local authorities."

"But you said he was fine. Why does he need a doctor?"

Seeing her worried look, Julian quickly shook his head. "He

386

doesn't, but a doctor must verify the cause of Sir Charles' death. And it won't hurt to have him take a look at Dominic's arm at the same time."

"Oh," Brie said, biting her lip.

"You realize, don't you, that the authorities will want an explanation?"

"But Dominic has done nothing wrong!"

"No, certainly not," Julian soothed. "Sir Charles fired at Dominic without any warning and Jacques shot back. But there will probably be an inquiry of some kind."

Brie lowered her gaze to her glass and stared at it for a moment. Then she looked up again. "What are you and Katherine doing here? How did you find me?"

Affronted by the question, Julian suddenly shed his fatherly air. "What do you think we're doing here? You disappeared the morning after that fiasco at the ball without leaving a note, without saying a single word to anyone. When Katherine discovered you gone, she came to me. She was frantic with worry, thinking perhaps that Dominic had kidnapped you."

Brie had the grace to flush. "Of course he didn't kidnap me. He never wanted to see me again. I followed him."

Julian frowned for a moment longer, then sighed. "I guessed as much. Either way, we were concerned for you. Whatever possessed you to go off like that?"

"I had to, Julian. I couldn't bear to leave things as they were."

There was another short silence before Julian nodded. "Dom had told me a little about the business with your grandfather, so when you disappeared, Katherine and I put the pieces together. We thought you might be in need of support."

Realizing her companion hadn't said a word during their entire conversation, Brie turned a questioning gaze on Katherine. She was sitting with her head bowed, nervously twisting the ends of her shawl while tears fell silently down her cheeks.

Brie leaned forward in her chair. "Katherine?" she said gently. "Katherine, dearest, you mustn't cry for Sir Charles. He doesn't deserve your sympathy."

Katherine buried her face in her hands. "Ah, child, if you only knew."

"If I knew what? Katherine, why are you crying? Please, won't you tell me what is troubling you?" When she received no response, her patience gave out. "Katherine, surely you don't condone what my grandfather did? My God, he tried to kill Lord Stanton! Not once, but several times. Sir Charles would probably still be alive if he hadn't shot first."

"Take it easy, Brie," Julian said, laying a restraining hand on her arm.

"And end such a spirited defense? No, Julian, by all means let her continue."

The cool voice had come from the doorway, and immediately three pairs of eyes swung to where Dominic stood with his arm braced in a sling. The reaction of the room's occupants to his appearance was varied. Julian frowned, Brie flushed and lowered her eyes, and Katherine stiffened.

Julian was the first to recover. "Dominic, I'm afraid there are some things you don't know about Sir Charles."

Dominic raised a dark eyebrow. "And I suppose you mean to tell me. Very well, then. Please get on with it." He strode into the room, taking up a position behind Brie's chair, resting one hand negligently on the tall back.

Julian threw an apologetic glance at Katherine, then cleared his throat. "Miss Hewitt knows why your father was arrested."

Dominic's gray eyes narrowed at Katherine. "Is this true?" he asked sharply.

"She was there the night—"

Dominic held up his hand, effectively quelling Julian's speech. "Allow Miss Hewitt to speak, if you will."

"Honestly, Dominic," Brie interrupted. "Must you be so harsh? Can't you see she is upset?" Intending to comfort Katherine, Brie rose halfway in her chair, but Dominic's hand firmly pressed her back down.

"Miss Hewitt?" he repeated softly, the underlying steel in his voice brooking no argument.

"Lord Denville is correct, my lord," Katherine whispered. There was a lengthy pause while she appeared to be gathering the nerve to continue. Then she clasped her hands tightly in her lap and began to speak. "I was here when the tragedy began—and it was a tragedy. I was Lisette Durham's companion then, as well as a governess of sorts for her daughter Suzanne. I know, Brie," Katherine added at Brie's sharp intake of breath. "I should have told you before now. But it seemed pointless. While she was alive, your mama forbid me to speak of it. And afterwards . . . well, there seemed to be no reason to dig up the past. It was such a sordid story that I thought you better off not knowing."

Katherine hesitated, her gaze momentarily lifting to Dominic's. Then she dropped her eyes and kept them trained on Brie. "It happened in '92. That spring and summer . . . Sir Charles was gone much of the time, travelling around Europe. He left Lisette alone too much of the time. She was French, you see." At Brie's blank look, Katherine leaned forward. "Lisette was . . . gentle. She didn't have your strength, Brie, nor your mama's for that matter. Suzanne was away at a finishing school and Lisette was lonely. She began seeing the Comte de Valdois.

"I tried to warn her that no good would come from encouraging a man like that, but she just laughed. She was like a butterfly, attracted to pretty flowers. Then one day she came home with her gown torn and dirty. There were . . . bruises on her body. She had such a stunned look on her face that my heart nearly broke. The comte had . . . the comte had forced himself upon her."

Since Dominic was behind her, Brie couldn't see his expression, but she could feel his fingers tighten reflexively on her shoulder. She wondered if he would challenge Katherine's statement, but he said nothing.

There was a tense silence while the elderly woman wiped at

her eyes with a handkerchief. Then she took a deep breath. "Lisette begged me to keep it a secret from her husband, and I agreed. Sir Charles was such a jealous man that he would have killed anyone who touched his wife. But I made her promise never to go near the comte again. I . . . I took Lisette to a woman in the village, and she was given a remedy that made her vilely ill. For a time I even feared for her life . . . but she recovered. She never again was as gay and carefree as she once had been, but I thought she was beginning to recover from her . . . her experience, as well.

"Some two months later, we received word that Sir Charles was coming home. Lisette seemed upset, but I thought . . . I thought she was simply nervous, you see."

When Katherine gave a choked sob, Brie couldn't bear watching such grief any longer. Shrugging off Dominic's hand, she went to sit beside Katherine and put an arm about her.

Katherine wouldn't be comforted, though. Tears were streaming down her lined cheeks as if they would never stop. "I should have known!" she cried with a vehemence that was startling to her listeners. "The day before Sir Charles was to arrive, I woke to find a letter beside my bed. It was from Lisette, addressed to me. I tore it open. . . . 'When you read this, I shall be gone.' That was how it began. At first, I thought Lisette must have run away, but then I read further. Lisette had realized she was to have a child, the comte's child. She . . . she took her life . . . because she couldn't bear the shame."

Sobbing brokenly, Katherine buried her face in her hands, while Brie stroked her hair gently, trying to comfort her. Brie wanted desperately to know how Dominic was taking all these revelations, but she couldn't bring herself to look at him. She glanced at Julian instead and saw he was staring fixedly at the carpet.

Dominic was the first to break the silence. "And I suppose Suzanne Durham discovered the reason for her mother's death and wanted revenge," he said in a tired voice.

"Monsieur le Comte, pardon-moi." The voice had come from behind Dominic, and they all turned to stare at the intruder. He was a man about aged fifty, well dressed, carrying a black bag—a physician by all appearances.

"Yes?" Dominic said impatiently.

"If I may be permitted, monsieur," the doctor replied in faltering English. "I have information to add to this lady's story. You are le Comte de Valdois?"

"I do not claim the title," Dominic answered, "but I am the comte's son. You are . . . ?"

"Henri Fontaine, doctor of medicine."

"I see. Well, then, Monsieur le Doctor, perhaps you will be so good as to come with me. I think a private conversation would be more in order."

"But Dominic," Brie said quickly, realizing they wouldn't hear what the doctor had to say. "Surely Doctor Fontaine's information cannot be so very private. Could you not remain here?" When Dominic turned to look at her, Brie hesitated, seeing the hard glitter in his eyes. But she felt she had a right to the truth. "Please, Dominic?"

He couldn't fail to see the justice in her plea. "Very well," he agreed. "Be seated, if you will, monsieur."

When the doctor was settled, Dominic took a seat across from the sofa and leaned back wearily, feeling a painful throb in his wounded arm. He wanted nothing more than to hear the last of these revelations and be alone with his thoughts. He needed time to digest what he had learned . . . and decide what to do.

As the doctor began to speak, Dominic found his gaze straying to Brie. She sat with her head bowed, her hand tightly gripping Katherine's. Watching her, he couldn't help swearing at himself. God, what had he done? Stripped her pride away, destroyed her reputation, doubted her honor, forced her . . . like his father. Only with a strong effort was he able to control his thoughts so he could follow the doctor's words.

"What Madame Briggs says is true," the doctor was saying. "My father, Pierre Fontaine, was Lady Durham's physician

391

during the last years of her life. He examined her body upon her death and confirmed that the cause was poisoning. He also discovered that she was with child."

The doctor glanced at Dominic, then at Katherine. "When Sir Charles returned home and learned of the death of his wife, he was very distressed. He did not know then about the child, for my father never told him. But later he discovered the letter, did he not, Madame Briggs?"

Katherine nodded mutely. No one interrupted the story to ask about her name, for it seemed a minor point.

"How much better it would have been had you burned the letter," Fontaine said with a sigh. "But you did not expect Sir Charles to search your rooms? No, naturally you would not. Yet that was how he found the letter and learned about the child. I believe that was when Sir Charles became crazed. He could think of nothing but revenge on the man who had dishonored his wife. So he turned Le Comte de Valdois over to the revolutionaries. A cunning sort of revenge, perhaps, but effective. He could not be certain of winning a duel."

"But I understood my mother had accused the comte," Brie interjected.

Fontaine's gaze swung to Brie, studying her. "Your mother was Mademoiselle Suzanne? You have very much the look of Madame Lisette. But where was I? Yes, M'amselle Suzanne. Bah, she had nothing to do with the comte's arrest. It was Sir Charles, believe me. In his anger he thought it would be . . . how you say? Using one stone to kill two birds. Mademoiselle Suzanne had returned home from school but a few days before, and she was beginning to fall under the comte's influence." The doctor gave Dominic an apologetic glance. "Pardon, m'sieur, but your father had great charm with the ladies."

Julian spoke then for the first time. "Doctor Fontaine, how do you know all this? Surely Sir Charles did not confess all this to you."

Henri Fontaine looked affronted. "Monsieur, I have not

been the physician and confidant of Sir Charles for twenty years without gleaning the facts of the situation."

"Then you know that Sir Charles tried to murder Dominic?"

The doctor gave a start. "Non, but I did not! He spoke of it many times, but I did not know that he had tried."

"Julian, pray let the good doctor continue," Dominic said wearily.

"Alors, where was I? Ah, yes, Mademoiselle Suzanne. She discovered what Sir Charles was about and went to warn the comte. But she was too late. That night she left her father's house with Madam Briggs. You went to England?" he asked Katherine.

"No," she replied in a hoarse whisper. "We stayed in an inn for a time, and when the comte was taken to Paris, we followed. Suzanne thought she could bribe the authorities to free the comte. But she could do nothing. Afterward, we went to London, where she met and married your father, Brie."

"Katherine, my father . . . Papa was my father?"

Appalled that Brie should have such doubts, Katherine stared at her. "Of course he was. You were born more than a year after Suzanne and Sir William married."

"She knew about her mother, then? About why Lisette had killed herself?"

Katherine nodded. "Yes, she knew. When I learned Suzanne meant to go to Paris, I had to tell her, though I think she had guessed beforehand what had happened. Lisette left a sort of warning for her . . . inscribed on a pendant. But Suzanne would not listen to me. She went to Paris, despite knowing what sort of man the comte was. I went with her, for I had lost my place here and I was afraid for her safety. It was so dangerous then—for all of us—but particularly for a young girl alone."

When Katherine bowed her head, Fontaine cleared his throat and continued. "During the war between our countries, Sir Charles was forced into hiding for a period, he being

English. But he returned, having obtained the proper authorization papers. Many years went by. I believed he had forgotten about the past." Fontaine paused, then addressed Dominic directly. "Monsieur, do you remember a boy by the name of Nicholas Dumonde?" The arrested look in Dominic's eyes confirmed the answer. "I see you do. Did you know that young Dumonde was the son—pardon mesdames—the bastard of Sir Charles?"

Dominic groaned, putting a hand to his eyes. "This becomes more absurd with each passing moment," he murmured. "Had I tried, I could not have become more involved with Sir Charles' family."

Everyone but the doctor was puzzled by his remark. "And the mademoiselle?" Fontaine asked curiously.

"Another coincidence," Dominic replied curtly, directing an enigmatic glance at Brie.

Julian, who had been trying to follow this odd conversation, finally became exasperated. "Would you mind explaining what the devil you two are talking about, Dom?"

Dominic shot his friend a hard glance, but then he sighed. "I was in Paris some four years ago," he explained, "spying for the British, if you must know. I had . . . discovered some valuable documents which I had to deliver to my superior. Before I left France, a boy by the name of Nicholas Dumonde tried to relieve me of them. I turned him over to a colleague of mine and then left for England. Later I heard that my associate had become . . . overzealous and that Dumonde had died. I assume Sir Charles discovered my involvement?" Dominic said to the doctor. "But that doesn't explain why he waited this long to seek me out."

"After his son's death, Sir Charles suffered a stroke. He was partially paralyzed."

"But he recovered enough to travel to England?"

Fontaine nodded. "Last September. But I thought he did not find you. You were travelling in the West Indies, or some such place."

"So I was. It was after I returned that Sir Charles' hirelings attempted to earn their pay."

The doctor stroked his chin thoughtfully. "Sir Charles was very angry when he learned you had recovered the Valdois estate. He meant to prevent you from taking possession. He even went to Paris a few months ago to speak to an attorney about this."

And in Paris he hired Germain, Dominic thought to himself. It wasn't difficult to guess the rest of the story. "Tell me, M'sieur le Doctor," Dominic said. "What do you gain by telling me this?"

Henri Fontaine shrugged. "A clear conscience, perhaps. I wanted you to understand why Sir Charles acted as he did."

Dominic's jaw hardened. "I understand," he replied grimly. "All too well, I understand."

He stood up then and crossed the room before anyone thought to stop him from leaving. At the door, however, he turned back to survey the company, his gaze lingering on Brie even though she refused to meet his eyes.

"Ironic, is it not, doctor," Dominic said slowly, "that the pattern of our lives can be so easily altered by circumstances? And that we can be so foolish as to wish it were not so? Superbly ironic."

Chapter Eighteen

"I am perfectly all right, Julian," Brie repeated for the third time. "And will you please stop looking at me as if I had lost my reason? I am sorry to have put you to so much trouble, but it really wasn't necessary for you to come after me."

Julian dismissed her remarks with an impatient wave of his hand and continued his agitated pacing of the floor. "Damn it, Brie, it was no trouble! What kind of friend do you take me for? Do you think I could merely turn a blind eye while you gadded about the continent with a man who could ruin your reputation with a few choice words, let alone his company?"

When Brie began to protest, Julian held up his hand again. "All right, perhaps you were not gadding about, and Dominic is one of my best friends. But that still doesn't change the fact that you were unchaperoned in his company for the better part of a week. Good God, Brie! Were you lost to all sense of propriety? Surely you must see what this means?"

"Julian, calm down. And please quit scolding me. You are beginning to sound like my aunt."

Julian snorted derisively. "At least Lady Arabella knows what is required in the conduct of a lady." He paused for a moment, then said in a milder tone, "There is no hope for it, Brie. You must marry Dominic—and at once. At least that will help scotch the rumors that are flying about. My guess is that

397

Dominic has already arrived at that conclusion."

Brie looked away. "You can see how overjoyed he is at the prospect. He has been gone the entire afternoon."

"I'm certain he meant no insult to you." When Brie didn't reply, Julian swore silently. Dominic should be the one trying to find a satisfactory solution to this mess, but he had ridden out after hearing the doctor's story and hadn't come back. Julian had been required to handle the French authorities alone. But even that hadn't been as difficult as trying to talk some sense into Brie.

"Come now," he said, adding to his argument. "It won't be so bad being married to Dom. He can be quite a pleasant fellow. He's rich and titled and not unattractive to women. I'd even lay odds that after a time, you'll be able to wind him around your finger the way you do me. I expect he'll let you continue to indulge in your passion for your horses and stables."

Brie had been keeping a tight rein on her temper, but when this comment was uttered, she looked up at him with a militant gleam in her eyes. "Thank you, Julian, for arranging my future so satisfactorily! Need I remind you, though, that I can indulge my passions quite adequately without being married to Dominic or anyone else? I have no need of his money or his titles, or for that matter, his protection. And I think you forget that he is selfish and arrogant and highhanded. . . ."

Brie paused in her denunciation of Dominic's character to dash a tear from her cheek. Seeing her, Julian couldn't be fooled by her angry protests. He eyed her pityingly. "Poor Brie. You're in love with him, aren't you?"

"I. . . . It doesn't matter."

"No?" he asked softly. "Then why are you crying?"

"I am not—" Brie took a deep breath and waited for the painful lump in her throat to diminish. "Please, Julian, just take me home. I'm tired and upset, and I can't think objectively."

"But we cannot leave until things are settled."

Brie stared down at her clasped hands. "There is nothing to settle."

"Of course there is. One would have to be a blind fool not to see that." When she said nothing, he went to sit beside her on the sofa and took her hands in his. "Brie, look at me." When she complied, Julian's breath caught in his throat. Her blue-green eyes were sparkling with tears and her mouth was quivering, looking soft and vulnerable. Julian had to restrain himself from offering the kind of comfort he still wanted to give.

"You aren't making sense, Brie," he reasoned. "If you love Dominic, there can be no reason not to marry him. And I can't believe he is completely indifferent to you. I'd say he's getting the better part of the bargain."

Trying to ignore the ache in her heart, Brie closed her eyes. How could she make Julian understand how impossible it would be for her to marry Dominic, especially now that the truth had come out? Dominic wouldn't want an alliance with her, not when their families had so nearly succeeded in destroying each other. And he wouldn't want any reminders that his father has assaulted a woman and indirectly caused her death. He would only want to forget the subsequent tragedies. But more importantly, she wouldn't be able to bear seeing the thinly veiled contempt in his eyes that would surely be present if he were forced to become her husband.

For the woman who stole Dominic's precious freedom, there would be misery indeed, and her own suffering would be magnified a hundredfold. Brie could clearly imagine what such a marriage would hold for her. While Dominic might be attracted to her now, he would resent being trapped into marriage, and it wouldn't be long before he found solace in the arms of a more desirable, more biddable female. As the years went by, he would engage a string of mistresses in assertion of his independence, perhaps even try to lose himself in an endless round of dissipation and debauchery as so many of his peers did. She herself would become more and more embittered by his infidelities, even while craving a sign of his affection.

No, the years of loneliness without him still looked rosy in comparison to the bleak future she envisioned as his wife. And the pain of being separated from Dominic now would be infinitely preferable to the inevitable anguish of loving him when her love wasn't returned.

Steadying herself, Brie opened her eyes to look at Julian. "You are a true romantic, Julian," she murmured. "You believe in fairy tales and knights in shining armor and living happily ever after. I appreciate your concern, my very dear friend, but I do not want to marry Dominic. Besides. . . . you are mistaken. I don't love him."

"Now who is speaking of fairy tales?" Abruptly releasing her hands, Julian rose and resumed his pacing. "You cannot have considered what will happen if you return to England unwed, Brie. You will be an outcast of society, a pariah! Your name will be bandied about in the clubs and by gossiping old cats who delight in spreading scandals, and even when some other sensation pushes your story in the background, you will be shunned by all the respectable, self-righteous hypocrites who set themselves up as judges. No, Brie, I can't let you ruin your life. If you won't marry Dominic, then I suppose I will have to offer for you."

"Thank you for your kindness," she said dryly. "But there is no need for you to sacrifice yourself for my sake. Oh, come now, Julian," Brie exclaimed when he stopped his pacing to scowl at her. "You know you wouldn't be happy with me as your wife. I expect your assessment of how society will view my . . . indiscretions is correct, but it makes no difference. I've never placed much value on the opinion of strangers or mere acquaintances, and I shan't start now. Of course, I hope my friends will not condemn me when I return to Greenwood and take up my life where I left off."

"Brie, why won't you understand? There will no longer be a cloak of respectability to protect you from—" Julian broke off, too angry to finish the sentence.

Brie raised an eyebrow. "From lecherous fortune hunters? Men who will consider me a female of easy virtue and therefore a pigeon ripe for plucking? Very well, if it will make you more comfortable, Julian, I will hire a bodyguard whose duty it will be to keep me from falling victim to seduction." When Julian merely glared at her, Brie gave an exaggerated sigh. "You could at least laugh at my sallies, poor though they may be. You, my friend, are showing signs of becoming an extremely poor travelling companion. Perhaps I should hire my own carriage and make the return trip on my own."

Aghast at that possibility, Julian threw up his hands in defeat. "Very well, damn it! I will have the coach made ready. But don't tell me you aren't running away, because I won't believe a word of it." Turning on his heel, he marched to the door, pausing only long enough to fling over his shoulder, "I never thought to see the day when you would give up without a fight!"

He was still seething with frustration when he reached the stableyard. "Where the hell have you been?" Julian snapped when he saw Dominic dismounting. "And what did you mean by disappearing for two hours and leaving me to handle this mess? I should call you out for that, not to mention your treatment of Brie."

Handing the reins to a groom, Dominic eyed his friend quizzically. "Am I to take that as a challenge then?"

"No, of course not ! I'm no fool. You're a better shot than I." Turning, Julian shouted for his horses to be hitched to the hired conveyance.

"Going somewhere?"

"Yes, blast it! Home. Brie insists on leaving at once."

Dominic cocked his head. "It appears that you have lost an argument."

"Not one. Several. I've never been able to get the best of her, not when her mind's made up."

"Perhaps I can persuade her to stay."

"The devil you will! Why do you think we are leaving? She doesn't want to talk to you, that's why. Doesn't want anything to do with you. And don't think you can set things to rights by marrying her. She won't have you. I talked till I was hoarse, but Brie said she didn't care about her reputation or what the scandalmongers will say. She doesn't want to marry you—or me either for that matter, although I offered."

A muscle in Dominic's jaw tightened. "You might have let me do my own proposing."

"Well, you weren't here. What was I supposed to do, tie her to a chair? Brie said she would hire her own transportation if I wouldn't take her home. Besides, I assumed you would feel obliged to offer. I thought if Brie knew you would marry her, she wouldn't run off—"

"Enough," Dominic said curtly. "I think I understand. Where is she?"

"I left her in the parlor, but I expect she went to find Katherine. Miss Hewitt was lying down for a while. Dom?" Julian said when his friend turned to leave.

"Yes?"

"Don't be too hard on Brie, will you? She has been through a lot lately."

Dominic's lips compressed in a thin line. "Of course," he agreed mildly. "I promise to stop just short of wringing her neck."

By the time Dominic reached the house, his temper was smoldering. He had spent the past two hours riding aimlessly about the countryside, coming to terms with the situation and himself, not an easy task for a man who prided himself on his ability to judge human nature.

When the doctor had concluded the story, Dominic's overwhelming impulse had been to escape. He had felt a desperate need to be alone, to sort out his thoughts and feelings. All his life, he had been governed by certain convictions—convictions that had been dashed to fragments in the short space of an hour. He had neither known nor cared where he was going, but had let his mount roam at will. A cold mist swirled around him, obscuring his vision and muffling the sounds of his horse's hooves, but even though it settled damply on his hair and clothes and attacked the bare skin of his face, he was oblivious to the discomfort.

As he wandered through the fog, long forgotten memories came floating to the surface of his mind. A boy raging silently against the fates, swearing revenge for the death of the father he had idolized. A young man out on the town for the first time, standing among a cheerful crowd of Christmas revelers but feeling a wave of loneliness so strong that it became a physical ache. A fully grown man, heart hardened against any tender emotions, triumphant when a slender, russet-haired beauty bowed to the force of his will.

Forcibly brushing aside thoughts of Brie, Dominic tried to summon a mental image of his father. Nothing came. The Comte de Valdois was a stranger. His death had been the foundation upon which Dominic had built his childhood plans of revenge, but he could no longer even feel anything for the man.

But his own feelings were unimportant. Leaving them aside, Dominic made himself review the facts, one by one, coldly, objectively, starting with his father. The comte had raped an innocent gentlewoman, then remained idle while she suffered the consequences of his actions. It had been murder, of a sort.

Dominic's lips curled in self-mockery. Had he been in Sir Charles' place, had it been his wife who had died, he would have torn the comte apart with his bare hands. Instead, Sir Charles had devised an alternate plan to avenge the honor of his dead wife. While his action had not been particularly honorable, having the comte arrested was just as effective as putting a bullet through his heart. And it had been justice . . . of a sort. The comte had received his punishment, a life for a life.

The story should have ended there, with the score even. Except that Suzanne Durham had become involved. Sir

Charles had suspected his daughter's growing attraction to the comte and used her name on the arrest warrant as a means to end it. The result, however, had been to drive the young woman from her home.

It was rather humbling, Dominic reflected, to admit he had wrongfully blamed Suzanne Durham all these years for his father's death. It must have taken considerable courage for her to go to Paris and attempt to influence the comte's fate. She had tried to save his life, even when she knew of the crime he had committed against her mother.

But the story had not even ended there. Dominic shook his head, hardly believing the irony even now. Had he systematically set out to destroy the Durham family, the results could not have been more devastating. Sir Charles had lost a daughter as well as a wife, and later the score had become even more unbalanced. Durham's son, Nicholas Dumonde, had died. Young Dumonde had been the victim of Germain's treachery, but Sir Charles had obviously been told differently. No doubt, Dominic thought sardonically, the matter would have come to a head sooner, had Sir Charles been able to travel then. Instead, he had suffered a paralyzing stroke, and it had been several years before he was able to seek revenge for his son's death.

Then, unbelievably, another member of the Durham family had entered the picture—Brie. By that time, however, Dominic had been unable to credit her involvement as being merely circumstantial. But not only had he mistrusted her, he had suspected Brie of betrayal. He had believed her capable of cunning and deceit, if not actually cold-blooded murder.

Dominic groaned out loud. How could he have been so blind? But he knew the answer to that. He had wanted to believe her guilty, for his own self-protection. He had been overwhelmingly attracted to her from the first, and when she had begun to penetrate his defenses, he had actually felt relief that he could arm himself with the knowledge of her treachery.

But Brie had not given up. She had stood firm in her

championship of her beliefs, and had shown a courage and determination that couldn't be broken by public ridicule or physical threats. And she had taken his side, even when her grandfather had been killed.

Remembering how badly he had treated her, Dominic groaned again. He owned her an apology, several hundred abjectly humble apologies to be exact—and not the least was for his cruel remark this morning in the inn. He had not meant to hurt her. He had only wanted to end the closeness that had recently sprung up between them, knowing he needed a clear head to face his past. Even so, he deserved to be shot for treating her so callously.

Feeling an inexplicable sense of urgency, Dominic turned his mount and spurred him into a canter. The mist had cleared somewhat, leaving the bare trees dripping with moisture, but he paid no attention to his surroundings as he rode back in the direction of the Durham estate. His thoughts were fully occupied with Brie.

What was it that Jason had said when they had parted at Dover? *You must marry her.* Well, that was true enough. It was the only honorable course. But his friend's conviction that he was in love was something Dominic wasn't yet willing to contemplate. He wasn't prepared to consider that he might have lost his heart to a hot-tempered, sharp-tongued vixen. It was enough that he was willing to sacrifice his freedom in order to preserve Brie's honor.

Realizing his thoughts, Dominic smiled for the first time that day. The idea of a sacrifice was distinctly humorous. It would be no hardship being married to Brie. In fact, he might find it rather enjoyable. Brie was no prim and proper miss who would treat her conjugal duties in the bedroom as obligations. She was as warm and passionate and beautiful as any mistress, and even if she possessed a hot temper and sharp tongue, she was intelligent and lively enough to keep boredom at bay. Of course, she was far too independent for a woman, Dominic reflected, but as her husband he could influence that. He would keep her in bed where there was less chance for argument. Brie was far more likely to obey him when he was plying her body with kisses.

Dominic grinned at that image, his teeth showing white against his bronzed skin. No, he had to admit that the idea of marriage didn't seem nearly so distasteful as it once had.

By the time he reached the stableyard, his plans were well formed. First he would take Brie to Paris where, with the help of the British Consulate, he would obtain a special marriage license and make her his countess. Then when they were married, he would buy her a magnificent wardrobe, befitting her station as the new Lady Stanton. She had left England with only the clothes on her back, and the outfits he had scrounged up in Dieppe would hardly suffice for a wedding trip. For the honeymoon, they would visit some of the other capitals of Europe, then perhaps rent a villa on the Mediterranean for a month or two. And when they returned to England in the fall, the scandal would have blown over.

Dominic's thoughts had so easily adjusted to this pleasant future that Julian's warning had the same effect as a dousing of ice water. The possibility that Brie might not want him for a husband hadn't even entered Dominic's mind. He had realized of course, that her pride had been wounded, both by his lack of trust in her and his subsequent behavior, but he had been certain that once he tendered his apologies, Brie would forgive him and forget the tragic past. But now it seemed she had thrown his magnanimous gesture back in his face before he had even an opportunity to present his offer.

Dominic's attitude as he strode determinedly toward the house was a mixture of simmering anger, disbelief, and apprehension. An unproductive search of the ground floor rooms did nothing to sweeten his temper, nor did his mood improve when all the servants shrank from him in fear. At last, however, Dominic cornered a trembling maid who said both ladies could be found upstairs in one of the spare bedchambers. Taking the stairs two at a time, he strode purposefully down the hall and rapped sharply on the door.

Brie was helping Katherine into a warm travelling cloak and had her back to the door, so she didn't immediately see Dominic when he entered. When Katherine visibly stiffened, Brie turned. She froze then, like an animal poised for flight. Even with one arm in a sling, Dominic looked every inch like a powerful predator ready to spring on its victim—and she was to be the victim.

"I would like a word with you," he ground out menacingly. "In private."

Seeing the chill look in his eyes, Brie tried to remember all the logical arguments she had prepared just for this moment. But all the rational arguments in the world didn't help the fact that her pulse began leaping uncontrollably every time Dominic simply came near her.

Mentally trying to bolster her courage, Brie finished tying the strings of Katherine's cloak and gave her a reassuring smile, before silently preceding Dominic from the room.

The moment they were alone, Dominic grasped her by the arm and guided her to the chamber across the hall. Brie gasped at his rough handling, and when Dominic had shut the door, she swung around to face him, her hands clenched at her sides.

Seeing the fury in her eyes, Dominic couldn't help smiling at himself. As always, that flashing green fire stirred his blood and drove any rational thoughts from his mind. He ached to take Brie in his arms, to kiss away her anger, to change her indignation to passion. He took a step toward her, intending to embrace her, but Brie retreated across the room.

"What do you want, Dominic?" she asked warily. "You said you needed to speak to me."

Dominic hesitated, suddenly unsure of himself. Was she playing some kind of coy game? She knew perfectly well what this interview was about, however ignorant she pretended to be. He meant to ask her to become his wife. But perhaps she needed to hear his proposal from his own lips.

Curbing his impatience, he replied rather stiffly. "Julian

tells me you wish to leave. Before you go, however, I should like you to know that I am willing to offer you the protection of my name."

Hearing the way he phrased his offer, Brie felt her last lingering hope die. Never, never could she marry this man loving him the way she did, being unloved in return. She averted her face, not wanting him to see the tears that stung her eyes.

"Brie, did you hear me?" Dominic said softly. "I am asking for your hand in marriage."

"Yes, I heard you. Julian said that you would feel compelled to offer for me."

"Not compelled, precisely—although in all honor I cannot allow you to suffer because of my actions. But—"

"In all honor!" She whirled to face him, wanting to lash out and hurt him as she had been hurt. "Is it honorable to propose marriage because of a misguided sense of guilt? Do you suddenly find you have a conscience? Well, you can rest easy, Dominic. I won't marry you merely to save my reputation. You aren't obliged to protect me, nor are you required to feel guilty because I allowed you into my bed of my own free will."

Dominic responded with a sardonic smile. "You are much mistaken if you attribute my motives to guilt."

"Indeed? Then what, pray, are your motives?"

His eyes narrowed as he studied Brie. What difference did it make why he married her, for Christ's sake? She was being offered a position that most women would be honored to accept. Dominic felt his own temper flaring. He wanted to shake her until she abandoned her absurd attitude and admitted that her reluctance was merely pretense. But when he saw the tired droop of her shoulders and the way she was wearily rubbing her temples, he realized she must be exhausted. "Brie," he said quietly, "this has been a very long day for us both. You should rest. Our discussion can wait until tomorrow."

"No!" she cried, the fire in her eyes flaring to life again.

"Then, damn it, what do you want? A recitation of my titles and an account of my various incomes? No?" he said savagely when Brie shook her head. "No, of course not. You have no need for titles and you have an adequate fortune of your own—which, by the way, would come under my control were you to marry me. A point against, surely. Let me see . . . points in favor.

"One, it is not unusual for a man of my station and age to marry, so let us say I am in need of a wife. Two, while you are perhaps a little too free in your behavior at times, your birth is unexceptional and your breeding adequate for the position as my countess. Three—no, back to two. I could be persuaded, perhaps, to let you continue some of your pursuits, provided you were discreet. Three, your beauty is unquestionable and given a little more training, your performance in bed should measure up to even my exacting standards. Four, you are in need of a husband, whether you admit it or not, someone to guide you and keep a firm hold on your bridle. Five—shall I continue?"

Brie stared back at him, white-faced. "No, my lord, there is no need to continue. Although you left out several points against. You are arrogant, overbearing, spiteful—"

"But we have not begun to extol my virtues," he observed dryly.

"Virtues? I wasn't aware you had any!"

Dominic hesitated. He wasn't proud of his vicious attack, particularly since he had meant to apologize. Yet when he saw how his one and only marriage proposal had degenerated into a shouting match, he felt his anger dissolve in amusement. "Brie, this is getting us nowhere," he pointed out calmly. "Perhaps tomorrow you will see that marrying me will be the best solution for us both."

Brie clenched her teeth. "I thank you for your kind offer," she returned, "but I will not marry you. Now will you please let

409

me pass? My friends are waiting for me."

Dominic made one more attempt to persuade her. Catching Brie's arm as she tried to slip by him, he gently grasped her chin and forced her to meet his gaze. "What if you carry my child?" he asked softly.

Somehow Brie managed not to flinch. She had no idea what she would do if she were pregnant, but she refused to let him know that the thought troubled her. She could not use a child as an excuse for marriage. "Unlike my grandmother," she said stiffly, "I do not have a suicidal nature. I will not kill myself, if that is what concerns you."

It was Dominic's turn to pale. His skin went ashen beneath his tan, while his grip tightened painfully on her arm. "That is not what I meant," he said acidly. "I was questioning the wisdom of bringing a bastard into the world."

Brie did flinch then, seeing the cold glitter in his eyes. "We are speaking of remote possibilities," she said, trying unsuccessfully to keep the quaver from her voice.

"Not so remote. You are young and healthy."

"Well . . . , that will be my problem, not yours."

Dominic's jaw hardened, as if he were considering using physical force to persuade her. But then he abruptly released her and stepped back.

Brie watched him uncertainly as she rubbed her arm. She had wanted to wound him as she had been wounded, but now she knew she couldn't leave without explaining her reasons for refusing him.

"Don't you understand?" she whispered. "I will not, cannot tie myself to you in a loveless marriage. You would never forgive me, nor would I forgive myself."

For a long moment, Dominic said nothing. When he finally spoke, his tone was as devoid of emotion as his expression. "Of course, you are right. The points against would win out in the long run. I wish you a safe journey." When she made no move to leave, Dominic gestured impatiently with his hand. "Go, Brie, just . . . go."

Brie turned and fled then, knowing if she stayed a moment longer she would break down completely. She didn't see the anguish that crept into Dominic's eyes as he watched her go, nor did she see how tightly he clenched his fists to keep himself from calling her back. Yet he stood and stared after her for a long while, listening to the silent echo of her retreating footsteps and wondering why his chest felt so achingly hollow.

Chapter Nineteen

Leaning back wearily against the cushions, Brie gave herself up to the ceaseless swaying motion of the coach. They were nearing the French coast, but the journey already seemed interminable since her parting with Dominic. Even so, time and distance had begun to work their healing magic on her fragmented heart. The acute pain had dulled to a mere throbbing ache, while the misery had faded to numbness.

Brie sighed. The exertion of pretending an interest in her surroundings during the past few days had been a severe strain on her frayed nerves. Yet keeping up an endless stream of conversation had provided occupation for her mind, and her attentiveness had helped reduce the frequency of worried glances which Katherine and Julian had showered upon her.

Realizing how uncharitable her thoughts were, Brie flushed guiltily. She ought to be grateful for the consideration her friends had shown her. Julian had been determined to entertain her, and Katherine had been equally determined to ignore the recent explosive events. Both had made her comfort and well-being their prime concern. Their affection for her had seen her through one of the most trying periods of her life, she admitted, stealing a fond glance at them both.

As the coach rolled into the yard of the inn where they were to stop for lunch, Brie made a concerted effort to shrug off her

413

despondent thoughts. When Julian gave her an engaging grin as he handed her down from the carriage, she responded lightheartedly for the first time in days, giving him a bright smile, then turning to plant an impulsive kiss on Katherine's withered cheek.

A melee of carriages, horses, and scurrying ostlers impeded their progress as they made their way across the yard, and the common room of the inn was no less crowded. Brie and Katherine waited in the hall, while Julian beckoned to the innkeeper and ordered a private parlor and a meal.

From her position, Brie had a good view of the crowded taproom. When her gaze wandered absently over the occupants, her attention was caught by a slender, fair-haired man sitting at a table not two yards away. Dressed as a gentleman, the man appeared to be English, although what might have been a ruddy complexion had deepened to a dull red beneath his leathery tan. She was surprised to see him staring so intently at Julian, but when the stranger transferred his gaze to her, Brie experienced a shock. The hatred shining out of those hooded eyes was unmistakable. She shuddered, trying unsuccessfully to break away from his malevolent gaze, and clutched involuntarily at Julian's sleeve.

Seeing Brie's pale face, Julian abruptly ended his conversation with the landlord and ushered his charges up the stairs to a small parlor. Brie went directly to the hearth, holding her chilled hands out to the cheerful blaze. But in spite of the fire and the warmth of her fur-lined cloak, she found she couldn't stop shivering.

She couldn't explain her reaction, for she had never seen the fair-haired man before, yet for some reason he terrified her. It was only after lunch had been served and she had drunk several cups of scalding hot tea that her fear began to dissipate.

The meal was pleasant enough—braised veal with chive sauce, baked cod, goose pate, an assortment of vegetables, and an excellent wine—but Brie hardly tasted it. She spoke in monosyllables, if at all, while Katherine kept up a polite stream of conversation with Julian.

Finally, though, Brie realized her silence was becoming obvious. Bestirring herself to contribute to the discussion, she asked Julian when they could expect to arrive home.

"We'll reach Dieppe by this evening," he replied, "and we should be able to sail tomorrow. They will be expecting us at *La Belle Fleur*, since I reserved rooms when we stayed there last week."

Brie listened to Julian elaborate their travel plans, but when she heard a squeak in the hall that resembled a creaking floorboard, she jumped and glanced wildly over her shoulder. The parlor door had been left partially open by one of the maidservants, and Brie stared at it as if she expected a ghost to waltz into the room.

Watching her, Julian frowned. He hadn't wanted to distress her further by being overly solicitous, but when her gaze remained riveted on the door, he grew concerned. "What is the matter, Brie? Dominic isn't coming. He's at least a day behind us since he intended to see Durham properly buried."

"Must we speak of that?" Katherine murmured, while Brie tore her gaze from the door to glare at Julian.

"Honestly, Julian. I wasn't even thinking of Dominic."

"Brie, I hope. . . . Well, no matter," he added with a shrug. "Your experience was far from pleasant, but it's over. You needn't ever see Dom again if you don't wish to."

When Brie heard the gentle consideration in his tone, a lump formed in her throat. Not wanting to make a fool of herself by crying, she rose from the table and began to gather up her cloak and gloves and reticule. Katherine and Julian shared a look of concern, then wordlessly followed her example.

They reached Dieppe just as the last lingering rays of sunlight faded. Even though it was twilight, the yard of *La Belle Fleur* was teeming with carriages and horses, and as their coach drew to a halt, several ostlers leaped forward to provide the excellent service for which the posting house was famous.

The landlord was just as solicitous. He sent a lackey to see to their baggage and then personally showed them upstairs to their rooms. Brie, noting her companion's weariness, told Julian she would help Katherine lie down. He nodded in reply, saying he would meet her in the private parlor in an hour for dinner.

Brie was just coming out of Katherine's room when she heard a voice call to her in a harsh whisper. She turned, searching the shadows in the corridor. When a man stepped forward into the flickering lamplight, Brie's hand flew to her throat. She had no trouble recognizing the slender, fair-haired stranger from the inn where they had stopped for lunch—and he had the same paralyzing effect on her now as he had had then.

He reached her in three strides, moving with deceptive speed, then grasped her arm as if to prevent her escape. His action was unnecessary, though. Brie could not have moved had her life depended on it.

"Mademoiselle," he repeated in that same urgent whisper. "You are a friend of Dominic Serrault, Lord Stanton?" He spoke in French, but when Brie didn't utter a sound, he switched to English. "Come, answer me. Are you Miss Carringdon? Do you know Stanton?"

When she managed to nod, the stranger relaxed. His eyes darted once around the hall, then returned to Brie as he spoke again.

Brie had trouble following what he was saying, but her heart lurched when she realized there had been an accident. Dominic had been badly injured and had called for her, the man said. She must come at once.

Brie swayed, feeling suddenly faint. She made no protest when the stranger's grip tightened on her arm, but allowed him to lead her downstairs and out into the crowded yard. A closed carriage was waiting for them. The stranger urged Brie into its dark interior, then climbed in after her and slammed the door.

The coach was moving rapidly away from the inn before Brie

belatedly came to her senses. She should have discovered their destination, she realized. At the very least she should have told Julian she was leaving.

She was about to ask that the coach be stopped when the fair-haired man spoke from the opposite seat, saying that Dominic would be grateful for her presence. Although Brie couldn't see his face well in the darkness, she caught a note in his voice that sounded oddly like amusement.

Realizing suddenly that she had been duped, Brie silently cursed herself for being a fool. There had been no accident. Dominic was in no danger. This was some kind of abduction, and she had let herself be led away like a sheep to slaughter.

She opened her mouth to give her abductor a scathing denunciation, but then thought better of giving herself away and clamped her lips shut. Perhaps if he thought he were dealing with a distressed female, she would stand a greater chance of escape.

Cautiously, she felt for her reticule with its hidden pistol. When she discovered the strings were no longer looped around her wrist, she realized the stranger had somehow taken it from her. Repressing a feeling of panic, she told herself to wait for her chance, then bit down hard on her lower lip till she could taste blood, hoping that the pain would keep her more alert.

The stranger must have sensed a change in her, however, for he let out his breath in a slow chuckle. "I was wondering when you would catch on. I had heard that you were clever, Miss Carringdon, but I assumed Martin was mistaken when you were so naive as to come without a struggle."

Brie didn't answer. She didn't trust herself to speak without her voice trembling.

"Of course, I already had reason to doubt Martin's report," the stranger continued. "Stanton never has held cleverness as a prerequisite for his . . . women, if you will forgive me for saying so."

Goaded by his insult, Brie found her tongue. "You can hardly expect forgiveness, sir! And certainly not before you tell me who you are and what you want of me." She could feel his eyes raking her in the darkness. His reply, when it came, repelled her but really didn't surprise her.

"Surely you have guessed, Miss Carringdon. I am Charles Germain. I expect you recognize the name, even though we have never met before. As for what I want . . . I want Dominic Serrault. And, now that I have made your charming acquaintance, I would be less than a man if I did not want you as well."

He chuckled at her silence, and his soft laughter sent a shudder up Brie's spine. "The next few hours should be rather pleasant," he said mildly, "for me, if not for you. And if you are particularly obedient, I may reconsider handing you over to Martin. You do remember Martin, do you not? He and his brother Freddie paid your stables a visit once. He wasn't at all pleased by his brother's death and is quite anxious to make your acquaintance. When he reported to me in London, all he could talk about was the revenge he would exact on you and your lover. I have first claim, however."

Germain paused, as if he were measuring the impact of his words had on her, and Brie dug her nails into her palms, trying to keep her fear under control. When he spoke again, she could hear the gloating triumph in his voice.

"I can just imagine Dominic's rage when he discovers he has shared you with his most hated enemy. But then I could be speaking prematurely. After you get a taste of my lovemaking, you may not wish to return to him. Nor would he want you, I suspect. He was rather angry when I stole his last mistress from him, beneath his very nose." Germain clucked his tongue. "Poor Cassandra. Dominic killed her, you know—for her faithlessness. But don't be concerned. He won't be able to harm you when he is dead."

Brie had difficulty following what Germain was saying, but she understood one thing quite clearly: she was to be used to bait a trap for Dominic. She was thankful when despite her mounting fear she managed to scoff quite credibly. "If you

418

think Lord Stanton will come after me, I'm afraid you are overestimating my appeal. You weren't present when I took my leave of him, so you couldn't be aware of his dislike for me."

That made Germain hesitate, but then he chuckled once more. "He will come. Dominic may not care a whit for you personally, but he has always been protective of his possessions. He will want you back, if only because I have taken you. Until then, my little dove, you will help me to while away the hours."

Brie had no response for Germain's observation. She doubted that Dominic cared enough about her to rescue her, but if he did attempt it, he would be walking straight into this madman's trap. She couldn't view either alternative with equanimity, but she knew she would find it unbearable if she were used to lure Dominic to his death. She could only hope for a chance to escape before this fair-haired demon could carry out his plans.

Watching him, she tried to steady her thoughts. Her eyes had become accustomed to the darkness by now, and she could see his gloved hand grip the seat, bracing against the sway of the coach as it rounded a street corner. When she felt their speed slacken, Brie decided to take the slim chance the slower pace offered. Making a desperate lunge, she flung herself at the carriage door.

It swung open when she twisted the handle, and she felt herself falling toward the rough cobblestones. But then Germain caught a handful of her skirts, preventing her escape. He swore violently as he jerked her back into the coach and threw her against her seat.

The impact knocked the breath from her body. Stunned and gasping, Brie was unable to duck when he drew back an arm and struck her across the face.

The vicious blow made her head snap back, sending it cracking against the wood panel behind her, and Germain's curses were the last thing she heard before fiery sparks exploded inside her skull.

She regained consciousness slowly, swimming in a painful black void. When the murkiness gave way to shimmering brightness, Brie moaned in protest. Cringing, she turned away and buried her face gratefully in the rough-textured cloth beneath her cheek. She slept.

When she next woke, there was a relentless pounding in her head and her stomach was churning. She opened her eyes, trying to focus, but the room swayed alarmingly and another wave of nausea swept over her, almost sending her back into oblivion. She closed her eyes, feeling herself break out in a cold sweat.

When she was able to open them without sending the room into a spin, she discovered that she was lying on a small cot. Her cloak was gone, but she was covered to the waist with a thin coverlet, and her hands were bound so tightly that all feeling in her fingers had disappeared. Seeing the rope, Brie remembered Germain and his threats. He must have brought her here after she had tried to escape, she thought with dismay. She looked around her, trying to force down her rising panic.

The room appeared to be an attic of sorts. Besides the cot, a rough-hewn slab of wood that improvised as a table was the only recognizable piece of furniture. A candle had been left burning there, and since no sunlight was streaming through the uncurtained window, Brie decided it must be evening.

Carefully, she shifted her weight upon the lumpy mattress, testing her body's reactions to movement. Aside from a stiffness in her muscles, the pain in her head and the numbness in her hands seemed to be the only apparent damage. Forcing her body into an upright position, however, required an unusual degree of effort, and Brie had to support herself with her bound hands while she waited for an end to the nausea that washed over her in merciless waves.

It left her weak and trembling, but after a time, she pushed herself to her feet and stumbled to the window, pressing her forehead against the pane to look down. Far below, shrouded in shadows, was a yard surrounded by a high wall of iron.

Her breath caught on a sob when she realized the hopelessness of her situation. How could she possibly devise an escape? She had no idea where she was, or how long she had remained unconscious, or even what her abductor meant to do with her. She was hungry and close to exhaustion and she had already begun to shake from the chill damp of her prison cell. And even if she were able to free herself from her bonds, breaking the window—which proved to be locked—would most likely rouse her captor and bring him running. Or, barring that, if she managed to reach the ground below without sustaining a severe injury, she would still have to scale the fence with its treacherous, protruding spikes.

Sinking to her knees, Brie buried her face in her arms and succumbed to fear and despair. Deep, racking sobs shook her slender frame as she began to cry.

Finally, though, her pride reasserted itself, making her aware that she had awarded her captor the victory before the fight had even begun. Anger began to burn within her then, giving her strength, and she dashed away her tears, realizing that defiance would stand her in far better stead than capitulation. And there was always the chance that Dominic might actually try and rescue her. That small ray of hope bolstered her courage immeasurably, and for the first time since wakening, she looked around in search of a weapon.

There was not much that could serve her purpose. A pile of dirty rags lay heaped next to faded newspapers, brittle with age. A coin shone dully in one corner, while in another, a child's rag doll lay abandoned and forgotten. A stash of broken sticks that had once been a rocking chair seemed to offer the best alternative.

Dismissing these for a moment, Brie turned her attention to her only light. The wooden candlestick was too small to be used as a weapon, but if her bonds could be burnt away. . . . With firm deliberation, Brie went to the table and thrust her hands above the candleflame, letting the fire lick the thick knot between her wrists. She winced as the heat scorched her skin, grinding her teeth when the pain became almost unbearable. Her patience was rewarded, though, for the rope at last began to send up tiny curls of smoke and the threads began to fray.

Brie was concentrating so intently on her task that she missed hearing the scrape of approaching footsteps. When a key turned in the lock, she jumped, then whirled as the attic door swung wide. She froze as she met the hooded eyes of her captor.

He was slightly more disheveled than when she had last seen him. His clothes were rumpled, while his blond hair fell across his forehead and a growth of new beard darkened his sunburned face. But he still wore that air of supreme confidence, and the predatory gleam in his eyes still had the power to frighten her.

His surprise at seeing Brie standing beside the table swiftly turned to outrage when he realized she had been trying to burn away her bonds. He leapt at her, reaching her side in two strides, and grabbed her by the arm. Then jerking her around, he flung her away with a force that sent her sprawling.

With her hands tied, Brie wasn't able to break her fall. She cried out in pain as she hit the floor, then lay there face down on the filthy wooden planks, gasping for breath and fighting the welling nausea as a stream of curses broke over her head.

Germain continued his harangue for nearly a minute before quite suddenly his tone changed. "Get up, you little bitch," he said rather calmly, "before I kick you. I want you in one piece, not fainting dead away as you did before. It was rather clever of you, I admit. . . ."

Brie heard the rest of his speech only vaguely, but she understood two things quite well. The first was that her unconscious state had been all that had saved her from ravishment. The second was that he meant to rectify the omission immediately. She watched in horror as he shrugged out of his jacket and tossed it on the foot of the cot. Yet when he slowly began to move toward her, she lay there paralyzed, too frightened even to try to scramble away.

They both heard the noise. It was no more than a whisper of sound from somewhere below, but they both reacted to it; Germain tensed and cocked his head in an attitude of listening, while Brie closed her eyes and held her breath, hoping desperately that she had somehow been offered a reprieve. Fear had made her almost numb, but she could feel her heart slamming against her ribs as Germain walked to the door and peered out.

After a moment, he called loudly and somewhat uncertainly to Martin. He apparently was not reassured by the lack of response, for he swore under his breath and pulled a knife from the belt of his trousers.

Brie shrank away instinctively when Germain returned to her side, for the wicked gleam of the blade mirrored the glitter in his pale eyes. But he only hauled her abruptly to her feet, then used the knife to cut away the rope binding her hands. She nearly screamed as the blood rushed to her hands, sending an agonizing pain shooting up her arms.

Hearing her involuntary whimper, Germain wrapped an arm around her waist and pressed the sharp steel against her side in silent warning. "Don't make a sound," he hissed. "Or you won't live long enough to greet your lover."

Her knees threatening to collapse, Brie managed to nod, but she swayed against him involuntarily. Germain snarled another oath, then lifted her up, crushing her against his side. Half carrying her, he propelled her from her attic prison and along the darkened corridor. He released her when they reached a flight of steep, narrow stairs, merely to shove her in front of him. Brie stumbled and almost fell, and only her instinctive gesture of throwing out her hands to grasp the rail banister prevented her from tumbling headfirst.

After what seemed like an endless number of flights, they reached the ground floor. Germain came to a halt, jerking her up by the collar, then stood listening, very much like a fox sniffing the wind. Brie took a long shuddering breath and cautiously looked about her, trying to get her bearings.

The front door was immediately to her left, shut tightly and well bolted. The sight of those heavy drawn bolts made her heart sink, but they must have reassured her captor, for he gave her a push toward the room across the hall. "We will wait in there," he said, forcibly directing her footsteps.

Light was streaming brightly from the open door, and Brie winced as it struck her eyes. She took three steps into the room, then halted abruptly, her heart leaping with joy and terror. Dominic sat in a large armchair facing them, looking very much at ease as he held a pistol trained on them.

Brie felt her fair-haired captor stiffen, but before she even had time to think, he had dragged her in front of him and was pressing his knife against her side. "How did you get in here?" he ground out, addressing Dominic.

A lamp stood on the mantle behind Dominic, the bright light casting his face in shadow, but Brie could see his lip curl. "My dear Charles, were you not expecting me?"

His tone was soft and mocking, but at the sound of his beloved voice, Brie swayed. Not even the bite of cold steel against her ribs could dampen her relief at seeing him again.

"How did you get past Martin?" Germain demanded, making Brie feel his rage as he held her so tightly.

"Jacques handled your henchman easily enough," Dominic replied. "You forget that I once was quite familiar with this particular house. But I might ask you a similar question. How did you manage to escape Jason's watchful eye? I shall have a word to say about his laxity when I next see him."

Charles raised his knife, pressing the sharp edge threateningly against Brie's throat. "You will put down that pistol if you want her to live."

Dominic hesitated, his gray eyes flicking over Brie as if he were seriously deliberating. Then he shrugged. "Do what you will with her. She is nothing to me. I've felt her claws once too often to care what becomes of her."

Hearing his casual denouncement, Brie paled. Her eyes were huge and haunted as she stared at Dominic, not wanting to believe she had heard him correctly. Then she saw his mouth twist in a sardonic smile. "Perhaps I should have adopted your method of silencing her," he said, sounding amused. "A knife is a bit uncivilized, but effective. I've not heard her sharp tongue stilled until this moment."

His cruel words cut Brie more deeply than any knife. She had always known Dominic didn't love her, but she had thought he might care enough to try and rescue her. That hope that had sustained her in her moments of paralyzing fear, but she realized now how foolish she had been. He had come, not to rescue her, but to carry out a vendetta against his enemy. It was nothing to him if Charles Germain ended her life with his blade.

Overwhelmed by pain and anger, Brie began to struggle, no longer caring that a ruthless madman was holding a knife at her throat. When Germain swore and ordered her to be still, Dominic laughed harshly. "See, the vixen would like nothing better than to carve out my heart and serve it on a platter. Keep a good hold on her, Charles, I beg you. Even unarmed, she can be dangerous."

"You're lying, Stanton! Martin saw you with her more than once. You were so hot for the bitch, you couldn't keep your hands to yourself."

"Can you fault me?" Dominic replied laconically, ignoring the taunt. "The pleasures of her delightful body are without peer—as you well know if she has shared your bed."

"Indeed," Charles smirked as his hand swept upward to fondle Brie's breast. Brie closed her eyes, shuddering with revulsion.

Dominic leaned back in his chair. "You're welcome to her, Charles, but I ought to warn you—she's only interested in marriage. She tried to trick me into offering for her just last week. I was even tempted to let myself be caught, she pleads

425

so convincingly."

Knowing that for a bold-faced lie, Brie opened her eyes to stare at Dominic. He was looking directly at her, the piercing intentness of his gaze at odds with his casual pose. It seemed as if he were trying to communicate something to her.

Reading the silent message in his eyes, she suddenly understood his intention; he was pretending not to care merely to direct Germain's attention away from her. A wave of relief washed over her, leaving her weak. Whatever Dominic's feelings for her, he wouldn't enjoy watching her die.

"But I didn't come here to quarrel with you over the lady," Dominic said, switching his gaze to Germain. "I came to discuss the boy I turned over to you here in this house, the one you later killed. You remember Nicholas Dumonde, don't you, Charles? You said his death was accidental—but it wasn't, was it? And you knew he was Durham's bastard. I thought perhaps you did," he added dryly, watching his opponent's face.

When Germain didn't reply, Dominic smiled a decidedly nasty smile. "You covered your tracks well, Charles, I must admit. Durham never knew. Ironic, was it not, that he later hired his son's murderer to kill the man he thought responsible?"

His voice lowered to a mere whisper then. "You will die for that, Charles. By my hand. I could shoot you. However . . ." His tone became normal again, sounding almost pleasant, as if he were proposing a stroll through the park. "However, I am prepared to be magnanimous and offer you a sporting chance. I brought a pair of foils for us to use. I imagine you are almost recovered from your wound, and as you can see," he indicated the sling that supported his right arm, "I have sustained one of my own. That will give you a decided advantage, since I will have to fight left-handed.

"You needn't look for your henchman to appear," he added when Germain threw a glance over his shoulder. "Jacques is keeping him occupied. Well, what is it to be, Charles?"

426

lipping his arm from the sling, Dominic transferred his pistol
his right hand but kept it trained on his foe as he stood up.
eaching behind him where a pair of rapiers lay on the mantle,
e grasped one in his left hand and tested the blade, making the
r hiss around him.

"Well, Charles?" Dominic repeated. "Shall we fight, or do
ou mean to hide behind a woman's skirts all evening?"

As Charles weighed his chances, Brie watched Dominic,
nable to tear her gaze away. When she felt the increasing
ressure of the blade at her throat, she held her breath, waiting
or the cold steel to pierce her throat.

But then Germain shifted the knife to his left hand in order
o free his sword arm. He deftly caught the foil Dominic tossed
im and stood holding Brie while Dominic divested himself of
is sling and coat.

Those moments passed with agonizing slowness for Brie.
ler mind felt strangely divorced from her body, as if she were
atching a stage drama as an impassive observer rather than an
ctive participant. She could feel Germain's tenseness, and
lancing over her shoulder, she could see the beads of
erspiration that had broken out on his forehead. When she
aw the brightly stained bandage that wrapped Dominic's arm,
owever, Brie caught her breath in a gasp. The sleeve of his
wn shirt was soaked in blood, and his silk waistcoat was
lready flecked with red. Dominic had been telling the
ruth, Brie realized with dismay. Wounded as he was, he
ouldn't just be at a disadvantage; it would be a miracle if he
urvived!

Brie couldn't bear to think of the outcome of such an
neven contest. Dominic's life was far more important to her
han his love, more important even than her own life. Her
nguished eyes flew to his face, and when she saw he was
atching her, she returned his gaze steadily, baring her very
oul in that timeless glance, her fierce love for him glowing
rightly in her eyes as she silently wished him strength and

courage and victory.

Dominic at last tore his gaze away. Tossing his coat in the chair, he lowered his pistol and turned to place it on the mantle his back making a wide target as he reached for the second foi. That seemed to be the moment Germain had been waiting fo for he flung Brie to one side and lunged at his opponent.

Brie cried out in warning, but she realized an instant late that her shout hadn't been needed. Dominic had given th appearance of letting down his guard, but he had obviousl been anticipating Germain's action, since he managed to war off the sudden attack with surprising quickness.

The clash of steel rang out, reverberating in the small room while Brie's heart rose to her throat and stayed there. Sh backed against the wall, out of range of the flashing blade where she anxiously watched the two combatants.

The fight seemed so unequal. In spite of his agility an superb physical conditioning, Dominic's skill was drasticall diminished without the use of his sword arm. His defense wa slow, even awkward at times, and the sweat glistening on hi brow told her that his reflexes were being strained to the limit When he barely parried a thrust in time, Brie's hand flew t her mouth, smothering a cry.

Germain, on the other hand, had not yet begun to labor. H fought conservatively at first, but he seemed to gai confidence each time he lunged. And his advantage wa beginning to tell. Although he hadn't yet broken through hi opponent's guard, he was continuously driving, pressurin Dominic to retreat again and again.

Brie had no idea how long they fought—it could have bee minutes or hours—but the interval stretched into an eternity She bit deeply into her knuckle when Germain gave a sudden leap and crashed into Dominic. His thrusting blade swun wide, but the impact sent both men hurtling over the back of a sofa to the floor. They were both on their feet in an instant warily circling each other once more.

Unwilling to give up his advantage, Germain pressed the attack. His foil hissed as it made a slashing arc, and the point found Dominic's left shoulder, slicing through his shirt and leaving a deep gash from which blood welled freely.

Dominic stumbled backward, but Germain didn't let up for even an instant. Once more he advanced, flinging a small table from his path with a snarl, sending it crashing to the floor. Once more Dominic retreated, whirling away at the last moment as Germain's blade sliced through the air.

Seeing the triumphant gleam in Germain's eyes, Brie shuddered. She had never seen such hatred and lust for blood as was on his face, and she knew if sheer malevolence could win, he would have been declared the victor before the battle had ever been joined.

He moved slowly toward Dominic, stalking him like he would wounded prey, while Dominic backed away, moving ever deeper into a corner of the room. When she saw how Dominic was boxing himself in, Brie wanted to scream out a warning. But she bit her knuckle until she tasted blood, knowing that any sound she made might prove to be a fatal distraction.

Dominic's back was pressed against the wall before he finally stopped retreating. Brie couldn't see Germain's gloating expression, since he was facing away from her, but she could see the slow, taunting smile that curled Dominic's lips. That mocking smile seemed to infuriate Germain, for he growled and made a wild lunge.

Forever afterward Brie would remember that terrifying moment when the two combatants stood locked together. The room became deathly still, and she felt her heart stop beating. An endless moment elapsed before anything happened. Then slowly, Germain slumped to the floor.

It was another moment before Brie even registered that it wasn't Dominic who lay sprawled on the floor, a rapier buried deep in his chest. She gave an anguished sob and took a faltering step toward him. In response, Dominic turned hi head to meet her gaze across the room.

One side of his waistcoat was stained a bright crimson, whil his face was ashen, the color of dirty snow. Brie saw his lip twist in a faint smile. Then, before she could break out of he horrified trance, Dominic swayed and sank to the floor besid Germain.

Chapter Twenty

A full thirty-six hours passed before Dominic regained consciousness. When he woke, it was to find Jason slumped in a chair beside his bed, looking disheveled and weary. Morning sunlight streamed in the open window and the cheerful dancing rays set devils pounding in Dominic's skull. He winced at the bright light, wishing he were still unconscious.

When he raised a hand to shield his eyes, Jason roused himself and sat up. "Well, at last! I was beginning to wonder if you would pull through. How do you feel?"

"Like the very devil," Dominic rasped, his voice sounding strangely hoarse. When Jason chuckled in relief, Dominic frowned. "Have you been here all night?"

"Yes. And the night before that as well. I arrived just before Jacques carried you in. I would have been here sooner except that I lost Germain's trail. He escaped by killing his guard, and—"

Dominic reached out to grip Jason's arm. "Brie . . . where is she? Is she all right?"

Jason didn't seem surprised by the anxious question. "I imagine she is in her room," he replied calmly. "After the doctor stitched that gash in your shoulder, he gave Miss Carringdon a draught to make her sleep. She hadn't stirred last night when Katherine Hewitt came in to check on you. And

431

yes," Jason added when Dominic's grip tightened, "I believe she is all right, or at least as well as any woman can be after an ordeal like that. I really didn't get a chance to speak to her about it. I was too busy preventing the doctor from bleeding you."

Dominic relaxed his grip and leaned back against the pillows, shutting his eyes. "Damn his soul," he cursed in a toneless voice.

Jason didn't have to guess whom he meant. "Well, I expect Germain is well on his way to perdition by now. You'd do better to concern yourself with Julian. He's still fuming because you wouldn't allow him to go with you to find Germain. He wanted to kill the bastard himself."

When Dominic didn't answer, Jason picked up a glass of water from the bedside table and held it to his patient's dry lips, ordering him to drink. He was prepared for an argument, but Dominic obeyed wordlessly.

"Don't let it eat on you, Dom," Jason said quietly when the glass was empty. "Brie's a survivor. She'll manage to get over it. She was rather pale when Jacques brought her here, but she had full command of herself. In fact she seemed more concerned about your injuries than anything else. She wouldn't drink her medicine until you had been sewn up, and I nearly had to force her to leave."

Clenching his black-shadowed jaw, Dominic focused his gaze on the window. "I want to see her."

Jason stood up, rubbing the stubble on his own chin. "I wouldn't advise it just yet. You look like death, and you need a bath and a shave more than I do. Besides, that bandage needs to be changed. I'll go fetch some clean linen to bind your arm and send a man up to help make you presentable. I can't allow Miss Carringdon to visit you when you aren't wearing a stitch to hide your naked splendor."

When Dominic scowled with a semblance of his former spirit and said adamantly that he refused to be nursemaided, Jason merely grinned. "Be quiet, Dom. You're my patient now.

and I intend to see that you have proper care. And," he added sweetly when Dominic flung a particularly violent oath at him, "you'll eat before you talk to Miss Carringdon."

Dominic swore again as Jason left the room, but as soon as he was alone, he raised himself to a sitting position. The effort was far harder than he had expected. By the time he had managed to haul himself from the bed, he was breathing heavily and his body was covered with sweat.

He struggled into his dressing gown, but when a wave of dizziness nearly overcame him, he clung to the bedpost and waited for the weakness to pass. He was still leaning there when the door to the bedchamber flew open.

Julian stood in the doorway, glaring, his feet planted in a belligerent stance, his face flushed with anger. He barely gave Dominic time to lift his head before he crossed the room in two giant strides and drew back his fist. The punch he let go nearly dislocated Dominic's jaw as it sent him sprawling across the bed.

Groaning in pain, Dominic clutched at his shoulder, while Julian flexed his fingers in satisfaction. "You bloody bastard! I've been itching to do that for ages, and you damn well deserve another. Brie's hands were burned, goddamn you! Blisters the size of walnuts on her wrists. And you're to blame."

Dominic made no attempt to defend himself. He merely lay there, gritting his teeth against the pain.

Still glaring, Julian leaned over him and realized that the stitches in Dominic's shoulder had broken loose. Blood was welling beneath his fingers and running freely across his chest. Muttering an oath, Julian grabbed a towel from the washstand and pressed it tightly against the gaping wound.

"You bloody well deserve to bleed to death," he said between clenched teeth. "Brie got those burns trying to get a rope off her wrists, damn you. That *snake* had tied her up."

Dominic shut his eyes. "Where . . . is she?" he asked in a tormented whisper. "I must talk to her."

"She's better off without your company, if you ask me."

Dominic flung a hand up to cover his face, as if to ward off some nightmarish vision. "God . . . I've never been more terrified in my life. I couldn't do a thing but watch while that bastard. . . . He held a knife to her throat and would have killed her had I shown the least concern. Damn it, Julian, I would have given my own life before I let that vermin hurt her! I wanted to kill him with my bare hands. God . . . what he must have done to her."

Hearing the tortured explanation wrenched from Dominic. Julian felt his own anger ebb. He had been frantic with worry when Brie had disappeared and a search had turned up no trace of her whereabouts. When a message had come from Germain, saying that Brie was his hostage and that Stanton should meet him, Julian had immediately sent messengers to intercept Dominic on the road. But then Dominic had insisted on handling Germain alone. Julian had been infuriated by his own helplessness, but when he had seen Brie's injured wrists and heard her recount the tale of her abduction, he had become livid.

Now, hearing the anguish in Dominic's tone, Julian experienced a twinge of guilt. "Germain didn't touch her, Dom," Julian said, wanting to console him.

"Yes, he did—"

"I mean that he didn't rape her. He hit Brie instead and knocked her senseless. She didn't come around until shortly before you arrived."

Seeing the intense relief on Dominic's face, Julian wondered how he possibly could have thoughts his friend didn't care about Brie. If that wasn't the agony of a man in love, he would never again pretend to understand human nature.

"Germain told Brie you had killed Cassandra," Julian said quietly, "but she had enough sense not to believe that drivel. She's no fool, Dom, even if she behaves impetuously at times. And I think she cares for you more than you realize. She went with Germain in the first place because he told her you had been hurt and needed her."

434

When Dominic said nothing, Julian sighed. "Well, then, I guess I owe you an apology for planting you a facer. Come on, get back in bed while I—"

"You *hit* him?"

Both men looked up to see Brie standing in the doorway. She swept into the room, her eyes flashing when she saw the blood on the towel. "My God, Julian, you've made his shoulder start bleeding again! Go and fetch Jacques, quickly!"

When Julian sheepishly obeyed, Dominic managed to smile wanly. "Still defending the weak and helpless, I see."

Brie gave him a quelling glance as she helped him under the covers. "What were you doing out of bed?" she asked, seeing him grimace. "Your wounds are too serious for you to be up this soon."

"I wanted to talk to you."

She avoided answering as she bent over him to inspect the damage to his shoulder. When she dabbed at his bloody chest with the towel, Dominic caught her arm. "Brie. Please . . . I want to apologize. I had no intention of putting you in such danger. Truly, I had not thought Germain would involve you."

"It was not your fault," she replied, uncomfortable with both the subject and Dominic's nearness.

Dominic glanced down at her bandaged wrists and his jaw hardened. "But it was my fault—for not being prepared. I knew what Germain was like and I should have expected his next move. He was a dangerous man, Brie, with abduction and murder only two of the specialties in his bag of tricks. He had already killed once, in that same house. The boy was your grandfather's son Nicholas."

"I . . . I realized that at the time, from your conversation."

"And can you forgive me?"

Feeling his penetrating gaze search her face, Brie looked away. "There is nothing to forgive. Indeed, I should be thanking you for rescuing me. I was never in my life so pleased to see anyone."

"I regret that you had to witness our fight, especially when I had to kill Germain. But I couldn't let him live, Brie, not after what he had done to you."

"He didn't harm me," she said quietly, remembering the pain of Germain's rough treatment and the greater anguish of Dominic's indifference.

"But I think you misunderstood my words at first. I had to say what I did. Had I given Germain the slightest indication I was concerned for you, he wouldn't have hesitated to use his knife on you."

Brie looked down at the towel she was twisting in her hands. "I realized that, too . . . when I had time to consider. But your . . . indifference was difficult to bear."

"Was it? Is that why you refused my proposal, Brie? Because you thought me indifferent?"

When she made no reply, Dominic felt hope surge within him. He took a deep breath and drew Brie down to sit beside him. "I wasn't at all indifferent," he said solemnly. "The moment you left, I realized what a fool I had been—for not telling you that I love you."

Slowly, Brie lifted her head to stare at him. "You love me?"

Dominic studied her face, noting the guarded expression in her eyes. Striving to find the right words, he lowered his voice to a mere whisper. "You refused me once, Brie, but I hope to God it was my manner of approaching you and not your feelings that prompted your refusal. I'm asking you again. . . . Will you marry me?"

When she still remained silent, he gently cradled her face between his hands, holding her gaze. "I want you for my wife, my love. Will you have me?"

Brie searched his face intently, looking for any sign that he might be playing a cruel game with her. But his gray eyes were completely serious, holding a touch of uncertainty in their depths that went straight to her heart. "Are you sure Dominic? I couldn't bear it if you—" She broke off, her voice choking with tears.

Seeing her weakening, Dominic pressed his small advantage.

"If it's your independence that concerns you, I'll have my attorneys draw up a contract leaving you in full possession of your fortune, to be given to your children or your designated heirs—whomever you choose. I'll even have them include a paragraph stipulating that your manner of dress is beyond my authority. You can wear those blasted breeches whenever you care to. I don't want to deprive you of your freedom, Brie. I only want you—on any terms you care to name."

When she lifted her gaze to his, he could read the answer in her eyes, could see the love shining in their clear depths. His heart soared with joy. But he wanted to hear Brie's answer from her own lips. "Will you marry me?" he repeated softly.

Brie nodded.

"Yes?"

"Yes, I will marry you."

Dominic closed his eyes in sheer relief. Drawing Brie into his arms, he simply held her, his cheek pressed against her hair. "How can I ever begin to say I'm sorry for all the pain I caused you?"

With tears of happiness running down her cheeks, Brie buried her face in his good shoulder. "You don't need to, just so long as you love me."

"God, Brie. . . . Do you know how humble you make me feel? I don't deserve you."

When she didn't answer, he leaned back a little and with a finger, tilted her face up to his. Seeing the tears trickling down her cheeks, he gave her a devastatingly tender smile. "No tears, my love. This is to be a joyous occasion."

"I know," Brie sniffed, wiping her eyes. "It's just that I don't believe this is happening."

"You should have accepted my proposal the first time and saved us both this misery."

"The way you phrased your proposal hardly inspired confidence in a rosy future, my lord," she interjected with some of her usual spirit. When Dominic's gray eyes filled with laughter, Brie pressed her hands against his chest and sat up.

437

"I would not have married you under any circumstances, since you thought yourself *forced* to have me."

He grinned slowly, a heart-stopping grin. "But you are still forcing my hand, cherie. I would rather cut out my heart than let you go." Still looking at her with that mixture of love and laughter and tenderness that held her spellbound, Dominic pulled Brie into his arms once more. "I do love you, you know."

"You do?" she murmured, her thoughts suddenly distracted by the way his hands were caressing her back.

"Yes, my darling Brie," he whispered in her ear. "I love you passionately, madly, desperately. And I'd like to show you. Unfortunately, Jacques will be along at any moment, not to mention that Julian would truly kill me if I made love to you right now."

Coming to her senses, Brie sat up abruptly. "Julian would kill us both," she said, self-consciously dabbing at Dominic's wound again.

Dominic grinned. "I think we should send him to London. Someone has to tell your family that you are safe, and he can make up some kind of story to reassure the Langleys. Perhaps he can phrase it so Sir Miles won't feel obliged to call me out."

"My uncle won't call you out. Not if you intend to marry me."

Dominic reached out to run a teasing finger over her lips. "Does that mean I can have my wicked way with you?" he said huskily.

Seeing the gleaming lights in his gray eyes, Brie flushed. "You're in no condition to undertake such an activity. You're wounded, remember?"

"I remember. It hurts like hell. But I'm not sure if I can wait till after the wedding."

Brie smiled, meeting his gaze fully. "Neither am I."

They did wait, for even when Julian returned to London, Katherine remained at the inn to act as chaperon. Dominic and Brie were permitted a chaste kiss or two, but nothing more.

When Dominic had recuperated enough from his wounds to travel, they returned to Rutland. They planned to be married by special license, but Brie wanted the ceremony to take place at Greenwood with her family and friends present. She was relieved to find the scandal Julian had predicted had never materialized. No one had even known about her journey to France with Dominic, since her aunt and uncle had made up a story to cover her sudden absence from London.

Dominic stayed at the Lodge during the week before the wedding and called daily at Greenwood, but even though he spent the majority of his time with Brie, he rarely saw her alone. Finally, the day before they were to be married, he was able to get her to himself—by the simple expediency of inviting her to go riding.

She was waiting for him in the stableyard when he rode up on Diablo.

"Still wearing breeches, I see," Dominic observed when he saw how she was dressed.

Brie glanced up at him uncertainly. "You said you didn't mind."

His eyes raked her body, lingering on the swell of her breasts. Then he grinned. "No, ma belle, I don't mind. I even find myself growing quite fond of your breeches. And at least you've rid yourself of that disreputable coat. Remind me, though, to recommend a decent tailor to you—one who can fashion you something with a bit more style."

Seeing the teasing glint in his eyes, Brie felt her pulse quicken. Dominic looked impossibly handsome, she thought as she gazed up at him. His flowing lawn shirt was opened at the throat, its whiteness contrasting with his dark features, while his ebony hair was ruffled by the fresh spring breeze, glinting blue-black in the sunlight.

"What was it you wanted to show me?" she asked, trying to dismiss her fluttering heartbeat.

"You'll see. Come here." He urged Diablo closer, reaching down to pull Brie into the saddle before him.

Brie leaned back in his arms, never suspecting what such intimate contact with Dominic would do to her. Immediately she sat bolt upright, startled by the throbbing tremor that ran though her.

She sat rigidly erect as they rode out of the stableyard, but Dominic's arm remained wrapped around her waist, his hand resting directly below her breast, making her skin burn. She could feel the strength of his muscled chest against her back, the iron hardness of his thighs against her legs.

"Is it a secret?" she asked breathlessly, trying to take her mind off Dominic's nearness.

"No, I merely want to show you a horse I recently acquired. I had considered asking you to train him for me."

"A simple business proposition, then? Why didn't you say so?"

Dominic didn't reply, since he too was trying to ignore the warm currents radiating between them. He hadn't counted on his body's instant reaction to Brie's soft thighs, but he could already feel himself stiffening. "Perhaps riding double wasn't such a good idea," he murmured, removing his arm from about her waist.

When he fell silent, Brie kept her thoughts occupied by concentrating on her surroundings. It was a mellow spring morning, one whose beauty couldn't fail to enchant. Lush green fields stretched before them, glowing emerald in the bright sunlight, and in the distance, cattle and sheep grazed peacefully. The hedgerows and coverts that dappled the rolling landscape were bursting with hawthorn, agrimony, and meadowsweet, their sweetness adding to the scent of new grass and damp earth, while black and yellow butterflies vied for space with larks, goldfinches, and hedge sparrows.

Dominic was more enchanted with the woman in his arms, though, than with the lovely morning. Brie's fragrant scent was teasing his senses, arousing a fierce hunger in him that was only aggravated by the feel of her warm, lithe body pressing against him.

440

When Brie squirmed in his arms, Dominic sucked in his breath. "Unless you want to be ravished, ma belle, you had better be still," he warned. "It's been far too long since I last had you to myself, and my control is rather tenuous at the moment."

They rode for a while longer, but when the ache in his loins grew too painful to ignore, Dominic touched his heels to Diablo's flanks and the powerful stallion bounded forward.

They cantered across a field, heading south when they reached a lane. About a mile further, Dominic checked their speed and turned off the lane into a wooded area. He followed the path until it ended, then brought Diablo to a halt.

"Here we are," he announced, gazing down at Brie to watch her reaction. The woods had given way to a meadow, and in the center, some distance away, a bay horse was grazing with apparent contentment.

When she spotted the bay, Brie leaned forward, narrowing her eyes. Then suddenly she gasped. "It couldn't be," she breathed.

Dominic's mouth twisted in a tender smile. "What you see in that sorry specimen of horseflesh I'll never understand. But, yes, it is Jester, alive and well."

Brie was off Diablo's back in a flash, her cry of excitement startling the high-strung stallion as she broke into a run. "Sorry, boy," Dominic murmured, soothing the nervous animal. "She isn't always this flighty, I promise you."

Dominic watched her race across the meadow, smiling when she flung her arms around Jester's neck in obvious delight. All the effort to save the injured horse had been worth the trouble, he decided. Swinging down from his horse, he tethered Diablo to a branch, the followed Brie across the meadow.

She looked up when he approached, and Dominic's heart skipped a beat at the lovely picture she made. The ribbon holding her hair had come undone, and the vibrant tresses cascaded over her shoulders, shining like fire in the sunlight. She had been crying and her eyes sparkled like emeralds through her tears. Seeing her happiness, Dominic wished it were his neck she had wrapped her arms around, rather than the bay's.

"Dominic, I . . . Thank you," Brie said simply, gazing up at him.

He took a step closer, reaching out to gently brush away a glistening teardrop.

Brie caught her breath at the tenderness in his gray eyes. When Dominic drew her into his arms, she went willingly. He looked at her for a long moment, then lowered his head slowly, just letting his lips brush hers.

Brie was lost. With an anguished moan, she melted against him, needing to feel his arms around her, needing his strength and warmth and love. Her hands clutched at his shoulders for support, digging into the rippling muscles beneath his shirt. When Dominic's lips grew more demanding, more insistent, she opened to his searching tongue, responding with all the passion she was capable of.

He kissed her fiercely, as if he were starving for the taste of her. His hands stroked her hair, her shoulders, her back, communicating his feverish need. Brie could feel her own desire mounting, and she knew she had to stop him soon, before they both lost complete control. She pressed her hands against his chest . . . yet when his kisses moved lower on her throat, leaving a fiery trail, she arched against him, wanting him with a fierceness that left her weak.

"Dominic!" One of his hands had slid up to cup her breast, making her ache with longing.

He didn't even raise his head. "Brie," he rasped huskily against her throat, "You wouldn't happen to be concealing a whip or pistol, would you?"

"No," she answered in a ragged voice. "Why?"

"Because I'm going to make love to you. Right here, right now." Working her shirttail loose from the waistband of her breeches, he slipped his hands beneath her chemise and slowly ran them up her ribcage.

Brie gasped at the warm shock that coursed through her when his fingers found her rigid nipples. "Here?" she said breathlessly, intensely aroused by the wicked things his hands were doing to her bare breasts.

"Yes, my little torment," he growled with mock fierceness. "You've been driving me mad for days and now I mean to make you pay."

As if he could wait no longer, Dominic swung Brie up in his arms and with long strides, carried her beyond the curve of trees where they would be sheltered from prying eyes.

He laughed as he lowered her to the sun-warmed grass. "This reminds me of the day I found you here," he murmured. "I would have made love to you then, only you held me off with your crop."

"Aren't you forgetting there was snow on the ground?"

Stretching out beside her, Dominic propped himself up on one elbow. "No, my sweet. The snow was all that kept you from being seduced that day."

Brie smiled as she wrapped her arms about Dominic's neck. "You, my lord, are a scandalous rake."

"Perhaps, but I intend to give up my rakish ways. You've ruined me for anyone else, you know." Wrapping an arm possessively around her waist then, Dominic gazed down into her eyes.

Brie arched an eyebrow. "Does that mean you intend to remain faithful to me?"

"I'll definitely give the matter some consideration," he replied thoughtfully. "Ouch!" he yelped when she made a fist and pretended to punch him in the shoulder.

Grinning, he pinned her arms over her head. His lips hovered teasingly over hers as he regarded her with a wicked gleam in his eyes. "You really ought to try persuasion, ma belle, if you wish to keep me from straying. In fact, I suggest you begin now. It just might take you all day and all night."

Brie's laugh was low and throaty, a sound that stirred Dominic's blood with its sensuousness. "Actually," she replied, "that sounds like a delightful prospect. But don't you think the nights are still far too cold to spend them under the stars? I wouldn't want the bridegroom to catch a chill and miss his own wedding."

"Oh, no, Brie. You won't be rid of me so easily," Dominic declared. "And in any case," he said huskily before his mouth covered hers, "I doubt if I will even feel the cold. I've found an accommodating vixen to keep me warm."

Three days later, a travelling coach pulled by four perfectly matched bays drew up in front of the imposing country mansion belonging to Sir James Torpal. The ebony-haired gentleman who stepped down from the carriage was dressed for a morning call, but he appeared to be in no particular hurry to carry out his errand. He stood on the gravel drive for a long moment, looking up at the house as if trying to determine a way to breach the walls without resorting to the normal mode of entering through the front door.

When the door was opened by an elderly retainer, though, the gentleman gave a shrug of his shoulders and made his way, somewhat reluctantly, up the broad flight of steps. He presented his card to the butler and stated his purpose for coming, and when the fellow had gone off to announce him, he permitted himself a faint smile; by not so much as a flicker of an eyelid had the well-trained servant betrayed either astonishment or curiosity.

The gentleman's arrival had a pronounced effect on the lady of the house, however. Upon learning the name of her visitor, Lady Harriet paled and clutched at the arm of the chair in which she was seated.

A tall, slender woman, Harriet Torpal had features that were elegant rather than pretty. Her dark, chestnut hair, graying at the temples, made her appear striking, as did her penetrating gray eyes. Her normally calm demeanor was not in evidence, though, for it had been badly shaken.

Needing to compose herself, Lady Harriet insisted on a few moments respite before the gentleman was shown into her salon, even though she doubted whether a week would be sufficient time to accustom herself to the idea of a voluntary visit from her son.

She had recovered outwardly at least when he appeared. He paused at the door, seeming to fill the entire room with his presence, and she clasped her hands together to still their trembling. "Dominic." The word was uttered with less confidence than she had intended, and her whisper almost went unheard amid the rustle of her skirts as she rose to greet him.

It had been well over three years since she had even seen Dominic, but it had been almost a lifetime since she had had the right to claim him as her son. He was a stranger to her, even though he was her own flesh and blood. But as she stood staring at the dark features that were so reminiscent of her first husband, she became aware of a subtle but unmistakable message in her son's intent gaze. The gray eyes that were so exactly like her own were speaking to her in silent communication, making her wince with their honesty.

It was the moment in her life that she had longed for, yet dreaded. The one moment she had thought lost to her. She had never been able to reach him, and now he was reaching out to her, without condemnation, without pity. He was offering himself.

She could hardly speak. "You know?" It was more a statement than a question, and even before Dominic answered with a nod of his dark head, her knees gave way.

Instantly he was at his mother's side, helping her into her chair. When she was seated, he knelt before her and carried her fingers to his lips. "You must not faint on me, my lady," Dominic said, giving her a tender smile. "Not when I have travelled such a distance to humbly beg your forgiveness. See, I am down on my knees."

Affection swelled in her breast as she gazed at him, and she hesitantly reached out to touch his cheek. "The blame was never yours, Dominic, but mine. You were only a child. You

445

could not have known . . . your father's failings."

"All these years," he said gently. "Why did you never tell me about him?"

"Would you have believed me?"

Dominic's lips curved ruefully. "Probably not. I've only lately come to realize that I have an extremely stubborn propensity to believe what I wish about people, even when the truth is staring me in the face. Rather arrogant of me, isn't it, to think that my judgment is infallible?"

Again she reached out to touch his cheek, and her gray eyes were shining with tears. "Please, Dominic, don't say such things. I deserved to lose your love. Your rejection was entirely understandable, although it broke my heart to see you turn from me."

He returned her gaze steadily. "You did not deserve my contempt all these years. I am truly sorry, *maman*."

Lady Harriet was clearly startled to hear Dominic address her as he had when he was a child, but she was also clearly pleased. She flushed and shook her head. "Even so, I will always regret that I couldn't find the courage to defy Philippe and take you with me when I left him. Things might have been so different between us, had I not been such a coward."

"I suspect 'coward' is rather too strong a word."

"Perhaps. But how did you come to learn the truth?"

She listened quietly as Dominic told her about Sir Charles Durham and the events leading to his death, all the while keeping her eyes trained on the Axminster carpet. Dominic spared her many of the details, only touching briefly on his shooting of Sir Charles and his later, nearly fatal duel with Germain.

When he finished speaking, Lady Harriet looked away, gazing blindly at the Adam fireplace. "It . . . it is difficult for me to think about your father, even now. I'm afraid the comte was . . . not a good man."

Dominic could see how pale her face had become and how

446

hard she was biting her lower lip. "No," he agreed. "He was not a good man."

Lady Harriet lifted her eyes to her son's. "I regret that you discovered it, Dominic."

"I only regret that I didn't discover it sooner," he returned grimly. "If I had, I might have realized why you so often avoided me when I was a child, why you kept to your rooms for days at a time. Your absences were not because you lacked affection for me, were they? They were due to my father's depravity."

She nodded, bowing her head to hide her tears. "I had always been told it was a woman's duty to submit to her husband, but no one ever explained to me exactly what that entailed. I was so naive I didn't recognize Philippe's . . . perversions for what they were. We had been married several years before he began to find even those . . . less than satisfying. Philippe began to beat me. Generally, I could hide the bruises, for he was careful with my face. It would not have done for his countess to appear bearing scars for all the world to see. After a time, I even became grateful for the beatings. They were nothing compared with what he preferred doing . . . in other ways."

It was well that Lady Harriet was avoiding Dominic's eyes, for the fury in the gray depths would have frightened her. She went on in a low voice, needing to explain to him why she had left her husband and young son. "That spring Philippe allowed me to visit my father. I didn't want to leave you behind, but I knew I could never force myself to go back to Philippe. I could no longer bear the . . . the degrading life he forced me to live." Her voice broke then, and she buried her face in her hands.

Seeing his mother's anguish, Dominic thought it best to change the subject, but his fists were clenched and he had difficulty keeping his tone level. "You did not seem surprised to hear about Lisette Durham. Did you know before today what

447

had happened?"

Lady Harriet took a shuddering breath. "I did not know of her death, but I did know what Philippe had done to her. You see, Philippe was furious with me for leaving him. He wrote to me, first threatening me, then you, Dominic. But I knew him well. He would never have harmed a hair on your head. He preferred women . . . weak and fearful women. It added to his feeling of power. It was August when I received his last letter saying he no longer wanted me to return. He had found someone else whose screams excited him more than mine."

She was silent for a time, and when Dominic silently offered her a linen handkerchief, she accepted it with a tearful smile. When she had dried her eyes, Lady Harriet reached out and grasped Dominic's hand, holding it to her cheek. "I have few tears left, but it is a relief to share them with someone. I have never told a soul what I have just told you, Dominic, not even James. For a while after Philippe died, I kept the letters he wrote me—as a sort of protection at first. Then later, I thought perhaps to show them to you. I burned them, though, when I wed again."

"Well," Dominic said softly, "there may have been many misunderstandings between us in the past, but now they are over."

"Yes. I only hope that . . . that we might become friends."

Hearing her wistful tone, Dominic gave her a tender smile, the kind that never failed to win female hearts. "Nothing would please me more, *maman*. But if you have no objection," he said, rising and dusting his knees with his hand, "I will begin our friendship from a more comfortable position. I always suspected that humbling myself would be painful, but I never realized just how hard it could be on the knees."

For the first time since his arrival, his mother smiled. Gazing down at her, Dominic found himself wishing to know her better. For years, Lady Harriet had been the stranger who had brought him into the world and then deserted him, but he

ould see now what a void her absence had left in his life. And it
had actually come as something of a shock to find himself
warming so readily to the woman he had always despised.

His meeting with her had not gone at all as he had expected.
She had greeted him without rancor, and except for shedding a
few tears, she hadn't allowed him to feel any guilt over their
past relationship. She had accepted him at once, without
question, sweeping away the years of neglect and antagonism
like so many cobwebs, in a manner that had allowed them both
to maintain their self-respect.

Something of his thoughts must have shown in his eyes, for
his mother reached out to clasp his hand. "Do not pity me, my
love," she implored. "Knowing I have you for a son has more
than made up for Philippe's sins. And since I married James,
I've realized that a normal relationship between a man and a
woman can be full of love and companionship and trust."

A soft, private smile curved Dominic's lips. "Indeed, it
can," he replied. "Which reminds me—I'd like you to meet my
wife."

"Your . . . *wife?*"

Dominic grinned at his mother. "We were married two days
ago by special license. We're on our wedding trip, in fact, but
Brie insisted we come to Hampshire before we leave for France.
She's anxious to meet you."

"She is here? Dominic, never tell me you left your poor
bride to wait outside!"

"Brie thought it best that I speak to you alone. And she isn't
'my poor bride'—but you'll soon see for yourself. I'll bring her
to you. She's waiting in the carriage."

"No, I shall come with you," Lady Harriet said quickly.

"You seem concerned that I'll vanish," Dominic teased
when she claimed his arm.

"I expect I am," she acknowledged, her gray eyes sparkling.
"But then it isn't every day that I gain a son—and a daughter.
I've had little practice in exercising my maternal instincts,

449

though, so if you find yourself suffering, you must bear it with good grace."

She beamed up at him so unashamedly that Dominic laughed. "Give me due credit, *maman*," he said as he bent to kiss her cheek. "When I return to England, I intend to play the prodigal son and allow you to spoil me to your heart's content. Now, come. I want you to meet my lovely wife."

Epilogue

Sitting cross-legged on the bed, Brie propped her chin in her hands and smiled at her sleeping husband. Dominic looked so handsome lying in the huge four-poster bed where the Earls of Stanton had slept for generations, in spite of the fact that his ebony hair was tousled and a faint growth of beard shadowed his jaw.

His coloring was a startling contrast to the white bedsheet, for his tan was darker than ever after spending most of the summer under the Mediterranean sun. He was lying on his back, one arm flung above his head, the sheet drawn up to his waist.

Brie let her gaze roam lovingly over his bronzed torso, admiring the corded, rippling muscles of his chest and shoulders and feeling a little disappointed to be denied a view of his narrow hips and iron-thewed legs. His nakedness no longer embarrassed or shocked her. As his wife, she had every right to look at him or even touch him whenever she liked. It was one of the joys of being married, just as waking up next to him in the morning was a joy.

As she watched Dominic sleeping, a surge of possessive pride swept through her, mingling with the love and happiness that filled her heart. She wanted to touch him, to draw her fingers along his sinewy length and arouse him the way he was so fond of doing to her—but it was still rather early.

When she had awakened, Brie had been unable to go back to sleep, all because of the burgeoning excitement within her. She had quietly slipped out of bed and opened the heavy damask draperies, letting the soft autumn sunlight stream in the windows and warm the large master bedroom they shared. Then she had put on Dominic's robe—a sapphire-blue dressing gown that he had bought just for her to wear—and had come back to bed, taking up a position where she could observe him to her heart's content.

Critically studying Dominic, Brie decided that he had changed during the past few months of their marriage. That hard, cynical look he had worn so frequently had softened greatly. Now, with his aristocratic features relaxed in sleep, he looked peaceful and content, even happy.

He stirred then, as if he had sensed her watching him, and opened his eyes. Seeing Brie, he gave her a devastatingly sweet smile and stretched lazily. "If you're trying to tempt me, my love," he murmured in a voice still muffled by sleep, "you are succeeding admirably." Reaching up, he threaded his fingers through her tumbled hair, lightly cupping the nape of her neck.

Brie returned his smile and bent to brush his lips with a kiss, but when she tried to pull back, Dominic's hold upon her tightened. He drew her down beside him, wrapping his arms around her and deepening his kiss.

It was several moments before he allowed Brie to come up for air. When at last he let her go, she snuggled against his hard length, resting her head on his shoulder. "Actually," she murmured, "I was wondering what had happened to the cynical, arrogant rake I married."

"He's still there," Dominic replied, pressing his lips against her hair. "Only he has mellowed considerably. I expect it's

452

because a sharp-tongued, enchanting vixen captured his heart."

Brie laughed. "Is that so?"

"You know it is, minx." Tilting her face up to his, Dominic kissed her once more, long and lovingly.

When he finally released her, Brie sighed with contentment. She no longer doubted that Dominic loved her, but it was reassuring to feel the passion in his kisses and to realize that his desire showed no signs of diminishing. She had always known that he had wanted her, of course, but even when she had agreed to marry him, she hadn't been certain that he truly loved her. Dominic had spent their entire honeymoon proving it to her.

Brie smiled, remembering the delightful wedding journey they had taken. After visiting his mother in Hampshire, Dominic had immediately whisked Brie off to Paris. He had shown her both the glamorous and seedy sides of the city, giving her a taste of the wild life he had enjoyed before meeting her, then had taken her to Italy to see the cultural beauties of Milan, Venice, and Rome.

From there, they had gone to Spain and rented a villa on the Mediterranean, spending two glorious months swimming in the sea and basking in the sun and making love on the beach in the moonlight. Brie had turned as brown as a gypsy, but when she had complained about the freckles sprinkling her nose, Dominic had kissed every last one, saying that ladies with lily-white complexions bored him and that her tan only made her a more fitting mate for him.

They hadn't stayed the entire time in the villa, but had spent a week in a mountain retreat belonging to a friend of Dominic's, just the two of them. Brie had been surprised to learn how close the mountains were to the sea—merely an hour or two by horseback—but she had been even more astonished by the accommodations. The place resembled a fortress. It overlooked a narrow pass and according to

Dominic, had been used as a hideaway by Spanish guerrillas during the Peninsular war. The enormous, crude dwelling which had been built into the rock served as their living quarters, while the adjoining caves stabled their horses and pack mule. The conditions were far more primitive than anything she had ever experienced, but Brie had never been happier.

Afterward, they had returned to England, going directly to Dominic's country seat in Kent. Brie had fallen in love with the place—a huge, sprawling brick mansion set amid a beautifully landscaped park and surrounded by orchards and fertile fields. Its loveliness made up a little for the fact that she had had to leave Greenwood upon her marriage. Dominic had promised that they would spend several months in Rutland each year, but still she missed her home.

Greenwood was being well cared for in the interim. Katherine continued to manage the house and servants, while Tyler, Greenwood's steward, had been given full responsibility for the farms. They had also hired a talented young man to assist John Simms with the stables and eventually replace him as head trainer.

Brie actually had little time for homesickness, though. Besides having to learn how to run Dominic's household, she had numerous other duties that kept her fully occupied. Initially she had been a bit nervous about assuming the role of lady of the manor, but she soon realized her worries were unfounded. Her background had adequately prepared her to fit into the simple Kentish farming community, even if she was the wife of a major landowner and a countess, as well.

She had found to her surprise that Dominic's tenants were delighted to welcome her. During their first month in residence when Dominic had taken her around the estate to introduce her to all the farmers and their families, Brie had been warmed by her reception. She had also been embarrassed t times when Dominic was congratulated upon his marriage, or he was frequently wished luck in siring an heir for the state.

Shortly after they had settled in, Brie had been required to lay hostess. Dominic, intent on showing off his new bride, ad invited Jason and Lauren for a visit, and then Julian had ome for a while. Following his departure, Dominic's mother nd stepfather had arrived. There had been a certain wariness etween Dominic and his stepfather at first, but when Sir ames had seen that the long-standing rift between mother and on had been totally mended, he had accepted Dominic wholeheartedly.

The Torpals' visit had been delightful, if a little unusual. ady Harriet had virtually taken over the garden where she had pent much of her girlhood, while Sir James had alternately livided his time between surveying Dominic's farms and ishing.

Thinking of the Torpals now, Brie smiled. Sir James was a ood-natured older gentleman with a balding head, a stout rame, and a passion for crop rotation. He must have been very lifferent from his wife's first husband, but it was obvious Lady Harriet loved him.

Lady Harriet herself was a delight, and Brie had greatly enjoyed getting to know her. She had an intelligence and a propensity for mockery that reminded Brie of Dominic, although the sarcasm and the sardonic wit, coming from Lady Harriet, had a gentler mein.

"I like your mother," Brie observed, remembering Lady Harriet's many kindnesses to her during the past month.

Dominic pulled idly at one of Brie's russet curls. "So do I," he replied soberly. "My biggest regret is that I spent all those years refusing to see her or even to speak to her."

"But she has forgiven you, Dominic."

"Mmm," he murmured noncommittally. "At least she seems happy now, married to Sir James."

Brie raised herself up on one elbow and gazed down into her

husband's eyes. "I'm happy, too, being married to you. I neve
thought I could be this happy."

Tenderly, Dominic drew a finger along Brie's cheek to he
lips. "Nor I," he said softly. "I never thought I would lov
anyone the way I love you. You fill my life completely, makin
me forget the void that once was in my heart. I couldn't liv
without you, you know."

Brie smiled, his admission making her heart swell with joy
But then Dominic tilted back his dark head and chuckle
"What is so amusing?" she asked him curiously.

When he met her gaze, his gray eyes were dancing wit
laughter. "Jason once said something like that to me abou
Lauren and I sneered at him. Now I find myself spouting th
same sentimental drivel and meaning every word of it. Wha
have you done to me, Brie?"

Pleased to think she had affected Dominic as much as he ha
her, Brie relaxed against him. But she listened with growin
alertness when Dominic spoke again.

"All I need now is to become a father. Jason has alread
chided me unmercifully about what a model husband I'v
become, but I expect he would really have something to cro
about then."

Brie threw him a concerned glance. "Would next spring b
early enough?"

For a moment Dominic lay very still. Then he grasped Brie'
shoulders and held her away to stare at her. "A baby?" h
asked, sounding shocked. "Are you sure? How do you know?"

She searched his face, trying to decide whether he wa
pleased or not by the news. He seemed a little stunned. "You
mother guessed somehow," Brie said hesitantly. "Yesterday
when you were fishing with Sir James, she had your docto
examine me. I'm nearly two months pregnant."

Dominic stared a moment longer, then rolled Brie over
pinning her beneath him and entangling her legs in the sheets
Almost reverently, he loosened the belt of her wrapper an
slipped his hand next to her skin, holding his palm against he

456

abdomen. "A child," he breathed. Then his gaze sliced back to Brie. "You've known for a whole day and never told me?"

Brie fought the urge to squirm in his penetrating gaze. "Last night was my first formal dinner and it hardly seemed the right time to tell you with so many guests present. Besides, I wasn't sure what you would say. I was a little afraid you wouldn't want a child."

"Why the devil would you think that?"

Relieved by his puzzled frown, Brie trailed a finger down a corded muscle in his neck to the fading scar on his shoulder. "I suppose because you never mentioned wanting children. And you still haven't told me how you feel about becoming a father."

"Feel? Why . . . I'm delighted . . . I think. I was hoping to have you all to myself for a little while." Then Dominic's mouth suddenly twisted in a grin as he did some rapid calculations. "Two months? I'll wager it happened while we were in the mountains—that night in front of the hearth."

Remembering the particular night he was referring to, Brie blushed in spite of herself. It had been a wild, delicious time she would never forget. She and Dominic had spent the entire night making love beneath luxurious furs in front of a roaring fire, for even though it had been summer, the evenings were chilly in the mountains.

"I wonder what he will be like," Brie mused, realizing that their child might have been conceived in a guerrilla's hideaway.

Dominic had been following that same line of thought and his grin deepened. "Staid and proper like his mother, I imagine. Unless it's a girl. Then she'll probably be feisty and uncontrollable."

Brie might have pointed out that she was no longer feisty or uncontrollable, and that she too had mellowed since their marriage, but just then Dominic lowered his head and began planting light kisses along the side of her neck.

Brie arched instinctively, giving him greater access to her

throat while she curled her fingers in his dark hair. She had not meant to linger in bed with him after telling him her news, for they had guests who would be expecting to see them at breakfast, but she found it difficult to move. The sheet had somehow twisted around her legs, and one of Dominic's muscular thighs was draped over hers, holding her prisoner. Even then, Brie might have escaped with a little effort, but his nibbling kisses were drugging her senses and lighting fires in her that were impossible to ignore. She could feel the heat of his naked body through the silk of her robe and knew she would shortly be feeling his bare skin against her unless she stopped him at once.

"We should get up," she murmured halfheartedly. "Your stepfather invited me to ride with him after breakfast."

Unknowingly, she had hit upon the one subject that was certain to grab her husband's attention. Dominic immediately ended his amorous advances and raised his head. "One moment, ma belle. Don't you think we should talk about this?"

"Talk about what?"

"Your riding. It could be dangerous. You might injure yourself or the child."

Brie searched Dominic's face, finding only concern for her in his gaze. "But the doctor said it was safe, at least until the baby starts to show."

"All the same I don't want you near any of the fractious beasts you are so fond of riding."

Her eyes widened. "Do you mean I can't ride for *seven months?*"

Seeing her half-anxious, half-mutinous expression, Dominic couldn't repress a smile. "I didn't say that. I merely want to approve your mounts."

"You'll probably give me only broken-down nags," Brie muttered, although she realized the wisdom of curtailing her activities somewhat.

Dominic raised an eyebrow at her. "Don't be insulting, my love. There isn't a horse in my entire stable worth under two hundred guineas, unless you count that bay of yours."

"But Jester has improved, Dominic, even you have to admit that."

"He hasn't improved enough to carry my most precious— my *two* most precious possessions," he amended, covering her stomach again with his hand. "And if I catch you near that animal, I'll beat you till you can't even sit a horse."

Somewhat mollified by his concern, Brie raised her arms and wrapped them around Dominic's neck. "Very well," she replied meekly. "I won't go near Jester."

He frowned, suspicious of her sudden capitulation. "I mean it, Brie. I don't want you endangering our child. I'll forbid you to ride entirely if I must. And just in case you are planning to use those feminine charms of yours to try and convince me otherwise, let me warn you this is one subject where no amount of persuasion will make me change my mind."

When Brie's eyes started to flash, Dominic though it wise to head off a direct confrontation. "As for this morning," he said, changing the subject, "I was hoping to have your company. A friend of mine in Wrotham has a mare who might be a good match for Diablo, and I'd like your opinion. Why don't you drive over with me? We could invite Sir James along, and my mother, too. We'll make a day of it."

"I'd love to," Brie admitted grudgingly, "but I think I'm being out-maneuvered. You just mean to keep me from riding."

The grin Dominic gave her was slow and wicked. "Not at all, cherie," he said huskily as he again lowered his lips to her throat. "In fact, I insist you ride this morning. My only stipulation is that you choose me as your mount."

Before she could reply, he had parted her robe fully, baring her breasts to his heated gaze. With his arms on either side of her, his weight braced on his elbows, he cupped the pale globes in his hands and bent his head. His mouth captured a taut nipple, making Brie gasp as a lightning bolt of sensation shot through her body.

"Your parents . . ." she reminded him breathlessly as he tantalized the sensitive nub. "They will wonder what has happened to us . . . if we aren't at breakfast."

"They won't wonder for long," Dominic replied, showing not the least concern. Shifting his weight in order to push down the sheet, he divested Brie of her robe and tossed it on the floor. Then he stretched out beside her, letting his gaze roam down her naked body. Following his gaze with his hand, he slowly caressed every inch of silken skin he could find.

Feverish with longing, Brie arched her spine, pressing closer to Dominic's hard, masculine length, trying to find release from the delicious torture he was inflicting on her. But when she raised her arms to draw him down to her, Dominic smiled lazily and pressed her hands back down at her sides.

"Let me look at you," he ordered huskily. Taking his time, he spread her hair across the pillow in a flowing wave. "You're like autumn leaves," he murmured. "Flaming and vibrant and beautiful." He bent his head again, letting his mouth work its magic on her breasts once more.

Brie sucked in her breath as Dominic first nipped a turgid nipple with his teeth, then let his tongue swirl soothingly over the swollen peak. The faint stubble of his jaw chafed her sensitive skin, but the pleasurable rasping only aroused her further.

"Dominic," Brie murmured, clutching at his shoulders. But he continued to lave her breasts, heightening the tension in her body with each tender caress. When she was aching with need, he moved lower, pausing to press a dozen loving kisses over her belly where his child lay safe and protected, before letting his lips glide down to nuzzle the curls between her thighs.

Brie shuddered. "Dominic, please," she begged, her hands gripping the mattress.

He seemed unconcerned by her plight. "You taste like autumn, too," he remarked thoughtfully. "Rich, earthy, and sweet."

Ignoring Brie's plea, Dominic positioned himself between her thighs, slipping his hands beneath her buttocks and raising her hips off the bed. Then leisurely, he lapped and nibbled at her soft flesh, drinking her sweetness until she was whimpering and pleading with him to take her.

At last, when she was writhing frantically beneath him, her breath coming in sobbing gasps, Dominic suckled in earnest, possessing her with his tongue, claiming her totally. He drove her over the brink into a swirling sea of sensation.

Brie returned to earth slowly, only to find Dominic kissing her damp brow and smoothing her hair away from her flushed face. Lifting her lashes, Brie regarded him with languid, passion-glazed eyes. "Devil," she whispered, hardly having the strength to voice the accusation. He laughed huskily, lowering his lips to the fragrant hollow between her breasts and starting his maddening caresses all over again.

Brie wasn't taken in by his casualness this time, however. She could feel the tension in the rippling muscles of his body and the heat of his skin wherever it touched her own sweat-dampened flesh. His masculine hardness was pressing hot and urgent against her thigh, loudly proclaiming his arousal.

Somehow she summoned the energy to push against Dominic's chest with her hands and make him roll over on his back. "Oh no, my handsome husband," she murmured, giving him a triumphant smile. "You promised I could ride, and I mean to hold you to your word." Draping her body over his, Brie stretched on top of him full-length, shamelessly pressing her slender hips against his throbbing loins and rubbing her breasts against his chest.

Dominic groaned, closing his eyes. "I am entirely at your disposal, my love," he said shakily. Belying his words the next instant, he grasped Brie by the waist and lifted her up to straddle his thighs. Then slowly, he drew her downward onto him, shuddering as he was sheathed in warm velvet. "Oh . . . Lord . . . Brie," he ground out in ragged gasps. "My sweet vixen. . . ."

461

Any thought of prolonging the exquisite moment left him when Brie began to move her hips in an ancient, rhythmic motion, and when she arched her back in wanton ecstasy, Dominic's rigid self-control snapped altogether. His arms came around her in a crushing embrace, pulling Brie down to him. He thrust into her again and again, his powerful hips surging upward, while his lips claimed hers fiercely, his tongue plunging hungrily inside her mouth, demanding everything she was willing to give and more.

Brie surrendered joyously, clutching at Dominic's shoulders and returning his kiss with a fierceness that matched his. She could feel his hard flesh throbbing inside her, filling her, igniting her senses.

When the explosion came, it showered them both with burning embers. Brie cried out as Dominic made one last searing thrust, and when the violent shudders that shook his body lessened, she collapsed against him, hardly hearing his ragged, rasping breath in her ear.

She had no trouble recognizing his tender words of love, though, when he tilted her chin up so he could see her face. "I love you, Brie," he said hoarsely, his gray eyes reflecting the depth of his feeling for her. "I think I've loved you since that morning in the meadow when you took your crop to me."

Brie regarded him dreamily. "I fell in love when you first smiled at me. You looked like a fallen angel."

"A *what?*"

"A fallen angel," she repeated, her voice fading. Dominic's lovemaking had drained her of energy, leaving her satisfied but exhausted. Sleepily, she let her head drop to his shoulder and her heavy eyelids close.

Dominic lay there a moment longer, a soft smile curving his lips as he remembered he was soon to be a father. Then gathering his sleeping wife even more closely in his arms, he, too, shut his eyes.

It was much, much later before either of them stirred again. When they finally rose, they dressed slowly amid much laughter and kissing and left the chamber, hand in hand, in search of breakfast.

Farley, Dominic's valet, was in the corridor when the two lovers emerged. Seeing Dominic draw Brie into his arms, then whisper something in her ear that made her laugh and blush, Farley shook his head. The earl's reference to autumn leaves was puzzling since it was only September and the trees had not yet started to turn. But then his odd behavior could be attributed to Cupid's influence. It was obvious that Lord Stanton cherished his beautiful wife, for his face was alive with love and laughter. And there was no doubt that the countess adored him in return, for she was glowing with happiness.

Brie and Dominic descended the grand staircase together and discovered that they had the morning room to themselves. Both Lady Harriet and Sir James had long since given up waiting for them and were each engaged in their favorite pursuits. Dominic sent a footman to the fields with a message for his stepfather, and when he and Brie had finished eating, they went out to the gardens in search of his mother.

They found her kneeling at the base of a giant topiary yew, clipping the ragged edges of a sculpted deer. She looked up at their approach and waved, then began gathering her gardening tools into a basket.

Dominic left the shaded path and strode forward to assist her, but Brie hung back, watching as he helped Lady Harriet to her feet. Seeing him smile so tenderly at his mother, Brie felt a warm glow flow through her. And when Dominic turned to meet her own gaze across a stretch of flowering shrubs, the glow deepened.

Realizing that the shadows of the past had at last been banished, Brie breathed a silent prayer of gratitude. Then returning her husband's loving gaze, she stepped into the sunlight and went to join him.